Theodore A. Dodge

Riders of Many Lands

Theodore A. Dodge

Riders of Many Lands

ISBN/EAN: 9783337390013

Printed in Europe, USA, Canada, Australia, Japan

Cover: Foto ©Andreas Hilbeck / pixelio.de

More available books at **www.hansebooks.com**

RIDERS OF MANY LANDS

BY

THEODORE AYRAULT DODGE

BREVET LIEUTENANT-COLONEL U. S. ARMY

AUTHOR OF

"THE CAMPAIGN OF CHANCELLORSVILLE" "A BIRD'S-EYE VIEW OF OUR CIVIL WAR"
"PATROCLUS AND PENELOPE, A CHAT IN THE SADDLE" "GREAT CAPTAINS"
"ALEXANDER" "HANNIBAL" "CÆSAR" ETC., ETC.

ILLUSTRATED

WITH NUMEROUS DRAWINGS BY FREDERIC REMINGTON
AND
FROM PHOTOGRAPHS OF ORIENTAL SUBJECTS

PREFACE

THE following pages, which ought, perhaps, to be entitled "A Globe-trotter's *Pot au Feu* of Horse-flesh, with a Seasoning of Chestnuts," recall to the author's mind the story of the old Yankee who, in default of other books, read Webster's Unabridged through from beginning to end, and then remarked that it was mighty interesting reading, especially the pictures, but it didn't seem to have much plot. May the author ask for the gentle reader's patience if he finds the same lack of sequence between these covers?

And yet there is a *motif* running through them, which the good American horse-lover will not find it hard to follow.

BROOKLINE, MASS., 1893.

ILLUSTRATIONS

	PAGE
AMERICAN POLO-PLAYERS	*Frontispiece*
"A COUNTRY BUMPKIN"	2
PANATHENAIC RIDER	3
OLD GALLIC SADDLE	8
AN OLD-TIME NORTHERN PLAINS INDIAN—THE COUP	15
STATUE OF ALEXANDER BY LYSIPPUS	19
A WHITE TRAPPER	31
AN INDIAN TRAPPER	37
THE TRAVAUX PONY	47
MODERN COMANCHE	53
AN APACHE INDIAN	57
UNITED STATES CAVALRYMAN	67
INDIAN SCOUT WITH LOST TROOP-HORSE	91
CANADIAN MOUNTED POLICE	95
COWBOY LIGHTING THE RANGE FIRE	103
THE INDIAN METHOD OF BREAKING A PONY	113
A MEXICAN VAQUERO	125
GENTLEMAN RIDER ON THE PASEO DE LA REFORMA	133
A SOUTHERN RIDER	145
A HUNTING MAN	151
GENTLEMAN RIDER IN CENTRAL PARK	161
COUNTRY GENTLEMAN'S TYPICAL SADDLE-HORSE	167
JOCKEYS	173
THE SPANISH WALK	181
CAPRIOLE	183
CROUPADE	185
HOW TO DO IT	202
HOW NOT TO DO IT	209
FRENCH ALGERIAN CAVALRYMAN ON BARB	221
CAVALRY LEAPING-DRILL IN ALGERIA	225
A SPAHI AND HIS BARB, ALGERIA	231

	PAGE
REMOUNT BARB FOR ALGERIAN CAVALRY	235
SPAHI RACKING ALONG THE ROAD	239
SPAHI, EQUIPPED FOR "FANTASĪYA," MAKING HIS HORSE REAR	242
COUNTRYMAN ON AN ASS	251
BICHARI CAMEL-RIDERS, UPPER EGYPT	265
READY FOR THE "FANTASĪYA"	267
"FANTASĪYA" RIDERS, ALGERIA	271
TUNISIAN HAT	274
MY FRIEND THE CALIPH	281
TUNISIAN WITH TWO-YEAR-OLD BARB	287
A TUNISIAN SHEIK	290
ARABIAN POLO-PONIES, CAIRO	293
ENGLISH OFFICER ON ARABIAN, CAIRO	295
SAÏS HOLDING ARABIAN, CAIRO	299
EGYPTIAN WOMAN'S STYLE	315
TIRED DONKEY-BOY	321
WELL-BRED SADDLE-ASS, CAIRO	329
CAMEL-RIDERS ON THE DESERT	335
AN ARABIAN SIRE	341
BEDOUIN ESCORT FROM JERUSALEM TO JERICHO	349
RICH BEDOUIN SHEIK	363
SYRIAN WOMAN ON AN ASS	367
POOR BEDOUINS OF MOAB	371
PALANQUIN CAMEL	375
TWO-CAMEL PALANQUIN	379
A HUNGARIAN THOROUGH-BRED	387
ONE OF THE SULTAN'S RIDING-HORSES	391
AN OLD ARABIAN FROM THE SULTAN'S STABLE	397
OLD ARAB OF THE SULTAN'S STABLE ON ARABIAN	400
MODERN GREEK COSTUME	405
COSSACK OF THE GUARD—FIELD TRIM	413
KING OF NEPAUL	429
MANIPURI POLO-PONY	437
CHINESE MANDARIN	453
MONGOLIAN HORSEMAN	473
HAWAIIAN BULLOCK-RIDERS	479
HAWAIIAN AMAZON RIDER	483

WE Americans are a many-sided people, and our equestrianism partakes of our many-sidedness. The greatest variety of riders which any one people has produced has thriven on the continent of North America. Going back to include the days, still in the memory of old men living, when the Indians who dwelt farthest from civilization were armed with bow and arrow, tomahawk and lance, and rode without a saddle, we can count within the boundaries of the Union almost every type of rider, from those who subdued the steed in the era which produced the frieze of the Parthenon to the Sunday rider of the present year of grace. As a matter of pure skill, as well as artistically speaking, the first-named, or bareback rider, stands in every age at the head of all equestrians, while the latter is a proper object-lesson of what to avoid; but, inasmuch as for practical work the saddle gives a distinct superiority in many ways, we can scarcely compare the bareback horseman with the modern rider, be he good, bad, or indifferent.

When we speak of bareback riding, we do not refer to the country bumpkin, a species indigenous to every soil, and most aptly illustrated in Rosa Bonheur's "Horse Fair." Especially where horses trot is this bareback horror at his worst. Leaning back, holding for dear life to the reins which give him a good half of his security, with elbows in air, or marking time to the horse's steps, and with a general appearance of a set purpose to contend with the

1

"A COUNTRY BUMPKIN"

impossible to the end of the chapter, this rider is the very
pattern of how not to do it. Take the rider on the big
gray in the "Horse Fair," and compare him with one of the
riders in the Panathenaic procession! How can two men
doing the same thing be so at odds? And yet each would
cast a slur at the other's horsemanship.

Qui s'excuse s'accuse, and I do not wish to offer an apology for what, in the following pages, may often on the
surface appear to be dogmatic. I hope that my brothers
in horsemanship will absolve me from narrowness—in all
things easily the first of vices. I have put a girdle round
the earth; I have ridden with all kinds and conditions of
men, from Mexican vaquero to Arab sheik; I have thrown
my leg across every species of mount, from a bronco to a

bridle-bullock; I have discussed horse-lore in the great *manéges* of Europe and on the Syrian desert, and I equally love to ride my pet horse and my hobby. You may disagree with me, my brother rider, but let us argue together. I will say my say now, and then you shall have your turn. I shall expect to learn much from you.

No intelligent horseman ever claims for his own method the *a* and *ω* of equitation. It is an axiom among all men who are not hide-bound by prejudice that the method of riding, and the bit and saddle which are best adapted to the animal to be ridden, to the needs of the work to be done, and to the climate, will, barring poverty of resources, be the ones to grow into use among all peoples and every class. This fact is well illustrated by the two almost

PANATHENAIC RIDER

extreme seats of the cowboy and the fox-hunter. The cowboy has to be astride his ponies from a dozen hours upwards every day, ropes steers, or drags out mired cows; has to stick to his saddle under the most abnormal conditions, and must if need be have both his hands at liberty. He rides with a short tree, horn pommel, and high cantle. He laughs at any other rig. The fox-hunter has nothing to do but to keep his seat; he has no occupation for his hands except by the play of the bits to get the very best performance out of his horse—a delicate enough operation by-the-bye, and not to be quickly acquired—and needs a saddle on which he can not only sit safely and comfortably over difficult obstacles, but which is convenient to fall out of if a horse comes down, and will prove the least dangerous should his horse come atop of him. He rides the flattest thing known except a pad. The very best authority obtainable—those men, to wit, who have done duty as cowboys, and have ridden to hounds as well (and many of us know from personal friendship that a man may be equally distinguished on the ranch, with the Meadow Brooks, and in politics and letters, too)—unite in pronouncing each saddle to be as closely adapted to the needs of each rider as it can be made. Long use will extract what is good from every style. Even the Arab, who would laugh to scorn the long stirrups of the cowboy, or the persistent road-trot of the fox-hunter, rides in a fashion which to us seems at first blush inexplicable, but which, when one has long dwelt among them, is found to be by no means ill-adapted to his needs. His entire rig suits the Arabian he rides vastly better than a flat English saddle would do, which latter, indeed, he deems the product of the always more or less insane Frank.

Leaving out the soldier, who is the lineal descendant of the knight in armor, with seat and saddle modified by his more modern weapons and equipment, and who is everywhere — barring some national traits — substantially the same, the home of the short seat and long stirrup is the Occident, that of the long seat and short stirrup the Orient; and these are varied in every locality to suit its own peculiarities, inherited or acquired. There are a few exceptions to this rule, but they only serve to prove it. Midway comes the Englishman, with his numerous civilized imitators, whose seat is a compromise between the long and the short. All other styles approach more or less to these, and each has, among the prejudiced, its uncompromising advocates. But whatever seat may be believed by its partisans to be the best, there are, after all said, so many unsurpassed riders who break every commandment in the civilized decalogue of equitation that we cannot even ask " Who is the best rider ?" but only " What is the best form for the peculiar wants of each of us, or of our climate, roads, and horses ?"

XENOPHON, whose work on horsemanship is the earliest which has been preserved to us, gives to some of our equestrians a commendable example by praising Simo, who had preceded him, and perhaps cut him out, in writing a horse-book. " We shall expect," says he, " to acquire additional credit, since he who was skilled in horses has the same notions with us." It is everywhere a good deal the fashion, and in some places a matter of faith, to claim that some particular brand of horsemen, as of cigars or whiskey, is the best; or, rather, that there can be no other really perfect brand. But this is a provincial trick. Whoso, like Odysseus, has seen men and cities, knows that there are everywhere equally good liquor, tobacco, and riders.

By-the-way, the author as well as the genius of the *Anabasis* was one of the most thorough of horsemen. Let me commend his " Horse Book " to your reading. You will find in fifty pages more horse sense than, I fear, there may be found between even these covers. And it serves to prove that man and horse have not much varied through the many centuries since this Yankee of a Greek marched through trials to the sea.

Apart from geological evidences, in which we riders of to-day are not as deeply interested as we might be, the Orient was the original home of horsemen, and war was the early training-school of the horse. Though this most useful of quadrupeds appears first in history and monumental record as a beast of burden, and though riding must be assumed to have preceded driving, there is evidence to show that chariots in great numbers were employed in war before cavalry came into common use. In the first home of the horse, his utility was all but limited to war; camels were the freight-carriers on a large, asses on a small, scale; bullocks were as much a usual means of passenger transportation as camels; and they were no doubt then, as now in parts of the Orient, steady and rapid travellers. No one who has not seen the trotting bullock has any idea of how fine a driver he is; as well bred as a racer, as quiet as the traditional (not the actual) lamb, he will go his forty miles in seven or eight hours to your entire satisfaction. But the bullock was of no use in war. He was lacking in character as much as his brother the bull was ungovernable. The utility of the horse as an adjunct to armed man soon impressed itself on his owner. The higher the warrior could tower above the common herd of soldiery, the more terrible his aspect, and the deadlier his aim with lance and arrow. To fight from above downward was always the desideratum in the days of short-carry jactile weapons; and from this ambition came the steed's early appearance in battle. But to debase him to the purposes of pleasure was, for many generations after he became an every-day matter, never dreamed of. He was altogether too noble an animal; and we can well imagine that he impressed himself upon the ancients with the same force he exerts on us.

We find the very best of cavalry in ancient times. The Greeks ran against a very serious problem in the Persian light horse when they first trod the soil of Asia Minor. While the best infantry in existence, they in nowise compared as horsemen with the Asiatics until Alexander's Companion Cavalry showed them what good material and intelligent drill would do. But Alexander's methods were forgotten, and the Greek and Roman cavalry for centuries after his day remained less apt than that of their barbarian neighbors.   It was Philip of Macedon who had first utilized the excellent little chunk of the Thessalian plains, and organized the Companion Cavalry, which his splendid son so divinely led, and which, to judge from its manœuvres and fighting, must have consisted of the most admirable horsemen.   The ancients all rode without saddle or stirrups, on a blanket, or on a pad, or bareback, and in spite of this fact, or perhaps by reason of it, rode extremely well.

The origin and era of the first saddles is hard to trace. Some authorities strive to prove the existence of a saddle-

tree several centuries before the Christian era.   The ancient Gauls unquestionably used a tree.   This is shown by some small terra-cotta figures found in France, dating back to the early centuries of our era.   But we know that the Greeks did not habitually use a saddle.

It is wonderful what feats of military horsemanship the bareback rider could perform in the age of what we might call gymnastic equestrianism.   Nothing but the personal knowledge of what our old-time Indian could do enables us to credit the historical accounts of the Greek's agility and skill.   They were simply wonderful.   The weapons he carried, his heavy armor, his baggage, all appear to

handicap him beyond possibility of marching or fighting
bareback; and yet we know that Alexander covered an
extraordinary distance in his pursuit of Darius; and Arrian tells us enough to determine beyond a peradventure
that no cavalry has ever been fought *au fond* as were the
Companions under the son of Philip at the Hydaspes.
But this was owing primarily to the Achillean fury of
Alexander.

When, after the lapse of centuries, saddles came into
common use, there grew up two schools of riding—that
of the mailed warrior, whose iron armor well chimed in
with his "tongs on a wall" seat in his peaked saddle, and
that of the Oriental, whose nose and knees all but touched.
The former was not what we really call a horseman; he
was a mere man on horseback. That some of them were
noble-looking specimens is vouched for by, say, the statue
of Bartolomeo Colleoni, in Venice, easily best of equestrian figures, and surely a splendid ideal in many ways.
But the horse was more of a lumbering vehicle than a
saddle-beast, a species of conveyance—a gun-carriage, so
to speak—for the bulky man of iron, who could no more
walk than ride, and when unhorsed was as useless as a
dismounted gun. Why the Eastern rider, who is at the
other end of the category, and really a horseman, should
cling to his extremely short leathers it is hard to say, unless it be from the same ancient motive—to place him
the higher above his horse, and therefore make him the
more imposing when he stands up in his stirrups to bran-
dish scimitar or matchlock. Yet he is a wonderful rider,
this same Oriental; as we shall see when we reach his
habitat; and so indeed is every man, whatever his style,
who from youth up is the companion of the horse. This
peculiar type—to come back to our original statement—
does not exist in North America, though some of our Ind-

ians ride with very short stirrups, and in a manner in some points not unlike the Arab of to-day. But every other style of equitation is found either among our aborigines, or in the thickly populated sections of our continent.

THE bareback rider was common among the plains Indians of forty years ago. Beyond trappings for mere show, the noble red man's pony was as naked as he. The bareback seat ought in theory to be alike in all ages, varied slightly only by the conformation of man and beast— the slimmer the horse's barrel, or the longer the man's legs, the straighter the seat. We are wont to ascribe variations from it to the use of saddles. This seat, in addition to giving the balancing trick, is supposed to train a man to grip his horse from breech to knee, and, unless when making unusual exertions which require all the grip a man has at command, to allow his leg from the knee down to hang more or less perpendicularly. It is at all events distinctly the model from which to start. The less the variation from it the better the results. And although many horsemen who wander furthest from this seat achieve singular success in equitation, the model, nevertheless, remains the best. This is a maxim in every school in Europe or America. Variations from the bareback seat are the result of peculiar habits or requirements.

This is only theorizing, you may say. True, but the best practice comes from following out good theory, however often practice alone may produce individual success. A man or a horse, or both combined, may accomplish astounding results in the wrong way; but the same skill, patience, and labor, properly directed, would have accomplished more. "Practice makes perfect," runs the old saw, but the word "perfect" has a limited meaning. To be perfect in doing a thing incorrectly is a misapplication of endeavor, the more so if the thing done is *per se* useful.

The average bareback rider of civilization is far from perfect. He pulls on his horse's mouth for dear life. If he quits his hold of the bridle or halter rope he is gone. He is, if any man, the typical three-legged rider—the very exemplar of what is vicious in the art. Good bareback riding, on the other hand, is one of the finest of performances. Did you ever try it? It is all very well so long as you have a bridle and a good tough mouth to hold on by; but drop your bridle, fold your arms, and see what happens. If your horse knows you and you him, or if you have been there before, well and good; but with a green beast, even if kind, you will find yourself all at sea; and should you happen to have caught a Tartar, you will be sent to Coventry in short measure, to be a trifle mixed in metaphor.

Now the old-time Indian did just what you find so difficult. He needed both hands for other things than holding on. When hunting, he must use his bow and arrow; on the war-path still less could he spare a hand to his horse. He was a consummate rider, who, despite what we call defects in style, could outdo in his way any rider who exists to-day. There are, of course, many things which only a man in a saddle can undertake; but that by no means makes him the better rider. We must yield the palm to the bareback seat.

What we have said of our old-time Indian applies with equal force to the cavalryman of antiquity. Livy aptly divides cavalry into "those with and those without the bridle," meaning regular and irregular horse. The former were the heavy horsemen. The latter guided their horses with voice or legs, or with a slender rod. "The Numidians, a nation ignorant of the rein, whose horses the wand, sportively waved over their ear, directs with not less effect than the bit," sings Silius Italicus, in a key which yields us a pretty bit of information. To those who have never ridden in the ranks it would seem as if horses could not be managed without bit and rein; but, in truth, if left to themselves and well trained, cavalry horses develop an intelligence unmatched in any other pursuit, and an ability to act together in the right direction which is marvellous. How many victories are due to this equine instinct only the *beau sabreur* can know.

WE have from all sources accurate and consistent accounts of the extraordinary riding of the old savage. Catlin and Parkman and Dodge depict him fully. A piece of buffalo-robe girthed with a rope over the pony's back stood in lieu of saddle, if even so much was used; a cord of twisted hair lashed round its lower jaw served both for bit and bridle. When hunting, in fact as a rule, the Indian wore naught but a breech-cloth and moccasins —not to lay stress on paint and feathers—and carried a buffalo-skin, which he threw around his shoulders or let fall from about his waist. He was often a splendid specimen of manly strength and activity—this old-time Indian. "By G——, a Mohawk!" exclaimed Benjamin West, when he first beheld the Apollo Belvedere. A heavy whip with elk-horn handle and knotted bull's-hide lash hung by a loop to the Indian's wrist. His bow and arrows gave full occupation to his hands; he was forced to guide his pony with legs and word alone, and to rely on its intelligence and the training he had given it to do the right thing at the right moment. Thus slenderly equipped, this superb rider dashed into the midst of a herd of buffaloes—a seething, tearing, volcanic mass of motion, of which no one who has not seen it can conceive an idea; but so quick was the pony and so strong the seat of his master, that, despite the stampede of the terror-stricken herd and the charges of the enraged and wounded bulls, few accidents ever occurred. The Indian on horseback has ninety lives,

not nine. His riding is not an art, it is nature. The cowboy has a task to tax the stoutest when he rides into a stampeded herd of cattle, but the cowboy has saddle and bridle-arm, the Indian had neither.

The Indian has never developed a system of training his ponies. Each man taught his own to suit himself, and except under imitation of some chief who had exceptional success in training his ponies, or a certain trick perhaps shown by father to son and thus perpetuated, there was none but individual knack in his horsemanship. The plains pony was quickly taught after a rough-and-ready fashion, more by cruelty than kindness; in a manner, in fact, as different from the system of the Arab as the fine shape of the horse of the desert as we see him in pictures differs from the rugged outline of the bronco as we see him in reality. All horses are more intelligent than man supposes; those most with men, or on which man most depends, most readily respond to training; and the Indian and his pony were every day and all day comrades. Before the Indian could trade for or steal a bit, he always used the jaw-rope—or nothing. With the rope in the left hand, he bore against the neck to turn to one side, and gave a pull to turn to the other; or else he shifted his pony's croup by a more or less vigorous kick with either heel. When both his hands were busy, he relied entirely upon his legs and the pony's knowledge of the business in hand; but as every Indian digs his heels into the horse's flanks and lashes him with the quirt at every stride, it is hard to see how the pony caught on to his meaning. The more credit to the quadruped.

This method of the Indian is nothing new. You find the same thing among all tribes on whose territory the horse is indigenous. Historically we know that the Numidians, several centuries before the Christian era, had the same success with their steppes ponies; that the Parthians, long before the Greeks came in contact with them, were riders of equal merit. To-day all natives of those lands where the horse is bred are practically what our Indian was, with whatever differences their respective national traits may have developed.

The riding feats of the Indian of to-day, such as shooting, casting the lasso, or picking objects off the ground at a gallop, or hanging to one side of his horse, concealed all but an arm and leg, while he shoots at his enemy from behind the running rampart, were equally performed by his bareback ancestor. The latter was wont to braid his mustang's mane into a long loop through which he could thrust his arm to preserve his balance, but he had not the advantage of the cantle to hold to by his leg. The only representative of such cleverness to-day is to be found in the sawdust arena; not many decades ago, every third Indian could have given odds to the best of circus performers. The old bareback Indian rider has disappeared; it needed but a short contact with civilization to show him the manifest advantages of bit and saddle. As the old men died off, the young bucks took to the tricks of the white man, quite as much from fashion as from an ability to put them to use. Whoso killed a pale-face would ride his saddle—galls or no galls to horse and man—as a matter of pure boasting; whoso could not get a rig by killing a pale-face was not happy until he stole one. And thus the fine old bareback trick was lost.

It is to be regretted that we can make no satisfactory comparison between the bareback rider of ancient times and our own Indian of the past generation. There are many men yet living to testify to the skill and strength of the Indian horseman; and Catlin has left us numerous pictures of the savage. But of the ancient rider we have in monumental and ceramic art few except very crude pictorial delineations, and in books yet fewer written ones, and it would not be easy to reproduce him were it not for a few works of exceptional art which remain to us.   One of the most precious relics of the past is a bronze statuette dug up at Herculaneum in 1751, and thought to be a copy of the equestrian statue known to have been made of Alexander the Great by Lysippus, after the battle of the

STATUE OF ALEXANDER BY LYSIPPUS

Granicus, when statues of all the brave who fell in this initial Greek victory were made by the famous sculptor. If it is truly a copy of Lysippus' work, we can judge from it how the Macedonians managed their horses in a hand-to-hand conflict.   The King is shown sitting on a blanket firmly held in place by a breast-strap and girth; without dropping the reins from his bridle hand he grasps this substitute for a saddle at the withers, and turning fully half-way to the right and looking backward, gives a swinging cut with his sword to the rear, covering as big an arc of the circle as the best swordsman who ever sat in a saddle-tree. The statue is full of life, and natural to a degree. If not Lysippus' work, it is that of a consummate artist. The position shows great freedom of movement on the horse, and a seat strong and elastic. That the Macedonians kept their heels well away from the horse's flanks, or rather that they did not rely on their heels to cling to him, is shown by their commonly wearing spurs, a thing the Indian is wont to avoid; and the same habit shows clearly in this piece of art.

And yet this does not prove much, perhaps. Our hunting-men wear spurs, and are supposed to keep them for the proper moment; still, whenever one chances to be photographed leaping an obstacle, even if only two feet high, you may see him with a good part of his glue resident in his heels. "Cruelty to animals!" you exclaim. Yes, but in the excitement of the moment the horse, brave, generous beast, has scarcely noticed the pain. So closely does the horse partake of the rider's enthusiasm and purpose that the high-school horse, in the airs requiring great vigor, will calmly receive a severe application of the spur as an indication of the thing he is expected to do, and this without the least resentment.

When riding merely and not fighting, the Greek sat on his breech in a natural position, took a firm hold with his thighs, but let his legs from the knee down hang free. His attitude, as shown in the Panathenaic procession on the frieze of the Parthenon, was singularly graceful in style; and that it was the common one is to be seen from Xenophon's rules for keeping the seat. He managed the reins with light and easy hands. The Indian, on the con-

trary, to judge from the pictures we have of him, was as
singularly awkward and ungainly.   He sat on his crotch,
leaned forward, with the thigh not far from perpendicular and the leg thrust back at almost a right angle.   This
he could do with the plains pony, whose barrel was far
from as well rounded as that of the Thessalian chunk;
and he got a goodly part of his grip from his calf and
heel.   The contrast between the statue of Alexander, or
one of the Parthenon riders, and any one of Catlin's pictures
is striking; but we must remember that the former are
the production of the ablest Greek sculptors, in the highest bloom of art, under the personal direction of Phidias;
while the latter pretend only to convey the idea of the
savage as he was; and though the old-time Indian was
the equal, probably the superior, as a mere rider, of the
Greek, it is the latter whom we must select as a model if
we wish to preserve any semblance of beauty in equestrianism.   And we may no more properly banish the idea
of beauty from our habits of riding than from any other
act of our daily life.   As a rule, clever performance is associated with what commends itself to the eye; what we
call style is often solely able performance; but no one can
watch the ungainly fad of swinging the legs or raising
the elbows without a desire to send the rider to school—
to the Elgin Marbles.

V

It is no wonder that the Indian rode well. Before he could walk, or talk, or remember, the lad had been tumbled into a parflèche with a lot of puppies or tepee stuff, and had travelled scores of miles a day; he had later been tied to a horse, or been set astride his neck, and told to hold on by the mane, or fall off and be left behind; and no Indian can recollect the time when he could not ride anything and everything which came along. The old knightly training—and why does it not, broadly construed, cover all that one wants to know?—to ride and fence and speak the truth, was carried out for two-thirds its value by the Indian. They could ride, and they could use their weapons. The boys from twelve years up do most of the herding among all Indian nations, and in this occupation they become familiar with every pony in the tribe. It is probable that the lads have roped and mounted in succession every one intrusted to their care, and have learned its individual qualities, while gaining in general horsemanship.

Even to-day the Indian always races bareback. His saddle weighs far too much, and he himself does not train down like our jockeys, except when he is starved on the war-path, and racing is a pastime of peace; so that at the starting-post he strips off all he can from both his horse and his own person. He is keenly fond of speed-matches, and is up to every known and unknown trick of gambling or jockeying. He can give long odds to the best race-track shark, and the sorrier he can make his pony look, if he knows he has speed, the better he is pleased. His pony will, of course, beat a thorough-bred at short distances; any pony can. He is half down the track before the racer has got his stride. At a mile or two miles the tables are turned, though there are many who insist that the bronco is the better at a ten or twenty mile gallop. This opinion is, I think, founded on an intimate knowledge of the bronco, but a lack of intimacy with the thorough-bred. In the late Berlin-Vienna ride the ponies came in with less apparent injury; but they were not the winners—and many other factors came into play.

The Indian does not rank high in beauty, strength, or endurance. There have been tribes in America which produced the finest of specimens; but if we read Parkman carefully we shall find the Indian of two hundred years ago much what he is to-day, bar a few nasty white man's tricks, learned to the eternal disgrace of the latter. While wonderfully agile and with the fortitude which all wild tribes possess, the Indian lacks the strength of our athletes; and in boxing or wrestling, even after a course of instruction, would be no match for an average American. A Sullivan—or rather a Corbett—could knock out two-score of them, "one down t'other come on." But for all that the Indian can perform equestrian feats which strike us as wonderful enough. It is a point of honor with him, as it was with the ancients and is still among many peoples, not to leave his dead or wounded in the hands of the enemy, liable to butchery or deprived of the rites of burial; and he will pick up a warrior from the ground without dismounting, almost without slacking speed, throw him across his pony and gallop off. This requires and receives much practice. Sometimes two act together in picking up the man, but one is quite able to accomplish it.

A buck represents the dead or wounded. He lies perfectly still and limp if the former, or aids as far as is consistent with his supposed hurt if the latter. It is rather rough handling he has to undergo, but by no means as rough as one sees in some of our favorite sports—say, foot-ball. Perhaps this is the best of the numerous feats the Indian can exhibit; but Dodge and Parkman tell us of many others. When I refer to Dodge, I mean Colonel Richard Irving Dodge, of the Army—a soldier, a sportsman, and an author, partaking of the virtues of each profession, and—well, I cannot say more an I would. Francis Parkman's unequalled knowledge of the Indian in our history is acknowledged in every part of the civilized world.

The Indians would be capable of making a superb irregular cavalry were it not for the divided authority from which all tribes suffer. There is no central power, no influence to hold the individuals to anything like what we call duty. The recent efforts to enlist Indians have not proven successful. Capable of immense exertion under circumstances which arouse his fanaticism, he is yet at heart a lazy brute, and when he has once sated his passion for adornment by wearing Uncle Sam's uniform for a few months, his greed for ease overcomes all sense of discipline, and he relapses into the indolent savage, of practically little use in any line but politics. Yet among themselves they have a certain organization, and in battle are able to execute a number of manœuvres, all, however, weakened by the lack of the one controlling hand. Nor can the Indian be easily kept in the ranks. In order to claim a scalp, the warrior must give the dead man the *coup*. This was in olden times a stab with a weapon, but Indians now have what are called *coup* sticks. Whoever first strikes the victim the *coup* can rightfully claim the scalp, and no authority known to his savage instincts can keep an Indian in the ranks when there is a scalp at stake. The fact that an occasional Indian turns out trustworthy merely furnishes the exception which proves the rule.

The Indians of to-day show a certain similarity in their style of riding to those of the last generation, so far as the constant use of the whip and heels is concerned, but the saddle has completely changed their seat, and the different tribes differ as greatly among themselves as saddle-riding does from the bareback. All Indians ride well. Living in the saddle, breaking wild ponies, and using half-trained ones at all times, they cannot help being expert horsemen. They remind me of the old horse-lover who once examined a fine mare I was riding—it was " Penelope." "She's a good mare, Deacon Dyer," said I. "That 'ere mare," replied he, after looking her all over with a true horseman's delight, and stopping in front of her to give one more look into her broad, handsome, courageous face—"that 'ere mare can't help but be a good un." So with the Indian ; but most of them ride in so ungainly a manner as to be hard to describe to one who has not seen them.

The first point of difference between them and the civilized rider which is apt to be brought home to a tenderfoot turns on the fact that the Indian always mounts from the off side. This was a common habit also of remote antiquity, though Xenophon teaches you how to mount from the near side. Perhaps the habit came from the same cause—that the lance or other weapon was naturally held in the right hand, and could not readily be thrown over the animal without fright or injury. The Greeks had a small loop on the shank of the lance, into which they thrust their right foot in order to swing themselves up on their horse. They had no weapons dangling from their waist to interfere with free action. But the long,

strap-hung sword of the mediæval cavalry soldier compelled him to mount on the near side, and as he is the
pattern from which we moderns have been cast the habit
has survived.

The average rider will be apt to deny that the soldier
is the prototype of the modern horseman; but every riding-school maxim is a distinct inheritance from the cavalryman of auld lang-syne; and only he who has learned to
ride, as it were, *au naturel*, can be free from these. Even
then imitation of or association with those who have ridden in a school will lend some of this color to his style.

To revert to our text, the white man who attempts to
mount an Indian pony in our fashion is very apt to get a
nasty spill before he has reached his back, for at the unusual attempt the half-trained beast will be apt to fly the
track with a quickness which the ordinary " American "
horse could in nowise rival. He is not so easily managed
either, this same pony. He is tractable and clever in his
way, but his way is not our way; and he must indeed be
a fairly good rough-rider who, once mounted on a fresh
and vigorous Indian pony, does not part company with
him before he has covered many miles of sharpish riding
or hunting.

VI

THE old-time Sioux was one of the earliest of the saddle-riding Indians. He was to be met with on the Northern plains some forty years ago. He managed his pony with a stick or the hereditary jaw-rope, and this when not in use he was wont to throw over the pony's neck, whence it would shortly fall and trail along the ground. But the pony never minded so small a thing. So well was he used to a rope thus trailing that he never blundered on it. This seems odd; but if you will study the clever way in which a horse will avoid the stones in the road he is travelling over, by stepping slightly within or beyond them, or on this or that side of them, all the while apparently paying heed to other things, you will see how naturally he may avoid treading on a trailing rope. A horse is apt to get his leg caught in a bridle, because it has two reins buckled together, but scarcely in a halter-rope if he breaks loose from you.

The home-made saddle of the old-time Sioux was constructed of a wooden or sometimes an elkhorn framework. The side pieces were well apart, and were held to the arches by the most ancient practice of shrinking rawhide upon them. No one who has not used it has any idea of how firmly rawhide will hold two such pieces together. A broken wagon-tongue wrapped with rawhide is as good as new—better. The pommel and cantle of the Sioux's saddle were very much alike; both rose perpendicularly from the arch of the tree to a height of sometimes eighteen

inches. There was no regulation pattern to them; each
saddle was separately made, and constructed and ornamented according to the momentary taste and fancy of
the maker, or according to the materials at hand. It was
not a saddle of commerce.

The bent-wood stirrups were lashed in straps also cut
from rawhide, slung loosely on the side pieces, and working back and forth into all conceivable positions. Such a
trifle as ill-hung stirrups the Sioux never heeded. His
seat was not so easily disturbed as a city swell's by one
hole difference in his leathers. It was generally immaterial to him whether he had any stirrups at all. His
seat was peculiar. His leg from crotch to knee gripped
in an almost perpendicular position; from the knee down
it was thrown sharply back, so that his weight was sustained solely on the crotch and the muscles of the thighs.
As a consequence of this seat, he pounded in his saddle
like a fresh recruit when riding anything but a rack or lope,
leaned forward like a modern track-jockey at a hand-gallop, and stuck his heels into his pony's flanks for a hold.
This matter of holding on by the heels is almost universal among riders not civilized into the soldier's method
above referred to. Nine-tenths of the daily riders of the
world hold on by the calf and heel. How the Sioux could
ride as he did and escape injury from the pommel is a
mystery. But though smashing to atoms all the maxims
of equitation, ancient or modern, the old-time Sioux was
a good rider, and his seat was strong and effective. It
has been referred to as ungainly; but in a certain sense,
no really strong seat can be such. Noteworthy ability is
generally handsome *per se.*

This savage tricked up his pony's mane and tail and
forelock with feathers, beads, or scraps of gaudy cloth,
and on occasion painted him all over with a colored clay,

very much as the Hindoo will daub red spots of paint all over a white horse, or dye his tail pea-green. In his fashion the Sioux was as much of a dude as if he wore a three-inch collar and a big-headed cane, or shook hands with elbow in the air, and was a singularly picturesque horseman, if not one who would appeal to the eye of a park-rider.

VII

AMERICA has been full of picturesque characters. Even the Orient to-day, which is much what it has always been, has no more of the odd and interesting than we have had. Civilization (*i. e.* newspapers, railroads, and telegraphs) brings us down to one pattern. Ready-made clothing is the archenemy of the graceful and appropriate—the demon in art. No greater advance in mechanics was ever made than that of building arms, machines, and tools to scale, and that of duplicate parts. But people nowadays are all duplicate parts, and while it works well in mechanics, it destroys originality and beauty in the human race. When you consider what our early frontier population was; what energy, intelligence, and pluck resided in the men who went out beyond "the settlements" into the *habitat* of the red man to hunt or trap, we can surely boast a more wonderful, and actually more picturesque set of actors on the stage of American history than can be found in any other land.

Among these was the trapper. Some of the largest cities on the American continent—St. Louis, as an instance—may be said to have been built from the profits of the fur trade. There had been stray trappers and small dealers from the earliest days; but the first man who discovered the immense extent to which the peltry traffic could be carried was a rover of broad views, who most likely hailed from Kentucky or Missouri, was of French or Scotch-Irish descent, and perchance came from the

A WHITE TRAPPER

blood which crossed the Alleghanies in the footsteps of Daniel Boone, intent on adventure or flying from civilization. The white trapper was as averse to association with his fellow-man as the hardiest of the old pioneers; in fact, he often fled the settlements for good and sufficient cause. He was not so much of a misanthrope as he was a law-breaker; but it is said that many had fled from the irate importunities of their respective Xanthippes. It will not do to class this trapper among the Ishmaels; many were pushed out beyond the frontier by their love of adventure and expectation of gain, and were as blameless in their lives as they were courageous in their calling. But it is also a fact that many of these hardy fellows preferred to live in a country where there was no sheriff to molest nor deputy to make them afraid. The white trapper has now all but died out with the buffalo, though a generation ago he was a common enough character in the territories north of Colorado. His descendants have mostly turned cow-punchers.

This famous hunter was a character more practical than poetic, though he has been made the subject of many fine phrases and the hero of many exaggerated situations. His unkempt hair and beard floated long and loose from under his coyote cap, and he had lived so continuously with the Indians that he had largely adopted their dress and their manners—could, if need be, live on the same chuck, and always had one or more squaws. He was apt to carry a trade-gun—perhaps a good one, perhaps an old Brown Bess cut down. At his side was slung an enormous powder-horn, for in the old days he could not so readily replenish his supply, far from civilization as he was wont to be. He rode a Mexican saddle, for which he had traded skins, or maybe stolen, and from which he had cut every strip of superfluous leather, as the Indian does to-day.

3

He rode the same pony as his Indian competitor in the trade, but with the seat adapted to a saddle rather than a pad, and still retaining a flavor of the settlements despite his divorce from their ways. In fact, a white man on the plains never quite acquires the redskin habit. He can to-day be told from an Indian as far as he can be seen by his style of riding, and it was no doubt always so. Nor had this trapper lost his pale-face instincts so entirely as to indulge in the Indian's usual atrocious cruelty to his horse. He can scarcely be said to have had the feelings of a member of the society with the exuberantly long name and truly benevolent method; but he had the sense to see the commercial value of the care he might bestow on his rough-and-ready companion, and at least treated him with common consideration. This the good little fellow repaid with a love and unselfish devotion which only an animal can show.

Right here and now I would fain pour out my heart-felt admiration for the truest of our four-footed friends, our dogs and horses. Have you never had a horse, my brother, to whom you told your secrets and your griefs? Have you never had a dog who was to you even as a child, for whom you wept bitter tears and honest when you had laid him at rest in some quiet spot, hallowed alone by his virtues and your sorrow; who, for his short term of years had grown into your very inmost heart by his faithful love, his unswerving loyalty, his spotless truth of character? If not, turn this page, read no more. But if you have ever given your affection to such a loving creature, if you have ever held his head between your hands and looked long and deep down into his tender, earnest eyes, in which lurks no thought of treachery, no ideal but yourself, which view you with a pathetic trustfulness of which you know you are not worthy, then, my brother, join me in laying on his grave a wreath of everlasting, and thank God that you have known that truth and honor and pure faith which we weaklings of so-called civilization have lost in our efforts to grasp a higher good not half so well worth seeking. Truly the poor Indian was right in believing that he should share the company of his faithful friend when both should be translated to that equal sky! If the hereafter is to be filled with the good we have known, will not many of us ask that such friends as these may be there? I am humbly conscious that, if honest purpose and loyalty to her ideal be the test, there is certainly one dog I have owned who should enter the gates in advance of her master, strive he never so well for what is upright. I am not so sure that she had not a soul—that she is not waiting for me now, even as she used to do when I went away from home. Dear, loving, white-souled Piccola! Many are the tears which the memory of thee hath evoked! Though I live to the term when life is but labor and sorrow, thou shalt daily have thy meed of a tender thought. Was not Buddha, indeed, a true prophet? But that is another story.

VIII

THE Indians were not long in finding out that peltries were a ready means of getting the guns and calico and fire-water of the white man, and the white trapper was not many years alone in the business. The Indian trapper whom Remington's clever eye and hand have depicted may be a Cree or perhaps a Blackfoot, whom one was apt to run across in the Selkirk Mountains or elsewhere on the plains of the British Territory, or well up north in the Rockies, somewhat antedating the outbreak of the Civil War. He was tributary to the Hudson Bay Company, whose badge he wore in his blanket coat of English manufacture, which he had got in trade. Wherever you met this coat, you might place its wearer. He had bear-skin leggings, with surface cleverly seared into ornamental patterns, and for the rest the usual Indian outfit. He rode a pony which had nothing to distinguish it from the plains pony, except that in winter its coat grew to so remarkable a length as almost to conceal the identity of the animal. Unless you saw it in motion you might take it for a huge species of bear—with a tail.

Such long coats are not uncommon among any breed of horses. We are wont to imagine that the Arabian always has a bright, glossy coat; but during the chill rainy season of the regions north of the Arabian desert— and it can be as bleak and cold on those treeless wastes as heart can desire—the Arabian puts on a coat all but as long and rough as a sheep. Unlike the Indian's pony, he

AN INDIAN TRAPPER

gets fed during the severe season, for his master is not quite so improvident as the red man; and he does not get so gaunt and miserable as his transatlantic cousin. But, like the bronco, it takes but a week or so of grass to scour him out into a coat as sleek as that of a race-track favorite.

The Indian trapper rode a pad which was not unlike an air-cushion, cinched in place and provided with a pair of very short stirrups hung exactly from the middle. This dragged his heels to the rear, in the fashion of the old-time Sioux, and gave him a very awkward look. By just what process, from a bareback seat, the fellow managed to drift into this one, which is quite peculiar to himself, it is hard to guess. Habits change by slow degrees, and each step is wont to bring a new condition somewhat resembling its predecessor. Here we have a seat which has wandered as far from the bareback as one can well imagine, and this in a comparatively short period. Among civilized peoples a novel invention may often immediately change a given method of doing a thing; among savages changes are very gradual; among semi-civilized peoples change is so slow that one may almost say that it never occurs.

Unlike the old-time Sioux, the Indian trapper would sit all over his horse, weaving from side to side, and shifting his pad at every movement. His pony's back was always sore. His pad-lining soon got hard with sweat and galled the skin, and the last thing which would ever occur to him would be to take steps to relieve his patient comrade's suffering. He never attempted to change his pad-lining or cinch the pad more carefully. On went the pad, up jumped the trapper; and why shouldn't the pony buck, as he invariably did? Sore backs are as much at the root of the bucking habit as the utterly insufficient breaking of the pony.

This matter of sore backs furnishes a curious study. In every southern country outside of the United States, and among all wild or semi-civilized nations which are not peculiarly horse lovers, no heed whatever is paid to saddle or pack galls. The condition of the donkeys in the East, in Africa, or in Spain and Italy, is as lamentable as it is short-sighted. It never enters the minds of the owners of these patient brutes that a sore back is a commercial loss; nor do they couple the idea of cruelty with dumb creatures at all. It is not until you reach Teutonic nations that both these ideas are extended so as to reduce the discomfort of animals to a minimum.

This is not so odd; one does not have to be so very old to remember the time when, even among us, calves were tied by all four legs and slung head down on their way to market; when common pity never extended to animals. Even to-day, not very far from home, one may find many breaches of the should-be commandment: "Thou shalt treat thy dumb servant as thou wouldst thy son." In those countries where the doctrine of transmigration has obtained a hold on the people, animals are better off; one does not like to abuse a creature which may contain the soul of one's great-grandmother. But bad as the cruelty of neglect may be, an American Indian is perhaps more actively cruel to his pony than any other person. He never wears spurs, not even as a matter of vanity, for spurs would prevent his pounding his pony with his heels at every stride, as is his wont; but he will ride him till he drops dead in his tracks, when there is no necessity of his making speed; he will lash him to the raw; he will even stick his knife into him to make him gallop faster, and an Apache will give his pony a dig with his knife from sheer malice when he dismounts.

IX

THERE is no horse superior to the bronco for endurance; few are his equals. His only competitor in the equine race is his lowly cousin, the ass, of whom I shall say much anon. The bronco came by his toughness and grit naturally enough; he got them from the Spanish stock of Moorish descent, the individuals of which breed, abandoned in American wilds in the sixteenth century by the early searchers for gold and for the Fountain of Youth, were his immediate ancestors; and his hardy life has, by survival of the fittest, increased this endurance tenfold. He is not handsome. His middle-piece is distended by grass food; it is so loosely joined to his quarters that one can scarcely understand where he gets his weight-carrying capacity, and his hip is very short. He has a hammer-head, partly due to the pronounced ewe-neck which all plains or steppes horses seem to acquire by their nomad life. He has a bit too much daylight under him, which shows his good blood as well as the fact that he has had generations of sharp and prolonged running to do. His legs are naturally perfect, rather light in muscle and slender in bone, but the bone is dense, the muscle of strong quality, and the sinews firm. Still, in an Indian's hands his legs finally give way at the knees from sharp stopping with a gag-bit, and curbs will start on his houghs, for a redskin will turn on a ten-cent piece.

The pony is naturally quick, but his master wants him to be quicker. His hunting and all his sports require work

which outdoes polo. One form of racing is to place two
long parallel strips of buffalo-hide on the ground at an
interval of but a few feet, and, starting from a distance,
to ride up to these strips, cross the first, turn between the
two, and gallop back to the starting-point. A fraction
of a second lost on a turn loses the race. Until one thinks
of what it means, a twentieth part of a second is no great
loss. But take two horses of equal speed in a hurdle race
with twenty obstacles. One pauses at each hurdle just
one-twentieth of a second; the other flies his hurdles without a pause. This lost second means that he will be forty-
five feet behind at the winning-post—four good lengths.
Another Indian sport is to ride up to a log hung horizon-
tally and just high enough to allow the pony but not the
rider to get under, touch it, and return. If the pony is
stopped too soon, the Indian loses time in touching the
log; if too late, he gets scraped off. The sudden jerking
of the pony on its haunches is sure eventually both to start
curbs or spavin, and to break his knees. Still the pony
retains wonderfully good legs considering.

The toughness and strength of the plains pony can
scarcely be exaggerated. He will live through a winter
that will kill the hardiest cattle. He worries through the
long months when the snow has covered up the bunch-
grass on a diet of cotton-wood boughs, which the Indian
cuts down for him; and though he emerges from this
ordeal a pretty sorry specimen of a horse, it takes but a
few weeks in the spring for him to get himself into splendid condition and fit for the trials of the war-path. His
fast has done him good, as some say sea-sickness will do
him good who goes down to the sea in ships. He can go
unheard-of distances. Colonel Dodge records an instance
coming under his observation where a pony carried the
mail three hundred miles in three consecutive nights, and

back over the same road the next week, and kept this up for six months without loss of condition. He can carry any weight. Mr. Parkman speaks of a chief known as Le Cochon, on account of his three hundred pounds avoirdupois, who, nevertheless, rode his ponies as bravely as a man of half the bulk. He as often carries two people as one. There is simply no end to this wonderful product of the prairies. He works many years. So long as he will fat up in the spring, his age is immaterial to the Indian.

It has been claimed by some that the American climate is, *par excellence*, adapted to the horse. California and Kentucky vie for superiority, and both produce such wonderful results as "Sunol" and "Nancy Hanks." Man certainly has done wonders with the horse upon our soil; and alone the horse has done wonders for himself. I have sought for great performances by horses in every land. One hears wonderful traditions of speed and endurance and much unsupported testimony elsewhere; but for recorded distance and time, America easily bears off the palm. We shall recur to this point hereafter. Ever since Brown-Sequard discovered that he could not always kill an American rabbit by inserting a probe into its brain, and enunciated the doctrine of the superior energy and endurance of the American mammal, facts have been accumulating to prove his position sound.

One peculiarity of the pony is his absence of crest. His ewe-neck suggests the curious query of what has become of the high, well-shaped neck of his ancestor the Barb. I was on the point of saying arched neck—but this is the one thing which the Arabian or Barb rarely has, being ridden with a bit which keeps his nose in the air. But he has a peculiarly fine neck and wide, deep, open throttle of perfect shape, and with bit and bridoon carries his head just right. There are two ways of accounting for the ewe-neck. The Indian's gag-bit, invariably applied with a jerk, throws up the pony's head instead of bringing it down, as the slow and light application of the school-curb will do, and this, it is thought by many, tends to develop the ewe-neck. But this is scarcely a theory which can be borne out by the facts, for the Arabian retains his fine crest under the same course of treatment. A more sufficient reason may be found in the fact that the starvation which the pony annually undergoes in the winter months tends to deplete him of every superfluous ounce of flesh wherever it may lie. The crest in the horse is mostly meat, and its annual depletion, never quite replaced, has finally brought down the Indian pony's neck nearer to the outline of the skeleton. It was with much ado under his scant diet that the pony held on to life during the winter; he could not scrape together enough food to flesh up a merely ornamental appendage like a crest. Most Moors and Arabs, on the other hand, prize the beauty of the high-built neck, and breed for it; and their steeds are far better fed. There is rarely snow where they dwell; forage of some kind is to be had in the oases, and the master always stores up some barley and straw for his steed; or in case of need will starve his daughters to feed his mares. The Indian cares for his pony only for what he can do for him, and once lost, the crest would with difficulty be replaced, for few Indians have any conception of breeding. The bronco's mean crest is distressing, but it is in inverse ratio to his endurance and usefulness. Well fed and cared for, he will regain his crest to a marked extent.

As we shall later see when we reach the land of the pure-bred Arabian, there are many more points of similarity than are generally supposed to exist between this steed of royal lineage and his country cousin across the sea. The city dwellers, or those who live near enough to

the busy haunts of men to cater to the wants of the
Franks who "have an eye for a horse," breed a well-
rounded, up-headed fellow—the one we all see painted.
But the real Arabian mare—the Anazeh—the progenitress
of all that is fast and enduring, the worshipped of the
sons of the Prophet, is quite another creature. She is for
all the world like a small thorough-bred in training—or a
bronco. But that, again, is another story.

X

From one kind of bronco we will skip to another. The Indian must have transportation as well as riding ponies, and as the patient ass is the follower of Mohammed, so is the travaux (or *traineau*) pony to the Indian. It is hard to say which bears the most load according to his capacity, the donkey or the pony. On the whole, perhaps, weight for weight, the palm must be awarded to the ass ; but either earns what he gets with fourfold more right than his master. The burdens the ass bears in the Orient break him down to the extent of forgetting how to kick. Fancy driving even an overworked Kentucky mule by the tail, as they do the donkey in many parts of the East, and guiding him by a tweak of that appendage, close to his treacherous heels ! In a later chapter I shall sing pæans to this noblest of the equine race.

The travaux pony is equally worked out of all idea of bucking. He furnishes the sole means of transportation of the Indian camp, except sometimes a dog hitched to a diminutive *traineau*, and managed—half for sport, half work—by a boy ; and, weight for weight, drags on his tepee-poles more than the best mule in Uncle Sam's service does on an army-wagon. When camp is broken, the squaws strip the tent-poles of their buffalo-skin coverings, and it is these poles which furnish the wheels of the Indian vehicle. Vehicle is, perhaps, an odd term to us who make the word synonymous with rotary progression ; but vehicles on runners are to-day used at all seasons in many

THE TRAVAUX PONY

parts of the Cumberland Mountains. They are of domestic manufacture, and are simply constructed of bent saplings lashed with green withes. As a rule, a cow or young steer is hitched singly into these sleds, which run with light loads all over the country—on mud roads in summer, and but for a short while on snow in midwinter. I have talked with old men in Eastern Kentucky who had never seen a wheel. That sounds odd, but it is true.

The Blackfoot makes the neatest trappings for the travaux ponies and pack-saddles. The pony is fitted with a huge leathern bag, heavily fringed and gaudy with red and blue flannel strips and beads of many colors. Over this goes the pack-saddle, which is not very dissimilar to the riding-saddle; but it is of coarser build, and has a perpendicular pommel and cantle. In the pommel is a notch to receive one end of the tepee-poles, which are sometimes bound together two or three on each side, and, trailing past either flank of the pony, are held in place by two pieces of wood lashed to them just behind his tail and a bit farther back. In the socket so made rides the parflèche, a sort of rawhide trunk, and this receives the camp utensils—plunder, children, sometimes an old man or woman, puppies, and all the other camp *impedimenta*—while a squaw rides behind the pack-saddle on the pony, indifferently astride or sidewise, with her feet on the poles, and perhaps a youngster bestrides its neck. Thus laden, the wonderful little beast, which is rarely up to fourteen hands, plods along all day, covering unheard-of distances, and living on what bunch-grass he can pick up in spare moments, with a mouthful of water now and again.

There are apt to be several ponies to carry the plunder of the occupants of one tepee, and often one of them is loaded down with the rougher stuff, while a second may be decked out with the finery and carry only one squaw—

4

particularly if she happens to be a new purchase and a
favorite of the chief.

A squaw is usually about as good a horseman as her
buck, and rides his saddle or bareback with as much ease
as a city woman rocks in her chair. She is often as plucky
as he is. Indeed, it is not uncommon to find women in the
fighting ranks, and doing a man's full duty ; and if the
squaw does not often join her lord in the killing and capture of the enemy, she can out-do him at all times in cruelty to prisoners. Perhaps no human being is so fiendish
in the pastime of torturing prisoners as an Indian squaw.
She out-herods Herod in barbarity.

XI

THE Comanche of the Fort Sill region is a good type of the Indian of to-day. He is the most expert horse-stealer on the plains, if we can credit the Indians themselves, who yield to him the palm as a sneak thief—with them a title of honor rather than of reproach. There is no boldness or dash in his method, but he is all the more dangerous. The Indian has been much misconceived. It is not strange that many novelists should have taken him as the hero of their books; few readers could check off their errors, and he was a new character who served as a vehicle for any number of qualities which might best fit into any given plot. But the red man has been as much overwrought as the Arabian horse. He is a brute, pure and simple, and has practically always been so. If you want the truth about him, consult people who have spent their lives among his ilk, not those who theorize on benevolent general principles at a judiciously safe distance. Read *Our Wild Indians*, and you will know more about him than most of those who think his vices are all attributable to the white man.

Not that we can avoid responsibility for much that is evil in the red man—vile disease of body and mind and character; but he is none the less a brute whose nature is a fit hot-bed for our worst vices. It is politics and dollars which have used him as a shuttlecock. The Indian problem is reducible to the simple question whether this broad land of ours is for the pale-face or the redskin. If,

as elsewhere, civilization has here a right to extend the
borders of its garments, the white man is responsible only
for his excess of wrong—for the manner, not the fact of
his taking. This excess is no greater than that attributable to any other nation which seizes and civilizes a bar-
barous land ; and, after all is said, the Indian is more sin-
ning than sinned against. He is and remains the most
vicious brute the sun ever shone upon.

The Comanche eats dog and horse flesh—as all Indians
do more or less—and is by no means above a diet of skunk
when other edibles fail him. Indeed, anything is chuck
to the Indian in case of need, and while he has his *bonne
bouche*, it is, as a rule, quantity and not quality he seeks.

The Comanche is fond of gay clothes, and has a trick
of wrapping a sheet around his body, doubling in the
ends, and letting the rest fall about his legs. This gives
him the look of wearing the skirts or leg-gear of the Oriental. He uses a Texas cowboy's tree, a wooden stirrup,
into which he thrusts his foot as far as a fox-hunter, and
leathers even longer than the cowboy's, perhaps the longest used by any rider. He is the only Indian who rides
after this fashion. He, if any one, has the forked-radish
seat. Between him and his saddle he packs all his extra
blankets and most of his other plunder, so that he is sometimes perched high above his mount. For bridle and bit,
he uses whatever he can beg, borrow, or steal.

In one particular the Comanche is noteworthy. He
knows more about a horse and horse-breeding than any
other Indian. It strikes one as rather singular that the
redskin has never developed an instinct for raising horses.
And yet it is not strange. The conditions themselves
have done so much for the bronco, and until of late years
wild ponies have been so easily procurable in unlimited
numbers, that he has not yet been pushed into breeding.

MODERN COMANCHE

And it is a rule with the red man not to do the unnecessary. "Never do to-day what you can by any possibility put off till to-morrow" may be said to be his motto—except on the war-path. Is it alone his?

The Comanche is particularly wedded to and apt to ride a pinto ("painted" or piebald) horse, and never keeps any but a pinto stallion. He chooses his ponies well, and shows more good sense in breeding than one would give him credit for. The corollary to this is that he is far less cruel to his beasts, and though he begins to use them as yearlings, the ponies often last through many years. In this he resembles his Oriental brother. Yearlings are very frequently seen under saddle among the Arabs. The Comanche is capable of making as fine cavalry as exists, if subjected to discipline and carefully drilled. But the process may be difficult.

XII

THE Apache of the present day is the exact reverse of the Comanche. His *habitat* is the Sierra Madre Mountains in Arizona. He is not born and bred with horses, he knows little about them, and looks upon ponies as intended rather for food than for transportation or the war-path; or, at all events, as ultimately destined for the *cuisine*. He at times outdoes the Frenchman in hippophagy, for he will eat every one of his ponies during the winter, and rely upon stealing fresh ones in the spring. He and the Cheyenne are the most dashing of the Indian horse-thieves. He raids down in Chihuahua, where the vaqueros raise stock for the Mexican army, and often drives off large numbers. When pursued, the Apache takes to the mountains, and is not infrequently compelled to abandon his herd. But such is his expert boldness that he rarely lacks a supply at his neighbor's expense. Not content with ponies, he steals his saddle and bridle in Mexico; he wears spurs when he can get them to drive on his pony, and if these do not suffice to make him go his gait, he will goad him with a knife. The Apache is hideously cruel by nature, even more so than other Indians, if this were possible; and his pony is often the sufferer. He takes no particular interest in him. Except for his summer's use and his winter's salt-junk, the pony has no future value. He takes a certain care of him only for the present value of the little fellow. In the mountains, where the sharp, flinty stones wear down the pony's unshod feet,

AN APACHE INDIAN

this Indian will shrink rawhide over the hoofs in lieu of shoes, and this resists extremely well the attrition of the mountain paths. Arrian, of Nicomedia, tells us that the Macedonians, under Alexander, did the same to their cavalry horses in the Hindoo Koosh, and no doubt the habit was much older than Alexander. On the whole, the Apache, *quoad* horses, is at the foot of the scale. There can be no comparative excellence to the Indian as a whole; it is comparative badness. In this, too, the Apache reaches the superlative.

In what I say anent the Indian I may perchance be accused of what many intelligent judges would call a criminal unwillingness to understand a really noble nature. But, so far as my experience goes, those men who maintain that the faults of the Indian are chargeable solely to the whites, and that he can be managed in any other way than by repression, either view the situation from an inexperienced and safe distance, or from a financial (*i. e.* Indian contract) stand - point, or from one of "practical politics." There are men, benevolent and noble men, who, after studying the subject, truly believe that the Indian can be civilized; but they only serve to prove the rule. Those men who have spent their lives among the Indians, and have nothing to make out of them, hold but one opinion. Narrow politics and the money in it are the curse of our country. If the Indian could be given over to the army to care for he would behave himself, for he knows that he receives justice, both in peace and war, from the blue-coats. But so long as Indian agents can grow rich fast, and there are a lot of fat jobs for the men who vote the successful ticket, so long will the Indian be cheated out of his rations, go on the war-path in revenge, and be doomed to fall under the sabre of the unwilling soldier. If there is or ever has been a more lamentable spectacle

in the political life of any nation than the cross-purposes
of our Indian and War Departments, I have failed to find
it.   We Americans, thanks to the inexhaustible riches of
our soil, are giants in all we do; and we are giants in
folly as well as in creation; witness our Silver Bill, our
McKinley Tariff, our Pension Legislation, and our Indian
Problem.

XIII

Previous to our Civil War, the lack of knowledge abroad with regard to the United States was singular. We were ignored in the economy of nations, in the schools and society of the Old World, as of no importance. To most people America was as yet undiscovered. Only the most advanced thinkers had divined that we were working out the problem of the future. To see their countries become Americanized was the nightmare of rulers, as it is now the dream of the more intelligent of the peoples. The blot of slavery was still upon us, and we were numerically among the smaller nations. When, sent to a monastic school in Belgium at the age of ten, I was led into the *petite cour* and introduced by the Père Supérieur to the crowd of eagerly expectant boys, "Tenez, mes enfants, voilà votre nouveau camarade, le jeune Américain!" I well remember a fair-faced lad (he was a son of a banished Polish noble) who went up to the father and plucked him by his skirt, with "Mais, mon père, il est blanc comme nous." His keen disappointment at my not being black, for he had never seen a negro, he always rather laid up against me. And when later I attended the Friedrich-Werderschen Gymnasium in Berlin, the only two ideas I could ever find that boys of my age had assimilated out of the shreds and patches they had been taught about America, were Niagara and slavery. How much did a Massachusetts lad who had left home in his first decade know about slavery, or

how many, in those stage - coach days, had been to the
great falls? "Ach, du bist kein Amerikaner," my play-
mates would exclaim, "wenn du Niagäära nicht gesehen
hast!" imagining, no doubt, that this world - famed cataract was at every man's back door. And my never even
having seen a slave stamped me still more of an impostor.

To wander for a moment from anything akin to horse-
flesh or America, to what, if imaginative, I would transform into a psychical phenomenon: The little Polish noble
before referred to and I became fast friends, and for years
wandered arm in arm around the playground. Nearly
forty years ago we separated, and neither, for four decades, heard aught of the other, nor made any effort to
hunt him up. In April last I landed at Constantinople—
as usual with tourists out of money—and repaired at
once to my bankers. My letter of credit and draft went
into Mr. A's private office for approval. Almost at once
out he came with, "Bless me, you are the very man!"
"No doubt," I replied; "I always have been, but why
just now?" "Were you ever at school in Belgium?" he
asked. "Yes." "Did you have a school - mate named
Ladislas Cz——ski?" "Why, yes." "Well, he is now
Mo——er Pacha, Inspector-General of Cavalry, and Aide-
de - camp to H. I. M. the Sultan, and only last week he
told me he once had a school-mate named Theodore Dodge,
and asked me to write to my correspondents in America
and see if I could find trace of him!" Here, then, had
my ancient school-friend, for the first time in forty years,
sought to hunt me up, and I, for the first time in my life,
had turned up at Constantinople. And yet it was mere
coincidence. Is not this such stuff as dreams are made
of—or superstition, or psychology? How easy to warp
this occurrence into something, let us say, spooky!

The ignorance on the part of Europeans concerning

us was, however, in nowise more curious, and was much
less culpable, than our own ignorance of to-day respect-
ing our South American neighbors, despite even the Pan-
Americans. How many of us can tell the form of government of half the South American States, or their
geographical features or limits, or their chief products,
or their population, or climate, or even their capital cities,
unless he is still in the grammar-school.

Our Civil War wrought a change. We hewed ourselves into notice by the doughtiest blows delivered in
war since the era of Napoleon. Yet were the most conservative among the military autocrats of Europe unwilling, till towards the very end, to look upon us in any
other light than as armed mobs, and even in the war of
'66 they declined to profit by our experience. But by
1870 the Germans, with their keen instinct for war and
more numerous ties with the States, had adopted many
of the methods we had first devised, and to-day, not
only are our campaigns studied as samples (of good and
bad alike, as almost all campaigns must be), but fair justice is done to our actual merit in the province of war,
and to the exceptional ability of some American generals.

Among other ideas, they have borrowed from the ver-
satility of our cavalry arm. Cavalry which fought on
foot had been sneered at for generations. It could not,
said the *beaux sabreurs*, be even good mounted infantry.
A cavalryman of this ilk must "ride like a hinfantry
hadjutant." He was of hybrid growth—neither fish, flesh,
nor good red-herring; and this, though history, among
other instances, shows us that Alexander's Companions—
as at Sangala, modern Lahore—dismounted and took in-
trenchments from which even his phalanx had recoiled,
while no body of five thousand cavalry ever held its own
in pitched battle so long by virtue of repeated and vigor-

ous charges, and with such heavy losses, as the Companions at the Hydaspes. We Americans were wiser; our cavalry was well suited to our needs, and when it became worthy the name, was singularly effective on our peculiar *terrain*. Our Western cavalry is now the pattern of the cavalry of the future. Even Prussia is about to abolish the peculiar scope of its cuirassiers, whose uniform Bismarck has so long honored, and cavalry will soon become largely irregular—if a regular dragoon, who mostly skirmishes on foot and rarely charges in the saddle, may be so dubbed.

XIV

Oᴜʀ frontier cavalryman is the beau ideal of an irregular. The irregular horseman of all ages was recruited
from among roving, unintelligent classes, and had, except
in his own peculiar province, as plentiful a lack of good
as he had a superabundance of bad qualities. Our trooper
is intelligent, and trained in the hardest of schools. Few
civilians, who find it so easy to criticise the operations of
the army in the West, would make much of a success in
hunting a band of a few hundred Indians in a pathless or
a waterless desert bigger than New York and New England combined. And yet, thus handicapped, what splendid work our cavalry has done! While one civil department of the Government has for years been busy sowing
the seeds of strife and furnishing the red man with arms
of precision, the best of cartridges and plenty of them,
how ably have our handful of blue-coats, under orders of
another, managed to quell the Indian uprisings! A force
of fifty thousand men constantly on foot, said that eminent
soldier, William Tecumseh Sherman (and he early made his
mark in estimating the number needed for a bigger piece
of work), would have been none too great to do justice to
our Indian problem since the war; the actual force has
been less than a third of this number. Let whoso is
tempted to criticise the army make himself familiar with
some of the deeds of heroism of the past twenty years by
our soldiers on the plains. Criticism blanches before
their recital. But the soldier is no boaster: you must
seek his story from other lips than his.

When in the field the cavalryman is allowed some latitude in suiting his dress to his own ideas of comfort, while kept within certain regulation bounds. It is thus our artist has represented him. He is apt to wear a soft hat— there is no better campaigning hat than the slouch, as thousands of old soldiers can testify— and boots *ad lib.*; his uniform is patterned on his own individuality after a few days' march. His enormous saddle-bags are much better filled at the start than at the finish, and a couple of canteens with the indispensable tin cup are slung at the cantle. His sabre he considers less useful than a revolver, and in a charge it is a question whether the latter be not by far the preferable weapon. Against Indians it certainly is so; for while your Indian is occasionally heroic beyond what the white man ever dreams, as a rule he is cowardly beyond belief, and you can rarely reach him with the naked blade. Cornered, or frenzied by superstition or passion or tribal pride, his constancy is marvellous; in open fight he will often shirk danger like the veriest poltroon. Like Sir Boyle Roche's Irishman, he would rather be a coward for five minutes than a dead man all his life.

No experience the trooper could possibly have could be a better training than Indian warfare, and at the end of his enlistment the intelligent cavalryman has perhaps no equal as a light dragoon. He labors under some serious disadvantages. His horse is an American, *i.e.*, one which comes from the States, and is in nowise allied to the bronco. This horse is larger and stronger, but less hardy, needs to be acclimated, and never can acquire the old hard stomach of the plains pony. Used to grain, he more speedily breaks down under lack of forage, and he is vastly overweighted. The cavalry pack is very heavy for pursuit of a foe who has nothing but his own precious

UNITED STATES CAVALRYMAN

carcass to transport, and never spares his many ponies, as
the soldier must his single horse. It has been suggested
that the California horse be tried, and in the South-west
this has been done, but without such results as to satisfy
all authorities. The California horse is small—fourteen
and a half to fifteen hands—weighs under nine hundred
pounds, and cannot well carry a heavy trooper and pack
whose weight overruns two hundred and thirty pounds.
But given light men of not exceeding a hundred and forty
pounds, recruited in the South-west, given a pack reduced
to the lowest limits, this horse would be of the greatest
utility. He is acclimated, has the much-enduring stomach of the old stock, is more active, and does not so soon
get used up.

In thus criticising the American horse, it will not do to
underrate him. He is capable of very great feats of endurance. Without question, the hardest continuous distance rides are those habitually performed by our cavalry
on the plains. This is partly due to the exceptional
knowledge of the capacity of the horse to perform which
our cavalry officers have acquired in their hard service,
but partly also to the horse himself. And when we note
that this animal is the common country horse, bought by
the Government at a low price—the horse which will not
command a price high enough to be worth sending far to
market—it speaks well for the quality of our American
stock. After a second summer in the ranks he becomes
used to exceptional feats, and can be kept on hard service
without grain for a month.

Considering all the circumstances—that the cavalry recruit is often a city-bred lad, who knows practically nothing about a horse, and has to be taught it all; that he
is employed too much on duties which unfit him for his
work; that he as well as his horse has to be acclimated;

and that the whole business which is new to him is an old story to the Indian — it is astonishing how well he does. His performances reflect unlimited credit upon his superiors. And when he has learned his business, he is certainly not surpassed by any cavalryman who bestrides a saddle.

Our cavalry seat in its best form is perhaps as good as can be. For long marches the saddle is comfortable, and the leathers are about the proper length for the work. It is neither the one extreme nor the other. You see some cavalrymen with stirrups altogether too long; but the well-trained United States trooper has as good a seat as any rider can have. I think it may be admitted that however good for rough-riding or for cross-country work, or racing, or polo, the English saddle may be, it is not as good for long-distance riding as a correct form of what we call a cavalry-tree. When a man sits in a saddle for thirty or forty consecutive hours, with but a few minutes' relief at a time, he can do better in a tree less long and flat. With some commands it is usual to girth a horse far back, so as to get the saddle well away from the withers, much as they do in most foreign armies, and thus save the weight from bearing too much on the fore-quarters; but the usefulness of the habit is still an open question. The place where the United States trooper rides is not far from the place where a man who sits in the middle of an English saddle rides. It is the withers which should determine the position of the saddle; and as the girth always slips more or less, it is the make of the tree and the way the saddle fits and the slant of the horse's shoulder which determine where the weight shall be. Some horses are bound to carry their weight more forward than others. If you seek to alter the place, you must alter the tree or look out for sore backs.

The proof of the pudding is in the eating. The skill of the soldier is measured by his performance. It is no doubt natural that we Americans should be a nation of army haters, but it is a pity that for the scruple of thanks our little regular army ever gets there should be so many ounces of grumbling. Uncle Sam has no public servants who work so faithfully and endure such hardships and danger. Why should sixty-five million Americans still harbor an inherited rancor against thirty thousand of our own countrymen because they professionally wear a uniform? The volunteers were always the pets of the nation; the regulars come in for more than their share of abuse. And yet what generals won our battles? What troops stood such decimation? That a volunteer deserves a certain credit beyond a regular for equal service no one will be found to dispute; but let us not forget the one in the services of the other.

XV

Wʜᴀᴛ has this to do with horsemanship, say you?
True, we seem to have wandered; but we can retrace our
steps. Let me quote some isolated facts quite apart from
the Civil War, to show that our cavalrymen on Indian
service have not only stout hearts under their army blue,
but stout seats in the saddle as well, and earn credit for
them both. Mention need not be made of the risk every
scouting party or detachment runs of perishing in an
Indian ambush, like Custer or Forsyth; nor of horrible
marches of many days with the thermometer at 40° below zero, like the command of Henry, when the bulk of
the men were frozen to death, or frost-bitten so as to lose
their feet and hands. Let us look at some good distance
riding, for it is in this that our men especially excel.

But to do this calls out another side issue by reminding
us of the celebrated ride between Berlin and Vienna, and
we may as well recall its incidents. There has been much
honestly severe criticism of this noteworthy performance.

> "But what good came of it at last?
>   Said little Peterkin.
> Why, that I cannot tell, said he.
> But 'twas a famous victory."

Let us view it from every side.

Imprimis: so far as the endurance of the riders is concerned it counts for nothing. The best time was three
hundred and fifty miles in three days — a mere trifle.

Why, in 1858, J. Powers rode one hundred and fifty miles
in six hours and forty-three minutes in San Francisco;
in 1868, N. H. Mowry rode, on the San Francisco race-
track, in the sight of gathered thousands, three hundred
miles in fourteen hours, nine minutes; and one Anderson,
in the same city, rode one thousand three hundred and
four miles in ninety hours. The fact that these men frequently changed horses only adds to the splendid character of the feat, so far as the man is concerned. But this
is not all there is to the Berlin-Vienna ride.

Many years ago Dr. Brown-Sequard, in a lecture to a
Harvard class, was illustrating how instantaneously death
followed any lesion to brain tissue or spinal marrow. "I
insert my probe between the vertebræ of this rabbit," said
he, taking up a specimen which was nibbling at a cabbage
on the table before him, "and you see that it at once ex-
pires." The doctor's remark was, to his surprise, followed
by a general titter throughout the class, for, though he
had duly suited his action to his words, when he laid it
down the rabbit went as calmly at the cabbage again as
if not in the slightest degree inconvenienced. This singular fact and other similar ones which he later noticed
here, but had never observed among European animals,
led Dr. Brown-Sequard, after careful tests, to enunciate
the theory that the mammal of North America has more
vitality than that of Europe. This theory is supported
by many facts, and was fairly proven sound by the numerous cases of recovery from extraordinary capital operations during our Civil War, when the antiseptic method
was unknown. It has now been accepted by all who have
studied the subject. The word "vitality," thus used, we
understand to mean the ability to perform exceptional
physical feats, or to endure excessive hardship without
death or material injury.

The ride of these seven-score army officers between Berlin and Vienna has two interesting aspects: the amount of endurance of the animals ridden, and the judgment of the riders as to the capacity of their horses to perform. How these two items compare with what our cavalry is daily experiencing on the plains is a fruitful subject of inquiry.

As the crow flies, it is three hundred and twenty-five English miles from Berlin to Vienna. By the road it is variously called three hundred and fifty to three hundred and seventy; it is certainly short of the latter distance. Count Stahremberg, the winner, covered the distance from Vienna to Berlin (which, owing to the mountainous section being crossed in the early part of the ride, is easier than the course from Berlin to Vienna) in some minutes less than three days. Three other men came in within three days and three hours. The best German rider, Lieutenant Reitzenstein, took a trifle over seventy-three and one-half hours. This sounds like a set of wonderful performances. Are they really so?

The race was go-as-you-please. The riders successively started from Vienna or Berlin at different hours, and rode at any gait or speed, and by any road they chose. The horses were the very best; no one not owning a horse noted for unusual endurance would have been fool enough to enter. There were many thorough-breds, many native horses, Prussians and Hungarians, some ponies from the Carpathian and Transylvanian uplands. The animals had all been prepared by weeks of careful training. They carried the least possible weight—the winner, *e.g.*, rides but one hundred and twenty-eight pounds, plus saddle and bridle. The roads were the very best. Under these most favorable conditions the winner rode one hundred and twenty miles a day for three consecutive days; the others less.

There has been a disposition among Anglo-Saxons to underrate this performance. The large number of horses killed or foundered with good right distresses our sense of pure sport. But for all that it was a famous ride, though open to serious criticism. Any horse ridden one hundred and twenty-five miles in twenty-four hours performs a great feat; one ridden two hundred miles in forty-eight hours, a greater; to ride three hundred and fifty miles in three days or a bit over is little short of marvellous, if you bring the horse in free from permanent injury. But there's the rub, and it is on this point that there is a word to say.

Comparisons may be odorous, as Mrs. Malaprop avers, but they are interesting and useful. Few people out of the Army know just what our cavalry is capable of, and this ride affords an opportunity, not to be lightly neglected, to point a moral and adorn a tale.

The nearest approach to the Stahremberg ride by an American which we can at the moment recall is that of the pony which Colonel Richard I. Dodge personally knew, and which I have already mentioned. His owner was a professional express rider, who carried the mail from El Paso to Chihuahua, thither once a week and back the next. As the country was infested by Apaches, the man had to ride by night and hide by day. His practice was to ride the distance, three hundred miles, in three consecutive nights, and rest his pony four days between trips. "Six months of this work had not diminished the fire or flesh of that wonderful pony," says Colonel Dodge. It is true that three hundred miles is not three hundred and fifty, but this pony—probably not over fourteen hands, and with rider, mail, and the usual plains trappings, carrying at lowest two hundred pounds—used to make the three hundred miles in some sixty hours (*i.e.* three nights

and the intervening two days), an equal average rate of
speed as that of Stahremberg and a much higher rate while
going, and no one pretends that the Count or any other
of the Berlin-Vienna riders could have turned round and
done the same thing over again the succeeding week;
whereas this little marvel kept on doing it every week
for six months, and no one knows how much longer, over
a country having no roads deserving the name, by night,
and feeding only on bunch-grass. Which of the two is
the better performance? This one cannot, perhaps, be
equalled; but to ride and repeat nearly as great distances
has never been and is not to-day considered an exceptional thing on the plains.

And if this pony outdid the winner of the great German race, by how far does he outrank the losers? The
horse ridden by Count Stahremberg was brought in in
fairly good condition, but died within a day or two. The
horse of the German winner died. A very high percentage of the others either died or broke down midway, or
were ridden home moribund or ruined. They were kept
up, *on dit*, by all kinds of stimulants and nostrums on the
road. No accounts have reached us showing the condition of the horses' backs under the saddle, always a prime
proof of careful or unintelligent treatment. In fact, the
number of dead or maimed animals seems to be purposely
suppressed. That it was the ponies which came in with
the least injury will not surprise our Western men. While
a thorough-bred may outpace a pony, a ride which will
kill him will not permanently disable the little runt of
the prairie. The latter's ancestry has had to struggle
with too much hardship to be easily killed, while the
thorough-breds have been warmly housed and artificially
handled. The pony's heritage is to do and endure; the
thorough-bred's to make pace.

XVI

Now, it may be interesting to give a few rides of our own cavalry on the plains, not as a contrast, but as a matter which all horsemen should be glad to know.

In 1879 several single couriers with the news of his imminent danger rode from Thornburg's "rat-hole" to General Merritt's column, one hundred and seventy miles, in less than twenty-four hours. The exact time of each was not taken. Rescue was more important than records. In 1891 two troopers of the Eighth Cavalry rode with despatches one hundred and ten miles in twenty hours, and Captain Fountain rode eighty-four miles in eight hours, and one hundred and ten miles in twenty-three. In 1876 Colonel Lawton rode from Red Cloud Agency, Nebraska, to Sidney Station, Nebraska, one hundred and twenty-five miles, with despatches for General Crook, in twenty-six hours. Rides of from one hundred and twenty to one hundred and fifty miles have repeatedly been made within the day and night by our ordinary troop-horses when not specially prepared for the work, and over very bad ground, and it is extremely rare that they have suffered serious injury.

There are few three-day rides by single horsemen which can readily be quoted; but other performances may be given, which are akin to this one. We put aside all mere hearsay rides. Of these there is no end; but it is well to put on record only such rides as are proven by official reports, and of which the distances can be measured by clear evidence:

It is plain that one man or horse travelling alone can go much farther or faster than two travelling together, and the more the individuals the slower the speed. The speed and endurance of a troop is that of the poorest horse. Extra weight infinitely adds to a horse's task and diminishes his course, and his capacity to go depends upon the chance to feed, water, and care for him suitably on the road. It is in marching detachments over great distances, under exceptionally difficult conditions, that our cavalry officers show peculiar success. Perhaps a knowledge of pace and the instinctive feel of the horse's condition is the highest grade of horsemanship. Civilians are wont to think that to play polo, or hunt, or win a race over the flat or over sticks, or perform high-school airs demand the highest skill; but let any one undertake to ride a horse, or, better, to lead a troop one hundred miles in twenty-four hours, and despite all he may have learned in peaceful sports, he will find his knowledge of real horsemanship distinctly limited. Not all our cavalry officers are equally gifted, but some have made rides which are unsurpassed.

It must be remembered that our cavalry horse is, *ab origine*, a very common fellow. He is bought by the Government at a price which brings out mainly those animals which are not quite good enough to command the top of the market, and are held for sale at a rather low figure. They go out to the plains, and are there got into condition while at work. They are not, as abroad, raised in studs boasting sires of the highest lineage. On the march the troop-horse carries very little less than two hundred and fifty pounds—eighty-eight pounds for equipment and baggage, and, say, one hundred and sixty for the rider. In camp he is well fed; on the march he cannot always be, and he is watered at irregular intervals. All these things tell against him.

In 1873 Colonel Mackenzie rode his command into Mexico after Lepan and Kickapoo Indians, beat them in a sharp fight, and returned across the border, making one hundred and forty-five miles in twenty-eight hours. In 1874 he again rode his command into Mexico after horse-thieves, making there and back, eighty-five miles, in fifteen hours. In 1880, Captain A. E. Wood, Fourth Cavalry, one of the most thorough horsemen I have ever known, rode, with eight men, in pursuit of a thieving deserter, one hundred and forty miles in thirty-one hours. Let him tell his own story. It shows just how the trick is done:

"In the month of September, 1880, I was stationed at Fort Reno, Indian Territory; the paymaster had visited us, and in those days, after such a visit, some desertion was expected.

"About noon one day the latter part of September, the post commander sent for and astonished me by stating that the first sergeant of his company—Twenty-third Infantry—had deserted, taking with him a considerable amount of the company fund, and he wanted me to catch him if possible. He had discovered that the sergeant had bought one strong Indian pony and had stolen another.

"The direction taken by the sergeant was not known, but under the circumstances I thought that he intended to reach the railroad as soon as possible. The nearest railroad was in Southern Kansas—the nearest point Arkansas City, one hundred and forty miles as the trail then went. I took a detail of two non-commissioned officers and six men from G troop, Fourth Cavalry.

"The detail was taken from the roster, except the first sergeant of G troop, who asked to go with me; the horses belonged to the riders; none were selected as especially qualified for the trip. I rode the same horse that I had been riding for months.

"I took two pack-mules with the men's rations; they were loaded with about eighty pounds each. We left the post at 1.35 P.M. The day was quite hot, and knowing what was before me, I did not push the animals very hard for the first twenty-five miles, which distance we had made by 6 P.M. This distance brought us to Kingfisher Creek, where we halted for one hour — unsaddled, got something to eat, let the horses roll and graze, then groomed their backs and legs, saddled up and started at 7 P.M.

"We started and walked for thirty minutes, then took a trot for fifty minutes, when we dismounted and rested for ten minutes; adjusted the saddles, mounted, and took the trot for fifty minutes, dismounted and walked for ten minutes. We thus trotted at about a six-mile gait for a little more than fifty minutes, and dismounted and walked for ten minutes, until 12 P.M., when we halted and rested for twenty minutes. We then mounted and kept up the trotting for fifty minutes, dismounting and walking for ten minutes, until about 4.50 A.M., a little after daybreak, when we were so overcome with sleep that I allowed the men to dismount, unsaddle, and sleep for about an hour. My mind was so busy that I could not sleep much, so I awoke the men. We groomed the backs and rubbed the legs of the horses for a short time and resumed the journey as before. When we had gone about one hundred and twenty miles we again halted, unsaddled, let the horses rest, and made some coffee. This rest took three-quarters of an hour, after which we started and travelled as before until we reached Arkansas City at 8.30 P.M. —thirty-one hours. Men and horses were extremely tired; one horse was quite lame in front. We rested the remainder of the night, the next day and night, and then marched to Caldwell, Kansas, thirty-five miles, the succeeding day. We remained at Caldwell two nights and a day, and

marched back to Fort Reno, a distance of one hundred
and fifteen miles by ordinary marches. All but one horse
seemed to be rested when we reached Caldwell. This
horse was unserviceable when we reached Fort Reno, the
others were apparently as good as ever. The above is
a record of the hardest ride I ever undertook. The fatigue was very great; but a good night's rest completely
restored all of us.

"At that time our mounts were purchased in Missouri
and Kansas. The horse I rode was twelve years old; the
others were a little younger. I think that the horse that
was rendered unserviceable was made so by bad riding.
His rider was not a very good horseman, and rode too
heavily forward. I tried to correct this, but it is impossible to teach all the niceties of horsemanship on such a
trip."

In 1870 four men of Company II, First Cavalry, bore
despatches from Fort Harney to Fort Warner, one hundred and forty miles, over a bad road—twenty of it sand
—with little and bad water, in twenty-two hours, eighteen
and a half of which was actual marching time. The horses
were in such good condition at the end of the ride that
after one day's rest the men started back, and made the
home trip at the rate of sixty miles a day. In 1879 Captain Dodge, with his troop, rode eighty miles in sixteen
hours, and Lieutenant Wood, with his troop, rode seventy
miles in twelve hours. In December, 1890, Captain Fechet,
with troops F and G, Eighth Cavalry, left Fort Yates at
midnight, reached Sitting Bull's camp, forty-five miles distant, at 7.20 A.M., drove off his band, and rescued the sur-
vivors of the Indian police who had arrested and in the
mêlée killed Sitting Bull. The two troops then scouted
the country for ten miles around and marched back, reaching Oak Creek at 2 P.M.—a total distance of eighty-five

6

miles in fourteen hours. "The roads were frozen hard
and half covered with ice and snow. At the end of the
ride there was not a saddle-boil nor a broken-down horse
or man." In 1880 Colonel Henry, with four troops, rode
one hundred and eight miles in thirty-three hours, being
in the saddle twenty-two hours. One horse dropped dead
at the end of the march, but there was not a sore-backed
horse in the regiment, and they started out again after a
rest of twenty-four hours. The same command made a
night march of fifty miles in ten hours.

General Merritt in 1879, with four troops, and hampered by a battalion of infantry in wagons, rode one
hundred and seventy miles to the relief of Payne in sixty-
six and one-half hours, and reached the scene in prime
order and ready to go into a fight. Very long distances
have been covered by cavalry regiments at the rate of
sixty miles a day. Colonel Henry, an expert on this subject, speaking of hardening the men and horses of a command by a month's drills of from fifteen to twenty miles
at rapid gaits, aptly says: "A cavalry command thus
hardened, and with increased feeds, ought to be able to
make fifty to sixty miles a day as long as required; and
to such a command one hundred miles in twenty-four
hours ought to be easy. The horse, like the athlete,
needs training, and when this is done his endurance is
limited only by that of his rider."

In 1877 General Miles organized in Arizona a plan for
accustoming men and horses to severe work by rides
across the plains by a party of "raiders," followed by
another of "pursuers." The parties were usually about
twenty strong. The pursuers were not allowed to start
until eighteen hours after the raiders, but the raiders were
bound to rest six hours after marching eighteen hours,
and again twelve after marching twelve more. The pur-

suers could "go as you please," but were ordered not to
injure stock by hard riding. Of these rides, which are
not under the spur of compulsion, a few may be given as
of interest. On September 17th, Lieutenant Scott, Sixth
Cavalry, and twenty-five men, started from Fort Stanton
towards Fort Bayard, and was overtaken in forty-two and
one half hours marching time, at a distance of one hundred and thirty miles. The pursuers, Lieutenant Pershing and twenty-seven men, made the one hundred and
thirty miles in fifty-four and one-half hours from start
to capture. On September 25th, Lieutenant McGrath,
Fourth Cavalry, and twenty-two men, started from Fort
Bowie to Fort Apache; he made one hundred and seventy-three miles in forty-two hours' marching time. On
September 26-27, Lieutenant Scott and twenty-five men,
in pursuit of Lieutenant Pershing, made one hundred and
ten miles in twenty-six hours ten minutes. On Novem-
ber 1-3, Lieutenant Pershing and twenty-two men, pur-
suing Captain Wallace, made one hundred and thirty
miles in fifty-seven hours. Captain Chaffee, in pursuit of
Captain Kerr, made on September 24-25 seventy miles in
twenty hours with seventeen men.

These are but a few instances which any of our cavalry
officers can duplicate from their own knowledge. I could
quote very many more. Now, if we take the conditions
under which these rides have been made, viz., a common-
bred native troop horse, not always kept hard and ready
for work; the exceptional weight carried, for all but the
courier work was done with full equipment; the fact that
most of the courses were over country without roads, or
only trails, which are the merest apology for roads, and
often hilly and badly cut up; that the pace must be made
for the slowest horses, and be such that weak factors in
the troop shall be respected; that the incentive was thir-

teen dollars a month and simple duty, and not a splendid money prize of five thousand dollars and the commendation of emperors; and, above all, that the commands have uniformly been brought in without injury to man or beast, we shall find matter for justifiable self-gratulation.

XVII

I HAVE from youth been reasonably familiar with the performances of European cavalry, and have studied the Arabian horse in the French army in Algiers, and in his native haunts on the Libyan and Syrian deserts. I have sought assiduously for records of great performances; but exceptional work is only called out by exceptional needs, and abroad these are apt to be wanting. Granted that the German cavalry, for example, is marvellously drilled; that it has the stomach to fight has been a notorious fact ever since the days of Ziethen and Seidlitz. Granted that it can perform precise evolutions or charge without confusion on the battle-field in masses greater than our entire cavalry force; yet this by no means reaches the heart of distance riding. Such a thing as our raider and pursuer drills would never be dreamed of in Germany. All our work on the plains tends to distance riding, and in no other regular army in the world does this obtain. The Austro-Hungarian cavalry is better fitted than the German for distance riding, and has, as a pattern, the steppes man and horse, who are unexcelled in this very thing. In Algeria, while the horse of the Nineteenth Corps d'Armée is all mounted on Arabians, there is apt to be no call for excessive marches, and there is no preparation for them. The Spahis, or light cavalrymen of native birth, are in constant movement all over the country, but they have the true Oriental trick of not overworking themselves; and so far as wonderful individual distance rides are concerned, I have been unable to pin down a single such ride to reliable evidence. An Arab sheik out in the desert, who owns a high-bred mare, will tell you of marvellous performances, but they are as nebulous as his own *Thousand and One Nights*. I once sought to purchase some speed—a drive of eighty miles over the excellent turnpike from Soussa to Tunis—in order to catch a steamer; but though the owner of some really fine Arabians had been telling about the three hundred kilometres (one hundred and eighty-six miles) a day they could do, no amount of money could induce him to agree to take me over the course of eighty miles with four horses and a light vehicle in less than twenty hours.

It used to be asserted that the Turcoman cavalry could ride in large bodies one hundred miles a day for a week, or even more; but, though all the steppes horses of the world, like our broncos, are incomparable stayers on their own *terrain*, this distance must be cut down by a large percentage. My ancient school-friend, now a pacha, major-general, and chief of the forty thousand odd Kurdish cavalry of the Turkish Empire, though absolutely familiar with the subject, was unwilling to vouch for such a statement. The Kurdish is practically the same as the Turcoman horse. In talking it over, this gentleman cited one of his own distance rides, fifteen hundred kilometres in forty-five days, as a great performance, which he thought established the reputation of the horse of Asia Minor beyond cavil. But this is only thirty-three miles a day. It was unnecessary to argue the matter, as it would not have elicited more accurate statistics.

After all said, the palm for distance riding must be awarded to our own cavalry officers. Taking all the conditions into account, there are probably no civilized horsemen who can ride so far with a body of men and bring them to the end of their journey in as clean a condition as the best of our officers on the plains. The talent to do this is by no means universal; but it is wide-spread. And though we may marvel at the recent three hundred and fifty miles ridden in from seventy-two to eighty hours by the most expert foreign horsemen on their picked horses, the record of dead and foundered steeds leads us to believe that we could have done as well and saved our horses.

This brings us again to the question of the endurance of the American mammal. Except the ass, there is perhaps no creature of the equine race as stubbornly enduring as the bronco. This is largely due to the American climate. The record of running and trotting time in America tends to prove the same thing; and our athletic records, considering how recently born our athletic fad is, are of high grade. The fact that the common States' horse can be taken and, after short training, made to do such marvels of distance work, not only proves the intelligence of our officers but sustains the claim of superior vitality in the horse.

XVIII

AND now, my hard-riding cross-country brothers, ye who win glory in the polo-field; ye who deem that twenty-five or thirty miles in fine weather, over the best of roads, without other weight than your own avoirdupois and a light saddle, is a good day's work for man and beast; ye who (I know you don't mean it, or do it without reflection) are wont to scoff at the West Point rider, or listen to the persuasive ranchman as he runs down the work of the Army because it does not always chime in with his own peculiar interests; ye who flatter yourselves that you and your ilk are peerless horsemen, and who run no risk beyond an occasional spill — will you not agree with me that the above Army rides are hard jewels to match? If you and I, on our thousand-dollar imported mounts — not to quote fancy prices — should cover even seventy miles in thirty-one hours (we should prefer to do it in two instalments, you know, chappie!), should we not have a good week's glory at the club, and be the cynosure of neighboring eyes? But do you think we should care, with Captain Wood, to double up that distance, sit thirty-one consecutive hours in the saddle, and do one hundred and forty miles for the sake of—thirteen dollars a month and duty? Not but what, in my youth and prime, I might have done; not but what to-day you might, under parallel circumstances, do that very thing! Good American grit is the same at all times and in all places. I am not discounting your ability to perform; and that your generous horseman's heart—for no man who loves a horse e'er lacks the touch of nature—must warm towards the blue-coats who can accomplish such feats it needs no words to tell. It takes gimp, brother, it takes intelligence, it takes that sympathetic knowledge of the horse which we all admire. Let me ask you to study these little items—you can find no end of others if you will take the trouble to hunt them up—and when you feel inclined to criticise the Army because it does not accomplish the impossible, just stop and think. Men who can ride such distances as these are apt to do all that flesh and blood can stand. Ta-ta!

XIX

In constant association with the cavalryman comes that most faithful servant—the only good Indian except a dead one—the Indian scout. There are numbers of these men enlisted in the Army, and many more when occasion demands have been temporarily in service. These men are not to be confounded with the Indians who have recently been recruited, with questionable results, in the rank and file. The scouts are men of exceptional reliability and intelligence, and as a rule have proved to be valuable in a high degree. Some have rendered unusual service. The Indian scout receives the pay and allowance of the cavalry soldier. He may have come of any tribe. He finds his own ponies, but has issued to him a Government saddle and equipments, and barring spurs, for which he substitutes the invariable quirt, delights in Uncle Sam's uniform, as, more's the pity, every soldier does not. Why is the profession which, honorably filled, is the noblest of all professions, if courage, endurance, and all the most manly qualities in their highest expression can ennoble a profession, looked on askance by all Americans? It is a fact of which we should be heartily ashamed, that the United States uniform, which has covered the breasts of so many heroes, from George Washington to Ulysses S. Grant, is to-day a badge of ostracism. It is this, more than any other one fact, which lies at the root of the numerous desertions from the Army.

Since the aborigines have been kept on the reserva-

INDIAN SCOUT WITH LOST TROOP HORSE

tions, the Indian scout has ridden an imitation of the cavalry seat, and has broken himself of kicking his pony's ribs at every stride. The Indian is vain and imitative, and these two qualities make him a servant of the republic equally tractable and reliable. We are indebted to him for much of the best service, and in his ranks have been numbered many men whose names are household words.

This habit of drubbing the horse's ribs is one by no means confined to the Indian, though he indulges in it to excess. You see it in Central Park, in Rotten Row, in all the cavalry of Europe, among the Arabs, on the steppes of Russia. Its special use among all these appears to be to keep the horse at a rapid walk; when a horse is on a faster gait, it is chiefly the Indian who keeps up the pounding. It is of no particular value; for, like the use of the whip, familiarity soon breeds contempt, and the horse performs no better for the punishment and less willingly for the worry. It is an ungainly trick, too, much on a par with swinging the legs at a trot. In a soldier particularly one wishes to see that sort of precision which should be a sequence of a perfect setting-up; and the trick of using the heels at every moment sadly mars the military seat. There are other ways of keeping a horse at his best which are not so objectionable as this.

XX

WE have travelled so near the border that we cannot well afford not to pay a visit to our neighbors. All except jealously conservative Canadians will acknowledge that there are many things which the Dominion might learn to advantage from the States ; and there are incontestably others in which the Dominion might give us points. Among these, what we have been discussing suggests its management of the Indian, which has always been in marked contrast to our own. Among other instruments of our neighbor's Indian Department is a brigade of cavalry known as the Canadian Mounted Police. This is an uncommonly fine body of men, numbering on its roster many of the better classes. They have the usual military organization, but are distributed in small troops all over Canada. Their duties are chiefly to suppress the whiskey trade—for fire-water has always been and is still the greatest of the red man's foes—keep the Indians in subjection, and aid the sheriffs of the various counties. These men ride a bred-up bronco. Their saddle is what is known as the Montana tree, and for this style of saddle they ride with rather too short a stirrup to suit our notions —a seat akin to the English military seat. On a trot they pound, as with such short stirrups they cannot well avoid doing. The seat of the United States soldier is apparently contrasted to theirs, and each method not only has its advocates, but produces in many individuals the best of horsemanship. The seat of this rider gives him a pur-

CANADIAN MOUNTED POLICE

chase with the thigh, the inside of the knee, and when he
closes his legs, as he must in the ranks, with the upper
part of the calf. It is in accordance with the old saw of
" 'ands and 'eels low, 'ead and 'eart 'igh," under which so
many splendid horsemen have grown up—except that his
bridle hand is raised by the blanket roll or carbine. He
seems to be sitting, as he faces us, in just the style he ought
not to sit. No one but a Mexican or the ghost of a knight
in armor rides in this form. It is not unnatural for a man
to thrust out his feet as a change of position, but it is the
very worst seat in which a man can indulge if he retains
it habitually.

The world seems to be sliding into other notions than
it used to have. The 'ands and 'eels low applies to the
hands only. The English cross-country rider of to-day
has his foot no more than level when at rest, and keeps
his toe well down when in motion. This has partly come
about from the trick of holding the stirrup in place when
leaping, and partly from the fact that the Briton, even
after hounds, does not ride with leathers as short as years
ago. We used to hear, particularly during our war, many
an Old Country man ridicule the American cavalry seat,
because our men hang their toes when in the saddle,
rather than depress their heels, as her Majesty's troopers
and school-riders are supposed to do. In some respects
this is not strange, for many an Englishman will, as a
matter of habit or of keeping his hand in, criticise everything he runs across, whether he knows anything about it
or not. It is merely a trick, a sort of weak offshoot of the
excellent character which gives him his energy and courage and stick-to-ativeness. And the veriest little London
cockney, who has never thrown his leg across anything
but a broken-down ninepence-an-hour 'Ampstead 'Eath
'ack, will undertake to criticise the riding of the cowboy
7

or the Southerner. But the variation between the seats
of the two soldiers in question is not great; they are, in
actual fact, nearly alike. Make a composite photograph
of five hundred American and another of five hundred
British troopers, and it will be found that the three lines
which establish the seat—the back-bone, the thigh-bone,
and the shank-bone—will lie with small variation upon
each other, while the position on the back of the horse
will in neither case be far from the correct one. The
low-carried toe merely gives the appearance of a straighter
leg; there is practically the same seat. One advantage of
"heels down" is that it lends a bit more griping power
to the upper muscle of the calf; but to gain the ankle-play
which is essential to comfortable riding with long stirrups,
the foot should be level, so as to yield as much up as down
motion. Neither extreme is beneficial. Though I have
always been an advocate of the old-fashioned seat, acquaintance with many wonderful riders with toes pendent
has taught me that this style has its advantages. It approaches nearer the bareback seat than any other, and by
far the greater number of civilized equestrians ride with
toe rather than heel depressed.

The Canadian Mounted Police is one of the most effi-
cient organizations which exist, and it accomplishes its
purpose because it is not interfered with. Its work tells
and is appreciated, as the much harder and more dangerous duties of our cavalry are not. There are some benefits
which accrue to the individual from a centralized government which our own does not so well afford. That a
true republic, well governed, is the best of governments
can scarcely be denied; but in an illy or laxly governed
republic abuses and hardships spring up as by magic and
thrive apace. By republic I do not mean the *soi-disant*
republics of the world. I know of but three real repub-

lics—Switzerland, Great Britain, and America. But this is politics; and, according to the Loyal Legion rule, whoever refers to politics at a meeting of the Commandery is for the first offence fined thirty dollars, and for the second is dismissed the Order. Let us consider this a meeting, and enforce the rule.

XXI

THE cowboy is in the saddle more than any man on the plains. He rides what is well known as the cowboy's saddle, or Brazos tree. It is adapted from the old Spanish saddle—is, in fact, almost similar—and differs sensibly from the Mexican. The line of its seat from cantle to horn, viewed sidewise, is a semicircle; there is no flat place to sit on. This shape gives the cowboy, seen from the side, all but as perpendicular a seat in the saddle as the old knight in armor. There are, of course, other saddles in use. The Texas saddle has a much flatter seat than the Brazos tree; the Cheyenne saddle a still flatter one, with a high cantle and a different cut of pommel-arch and bearing, and some individuals may ride any peculiar saddle; but all must have the horn and high cantle. In no other tree would the cowboy be at home or fit for service. Not only this, but in a flat English saddle the cowboy cuts a sorry figure. One of the best-known men in America, the owner of a big Western ranch—where, of course, he rides *à la* cowboy, and when East noted as a bold and skilful rider in the Meadow Brook Hunt, where of course, too, he rides a flat saddle—told me that once his ranch superintendent, a well-known bronco-buster, when East, was compelled to ride an English saddle, and that the man was fairly slipping off sidewise every minute or two. He simply could not ride the thing at all, nor for a long time get the hang of it.

The cowboy is careful of his ponies, not only from a

horseman's motives, but because he is held to account for them. Unlike the Indian, he rarely has a sore-backed nag. He often uses a gunny-bag saddle-cloth next the pony's skin, the hempen fibre of which keeps the back cool, and over this, for padding, his woollen blanket. In the Southwest he is apt to sport a variegated saddle-cloth with fringed edge, such as the Mexicans parade; and if he can manage to get hold of a Navajo blanket he is fixed. These wonderful bits of handwork, of bright, agreeable colors, are worth from fifty dollars upwards, never seem to wear out, are cool and pleasant to the pony's skin, do not gall, and are by long odds the best thing under a saddle which exists. The Indian will give from two ponies upwards for one of them, when he can buy a wife for one pony, and not a very good pony (or wife) at that. The cowboy's saddle is held in place by one very wide or two narrower hair cinchas, though the single cincha is more a Californian than a plains habit; if one, it is, among plains riders, always put a full hand-breadth back of what in the East we call the girth-place. The rear girth gets a purchase on the back slope of the ribs.

The cowboy's bit is any kind of a curb with a long gag. He rides under all conditions with a loose rein, the bit ends of which are often made of chain, to prevent the pony from chewing it off, and this clanks a rhythmic jingle to his easy lope. His pony is as surefooted as a mountain goat, and will safely scramble with his big load up a cliff, or slide down a bank which would make our tenderfoot hair stand on end. The loose rein and the sharp gag enable the cowboy with the least jerk to pull his pony back on his haunches, for the pony is unused to a steady hold. The cowboy is assuredly no three-legged rider. The bit hangs in a fancy trade-bridle, which the cowboy ornaments in various fashions to suit his own

ideas of style. The effect of its use on the pony is precisely the reverse of that which is made by a bit on a
horse suppled by school methods or even bitted, and
which has been ridden on a light touch. The latter
brings down his head to the hand, with an arched neck,
easy mouth, and a give-and-take feel of the hand. The
pony, at the least intimation of the bit, long before the
rein is taut, jerks up his head, and must have a tough
mouth, or an exceptional fright, to make him take hold
of you.

This habit of using a severe bit and of never allowing
the horse to take hold of it is partaken by the majority
of the riders of the world. All Orientals, without exception, bit a horse in this fashion. I have at intervals seen
a man in the Orient with an easy bit, playing it with a
light touch — by touch I mean an actual feel of the
horse's mouth—and with a neat and easy hand ; but it is
very rare. A loose rein gives no useful touch. You can
start your horse with the spur or whip, or with a word :
you can stop him with the merest touch of the rein ; you
can guide him by the rein on his neck. But I deem it
impossible to communicate with a horse as intimately
with this loose rein as you can with the touch of a bit
and bridoon, well adjusted, and which you always hold so
as to have the least possible delicate feel of the horse's
mouth. Such a touch not only yields a sense of compan-
ionship between man and beast, but the horse unquestionably likes the pleasant conversation which thus goes on.
A man may talk with his horse in words, and of these an
intelligent horse is very fond ; but they will at least be
rare. If he is in the habit of talking to him through the
rein and bit, his hands will be always talking—and it is
this that pleases and controls the true saddle-beast. I
will discuss this point again when I come to speak of

COWBOY LIGHTING THE RANGE FIRE

school methods. Even though the discussion may be quite one-sided, I fancy we shall not disagree.

The most striking part of the cowboy's rig are the chaparajos, or huge leather overalls, he is apt to wear. These originated in the mesquite or chaparral country, where the cattle business had its origin, and where jeans or a pair of the best cords will be torn to shreds in a day. When the chaparajos are seen out of this region, they have been retained from force of habit. This singular garment is made of cowhide, weighs five or six pounds, and used invariably to have the edge cut into a long fringe; but this ornamentation has begun to disappear. It boasts no seat, which could with difficulty be made to fit. On the left leg of the chaparajos is a pocket for cigarettes or chewing-tobacco, matches, and small sundries. The chaparajos could not comfortably be worn in any other saddle than one which gave a short, upright, "forked-radish" seat. They are too much like trousers made of stove-pipe.

At the cowboy's saddle-bow usually hangs a rawhide or hair or Mexican grass rope, from forty feet long upwards, to use for every purpose, from roping cattle to hauling out a mired team; and his rifle, a 73-Winchester, rests crosswise at the horn, in a broad pouch-like strap, which protects the lock from injury; or is slung under the left leg, where it can lie with equal security. He boasts few riches. What he has is apt to be in dollars, or owed him by the ranchman, or occasionally in a few steers. He buys a pair of eighteen-dollar boots, a pair of fifteen-dollar gloves, and the rest of his rig and dress is scarcely worth a five-dollar bill. This is by no means from extravagance. He must keep his feet well shod and his legs protected. Without the very best gloves he would shortly have no skin left on his hands. It is self-protection and well-

studied economy that makes him spend so much on these
two articles of attire. And so long as they are ornamental as well as useful, he is as well satisfied with them
as a New York swell used to be with a cover-coat with
long swallow-tails sticking out from under it.

Broncos with manners are fewer and farther between
than even angels' visits. The cowboy's bronco is never
what we should call half-broken. By the time he has
been ridden enough to be well broken in he is usually all
broken up. He is a difficult fellow to mount, being ridden but once every four or five days. If he were not so
small one could never mount him without assistance. He
will back away, plunge forward, swerve, kick, strike,
squeal, rush full at you with mouth wide open, or perform a hundred other antics, any one of which would
compel us simple-minded park riders to hurry him off to
the nearest auction-room — or advertise him at private
sale as a horse of exceptional courage and unflagging
spirit. He is, in every sense, what we are wont to characterize as a dangerous brute. But the cowboy can always see him and go him one better. Familiarity breeds
contempt. For what he calls violence he ropes the
bronco and chokes the violence out of him with the wind;
to what we call violence he pays no manner of heed.
He approaches him at the left shoulder, with a wary eye
to what the pony may be up to, and gathers the rein in
his left hand. Not infrequently he puts his hand over
the pony's eye while he grabs the left stirrup and gets his
foot in it, following up the bronco's antics as best he may
—man and horse not unlikely executing a most exhilarating *pas de deux*. Then, grabbing the pommel with the
right hand and the pony's withers with the left, and if
possible getting his left elbow in the hollow of the neck
just forward of the withers, nothing which the pony can

do can keep him out of the saddle. In fact, a plunge which drags him from his feet will all the more certainly swing him to his seat. Then, after a series of bucks more or less severe, according as to how much the pony has been "busted," during which exercise the cowboy's spurs go time and again into the pony's flanks, and the pony acts like the veriest wild beast, the mastery is established where it properly belongs, the pony steadies down after a fashion, and harmony, such as it is, reigns till the next time of mounting.

The cowboy universally rides a lope, as do all people who use wild horses. The bronco has no other gait, in fact, unless a sort of fox-trot. The cowboy's seat is unsuited to an open trot. He won't ride it if he can help it, and it may as well be confessed, he cannot—and no one can — sit close without pounding to the long rangy trot of a big thorough-bred, though it is the perfection of gaits if you rise to it. There is a good deal of nonsense talked about rising to a trot—almost as much as there is about drinking iced-water. The fact is that all peoples, wild and semi-civilized, who are used to horses, rise to a trot. They don't do it often because they prefer and train their horses to other and better gaits; but if their mount falls into a trot, or they happen to ride a trotting horse, they naturally rise, as a matter of course. It is only those who stick exclusively to the old ramrod pattern who do not do so.

I seem to have roped iced-water into the question, but I will use it only to quote a clever friend of mine, a doctor of no mean repute. Said he to me one day: "Why do you all declaim against iced-water? Of course it can be abused by drinking in a heated condition—so can any other food or drink be abused. But all animals drink iced-water a good part of the year. When you water a

farm-horse or your cows at the brook in January, what
else are they drinking? And yet, does it hurt them?
No," suiting the action to the word, " iced-water is a healthful drink, properly used."

We hear from many that the cowboy can do everything. Rumors run that some of Buffalo Bill's cowboys
rode English horses in their own saddles and beat everything to hounds somewhere in the Midland counties—
we won't be specific and say the Belvoir. Those who
know the country this implies and its riders accept this
statement *cum grano*. But assume its truth. One often
sees a dare-devil of an English lad just out of college
who imagines, because he has once or twice led the field
on one of the squire's crack hunters, that he is the best
rider in it. But, in truth, he is risking his horse's, not to
count his own less valuable neck, at every obstacle he
clears, and pumping the last ounce out of his generous
beast, while wiser and older riders close behind him are
saving their horses and bringing them in fresh and able.
It is not riding a fabulous distance, or at the greatest
speed, or with the most conspicuous daring, which is the
test, but getting in at the death with the least exertion to
man and beast. The highest proof of artistic horsemanship is to accomplish your task with the least expenditure
of physical force. To keep the horse in good condition is,
among civilized people, a greater test than the speed or
daring of the rider. Witness the Berlin-Vienna ride. So
in the great tests of distance made by plains ponies and
civilized horses one element is apt to be forgotten. The
latter must be brought in without injury; the pony may
be killed by the feat. No question whatever that if the
pony and the thorough-bred, under even conditions, be
ridden until both fall in their tracks, the pony will be
beaten in speed and distance. It seems to me clear that

thorough-breds have always beaten ponies; but that the pony will recover from what may kill the thorough-bred is equally clear. In the Berlin - Vienna ride no doubt fewer of the ponies died; but those thorough-breds which died a day or two after could probably have gone much farther and left the ponies still farther behind, before they dropped. The grit of the thorough-bred is a wonderful element. So long as you keep him moving he will resist death in a manner utterly inexplicable; when, if you stop him, he may die in a few hours.

But the cowboy is unequalled in his own province, and this is enough of fame. His seat is astonishing. It is a common feat for him to put a playing-card on the saddle, or a dollar piece under each foot in the stirrup, or under his knees, and ride a vigorous bucker. Still he cannot ride a flat saddle until he learns the trick of it. And while no cowboy, without serving his apprenticeship in the hunting-field, would hold his own with practised riders there, it is certain that he would much sooner learn to ride across country well than even the best of cross-country men could vie with him in controlling a vicious bronco, or indeed, in riding over the rough country he is wont to cover. It is the universal experience of the plains that the best English rider fights shy of ground which the cowboy will gallop over, until he catches on to it and confides in the sure feet of his little mount. Some men never learn to ride; but it stands to reason, *caeteris paribus*, that the man who makes riding his business will be a stouter horseman than one to whom it is a mere diversion.

XXII

As a rough-rider the cowboy is *facile princeps;* as a horse-breaker he devotes too little time to his task, nor does he go to work in the way best calculated to produce a quiet nag. Bronco-busting is a distinct art. The bronco-buster may be a "professional," who has originally taken up the work to replenish his exchequer, depleted by whiskey or poker, and sticks to it for lack of an easier job, and because he is at low-water-mark; or he may be a cow-puncher in slack times. As a rule he cannot stick it out very long, for the business is sure to end by busting the buster. It is unquestionably the most violent form of athletics, and the bronco-buster, though he must be strong and active, is not, as a rule, in the exceptional condition necessary for great feats of strength and endurance. Indeed, training would scarcely help him much. Whatever his strength and health, the bronco-buster is sure to get hurt sooner or later. He works it off and on at ten dollars a bronco. All cowboys do more or less breaking, and some ranches always break their own ponies, and generally have better ones for so doing, because they give each pony more time.

The typical bronco-buster should weigh a hundred and seventy or a hundred and eighty pounds. Weight does the business when a light man can accomplish nothing, though one of the most successful bronco-riders of whom I ever heard was a long-geared, lank Texas lad, who would stick to his horse till his head would snap

like a whip with the bucking, and he himself lose con-
sciousness. Indeed, it is not uncommon for violent pitching to produce hemorrhage of the lungs, while hernia,
cracked bones, and serious sprains are frequent disasters.
There is no creature in the service of man which can
put its master to such violent efforts in its subjugation as
the bronco. Of course a better plan would be the more
gradual one of civilized trainers, but for this there is no
leisure.

The whole secret of "busting" (the word is advisedly
used, as picturesquely expressive of the process, in contradiction to breaking) lies in completely exhausting the
bronco at the first lesson; he will never buck "for keeps"
more than once. Buffalo Bill's ponies have been allowed
to throw their riders, or the rider has judiciously slipped
off at the right intervals, thus impressing the idea on the
bronco's intelligence that he can surely throw his man if
he sticks long enough to his bucking. But once ridden
to the verge of falling in his tracks, the pony will not do
his level worst again, but content himself with grunting
and yelling, "knocking his teeth out" and playing the
devil generally. The buster must be careful to keep well
away from sheds and timber, and have room enough to
cut a wide swath. He must be able to stick to his saddle
like a leech, with or without stirrups. If, indeed, he needs
his stirrups for a hold, he is not looked on as much of a
rider; and it is a matter of pride with the "sure enough"
buster not to rely on anything but what old horsemen call
glue. To show his contempt for the bronco's power, he
will ply the quirt at every jump. It is a fair fight and
no favor between man and beast. But the buster has
been there before, and knows exactly what he is about;
the bronco is new to the business, and though he invariably makes a good fight, he is sure to have to give

in. Some ponies take more busting than others, and
some always buck more or less, however well broken.
In fact, when the punchers turn out of a cold morning,
the ponies will pitch through the entire outfit, and the
crowd stands around to see each man mount, watch
the fun, and chaff the rider. If a pony chances to win
a heat and his rider comes a cropper, it is what genial
John Leech calls a "little 'olliday" to the rest of the
boys.

Two rides will usually bust a bronco so that the average cow-puncher can use him, but he would scarcely keep
company long with most Central Park riders. Two men
generally work together. They enter the corral, where
there is apt to be a good bunch of ponies; and these, as
if guessing what is to come, at once jump away, and go
careering madly around the enclosure. One man handles
the rope, which he trails along the ground until he selects
his pony, and then, with a sudden and dexterous snap,
drags it over his head. A good roper can cast twenty-five
feet. Then both men seize hold, dig their heels into the
ground to stop the pony—knack will enable even one
man to jerk him up, if need be—and finally get a turn
round the snubbing-post in the centre of the corral.
There they have the pony fast, and they gradually work
him up to it. The pony does not submit to this vigorous
coaxing in any amiable mood. He bucks and plunges,
kicks and squeals, and charges straight at his tormentors,
who have to play a regular game of hide-and-seek behind
the snubbing-post to save themselves from broken bones.
But even a bronco with his lungs pumped dry will suc-
cumb, and finally the men get the winded pony snubbed
up close to the post, where one can hold him while the
other gets behind him and catches another rope on one
fore-foot. Then, as the pony starts, he yanks the foot

back, and in nine cases out of ten down goes the pony;
but not always. Some obstinate ones will sink on the
other knee, and with the nose on the ground still have
four points to stand on. But by-and-by down he must;
the snubbing-rope is made fast, the saddle is fitted on *tant
bien que mal*, the cincha worked under, and the whole
made fast. Sometimes it is difficult to get a bit in the
pony's mouth, and they put on a hackamore, which is a
halter-like rope arrangement, a sort of Rarey hitch, with
an extra twist around his jaw, instead. Then the second
rope is loosed and the pony is let up, still held by the
snubbing-post rope. This is gradually loosened so as to
let the pony have a little fun all to himself, which he is
sure to do, pitching round in a pretty lively fashion for
twenty minutes or half an hour to rid himself of the saddle, despite the choking of the rope. This takes the feather
edge off him, and he will end up his play covered with
foam and quite a bit tired. Some extra vigorous busters
ride the pony right off, but the more judicious prefer
to let him tire himself out first. When this is done the
pony is gradually worked out on the prairie between
two ropes, and may perhaps have to be thrown again
to cinch him up and get ready for the ride. To keep
him down while the rider gets ready, the other man
sits on his head, and the rider puts aside his six-shooter
and hat and coat and everything superfluous, but keeps
his spurs and quirt. Then he seizes the saddle and
gets his left foot in the stirrup, the pony is gradually
unwound, and the instant he reaches his feet the buster
is in the saddle. It is incredible how active these men
can be.

Now the real fun begins, and the rider and pony go at
it in earnest. The other man sometimes goes along on
another horse, with a rope to catch the pony if things

work wrong; but he is a wall-flower, and takes no part in the dancing. It is pretty rough sport. The pony may be a running bucker, or may stand stock-still and pitch in place at unexpected intervals; he may buck over a bank; he may pitch a somerset forward; he may rear and fall over backward. The rider wants both to stick to his pony and be ready to vault off in short measure if essential. He uses all the legs nature has given him, stirrup or no stirrup, and lashes his pony at every rise with all his might. The *suaviter in modo* is absolutely sunk in the *fortiter in re.* When the pony rises the trick is to get away from the cantle, and the heavy buster has a fashion when the pony comes down of settling himself in his seat with a hard jolt and a sort of an " Ugh !"—a thing that helps fag out the little fellow, which weighs barely four times as much as the man, was tired before he began, and is now working a dozen times as hard. One way or other the pony will keep his resistance up for a certain length of time, according to disposition; but in a couple of hours he will be ridden down. Unless he gets his rider into a snarl, and thus earns a let-up, he will be so played out that he will go along pretty quietly, with but slight attacks of his bucking fever. He has found his master, and he knows it.

One more ride will be the final polish of his primary-schooling. The kindergartening has been omitted. The second ride will be a repetition of the first in a slightly modified and less dangerous form. After this the pony is considered "busted;" but his grammar-schooling he gets from the cowboy's use. He never reaches the high or normal school, let alone the college; but he has a true Yankee knack of educating himself, and the amount of information and skill he will pick up of his own accord at cow-punching is wonderful. He is, of course, taught to

guide by the neck, and he twists and turns in the performance of his duties with extraordinary intelligence and
quickness; but a good deal of what he does is not so much
taught by an educational process as picked up by repetition of the same work, which, after all, is the only way a
horse ever learns.

XXIII

I HAVE above referred to "Buffalo Bill." There has probably been no American in Europe since General Grant who has become so universally known. Not to know "B. B." argues yourself unknown. You see him mentioned in print, or hear him spoken of on every street corner as "*Boofalo*" or "*Beel*," in every part of the earth where men and women like amusement. He has familiarized the Old World with America; or, I should say, has given the Old World a certain conception of America which is ineffaceable. Whether it is to our advantage to have the universe believe that our common sports are riding pitching ponies, or shooting glass balls from the saddle, and that an American Vestibule Limited is, after all, really nothing but a Concord stage-coach, liable to be attacked by savages, is perhaps questionable. We all know Colonel Cody, admire his manly qualities, and feel happy at his financial success—thoroughly well-earned by a capital "sho," than which Phineas T. himself never originated a better. But it gives people a queer idea of us sometimes, and lends color to the plausibility of the statement I recently saw in *Galignani's Messenger* anent one of our well-known publishers, that "he had been very carefully brought up, and had even had the benefit of an university education." And once I earned the suspicion if not the positive dislike of a very charming woman, *à laquelle je contais fleurette*, as we were riding through the Gap of Dunloe by mildly denying her positive assertion that

Colonel Cody was a regimental commander of our regular army. In fact, she became convinced, to my keen chagrin, that I myself was no army officer, for, said she, "I know a gentleman who has seen his commission." "Buffalo Bill" represents one phase of our civilization most admirably; but we have, in the eyes of the semi-intelligent abroad, fallen as a nation to the estate of Indian fighters and bronco-busters, partly owing to the education given the average circus-public by the otherwise irreproachable Wild West. For all that, hail to "B. B.," and here's a bumper to his future!

The cowboy will stay in the saddle an almost unheard-of period, often forty-eight hours at a time, when holding big bunches of cattle. He is up by daylight, and works till dark, and then well on into the night, or all night long by turns. He is faithful and untiring, and wedded to his master's interests. Much of the vice attributed to the cowboy must be laid to the score of the "bad man" of the plains, a class which used to exist in great numbers, but has been for the most part hunted down and run out by the ranchmen, who were the greatest sufferers.

This term "bad man" always strikes me as an odd coinage for a set of fellows no more noted for abstemiousness in language than mule-drivers. Its very moderation, however, lends it force, though at first blush it sounds like what the children call goody-goody. And out on the plains there is far less overwrought language than in the slums of cities. The language is picturesquely forcible, but rarely flavored with Billingsgate. The cowboy is no saint, but he is a manly fellow, and averages quite as well as the farmer or mechanic; the stranger who has been cast on his hospitality, and has accepted it as frankly as it was tendered, would say much higher.

The cowboy rides with the easy balance bred of constant habit, swaying about in the saddle much like a drunken man, but with a graceful method in his reeling. He does not, however, ride all over his horse like the Indian on his pad or bareback. When he ropes a steer or a pony, he gets well over on the nigh side, and throws his weight against the strain, resting the back of the right thigh in the saddle. He can perform all the tricks of the Indian, and much of his fun as well as his work is astride his ponies. On foot he reminds one of Jack ashore, partly from the stiffness of his chaparajos, partly from his own stiffness bred of the saddle habit; but with his loose garments, his bright kerchief, and his jingling spurs, he is a most attractive fellow, in perfect keeping with his surroundings.

The best cowboys are usually bred to the business, which is by no means an easy one to learn. The Southwest yields the best supply. They are apt to claim kinship with the South rather than the East. The term "round-up" originated in the southern Alleghanies, "corral" in Mexico. The cattle business is of Mexican origin, and the dress and method of riding are unquestionably of Spanish descent; but, as in every other business, there are men from every section who succeed, and vastly more who fail. As a whole, with all his virtues and all his faults, he is distinctly an American product, and one, take him for what he is, and what he has done, to be distinctly proud of.

I fear I have unintentionally given the bronco a bad reputation for manners. He has no worse than any wild horse with equal grit and strength would have; and I have been referring mostly to the simon-pure, uncracked article. After much use and care, the pony often becomes very reliable. Roosevelt speaks with great affection of his pet hunting-pony, and many a ranchman I have known has had quiet. well-behaved broncos all through the outfit. As a rule, the bronk is rough and ready because his master is so; but gentle treatment has its effect with even him. Broncos become tractable to a degree scarcely known where the demand for steadiness exists less. It is a common habit in some localities, when you want your pony to stand and wait for you, to toss the bridle-rein over his head and let it dangle. Many a pony by this simple device will stand all day and scarcely move from place. It, or an equivalent to it, is very necessary on a plain where there is nothing to hitch to. Moreover, the bronco will face the music in hunting or on the war-path as it is difficult to teach a civilized horse to do.

Many busters, when they have earned a little money, like to take to quieter pursuits as a rest from the violence of their life. But the instinct comes back again, and a man will go to his old work on slight provocation. A friend of mine who keenly enjoys fun of the cowboy kind told me a good story of the cook of an outfit he was once with when on a mining tour. Jim was a quiet slouch of a fellow, mighty clever over his pots and pans, and the boys lived in clover all winter long; but he couldn't be got near a pony. He seemed to have a special aversion to anything on four legs unless he could cut it up for the kettle. Finally, in the spring, when the ponies had to be got to work again, there was a deal of talk each day about this or that bronk, and a lot of swearing at the hard work each man would have to do to get the little brutes into order. Jim used to join the circle sometimes after he had washed up, and would sit and watch the pitching, while many a jeer was flung at him because they couldn't get him to take a turn.

Finally, one day when one of the best of the outfit had tried all his ponies except one piebald, a notorious outlaw,

which it was really a risky business to touch, but which
looked sheepish enough when let alone, Jim was asked if
he didn't want the job of saddling and riding him. Jim
said he guessed not, but he thought he "would be spryer
about doin' it if he'd got to," which piece of bravado
elicited universal laughter, and numerous taunts to Jim
to try. "Wa'al, boys, I don't know much about them
bronks," said Jim, "but I've got a dollar or two laid by
for a rainy day, and I'd like to bet I *kin* ride him." In a
moment every man's pocket was empty, for they thought
Jim didn't know what he was about. The old cook acted
rather foolish, but said if the boys would rope and saddle
the bronk, and would help him mount, he'd take a bet or
two, and in five minutes he stood booked to win more dollars than he could earn at the fire in five years, at odds
which left him with a goodish margin of ready money in
case he failed.

Jim made a good deal of fuss getting ready and putting
on a pair of spurs, but stood the chaff pretty well. "Made
yer will, Jim?"   "Why not tie a pot on yer head, Jim?"
"Said yer prayers, Jim?"   "Where shall we plant ye,
Jim?" and so on, *ad infinitum*. Finally Jim was up, and
the crowd backed away, for they all knew the old piebald outlaw. For an instant the bronk stood still, ears
back, and eye full of vicious mischief. He had not been
mounted for months. Then he arched his back and gave
a little hoist and a lash-out with his off hind-leg. The
boys all looked to see Jim topple; but the quondam cook
was transformed beyond recognition. The slouch had all
gone out of him; he sat like a Centaur, heeding neither
rein or stirrup. Nettled at Jim's strong grasp, which ordinary exertions did not appear to loosen, the bronk now
started in in earnest. He reared and plunged upward, he
plunged forward head down, he kicked as only a Kentucky

mule or an outlaw bronk can kick, he pitched and came
down on stiff legs with a force which would have unseated
nine out of ten of all the boys in the outfit. Jim never
budged from the saddle. He seemed lashed to it. The
boys stared with eyes like saucers. "Hollo!" and a long
"Whew!" was all you heard. The fun went on. Jim appeared to care for the piebald's pitching no more than for
the rocking of a chair. Finally, after some minutes of the
hottest kind of work, he seemed to wake up to it, as
the piebald began to find he had caught a Tartar. It
was a "game" Jim "did not understand." He chuckled
audibly, grabbed off his hat, slapped the bronk over the
head, kicked him between hoists, rolled all over him as he
plunged around, laughed outright, and screamed to the
blue-looking crowd, "Cotched a tenderfoot, boys, didn't
yer? Be gad, ye didn't know I'd been four years buster
for the 101! Go it, ye divil," he yelled, as he slapped the
bronk again and again with his storm-bleached hat, snap-
ped up the reins, dug his heavy spurs into the outlaw's
flanks, and drove the half-frightened, half-astonished brute
hither and yon at will. "Guess I'll go bustin' agin! Feels
like old times! Ha'n't had so much fun for a twelve-
month! Hooray!"

A sorrier crowd or a poorer you never saw, but no one
opened his mouth to Jim. Every man paid up without a
question. It was the event of the spring in all that section.

XXIV

THE American cowboy has a Mexican cousin, the vaquero, who does cow-punching in Chihuahua, and raises
horses for the Mexican cavalry and occasional shipment
across the Rio Grande. The vaquero is generally a peon,
and as lazy, shiftless, and unreliable a vagabond as all
men held to involuntary servitude are wont to be. He is
essentially a low-down fellow in his habits and instincts.
Anything is grub to him which is not poison, and he will
thrive on offal which no human being except a starving
savage will touch.

In his way the vaquero is a sort of tinsel imitation of a
Mexican gentleman, and very cheap tinsel at that. Our
cowboy is independent, and quite sufficient unto himself.
Everything not cowboy is tenderfoot, cumbering the
ground, and of no use in the world's economy except as a
consumer of beef. He has as long an array of manly qualities as any fellow living, and, despite many rough-and-
tumble traits, compels our honest admiration. Not only
this, but the percentage of American cowboys who are
not pretty decent fellows is small. One cannot claim so
much for the vaquero in question, though the term "vaquero" covers a great territory and class, and applies to
the just and the unjust alike.

Our Chihuahua vaquero wears white cotton clothes, and
goat-skin chaparajos with the hair left on, naked feet clad
in huarachos or sandals, and big jangling spurs. A gourd
lashed to his cantle does the duty of canteen. He rides

A MEXICAN VAQUERO

the Mexican tree, and his saddle is loaded down with an
abundance of cheap plunder. His seat is the same as the
Mexican gentleman's—forked, with toe stuck far out to
the front, and balancing in the saddle. He is supposed to
be a famous rider, and is a very good one. He breaks his
own ponies, which sufficiently proves his case. He likes
to show off, in the true style of the Latin nations and
their offshoots, and will often ride a half-busted bronco
with his feet stuck out parade fashion, much as a Yankee
boy would carry a chip on his shoulder on the school-
ground; but in breaking in his pony he gripes with thigh
and knee and calf and heels besides, as any rider perforce
must.

The Mexican cow-ponies are proverbially tough and
serviceable; but the vaquero has to turn in most of his
good-sized ponies, and is apt to be seen on a rackabones
of undersized or old stock, or on a mare with a foal at
foot. His gait is the lope, with an occasional fox-trot,
and he uses his quirt as constantly as an American Indian.
No savage can be more cruel to his pony than a vaquero,
or pay less heed to his welfare. Averaging the vaquero
of Northern Mexico, one American cowboy is worth half
a dozen of him to work; and, though he is used to Apache
raids, worth more than a gross of him to fight. In view
of the origin of both these cow-punchers, this is not a singular fact.

And yet it is strange that the vaquero should bear so ill
a reputation. Let us not be unjust. No doubt there are
good vaqueros; but are they, like the good Indian, all
with the "great majority?" I trow not. Give a dog a
bad name, and— Well, the vaquero has the bad name;
let us hope that he has not quite earned it. Even Judas
Iscariot has had learned defenders, and an excellent technical case can be made out for him. Shall the vaquero

lack an advocate? He comes of good stock; I have, in many qualities, rarely seen a finer subject-race than the Mexican Indian. I do not think the Spaniard on American soil has thriven, in body or mind; but the aborigines of Mexico have kept their fine physique, their good looks, and their amiable character; they have had no chance whatever to gain in intelligence, though they do not lack mother-gumption. I hardly think I have ever seen a greater percentage of pretty women than in Mexico, among the peasants. One must, to be sure, conjure away dirt and some rather trying habits; but then beauty, abstractly speaking, may no doubt reside beneath a grimy exterior. I do not refer to that peculiar quality of beauty neatly called *appetitlich* by the Germans. To evoke one's appetite requires cleanliness rather than the thing we call beauty, and I do not know that I ever saw a Mexican Indian girl whom I would care to embrace: but they are well-grown, plump, straight, have fine eyes and teeth, and in their unsewn garments of dirty cotton cloth, with a xerapa loosely thrown about head and shoulders, they are certainly fine specimens of womanhood, and graceful beyond the corseted beauty of civilization.

But the skin! say you. Well, the skin is brown, but it shows the red blood gushing heartily beneath; and—let us see—even so good a judge as the King of Dahomey preferred his lustrous, black-skinned, fattened beauties to the most exquisite of pale-face women. And let me confess to a weakness for a brown skin. I am sure that three out of four of my travelled, susceptible male friends —at least, if they will be honest about it—have grown to like the brown skin of the maidens of the Orient. Ought I to acknowledge that I, too, stand midway between the King of Dahomey and the European connoisseur in beauty?

> "I am black, but comely,
> O ye daughters of Jerusalem,
> As the tents of Kedar,
> As the curtains of Solomon,"

has a more distinct meaning to me to-day than before I
learned to know the East. I scarcely dare confess to having felt a momentary disappointment in the matter of
complexions when I once emerged from a burial of several weeks among Orientals, far from the contact of
whites. That the disappointment was due to the fact
that I came out upon a lot of unwashed humanity, and
that on a white skin dirt sits less gracefully than on a
brown one, in nowise alters the captivating quality of the
dark-hued women of the far East.

All of which reminds me of a story. I find, as I grow
older, that I am more and more frequently reminded of a
story. I hold the dangerous tendency in check; I shorten
the curb-chain by a link; but the tendency will now and
then shy at some statement made in perfect innocence,
and give a mad plunge off in the direction of a story.
And my gripe on the rein is more lax than of old. It is
not my fault, it is your misfortune; I am incapable of
kicking a supposititious canine under the table in order to
tell a good dog story, but this one must out.

Many years ago, down in Richmond, I was standing
with a friend at his doorway while he gave instructions
to an old colored servant. There chanced to pass one of
the beauties of the city—and there were beauties in those
days. We both took off our hats, courtesy in our attitude, admiration in our hearts. "Isn't she a beauty?"
said I. "*Isn't* she a beauty?" echoed he. "Just isn't she,
Uncle Jed?" said my friend. "Miss Ellen's a mighty fine
leddy," responded the old servitor, in a deferential but
somewhat hesitating tone. "Why, what do you mean,

9

Uncle Jed?" insisted my friend, rather nettled, and curious withal, at the old darky's manner. "Well, Mars' Tom," stuttered out the old man, "to tell de hones' truf, we niggers doan tink de white leddies is so hansum as de brack ones." This was a revelation to me, not then understood, but now very clear.

Our muttons, or lambs, *i.e.* the Mexican maidens, have been strayed from. Let us return cross-lots to them, and thence along our highway.

XXV

THE prototype of the vaquero, the Mexican gentleman, is a rider of quite another quality. No city man ever acquires the second-nature seat on a horse which one can boast who spends all the working-hours of the day, and at times most of his nights, in the saddle. He may be a better horseman; he may have a better style, actually or according to local notions or traditions; he may be able to ride on the road, or do some one special thing, such as riding to hounds, or playing polo, or tent pegging, or tilting, exceptionally well; but, for all that, a chair is more natural to him than a saddle; and to ask him to ride sixteen consecutive hours, which the cavalryman or the cowboy does every day, and will double up with a smile, is to ask him to work to the point of complete exhaustion.

Horsemanship is a broader term than mere riding. It of necessity comprises the latter to a certain extent. A good horseman must be a good rider, though he may not be a perfect one, from age or disability. But the best rider may be a very poor horseman. The best wild rider never spares his horse; a good horsemen's first thought is for his beast. Still the horseman may by no means be able to equal the rider's feats of daring, endurance, skill, or agility. Whether horseman or riders, we city folks, compared to the saddle-bred man whose lifework is astride a horse, are and remain tenderfoots.

I used myself to be something of a rider once, though it is not for me to say so, and age has withered my once good performance. I am something of a horseman yet, but old army wounds have kept me out of the saddle now some five years past, and threaten to end what for nearly four decades has been my happiest pastime. I have long ago yielded my place to the younger generation, to whose sturdy courage and fast growing skill I yield my very honest admiration. But though they must increase as I must decrease, they will not take it amiss if I descant upon what I once could do, and still well know, though performance be of the past; and they will not feel that I criticise unkindly. From the mass of chatty chaff they may perhaps glean a few kernels of grain ; for it has not fallen to the lot of every horseman to study the horses of so many lands. Moreover, I fancy that my hand has not yet lost its cunning; and that, when I find a promising young horse, I can still vie with many another man in making him a perfect saddle-beast. I should scarce dare compete with the rough-riding "trainer" or the bronco-buster; but I feel that I might still accomplish results in the way of the niceties of equitation.

The Mexican gentleman, like most Southerners, is a good rider within his limits. He is the very reverse of the Englishman, who, with his *reductio ad simplicitatem* of everything, has stripped the beauties of equestrianism to the bone. With his tweed suits and his brusque manners, with his disregard of everything which lends a touch of charm to daily life, he has driven out much that is beautiful and more that is gallant in social and equestrian pleasures alike. With lace ruffles and buckled shoes have quite disappeared not only the beauties of equitation, but the graceful outward courtesies to the other sex ; and the place of the latter has not been filled by the acknowledgment conveyed in the cavalier manner now in vogue that women have grown in wisdom to the point of taking care

GENTLEMAN RIDER ON THE PASEO DE LA REFORMA

of themselves. Women are glad, no doubt, of some emancipation, but does she whom we love and admire as the
real woman of to-day want to be left to her own resources
any more than did her grandmother? Has she tired of
the willing ministration of the other sex? We have by
no means lost our heart courtesies, but whither has the
old-fashioned polish taken its flight? We are indebted
for much to the Old Country; do not let us borrow too
largely. Despite our *ante bellum* accusation that the
South affiliated with the British aristocracy, the Southron
has retained his gallantry to women, as we of the Eastern
States, to our serious detriment, have not. The best rule
in equitation, as in other arts, is first the useful, then the
ornamental; but, having the useful, by no means let the
ornamental elude you, unless the twain be incompatible.

Our artist has drawn the typical rider on the Paseo de
la Reforma, the Rotten Row or Harlem Lane of the City
of Mexico. It is to be regretted that telegraph and railroad are spoiling national types. Whatever country is
invaded by news and cheap clothing loses first its national costume and then its national characteristics. Can
you remember how things looked forty years ago on the
Continent of Europe? You could tell an Englishman, a
Frenchman, a German, an American as far as you could see
him. Not so to-day. The travelled man is cast in about
the same mould, and unless the type is pronounced, all nations look more or less alike. The rubbing up against one
another of the various nations robs each of the piquancy
it used to possess. Italy to-day is no longer the Italy you
once posted through in your own carriage; and Mexico
is going the same road. In another decade there will
scarcely be a sombrero left. But one still sees an occasional swell who clings to his national costume, and a fine
bird he is, too, afoot or a-horseback.

In this style ride both the statesman and the swell, the banker and, when he can afford it, his clerk. And very much so rode the Englishman of half a century ago. I have of late years heard excellent English horsemen brush aside all reference to the high-school of equitation as worthy only of a snob. But there were some very decent "snobs" in England back in the thirties, when celebrated members of both Houses, the leaders of fashion, the most noted generals—the very heroes, indeed, who had beaten Boney—and every one pretending to be in the social swim would go prancing up and down the Row, passaging, piaffing, traversing, to the admiration of all beholders. The brave men who served under Wellington and Nelson were not cut on the tweed-suit pattern by any means. Even the M. F. H. fell into the trick of it in the park. They were not called snobs then; the initial letter was dropped; and when a Briton slurs at the better education of the horse to-day, he casts a stone at his own ancestry over the shoulder of the lover of the high-school. I shall recur to this high-school business.

The first thing in our Mexican friend which strikes us is his horse. This is not the bronco of the plains. He is evidently imported from Spain, or lately bred from imported stock without that long struggle for existence which has given the pony his wonderful endurance and robbed him of every mark of external beauty. Here we revert to the original Moorish type. The high and long-maned crest, arched with pride, the full red nostril, large and docile eye, rounded barrel, high croup, tail set on and carried to match the head, clean legs, high action, and perfect poise. How he fills our artistic eye, how we dwell upon him!—until we remember that performance comes first, beauty after, and that the English thorough-bred, which can give a distance to the best of this exquisite

creature's family and beat him handily, has developed
from the same blood far other lines than these; or, indeed,
that the meanest runt of a plains pony, on a ride of one
hundred miles across the Bad Lands, would leave the
beautiful animal dead in his tracks full twoscore miles
behind!

There is one point in which our steed is not Moorish—
and it was the Moorish horse, or Barb, which came across
with the Spaniards.   This is the croup and tail.   The
Barb carries a poor tail; it is the Arabian whose tail is so
high-set. And in Spain, too, the tail is, as a rule, low-carried, showing its evident origin.   You must cross the Libyan desert to the east before you get the best tail.   And
in Mexico one does not often see as perfect a croup as the
saddle-beast depicted.   He may have been imported from
the Orient.

The Mexican swell rides on a saddle worth a fortune.
It is loaded with silver trimmings, and hanging over it is
an expensive xerapa, or Spanish blanket, which adds to
the magnificence of the whole.   His queer-shaped stirrups
are redolent of the old mines.   His bridle is in like manner adorned with metal in the shape of half a dozen big
silver plates, and to his bit is attached a pair of knotted
red-cord reins, which he holds high up and loose.   He is
dressed in a black velvet jacket, fringed and embroidered
with silver; and a large and expensive sombrero, perched
on his head, is tilted over one ear.   His legs are incased
in dark tight-fitting breeches, with silver button and chain
trimming down the side seams, but cut so as, in summer
weather, to unbutton from knee to foot and flap aside.
His spurs are silver, big and heavy and costly, and fitted
to buckle round his high-cut heel.   Under his left leg is
fastened a broad-bladed and beautiful curved sword, with
a hilt worthy an hidalgo.

The seat of the average Mexican exquisite is the perfect pattern of a clothes-pin. Leaning against the cantle, he will stretch his legs forward and outward, with heels depressed in a fashion which reminds one of Sydney Smith's saying, that he did not object to a clergyman riding if only he rode very badly and turned out his toes. It is the very converse of riding close to your horse. In what it originates it is hard to guess, unless bravado. The cowboy, with an equally short seat and long stirrups, keeps his legs where they belong, and if his leg is out of perpendicular, it will be so to the rear. Not all Mexicans ride the clothes-pin seat. There are many riders of good style to be seen in the City of Mexico, and there are good horsemen. But when the pure Mexican rider puts on a bit of "side" he is deliciously ungainly in a horseman sense, though always picturesque to the every-day beholder.

The rack rarely, the canter all but universally, is ridden by the Mexican. It is only the Englishman and those he has taught who ride what can be called a trot. With all others the trot is a mere jog, though a good open trot is one of the easiest gaits for a horse to go, and, risen to, one of the most delightful on the road. Luckily, as the horses of the world gain in breeding by the infusion of English stock, so the world is learning the English habit of rising. When I was a school-boy in Prussia I was fairly hooted out of rising to a trot, a habit I had previously learned in England. But now you see the Prussians—all the Continental officers, in fact—riding à l'Anglaise in full uniform, and one may see a lancer or hussar trotting through the streets with a handful of despatches, leaning over his horse's neck and rising to the gait in a fashion which would have court-martialled him in the old ramrod Anglophobia days of Frederick William IV. For all they laugh at England for her military pretensions, they adopt many good things

from her, not the least of which is the course of cross-
country riding which all foreign officers are now required
to take; or rather a course of as near its requirements as
non-hunting countries can conjure up. Jumping has always been part of the drill of the Prussian cavalryman;
but since the growth of English ideas this exercise has
been broadened and made more of. It is, however, not
mere jumping of a thirty-inch obstacle but steady drill
which really helps shake a man into his saddle in the form
needed for cavalry evolutions.

The canter of the Mexican is the old park canter, with
a superabundant use of the curb to make the horse prance
and play and show his action. The horse is as fond and
proud of this as the rider. The best saddle-horse is, of
course, the one which will absolutely follow his master's
mood; upon whose neck the reins can be flung if one
wishes to saunter along the road, or if one wishes to dismount and rest *sub tegmine fagi;* and who, at call, can
show his paces to the best advantage. Most horses are
treated solely as a means of transportation, even in hunting and polo; few receive the training every intelligent
horse is as much entitled to as the American child to his
common schooling. And in a sense the Mexican has educated his horse to better advantage. Because his horse is
prancing it is no reason why we should look down upon
him. He is doing nothing more than the men who used
to go titupping down Rotten Row every fine afternoon of
fifty years ago; and he may be a better rider than he
looks. The steady, business-like gaits of the English nag
of to-day are in perfect keeping with his rider's business
suit; but you notice that the Mexican wears a different habit. Why, then, should not his riding be in keeping with his dress?

This trot and canter controversy is not yet settled. The

Englishman claims that his horse can go seven miles on a
trot for six he can go on a canter with the same exertion.
Our cavalry officers on the plains—and they are the best
judges of distance riding alive—have arrived at a similar
conclusion, and all long marches are made at alternate
walk or trot, or walk alone. Most cavalry does this. It
is astonishing how fast a walk can be, not in the exceptional horse, but in a large body of cavalry. General
Forsyth marched four troops of the Seventh Cavalry from
Fort Meade, Da., to Fort Riley, Kan., a distance of seven
hundred and twenty-nine miles. This was measured by
odometers, checked off by the railroad mileage when travelling along it. "The maximum rate per hour was 4.91
miles ; the minimum rate was 3.20 miles. The mean average per hour for the entire march was 4.11 miles. It is
to be understood that the gait considered is the walk, as
that was the one pursued during the march." Now the
speed of the average saddle-beast on a walk is, in the
Eastern States, barely three miles an hour, because he is
not educated. If you have owned a horse which could
walk four full miles, you have been lucky. Most men,
walking a three-and-a-half-mile gait, out-pace the riders
they meet who are walking their horses. It takes a very
busy horse to out-walk a fair pedestrian. Yet here, by
training, we have four troops of cavalry averaging over
four miles an hour.

The trot is unquestionably an easy gait for the horse.
But you cannot make a Southerner or a plainsman adopt
this theory. The Southern horse goes his so-called artificial gaits, or canters ; you cannot give away a trotter
for the saddle. The bronco canters all but exclusively.
The matter seems to depend on inbred habit, and comparative statistics on the subject, however interesting, could
scarcely be made accurate.

Altogether, the horsemanship of our neighbor in Mexico is not entirely to be commended. That the cattle business originated there, and that that admirable rider, the cowboy, traces his descent to that peninsula, is the best that can be said of the land, in an equine sense. Indeed, Mexico has all but outlived her usefulness. I do not believe that even railroads will do for her what it has been expected they would. Given certain factors of land and people and civilization, such as we understand it, is of no benefit, and cannot be made to grow.

XXVI

To return to the States, and to follow out the text on which we have been so far preaching. It will be accepted as a truism that the man or people that does any given thing the most constantly will be apt to excel in that one thing. Let us apply this to the riding of the Southerner and our own riding in the East. Now the climate and soil, the thicker population, the more industrious habits of the Eastern and Middle States produced excellent roads at a much earlier period than in the South. In fact, there are few places in the South to-day where the highways can be called even tolerable. The soil is intractable for roads. Good roads are wont to be followed by wheeled transportation, poor roads force people to cling to the saddle. When the Northern farmer goes to the nearest town he drives, because the roads are good, and he can carry his stuff to better advantage; the Southerner rides, because the roads for a great part of the year are impassable to wheels. This breeds the universal habit of horseback-work. The same thing applies to women. To visit their neighbors, go to church or shopping in the nearest village, the women must make use of the saddle. This necessity of the country, where the roads are bad, becomes habit of the city, where the roads are better. The Southerner has been in the saddle constantly for many generations, and to-day boys and girls alike ride the colts in pasture with, like the Numidian of old, only a stick to guide them. In the North these conditions and habits ceased long ago. Riding is a mere fashion of very recent origin, though it has acquired such an impetus that it has doubtless come to stay.

It is curious how short the period is since riding became even a fad, let alone a fashion. I was put on the retired list of the Army, and went to Boston in 1870. As I had always done, I kept up my habit of daily riding, and for years after that time, so unusual was the sight of a man in the saddle, except on procession days, that the urchins on the street used to hoot at me, or even throw a derisive pebble in my wake. Up to 1882 you could count the habitual riders of Boston on your fingers, and it was about the same in New York. For several years I rode in and out of Boston a handsome mare sired by Alexander's " Norman," and the opinion of horseback-work was well voiced by a noted horseman who once said to me, " What are you doing with that mare in the saddle? Why, she belongs on the track!" as if you ought not to disgrace a fine horse by throwing your leg across him. Shortly after began the fad, and in a dozen years we have made such vast strides forward that riding now appears to be a matter of ancient history. You surprise a young man to-day by telling him that in 1880 practically no one rode ; yet such was the fact all through the Eastern States.

It is noticeable that we Eastern riders are touchy on the subject of equestrianism, like most people not to the manner born. We are fain to believe, perhaps, not that the Southerner knows nothing about riding, but that what he knows is either all wrong or else not worth our learning. It must be confessed that for the very few years we have been at it we have accomplished wonders, and our riding to hounds, though the poor benighted pack may be all too often wheedled into chasing aniseed, has, so far as concerns pluck and enthusiasm, grown to be almost be-

yond criticism. This and polo are the things in which we
have made marked progress, and we have done well to
take our model from our British cousins, for in these
sports they are masters. But in road-riding the English
can teach us nothing. Much as the English ride they
know little of the niceties of equitation. What is called
a good saddle-beast in England will not pass muster among
those who breed exclusively for the saddle, and ride vastly more. Thoroughly familiar with the saddle, their style
of road-riding is none the less far from perfect. They are
so permeated with the hunting idea that they are constantly riding to cover in the park.

Now it is incontestable that the Southerner—though he,
too, shows points of criticism, as of necessity any class of
riders must do—is on the whole a better model for road-
riding than exists elsewhere; and it is also true that he
breeds and trains far better saddle-horses than England
has known for two generations. We Yankees are too
new and narrow in our recently-acquired sport to be able
to see this fact, though it is under our very eyes. This is
natural enough, for we got our riding fever along with our
athletic fad from across the pond, but it is regrettable.
Fox-hunting, though on a distinctly cruder plan than in
the old country, has been a constant practice in the South
for two hundred years; despite which the English hunting model is indisputably better. But in road-riding the
Southern gentleman is far ahead of the Briton as to his
gaits and seat and style. A man who hunts regularly
rides on the road a half-dozen times to once he follows
the hounds; one who hunts occasionally does so a hundred times as often. And yet each, as well as the man
who never hunts, patterns his seat for the road on the
hunting model, which was intended for as different a purpose from mere road-riding as the cowboy's. And each

persists in riding a constant, never-varied trot. The nice balance and quick response of the accomplished saddle-beast are overlooked. A horse is nowadays not even permitted to guide by the neck, while as for suppling his croup, or giving him a light forehand, no one ever dreams of it. All this is, to say the least, a distinct loss. Some men deem such education superfluous; some cross-country men brush such things aside as trivial and unnecessary. The world could doubtless have wagged along without many of the good things it has—Homer, Michael Angelo, Beethoven. But by how much is it better for having them! So with equitation. The opposition to the horse's education among hunting men is the mediæval outcry of class prejudice. The more liberal the world, the less there is of it; the more we ride, the more we shall find that a horse well educated is a horse twice told.

Our imitation of the English comes of a sincere desire to flatter; and imitation is what oils the wheels of prog-ress. When we have not what is worthy of imitation at home, let us by all means go abroad; but when we have the best in our very midst, it is little to our credit to go searching elsewhere.

The first duty of the cross-country rider is to save his horse, because the service required of him on each occa-sion of use is exceptionally great. The performance of a good hunter throughout a hard day's sport is very taxing. The road-rider need not seek to save his horse, because he covers but a tithe of the distance at any one time. Hence the rule of the road is that the horse shall, first of all, sub-serve his rider's comfort. The most comfort resides pri-marily in ease, next in variety of gaits. And no one who has learned the Southern gaits can deny their superior ease. The proof lies in the fact that they enable a man to ride without undue exertion in hot as well as cold

weather.   To one who knows it, nothing can be more in-
spiriting than a fine open trot; but a horse which can
go Southern gaits can trot besides, and, if the rider is as
clever as he, without injury to his other paces.

The Southern seat is practically the same as the true
military seat; and except that the bridle-hand is wont to
be held a trifle too high—which is a habit caught from the
high pommel or roll of blankets or other baggage in
front of the soldier—this seat, when not exaggerated, is, all
things considered, the best for road - riding, and perhaps
would enable a man to do a greater variety of things in
the saddle than any other one style.   And though the
English pigskin is perhaps a neater and more available
rig for our city needs, the Southerner is, in gaits and style
and knowledge of road work, by far the best model for
us to copy, as his saddle-beast is the best for us to buy.
This question of gaits is one to which we shall specially
recur when, in our equestrian trip across the water to the
original home of the horse, we find the habits that obtain
there.

XXVII

TAKING him as the type of a class, the Central Park rider has his good points and he has his bad ones. When he is new to his work and over-imitates the English style, he is at his worst; when he is used to the saddle he throws aside blind imitation and rides well. He steers clear of the showy tendencies of the Gaul, the military flavor which still clings to the civilian Teuton, and the extreme hunting type of the Briton.

I am aware that in what I say I am liable to be misconstrued by many of our riding-men, to be looked upon as impregnated with Anglophobia. This is an error. I have lived many years in England, and yield to no man in my admiration for the open-hearted, generous, plucky, prejudiced, self-adoring Briton. But love me love my—horse is unintelligent if proverbial. "How can you love that drunken wretch?" asked a sympathetic friend of a lachrymose wife. "You be still!" came the quick and positive reply; "I love every bone in his body—but confound his nasty ways!" Here is a neat distinction. We may love our British cousin and yet not adopt his style.

There is no better horseman than the Briton, no better rider. Few are as good. At his own sports—hunting and polo and racing—he may almost be said to be unequalled. But from these premises one must not draw the conclusion that he is master of everything else. Too many hard-riding English cross-country men have found on our plains that they could not hold a candle to the average

cowboy, to make this assumption safe. Very few English
cavalry officers could ride across our plains as our own
have learned by rough experience to do. And the color
which fox-hunting lends to road-riding seriously limits
the average Briton's skill in the park. Still the best rider
of England is well worthy of imitation. The trouble
with our young men, whose few months in the saddle
makes them feel as if they had nothing more to learn, is
that they imitate the English groom—and the poor one
at that—and not the English gentleman. As well study
art from prize-package chromos! Some of the tricks
which one sees taken up from time to time have their
origin among the poorest horsemen. The elbows akimbo
or the swinging legs illustrate my meaning. Of course
Swelldom must have a new shibboleth every now and
then. Hands must be shaken just so, or hats must be
taken off or kept on by some mystic rule, or some un-
meaning lingo must be used at meeting or parting. This
is all well enough as a pastime, or as a *cachet* of the
order, as a password; but when tricks in the saddle are
adopted from some questionable source, they may in
truth indicate that a man belongs to a certain clique, but
they do not demonstrate that he knows how to ride.
And this last happens to be the point of view we are taking. Such things are as harmless as they are ephemeral,
but it must be expected that they will evoke the smile
rather than the admiration of those who know.

To recur to our British-Southron controversy, and putting aside the peculiar uses of the English seat, let us suppose an Englishman and a Southerner passing under the
eye of an unprejudiced Arab, a man riding in the style of
neither and yet a born horseman. The former trots by on
his rangy thorough-bred, with stirrups short, leaning over
his horse's withers, both hands busy with his reins, but

A HUNTING MAN

showing entire familiarity with and control of his splendid mount, and his legs perhaps swinging to and fro with the motion. The latter comes along on an equally well-bred horse with longer leathers, upright in the saddle, one hand with a single curb lightly reining in his quickly moving single-footer. Though the Arab is used to both the shorter stirrups and the leaning seat, think you he would hesitate on pronouncing the Southerner the more graceful and expert? It is not that the Englishman is not a good pattern, but that for road-riding we have a better one at home. Assertions such as these are wont to provoke a sneer from the Anglomaniac; but a sneer is not argument; it is the resort of ignorance. Answer there is none, unless a man will in the same breath maintain that education is unfitted for a horse, as some assert that it is lost on women. Despite our slight veneer of Anglomania, however, we are sound American within, and shall not long neglect what can be taught us by our own countrymen, who have been in the saddle as many generations as the English, and been compelled to a much greater degree to use horses for daily work as well as pleasure. One may see it coming now. The Kentucky horse is by no means as often despoiled of his accomplishments when he reaches a New York owner as he used to be, and a better welcome is given him at the Horse-show. But either the Southern gaits should be recognized as suitable ones for a park hack in addition to the walk, trot, and canter, or else a special class should be provided. It is a mistake to overlook these gaits—the most universally employed of any among all peoples which are adepts in horsemanship.

I have often seen in England a man who prided himself on the speed of his park-hack's walk. He called it a "walk"—so would a Southerner; but it was a "running-walk," not a flat-footed one, which, as horses sometimes will, his nag had inherited from some distant ancestor or picked up of his own accord. No horse, except one specially trained, walks flat-footed more than four miles an hour. The running-walk will add a mile or a mile and a half to this speed. The Englishman saw no difference, even if it was an amble or a rack his horse fell into; he still called it a walk, because it was neither trot nor canter. But the flat-footed walk, the running-walk, the amble, and the rack are all as distinct as trot and canter. The English in Egypt will ride the racking donkey week in, week out, and yet I never met one who knew why the little fellow was so easy, or what gait he was going. They will condemn in the horse what they like in the ass.

These so-called artificial paces are not such in fact. Every horse under the excitement of the whip or of fright will fall into one or other of them. Every people which habitually rides at a walk—*i.e.*, travels on horseback—trains the horse, by simple urging, into these paces; even the ass-colts in Southern Europe or in the Orient running-walk. I have seen many a racker of true Norman blood. You find the gaits among all sorts and conditions of horses; but the Southerner has caught the idea, and has developed it into an art; he has trained his saddle-beasts to perfect paces, and has bred for their perpetuation. These are no more artificial than the trot, which is, indeed, by some of the best English authorities, pronounced an artificial gait. The marvellous Cossack pony " Seri," whom Sotnik Dmitri Peshkof rode in the winter of 1890–91 across Siberia from the Pacific to St. Petersburg, five thousand five hundred miles, in one hundred and ninety-three days—over twenty-eight miles a day, including several detentions, or thirty-seven miles per travelling day, mostly on roads covered with snow-drifts—was a

running-walker, and did the bulk of the distance at this
gait. This is one of the very best records of extreme distance ridden on the books—meaning a course of thousands
rather than hundreds of miles. No comparison of endurance required can well be instituted between this performance and the heretofore quoted ride of three hundred
miles in three consecutive nights, repeated weekly for six
months and over, though the latter strikes me as by far
the greater feat; for the average per day is nearly forty-
three miles for an equal or longer period, and the exertion of the long night rides vastly more taxing.

My daughters for years rode a noble little thorough-bred
Kentucky saddle-horse, handsome as a picture and easy
as a cradle, who could walk flat-footed four miles and
a half in sixty-minutes; could running-walk five and a
half, rack seven, single-foot up to twelve, and in harness
or under saddle trot a 'forty-gait as square as any horse
ever shod. This does not count his canter and gallop,
manners, or divers other accomplishments. Each gait was
so distinct that you could call it out by a word or a turn
of the bridle-wrist, and tell it from the others with your
eyes shut. Was "Pea Vine" not a better park hack than
if he were confined to the plain walk, trot, and canter?
And yet most of our Eastern fashionables would answer
nay, and on general principles our above-cited Briton
would sneer at the idea of riding "artificial" gaits, though
he has, without knowing it, been felicitating himself on
his nag's possessing such a gait. I must, however, say
that I think a Briton would be more open to conviction
by a proper demonstration than some of our home imitators of his methods.

It is odd how obtuse even an old horseman can be who
has not studied these gaits. I have seen judges at horse-
shows and prize competitions give a walking prize to a

running-walker over flat-footed walkers who were going a superb gait. Of course the "runner" (as they often call him for short south of Mason and Dixon's line) out-footed the others. You might as well give a prize for speed to a horse who won a trotting race at a gallop. The amble is often called a walk. "You have no idea how easy and fast my new horse can walk!" I have frequently heard from people whose recent purchase couldn't *walk* three miles an hour, but would *amble* a four and a half gait. Perhaps it is no wonder. I have known few horsemen who could analyze the several gaits, though they might recognize them. It was only when Muybridge's lens told the story that people found out how a horse moves his feet at a gallop. I think I have met not exceeding half a dozen men in the course of my life who could describe the sequence of a horse's feet at every gait, the intervals at which they reach the ground, and especially what a horse does when he changes gaits or changes lead in the canter or gallop, though I have met thousands who knew all the gaits blindfolded. These are pleasant technical studies, but they are perhaps rather beyond the domain of essential knowledge. We do not need to be philological critics in order thoroughly to enjoy "Hamlet." It is not through lack of technical knowledge, but by disregard of the thing itself that the refinements of equitation have disappeared.

The day of practical horsemanship has come, and well it is perhaps. No one doubts the superiority for average use of a hack well trained *à l'Anglaise* over the nervous, fidgety, watch-springy creature of the high-school. But is there not a middle point between ignorance and overtraining? A small amount of knowledge of a great art, or intimacy with a small art, are wont to make the possessor "feel his oats." "Oh, you play the violin, do you?"

says the chappie who carries a felt-covered banjo under
his arm on the way to the sea-side, or to an evening call
on some pretty girl; " the fiddle isn't of much account
nowadays." It is true, is it not? And yet when a man
has devoted over forty years to the instrument, has played
the sonatas of Beethoven and Mozart for a generation,
and owns a Stradivarius, does not this crude criticism
sound harsh? The pity of it is that life is not long enough
to explain the A B C of music to the banjoist. Certes, he
can amuse his audience better than the man with the bow,
who has not the remotest desire to compete with him; but
is it because the violin is not the superior instrument, or
because the player and audience lack equal cultivation?
That there is a time to weep and a time to laugh, a time
to mourn and a time to dance is recognized by even the
violinist, but—well, I was going to say that the banjo-
horse is a capital mount for the banjo-boy or the banjo-
girl; but if a man with loving persistence has embraced
his Cremona for twoscore years, has drawn forth its delicate tones as a comfort through the gloom of nights of
sorrow, and has burst forth with it at the daybreak of re-
newed hope in anthems of gladness, both his soul and the
quivering song-laden wood wrapt in mutual affectionate
bliss, he prefers this poet of instruments to the banjo;
when a man has once studied equitation in its finer features, and has trained his horses to perfect gaits and manners, he prefers the educated steed. But we have not yet
reached the point where brains go for as much as money,
or for what some people are pleased to call Society, though
we are fast getting there. The Chinese are ahead of us;
among them the school-master ranks as he should. When
one thinks of the society which clusters about our College
greens and the world-famous work which emanates from
their studious closets, and then goes to his book-shelves,

takes down a certain light blue book, entitled *Society As I Have Found It*, reads a page or two, and then contemplates this outcome of what some people consider all that is choicest, may he not truly rejoice that his life's ticket is numbered in the thousands and not within four hundred? Did not the genial Autocrat say something anent the clergymen and doctors—the Brahmins —of New England being good enough ancestry for any one? And is not a pedigree honestly traced back to the brave men who landed at Plymouth Rock better than a coat of arms got up by a heraldry expert (!) for some *nouveau riche* who doesn't know who was his great-grandfather? I for one am proud that my grandfather was pastor of First Church, Haverhill, and that my great-grandfather was one of the heroes of Bunker Hill; but I would give more to-day for old Seth Pomeroy's anvil, or the vice which clamped the muskets he repaired for the Massachusetts militia, than for the sword he wore as a colonel in the French wars. The Dodge who landed with the Salem company in 1629 is a forebear who satisfies all my ambition for ancestry. If we Americans cease to be proud of the thew and sinew of our forefathers, of the soil and the laws which have brought forth such a man as Abraham Lincoln and made him President of the Republic, what have we left? Are we to become a plutocracy pure and simple?

XXVIII

WHEN we reach the cross-country rider of our Eastern States, as typified in such hunts as the Genesee Valley, the Meadow Brook, the Radnor, or the Myopia, we touch our hats with a thrill of admiration as the red-coats ride to the meet, and wonder at the genuine Yankee grit and intelligence which have so soon popularized this sport among us. Not that we can have the real article in hunting in our severe northern climate, or under conditions which substitute a drag for Reynard's nimble legs and cunning twists and turns. Still, it is rare that a fox in our Eastern States will give you as good a run as a drag. The country is such that you cannot ride over it in every direction at will, as you can in England, and a fox has so many covers near at hand that you can never be sure of even a short run. This does not apply to the Genesee Valley. Fox-hunting there is the rule, and a drag is laid only to accommodate those who ride to jump fences instead of jumping fences because they are hunting across a country and won't be left behind. But the boldness, skill, and enthusiasm of our hunting-men are beyond praise, and there is plucky riding and good among them. It is, moreover, certain that in no part of the Old Country is there such breakneck timber as we find in several of our hunts—say the Meadow Brook.

I have often thought that as fine an exhibit of horsemanship as can be found is that of the middle-aged English country-gentleman, who has ridden to hounds since

boyhood, has outgrown the dare-devil, and lost somewhat
of the muscle and elasticity of his youth, but who still, by
his fine sense of the capacity of his horse, his light hands,
and perfect judgment, is able to keep in the next field
with the hounds throughout a long run over a stiff country.   As there is perhaps no animal equal to the best
hunter in his all-round qualities, unless it be an A1 Kentucky combined horse, so there is perhaps no more perfect
thing in equitation than this intelligent riding.   It soars
above the breakneck performance as a line of Milton
above the epic of Commencement.   We do not often see
this kind of thing here; the dare-devil still predominates:
but none the less, hail to the youth and strength and man-
liness which have sought an outlet in this splendid sport!
A generation ago the same spirit thronged the tented
field, and marched up to the Bloody Angle with teeth set
and heart aglow with heroic passion.   And it is this true
Anglo - Saxon mettle which can always be relied on to
come to the fore in our times of need.   May it never die
out!

In a few sections of country fox-hunting is older; in
fact, has become not only almost an hereditary sport, but
one in which the farmers take an equal part and interest.
This is as it should be.   Hunting can never thrive when
only the rich may indulge in it.   When a country is so stiff
that none but exceptional horses can get over it, and a
field is limited to a dozen men on nags averaging a couple
of thousand dollars each, it is hard to see a future in the
sport.   Were it not for some localities where the sport
has run through a generation or two, even though there
has been no regular Hunt and M. F. H., one would fear
its extinction when fashion shall have brought some other
form of athletics into prominence.   But it is probable that
hunting has taken firm root; and though our climate can-

GENTLEMAN RIDER IN CENTRAL PARK

not be coaxed, nor foxes quickly bred, there is small danger that the riding part of the sport will soon be lost.

This sport has shown us what capital material we have in this country for hunters. Our American horses are wonderful in their serviceableness. They have done better across our country than the expensive imported English and Irish ones. The difficulty of acclimation of the latter has something to do with this; but few things have shown the adaptability of our stock to any work better than the number of horses of trotting blood that have turned out fast gallopers, big timber-jumpers, and stayers besides.

There seems to be a growing tendency to breed for size. May it not be a mistake? It is doubtful if the hunter of over sixteen hands averages as well, all things considered, as the one which is somewhat under this measure, though big thorough-breds are needed for some men. Certainly, for plain saddle-work fifteen-two is a better size, commanding vastly more activity if less stride. Moreover, big horses are not always weight-carriers any more than they are weight-pullers. The work of the world is done, the speed of the world is attained, the races of the world are won, by the smaller specimens; but to-day's fashion is set for either a polo-pony or a sixteen-and-a-half hands thorough-bred. The ten inches between the two are skipped, though the best performances have almost invariably been between these two limits and well under the higher one.

I may here say a word anent the American horse as a racer. Some Englishmen are wont to underrate our climate, so far as it relates to horse-breeding; but this has never been a country of racing. Our national sport has, until lately, been trotting; and a country which has produced a "Sunol," an "Arion," and a "Nancy Hanks," may well claim pre-eminence for its effect upon the horse. There is nothing in breeding to parallel our reducing trotting speed from 2.26½ by "Lady Suffolk"—which many men still remember to have seen—down to "Nancy Hanks's" 2.05 in 1892. Nor need we feel like taking a back seat in racing. We have had altogether too much good-luck, even by our second-raters, on English turf, to feel discouraged, and our records are of the very best. So good an authority as Count Lehndorf, in his *Horse-Breeding Recollections*, says:

"Experience points to America as the source from which to draw in future the regenerating fluid, for, although the American thorough-bred takes its origin from England, and is still more or less related to its English prototype, the exterior appearance and the more recently shown superiority of American horses lead to the conclusion that the evidently favorable climate, and the, to a great extent, virgin soil of America—in every respect different from ours—gradually restore the whole nature of the horse to its pristine vigor, and make the American racer appear eminently qualified to exercise an invigorating influence on the condition of the thorough-breds of the mother-country, enfeebled, perhaps, by oft-repeated inbreeding."

This is from a source entirely impartial, and one often quoted in England.

XXIX

WE have during the past dozen years drawn from our tap of Anglomania a mug brimful of good. How easy it is to blow away the froth which rests on the excellent draught below! One of the most exhilarating of our imported sports is polo, and as it happens that our plains furnish so excellent a mount, and our increasing out-of-doors habits so many players, the game may well become a national one. The motto of the day in English sports is speed. Fox-hunting of the last generation was a modest performance at a hand gallop; Sir Roger de Coverley rode to hounds at a canter. But within twoscore years the cross-country pace has been run up to racing speed. More and more thorough blood has been called for in both park and field, and the old-fashioned hunter of our sires could not live through the shortest burst to-day. The same thing applies to polo—the faster and more able the pony the better the performance of his rider. You can get enormous weight-carrying capacity in an underbred pony, as well as remarkable endurance, but not at speed. When you call on a fourteen-hands pony to carry a hundred and sixty pounds and upwards at speed, you must have blood. Even the veriest weed of an undersized thorough-bred will do wonders in this way. The sudden bursts of racing pace called out at polo have made the English breed for small thorough-breds. Capital polo mounts have been raised from the handy little Exmoor pony with blooded sires. More barrel comes of this cross

together with a certain hardiness; but the little knife-
blade thorough-bred will often carry as big a man, and *endurance at speed* is the inheritance only of his race. These
words, in fact, sum up that peculiar quality which has not
yet been reached in any other animal, except, perhaps, in
the greyhound. But when we say thorough-bred there
is a limited and a broader meaning. The pure Arabian is
not, *quoad* the Stud Book, a thorough-bred; *quoad* blood
he is so. But to speak of the good blood in the plains pony
sounds absurd until you reflect upon where he came from.

So much for the English pony. When we come to
riders, it will be many years before we can boast the skill
of our transatlantic cousins, or either of us that of the
Japanese, with their light cup-wands for mallets and
feather-weight balls. The American polo-fields by no
means exhibit the play you see in England. Many a man
here indulges in recklessness which would warn him off
the ground at Hurlingham, though our cracks are really
experts. It takes years at the game to produce the at-
mosphere which breeds perfection, and in the twenty it
has been played in England it has wellnigh reached this
point. But it is well to persevere. We are making marked
progress in all our sports, and polo may yet become as
much of a national game as base-ball, though let us hope
without its commercial aspect.

The American polo-pony is no other than our little
bronco friend. Many come from Texas, Wyoming, Montana. The clever cow-pony is ready trained for the polo-
ground. He will catch the idea of the game as quickly
as he caught the trick of cow-punching, and he has already learned to stop and turn and twist as only he can
do. It must not be forgotten that he has precisely the
same blood in his veins which has placed the English thorough-bred so far above all other horses. He has increased

COUNTRY GENTLEMAN'S TYPICAL SADDLE-HORSE

his stock of endurance and hardiness by his struggle for existence on the plains, and for this game he is, perhaps, the equal of any pony, whatever his breeding, and within the limits of the polo-field his speed is as great—some good judges say greater. That is an open question. He is fast enough.

When he is taken off the cars on arrival here from his familiar haunts on the cattle-ranges, he is the sorriest, gauntest, most miserable equine specimen one can find in a day's tramp. He doesn't look worth a peck of oats. But he will reward your care. In a month or two you would never guess your plump, handsome, able little pony to be the same individual. You cannot kill a bronco. No other animal will recover from such *Strapazen*, as the Germans phrase it. And when he has undergone the torture of docking, and is finally invested with the pig-skin, nothing but the brand remains of the ragged little hero of the plains.

The pony is used to a single gag-bit; but he is tractable in his own odd way, and not a few will learn to work perfectly in a snaffle. So many of our polo-players require the bridle as a means of support that the loose rein of the cowboy will by no means do. The perfect polo-rider has not yet made his appearance. Under him the bronco would more quickly become the perfect polo-pony. It would take but a few months' training to teach him to guide by the legs alone, if need be. Indeed, his Indian master made him do just this. He learns to follow the ball in a few days. There is no sport in which training would be better rewarded than in polo, and though it would be useless to aim at the delicacy of the *haute école*—for the sharp runs and stops of polo make this as practically impossible as it is in hunting — still, given a rider with perfect seat, without a suspicion of

riding the bridle, and a pony which was taught to guide
by leg-pressure alone, and it would seem that they should,
other things being equal, be the best players in the game.

The polo-player's seat varies very little from the natural, and the best of them are consummate horsemen.
Few things call out good riding more than polo; nothing
trains a man quicker or better. While hunting can never
attain more than an imitative standing in our rigorous
climate, polo may become domesticated, and, except that
it must be played on ponies, is as good an educator in
horsemanship.

XXX

IF there is any one kind of riding between the worst of
which and the best there is a great gulf fixed, it is the
jockey's. Unless that demolisher of pet traditions and
shams — instantaneous photography — had shown us the
extremity to which bad jockeyship could be carried, we
should scarcely credit the mechanical possibility of some
of the positions the track-rider can assume. The average
jockey has no more to do with winning a race than the
time-keeper — in a neck-and-neck race by no means so
much. You will see him suspended, as it were, in fourfold straps — his stirrups and the bridle-reins — one quadruped bestriding another, and not the more intelligent atop.
He relies as much on the reins as he does on the leathers,
and has no control over his horse, no power to save or
coax him whatsoever. Considering who the jockeys are,
what their training is, and what the average race is like,
this is no great wonder. But Fordham and Cannon and
Archer did not ride this way, not to mention older celeb-
rities; nor do our own better jockeys. It is a thousand
pities that we have no photographs of Archer stealing
one of his celebrated races. The ability to ride a puller in
a snaffle-bridle, or to win with a slack rein without whip
or spur, is as unusual as the art of coaxing a horse, and of
making the most of his courage or nervousness or obsti-
nacy. How many modern jockeys study their horses, or
can cut and whip a race out of a slug, or wheedle it out of
a sulky jade? They use steel and whalebone on the will-

ing and unwilling alike. Delicate mouth-touching is the
rarest of the jockey's arts; almost every jockey here
" rides twice as fast as his horse is going."

Waiting races are not run in America. Running is
made from start to finish in the majority of cases. But
when a race is run between a few good jockeys, this rule
is not always followed. There has as yet been no phenomenal jockey produced in the States; but it may
fairly be claimed that our best jockeys come well up in
the second rank. Do not misunderstand this phrase.
Among great captains only Alexander, Cæsar, Hannibal,
Gustavus Adolphus, Frederick, and Napoleon are placed
by the best critics in the first rank; such men as Philip,
Pompey, Turenne, Marlborough, Prince Eugene, Wellington, Lee, and Von Moltke come only in the second rank,
which, after all, is good enough for any one but a demigod.
That the common jockey here is less good than in England is simply due to the fact that there he serves at least
a species of apprenticeship, while here he springs full-
armed from his own brain.

Please note that I am not undertaking to criticise the
riding of our better jockeys; I have seen some beautiful
work at home. I purposely use no names, lest some
should think me partial or unsound—you see I am wise
in my generation—and refer only to individuals who are
now translated. Nor am I an *habitué* of the race-track; I
do not consider my opinion the *ultima thule* on this subject, as I might on—well, never mind now. But that we
have not had a man who could, by his profession alone,
before he had got within a distance of middle life, accu-
mulate a fortune of over a million dollars, is clear; yet
Archer did it. With our running-horses we have done
great things; our American records are not to be questioned, and we need not be ashamed of our records in

England, from the days of game "Prioress" down. But while we have had truly phenomenal drivers of trotting-horses — among the dead let me piously refer to that noble horseman, Hiram Woodruff—I do not think we can claim to have developed a genius among jockeys. It is perhaps no wonder, for great as are the strides made by us in raising and running thorough-breds, the sport is not what it is in England; whereas trotting has long been our national sport, and at this we are so far beyond the rest of the world that trotters from any other part of the globe are "not in it." Those beautiful black Orloffs which came over from Russia to out-trot us some twenty years ago, and which were really able ten or twenty milers, were simply nowhere. They would have gone into the 'thirty class.

In olden times cathedrals were built, as they cannot be to-day, because then the whole sentiment, love, and ambition of the people were centred in the work. Unless a thing is a national institution, so to speak, it can never become truly great, as it surely will if it is upheld by the entire community. So with any sport. Base-ball thrives in America, cricket in England, because each evokes the popular interest. Racing is a more national affair in Great Britain than it is with us.

XXXI

THERE have always been in America a few isolated ex-
ponents of the high-school of equitation. Very naturally
they have as a rule been foreigners, in most cases riding-
school teachers, sometimes men stranded on our coasts
with no resource but what they had learned in better
times at home. In our old regular army there used to
be many high-school riders; to-day there are few; the
old style has given out with us as it has in England. We
are in the era of the practical; the artistic has been lost
sight of. No doubt this is for the best; it is our immense
American practicality which has taught the world what
the doctrine of the greatest good to the greatest number
can accomplish. But, stripped of all its artistic qualities,
life becomes sadly prosaic; and no one, I ween, will claim
our age of telegraph and telephone, of sixty miles an hour
on the rail, and five hundred knots a day at sea, to be an
artistic age. When a painter cannot, for love or money,
buy colors which have not in some measure been adulter-
ated, how can he expect his pictures to last? The old
Dutch masters of the fourteenth century still show up in
their original colors, as bright and glowing as the day
they were laid on. It is a serious question whether any
canvas or fresco produced to-day can last two generations. We can indeed build a Brooklyn Bridge, but
whom could we select to decorate a Vatican?

The high-school rider does not thrive because he fails
to appeal to our practical side. He will begin by telling

you that it will take you five years to learn the rudiments of horsemanship, when you want to ride with the hounds, at least as far as the first wall where you and your steed part company, so soon as the next fixtures are made; and as a result you turn your back on his *manége* and go to a more humdrum school. You want to ride *à la banjo*—and right you are!

At his best, however, this rider is in his way more of an artist than any other man who makes horsemanship his profession. My former simile of playing the violin is distinctly applicable to him. Some of the work he can do is like Paganini's "Carnival of Venice;" some of it like a smooth adagio of Kücken. The art to-day threatens to be lost; there are few masters left, but we have had some American experts who have done great things. Fancy bringing a horse to such a degree of confidence in your power and his own that you can back him up to an obstacle, however small, and make him jump it backward! Yet this has been done, while the trot and gallop backward have always been high-school airs. By trotting and galloping backward I do not mean that a horse attains any speed; he merely takes the gait, *i.e.* uses his feet in the true sequence of the gait, and progresses backward at a very slow rate. Nor is it a gallop; it is more properly a canter or a prance. The name "gallop backward" was given when the mechanical action of the gallop was not understood, and it still clings.

The chief point of criticism of the school-rider is perhaps that he is too little tolerant of the knowledge of others. This is a common error in artists of every profession. "They were all wrong, those old chaps!" is still the cry of the long-haired fraternity. I speak feelingly because I have at times been imbued with the spirit as I have enjoyed the delights of the high-school. But I have

12

seen too many splendid performers in the saddle all over
the world, who were anything but school-men, to have
a grain of prejudice left. I think I can see the high-
school horse and his rider as they actually are.

I once knew a charming old maid in England. And,
by-the-way, do you know, my friend, how much you lose
by not cultivating the society of old maids? As the med-
dlesome mother-in-law has been chosen as the type of a
class whose power for evil or good we all recognize, but of
which we know many lovely members, so has the physically, mentally, and morally weazened old maid been ig-
norantly chosen as a type of a class that is, if you will
take the trouble to study it, as full of admirable quality
as an egg is full of meat. Why some poet has not arisen
to sing aloud their virtues I know not. Their very charm
is their delicate quaintness. We go wild over a dainty,
odd, old-fashioned bit of china—why, that's just what your
old maid is, if you'll study the class as much as you have
bric-à-brac! We all crowd round and do homage to a
bud, and neglect her maiden aunt yonder. Unquestionably the bud has her charms; what bud has not, carti-
laginous though she be? But that it is imitation—emulation if you will—rather than judgment which makes us
crowd around her, is well shown by the fact that equally
charming, and often far more intelligent buds, are at the
very moment lying *perdues* in the corner by the sides of
their mammas or their duennas, and sobbing their dear
little souls away—if, forsooth, they are not indulging in
hatred, malice, and all uncharitableness. Moreover, the
bud fades or opens, and in either case is lost, while the old
maid is perennial, always delightful, always fresh. If you
know her not, it is your blindness, not her lack of charm.
Study her, friend; she will reward thee as no tenth part
of a popular bud can possibly do.

But to my own old maid. Lovely woman, she once wrote some charming verses to an entrancing little Danish air I had exhumed from the relics of a deceased musical antiquary—I am talking of thirty-odd years ago, and she was fifteen years my senior then. Well, one day she said, at a concert to which I had taken her at St. James's Hall, where we had listened to Joachim's wondrous playing, " If the organ is the king of instruments, surely the violin is the poet." Now, the high-school rider is much like the violin—mind you, I have not used the word "fiddle," which is quite another instrument, of the banjo order. There is no more delicate thing in the world than a horse's mouth, and the high-school rider works on its delicacy, while all other riders seek to harden it to their own less sensitive hands. The fact is undeniable ; the hands of the high-school rider are not to be equalled. He must have good hands ; he can accomplish no result without them. Nor is it the light hand and loose rein of the cowboy or Arab, for he feels his horse's mouth at every instant ; he talks to him through the bit as no one else ever can. The jockey stimulates his horse by the bit, sometimes in a marvellous way ; the cross-country rider does the like, and rouses his every power at a difficult obstacle. But the high-school rider talks a language to his steed which is, indeed, Greek to those who have not studied it, which is Homeric in its graceful touch and powerful effect.

Associated with this fact is the question whether such a delicate mouth is what one wants. Well— to be quite honest, no ; not as a rule. A man who is travelling needs a Baedecker rather than a Shakespeare ; we admire, if you like, the man who reads Browning before breakfast instead of his newspaper ; but—

Alas, my steed has positively got hold of the bit again, and I fear he will gallop into yonder chestnut grove. But there used, in my youth, to be a story of a Briton who was fed pretty constantly in America on that questionable confection yclept Washington pie. Being of a quiet and unresentful habit, he protested not; but one day, after an undue and perhaps underdone infliction of the *entremet*, he is said to have quietly remarked that "doubtless General Washington *was* a great and good man, but d—— his pie!"

So with the Browning man. We admire his taste, but —do not always agree as to his discretion.

Now, a man who is hunting or playing polo cannot possibly utilize or preserve a Browning, *i.e.*, too fine a mouth; he needs a newspaper-mouth. Both these sports originate in the rough-and-tumble instincts of our nature, though now grown somewhat beyond the crudely physical. Neither belongs to the same category as school-riding. They are arts in their way, but not arts in the way poetry or painting or music is an art, while school-riding is just this. How many men fence to-day? I do not mean the broadsword (though there are few enough of these), or that vigorous if crude imitation of it, single-stick; I mean the foils. It is too delicate, too difficult an art to please most people. We can learn to spar, if we have strength and courage, "in six easy lessons." But the small sword, of which foils are the practice-weapon, is the study of years and years, and yet years. And it is of that nature, like all true arts, that it is not necessarily lost by age. None of the finer arts depend upon brute strength. When a man grows less able physically, he must yield the palm to the younger men in the coarser arts; but not so in fencing. The crack fencers are almost always middle-aged men, whom study of their weapon has made perfect, not muscle. It demands patience to study fencing, not mere vigor. So with high-school riding. It is not a sport like

THE SPANISH WALK

hunting or polo, it is an art like fencing or playing the harp. In these days of sports, fencing and high-school riding are tabooed. Where school-riding is conserved, so is fencing, and vice versa. And, to recur to our initial idea, you do not require the same delicate mouth and hands for the sports that you must have for the art of horsemanship.

Again, as to legs and the spur. The only rider who uses his legs for any other purpose than holding on is the school-rider. I do not refer to kicking a horse's croup around by violent use of the legs, which the Indian and an occasional civilized rider indulge in. The school-rider's seat is very firm; it must be so or he cannot acquire or keep light hands; and in addition to using his legs to keep his seat, he uses them intelligently to talk to his horse. The delicacy of this use of the legs is equalled only by that of the schoolman's hands; nothing but to study the subject, and then to watch a master of the art ride, can give any idea of what a height this delicacy can reach. It is such that unless you know something of the art you cannot understand what the master is doing. Any one can see the skill of a rider who pilots his animal over six feet of timber; any one can appreciate "Hail Columbia" by a brass-band. But it is not every one who can understand what a master is doing when he makes his horse piaffer; nor can every one appreciate the over-ture to "Lohengrin" at its true worth.

The spur, moreover, by the school method is used not to punish or urge on the horse, but to convey certain ideas to him. Like the use of the curb-bit, in contradistinction or in addition to the use of the snaffle, the spur finds in the school - rider a new power—one never dreamed of by the rough - riding, cross - country man, or by the active, hearty polo-player. There is no question that, so far as the pure art of horsemanship is concerned, the fine work of the high-school rider soars above any mere sport, just as the "linked sweetness" of the 'cello, or the small circle of the small-sword hover above the rugged blows of the single-stick, or the lascivious pleasing of a lute. Whether there is to any given person more enjoyment in the sport or in the art is a question of each man's habits, tastes, and tendencies. I am far from seeking a quarrel with these.

Do not imagine, because you give your horse a fairly delicate mouth, that this will necessarily spoil him for an

occasional bit of rougher work. By no means. My "Patroclus," the instant I took up the reins, used to give me
the most delicate touch of the bit, and keep it so hour
after hour; but if I wanted a mile or two with the
hounds, I could let out a link of his curb-chain, use the
bridoon rather more than the bit, and Pat would take

CAPRIOLE

hold of me enough not to mind a twitch on the bit if, in
going over an awkward place, I did the trick less well
than he; and at once, on stopping him, fresh or winded,
he was ready to give me his school-head again without
fret or bore. Any horse can learn to do—almost as much.

What can the high-school rider do? you ask. Well,

he can do many wonderful, many beautiful, many useful things, not to speak of what he has done for horsemanship in the past. Some of the so-called "airs" of the high-school are truly wonderful—such as the croupade or the capriole, or galloping backwards; some, such as the piaffer, or the Spanish march and trot, are of singular grace; and the fact that by a school-training a dangerous horse may be made safe, or a chronic stumbler be taught to catch himself always, or the average ungainly, clumsily-moving brute be made light and handy, and responsive to the bit and legs, demonstrates its usefulness. Is it not useful to take a puller, or a horse so high-strung that it is a risk for any one to ride him, and make him moderate and safe for even a woman to ride, if she is taught what his training is, and is trained herself? Have you ever watched horses let loose in a pretty paddock after a long confinement in the stable, and paid heed to their free step and splendid bearing? Well, everything they do of their own accord they can be made to do at the bidding of man by a high-school training. All this, you think, has no value except from an artistic stand-point; but neither, it might be claimed, has hunting except as an exercise—in other words, it is art *versus* exercise. Neither statement is an argument; and a moderate use of high-school methods has a distinct value which we will discuss when we come to talk of road-riding as a separate matter.

The high-school has been of inestimable use in the past; to-day, when we think of nothing but athletics, its uses are not so apparent—to the athletic rider. Although it can be theoretically demonstrated that a school-rider on a school-horse ought to do anything and everything better than any one else, the truth is that he does not. Given the perfect rider and the perfect horse, and he would, no doubt, do so; but no horse or rider ever is perfect. It is like a republican form of government—perfect in theory, but mighty hard to make as perfect in practice with a somewhat mixed population; and in the hunting-field it is, even to an expert, practically impossible to ride on the delicate school-rein. On the polo-ground it might perhaps be done. A hunter or a polo-pony must not mind frequent and sometimes severe twitches on the mouth; but twitches, unless your bit is very light, ruin the school-horse. It will not do to forget that each occupies a field by itself, and that art and the sports can hardly mix: they are as unlike as oil and water.

Perhaps, to-day, the best uses for school-riding are in winter, when, on days too disagreeable to be out with sat-

CROUPADE

isfaction, one may ride in a *manége* to the manifest gain
of man and horse; or, in the extreme summer heat, the
well-ventilated school ring is not to be despised.

I wonder, *en passant*, whether I am living too much in
the past. It is the weakness of—shall I say middle age?
I often feel like the old darky who was modestly standing beside a visitor to the "family" on the porch of the
old plantation homestead in Virginia one fine bright night
when Luna was out in her full majesty. "Isn't that a
fine moon, Uncle Joe?" said the stranger. "Yes," slowly
assented the ancient, now somewhat threadbare servitor,
"dat am, fo' shure, a mighty fine moon, Massa Temple,
but yo' orter seen dat moon 'fo' de war!" Many a thing
seems to have lost a part of its *ante-bellum* flavor in these
later days. Draw the rein on me if I offend too much—
or, better still, be tolerant.

XXXII

THE chief value of school methods lies in the application of the simplest of them to plain road-riding. The term "saddle-horse" threatens to be lost. Any man who owns a horse which will allow itself to be ridden, will quietly walk and trot along the road more or less easily, and has endurance and good-temper, says that he has a saddle-horse, and really thinks so. Every second man will tell you he owns "the best saddle-horse in the State." The hunting-man calls his hunter a saddle-horse; the scrubbiest polo-pony with any sort of manners is so dubbed, and nearly every carriage-horse, too. Now this is all wrong; the saddle-horse is a creature and a creation *per se;* he must be bred and trained as such. Not that it does him any harm to work in light harness now and then—all my saddle-beasts do—but this must be a subsidiary thing. His saddle qualities must be first considered, and everything done to conserve them.

It is in this that our friends of the Southern States excel. They have distinct breeds of saddle-horses, which for generations they have been improving for this purpose alone, and they have made the strain as nearly perfect as can be. On the whole, the Southern "combined" horse, which, in addition to perfect saddle gaits and manners, will work true in harness, is the best general horse in existence. A pair of such, well mated, are beyond price. I have owned a few such pairs, but they are rare, and the difficulty of bringing them East and acclimating them enhances their value and rarity.

What is this paragon that you call a saddle-horse? you ask me.   Let me tell you, but without enlarging upon his "points," which we all of us know and appreciate alike. If he moves quickly, smoothly, and true at all his gaits, he is all right; motion is the test.   I have seen horses with "points" enough on the stable floor to make you fall down and worship them, that weren't worth a shilling a dozen when you got them out on the road.   "The perfect hack," says my good friend the editor of the *Sporting and Dramatic*—and I love to quote a thorough horseman —"must have a variety of excellences, such as are very rarely indeed found in one horse."   He "bends readily and obediently to the rider's hand, though his neck has never undergone the process of suppling."   True, indeed, but how often do you find this rare bird, whose price in the Old Country appears to be about two hundred guineas? Or how many of us can afford to buy him when found? It is just here that the school comes in and enables you to buy for a quarter of that sum an average young four or five year old, and in six months of pleasure, for training is one of the greatest of pleasures, make him the perfect hack.   And the veriest Philistine, presupposing intelligence, can begin with a green horse and, if he is half as apt at studying his manual as his nag is clever at catching the trick of it, can educate his purchase and himself at the same time.

While the price of choice horses in the big marts of Kentucky—such as Lexington, Mount Sterling, or Paris is to-day very high, you can still buy in the country for from two hundred dollars upwards a well-sired combined colt, who has been taught to "walk," or rack, canter, and trot, and of course to guide by the neck.   I recently rode a beautiful three-year-old in Bath County, who was fifteen three, as well rounded up as most five-year-olds, perfectly broken, who had as exceptional manners as he had beauty, and who was on trial in a friend's hands at one hundred and fifty dollars asking price. I have paid five hundred for less good ones, and would willingly give a thousand for a couple well-mated. Beyond simple training the accomplishments of the country horse will not extend; it is for you to teach him. Or, if you still insist that a trot and canter are all that you want, you can for the same price, or fifty dollars more, buy in New York, Philadelphia, or Boston a nice moving colt, broken to harness, and willing to trot kindly under saddle. The latter will need much more to make him a saddle-horse, for he has had no saddle ancestry. Still it can be done.

Where, you say, shall we learn how to teach this colt? Well, now you have asked me a delicate question. But if a man will not cry his own wares, how can he expect others to advertise them for him? I have tried to tell the how in a little Chat in the Saddle, named after "Patroclus" and "Penelope," two capital nags of mine, still alive and at work, hale and hearty, at near twenty years old. And for fifteen years they have not skipped a day's work—or, rather, seen a day when they were not fully up to a good bit of work. If you want higher training, Col. Anderson's *Modern Horsemanship* will help you. Any of the Baucher manuals will do; and there are a number of others. But all this is apart, for the *Ad.* is really not a paid one.

How much must the colt learn to be worthy the name of "saddle-horse?" According to my standard the least education which will make him perfect should include:

1. A busy walk, well up to four miles an hour. If your colt is naturally a slow walker—many good ones of trotting ancestry are—and you cannot appeal to his ambition so as to encourage him into a good walk which he

will maintain of his own accord, he ought to have an amble, or a rack, or a running walk. A slow walker under
saddle is intolerable. You must have at least one loose-
rein gait which gets you along at a minimum of four
miles an hour.

2. A quick, active, nimble trot—not the extended flying
gait of the trotting track, but one which keeps his legs
well under the horse and makes speed by quick gather.
Many a thorough-bred with very limber fetlocks will trot
with a long, rangy gait in the easiest manner possible to
himself and his rider. But his other gaits will not be
collected enough if he has too rangy an action. His inheritance is long stride and quick gather, too; but the
former is wanted on the track, not the road.

3. A good canter. Some people think that the faster
the horse canters the better. This is all right for a cov-
ert-hack, who is to take you as speedily as possible to the
appointed place fixed for the meet, where your hunter
will be waiting for you, fresh and able. But a saddle-
beast's canter is properly measured by its slowness, not
its speed. I by no means refer to some of those lazy
brutes which can canter as slowly as they walk, and impress you as being members of the vegetable rather than
the animal kingdom. I mean that a horse, who feels fresh
enough to jump out of his skin and would prefer a sharp
hand-gallop, shall be able to curb his ambition to your
mood, and put all his action and elasticity into a five-mile-
an-hour canter; that is luxury. But, you object, he is
working a ten-mile gait for a five-mile progress. Exactly
so. If, my brother, you go riding in order to cover distance, English fashion, you are not doing saddle-work
proper, according to my notion. Remember our rule: If
you are hunting, you must save your horse, because he has
got a big day's work to do; if you are riding, even on

your saddle-horse, to make any considerable distance, regulate yourself accordingly—but then you are travelling, not riding for pleasure. If you go out for the mere ride, it is for your nag to subserve your comfort, not for you to save his strength. Do you measure a painting by superficies or by execution? Is not a square foot of a Gerard Douw or a Hans Memling worth more than one hundred square feet of - well, let us say even a Rubens, after he had descended to political wall-paintings, oblivious of his work in Antwerp? So a saddle-horse's ability is to be measured by his gaits, not the distance he can go. Would you ask to go for a pleasure ride on a "Captain McGown" or a "Nancy Hanks" because, forsooth, the one might take you forty miles in two hours, or the other a mile in 2.05? Speed is a corollary of the Sunday rider's problem, not yours and mine, dear boy, when we ride along the pretty suburban roads, or on the soft bridle-paths of the Park.

I have often heard it said of a man with a well-trained horse that he appears to be putting on airs. But why is he showing off any more than the man who rides along with his elbows up at an angle of sixty degrees, or swinging his legs, or acting as if he were bestriding a Genesee County hunter, when he is atop of a three-dollar livery-hack? A man who makes his horse show his paces within in reason is as little to be accused of bumptiousness as the other; and if he were, he has a sounder reason for his vanity. If your nag can canter a well-collected four-mile gait, with all the proud bearing which such an accomplishment lends, why must you let him go an uncollected eight-mile gait, when the slower one is the very poetry of motion? To dub this "putting on airs" is on all fours with the outcry against "those d—— literary fellers."

4. A rack or singlefoot is not a *sine quâ non;* but I would vastly rather have a racker who could trot besides,

than a trotting-horse with an amble. You may not see
the difference; but there is one, just the same, as there is
'twixt tweedledum and tweedledee. If, for saddle, you
have to choose between a good singlefoot and a good trot,
by all means take the singlefoot, unless you prefer fashion
to comfort. Still, the trot is one of the finest of saddle
gaits in its place; it is out of place only when you
use it to the exclusion of everything else; it then becomes
a species of treadmill.

5. To say that a saddle-horse must guide by the neck
is as absurd as to say that a well-educated man must
know some grammar. Still, in these two-handed days,
when a man cannot blow his nose, let alone assist his
équestrienne, without losing partial control of his horse,
the statement must be ventured. The saddle-horse's
neck must be suppled so that, so soon as you take up the
rein, he will give his head to your hand and keep it there.
He must be able to execute the pirouette, *i.e.* move in a
circle in either direction about one hind-foot, which shall
not leave the ground. His hind-quarters must be suppled so that the use of the spur, or the closing of the legs
shall bring his hind-feet under him, to collect his forces;
in other words, he must readily come in hand. As a sequence to this he must execute the reversed pirouette
round one of his fore-feet. He must traverse—move sidewise—at least a dozen steps, without effort.

6. He must pass from any one of his gaits to any
other at the slightest indication, and without flurry. He
must start into the canter with either shoulder leading, or
change lead at will when in motion.

7. He must be able to jump handily and in cold blood
any reasonable obstacle, say a fence or wall up to three
feet and a half. If he will face four feet at call, he is an
able jumper.

8. He must, with good courage and endurance, have perfect manners, and never sulk, get nervous or flurried, alone or in company, or act otherwise than as a horse treated with uniform kindness and firmness should act. His mouth must be velvet, but still capable of feeling your hand, and all his instincts must be keen and lively.

With these accomplishments you have a " saddle-horse " sufficiently well trained for any ordinary purpose of pleasure ; but you have only laid the foundation for a high-school education. Your steed has merely got the three *r*'s—*r*eading, *r*iting, and *r*ithmetic.

To give a horse this knowledge presupposes some skill in the trainer; properly to ride such a horse equal knowledge. Every one who rides habitually has time to learn the art to the above quoted extent ; and a horse so trained need by no means be so delicate that he requires an expert to ride him. With courage, intelligence, and good manners, this education will only make him more tractable and more handy in whatever place you put him.

To do all this is by no means beyond the skill of any one who is really fond of horses and horsemanship. To him who rides merely because his doctor has confided to him that he has a liver, or because every one else rides, I would say, buy your article ready-made.

But wherein is such a horse the better for road-riding ? asks our chappie with the crop and irreproachable nether garments. No whit, friend, unless education be better than ignorance. If Mother Goose satisfies you, you do not need Homer or Dante or Shakespeare or Goethe—and Heaven forefend that I should underrate Mother Goose! Mind you, I have not said that a hunter or a polo-pony needs these accomplishments, though he would undeniably be the better for some of them. But these horses

13

have a definite work cut out for them; the saddle-horse is merely a companion along the road.

Each and every one of these accomplishments is distinctly useful. A busy walk enables you to rest your horse frequently without either of you being bored or losing ground by lack of speed. The trot enables you to change gait and equally ease yourself and your steed's muscles. To change lead in the canter saves the fore-feet, for a horse which always leads on one foot runs danger of going lame by-and-by. It also saves the houghs. The rack is the easiest of all paces, and is, *par excellence*, a hot weather gait, when a trot is all but impossible except to a man in training. To shift the fore-quarters quickly means handiness in turning and less danger of tripping a horse up; and the same applies to the shifting of the hind-quarters. Moreover, without the latter, how can you place your horse where you want him, as to open a gate, or to keep your place in a group of riders? The utility of the rest goes without saying, and this is but a little of the practical side; while the pleasure of it all is hard to be explained to a man who has not been through it, or to a horse which is not thus trained. For the horse, be it said, is as keen in his enjoyment of it all as the man; I sometimes think more keen than most men.

To whatever horse-owner there may be who cannot hunt or play polo or breed, or who has not a long enough purse to own racers, let me prescribe the study of pure saddle-work; he will be rewarded a hundredfold for his experiment. And this especially if he is getting on in years, and wants a quiet rather than a boisterous pleasure.

To revert to the text, though we seem to have reached a sort of Fourteenthly: it is not to be wondered at that we Americans have sought our models in the Old Country. It is the English who have taught us nearly all our sports.

Anglomania in its proper sense is as excellent as in its
forced sense it is absurd.   If to learn from the Briton
how to race or hunt or play polo be Anglomania, let us
all be inoculated for the disease, and speedily.   If to
swear by everything English, from togs to manners, just
because it is English, be Anglomania, the sooner we are
rid of it the better.   The word must be advisedly used.
In its better sense, we are all Anglomaniacs who are not
sick with Anglophobia, a much worse type of the disease.
But give Americanism a chance, especially in horsemanship.   We have no cause to be ashamed of what we have
in horses, nor of what we can do in the saddle.   And a
judicious choice in the field and on the road of what is
best at home and abroad ought to put us in equestrianism,
if not where we stand in yachting, at least on a level high
enough to satisfy the most critical.

XXXIII

COME with me across the ocean. If thou fearest the sickness of the sea, friend, come with me but in spirit, for old Neptune hath ordained that the particular part of his domain which is the most frequently crossed, the North Atlantic, shall be the most constantly stormy. It is thus he punishes him who dares his authority by ploughing through his purple waters. I wonder whether the ancients sacrificed to the fishes any the less for sacrificing to Neptune before they went aboard. However this may have been, libations poured out to the grizzly God of the Trident were assuredly less foolish than many nostrums against sea-sickness in our own day and generation.

Well, here we are in England. Mother-country, all hail! Years have I tasted thy bounteous hospitality, hearty thanks have I laid at thy feet! And as I am about to speak of thy horsemen, I begin by a cordial bow of admiration, for they are truly to be admired, in the good old Latin sense.

I will but take the chair, as it were, and begin by introducing better speakers. Says my ancient comrade, Colonel Edward L. Anderson—of the fighting Andersons, and once of General Sherman's staff—in that most authoritative of modern series, the Britannica of sports, the Badminton Library, to wit: "In breeding horses, in rearing and in caring for them, in racing them and in riding them across country, the Englishman is easily first." To which I say amen. In the same volume (*Riding and Polo*), one

of the best of horsemen, sportsmen, and critics, known to
us all as " Rapier," of the *Sporting and Dramatic News*,
Alfred E. T. Watson—may his shadow never grow less!—
remarks that "an Englishman's highest ambition, apart
from success in sport between the flags, is to ride straight
to hounds in the manner which, causing no unnecessary
exertion to himself or horse, enables horse and man to
last the longest without fatigue." "The Englishman has
no sort of desire to practise the 'high airs' of the school.
To him it seems an utter waste of time to induce a horse
to piaffer, execute the Spanish trot, or perform other
feats of school training. If he can make his horse lead
off with either leg as he may indicate, and perhaps swing
his croup as well as his fore-hand, the animal is looked on
as possessing a superfluity of accomplishments."

These two statements cover the entire case. It is true
that the Englishman is unapproachable in his own province; it is also true that he despises the high-school, and
that he doesn't know a saddle-horse as we know him in
the Southern States. I have interlarded so many observa-
tions on the English method in my chat about our own
ways, that there is scarce a word left to be said. I cannot overstate my unswerving fealty to the Briton's horsemanship as above construed, any more than I could overstate my affection for his frank and manly, if often
brusque and pushing, habit the wide world over. Why
should he not, if he chooses so to do, plume himself on
owning, if not, as we are said to do, on beating all creation?
It is a refreshing thing to see and hear him assert it. If we
fondly imagine we know better, and inwardly chuckle at
his unconscious intolerance along the highways and by-
ways of life, it does him no harm; and surely we, too, are
chips of the old block. British narrowness has wrought
great things—as narrowness has everywhere. Antislavery

was narrowness, and yet the extremists were the men who roused us to the efforts which culminated in freedom to the slave. Too great breadth will not keep the world a-moving. St. Paul makes a mistake in urging content-ment at all seasons — at least, in the way his translators have quoted him. Had he himself been one of your con-tented men, he would scarcely have accomplished what he did. And the Englishman's self-contentment and self-assertiveness are coupled with a fine habit of putting in big licks, hitting straight from the shoulder, in every part of the world. Just what right, for example, he has to be here in Egypt (where I happen to be penning these lines), I fail to see, and yet what a change he has wrought for the better! The poor fellahin to-day know that their land will be irrigated in its due turn, and for the first time since the Sphinx was hewn from its native rock can gauge the tax they will have to pay. So works the Briton everywhere and in most mundane affairs—but this thing militates against just what produces the niceties of equitation.

The English army officer rides well, just because he rides like an English gentleman. The British trooper rides no worse, no better, than any other regular cavalryman. Seat is largely an individual habit. I have seen men in the English cavalry, just as I have seen men in our own regiments, ride extreme forked-radish style, sitting bolt up-right on the crotch, while other men in the same troop would have in the saddle a regular cross-country seat, barring the fact that their toes were in the stirrups instead of riding "home."

The only difference I have ever been able to perceive between our own and the British cavalry seat is, as be-fore stated, that our men are wont to depress their heels a trifle less, riding in a more natural, less drill-stiffened

way.   The Horse Guards ride with particularly long stirrups, though part of the appearance of this is due to their
superabundance of leg.

But, good or bad, the Briton has enough to be proud
of; let us leave him alone in his glory.

XXXIV

WOULD that the times still were when one might cross the Channel dry-shod! Why did the sea ever encroach on that invaluable neck of dry land? If there is an uncertainty of travel in any part of the commonly trotted universe, it is that nasty bit of water. Nasty is said not to be a nice word, but it literally describes man and the elements on the Channel. Yet if we Americans, easily first in travelling conveniences, should have that water between our two biggest cities (not to mention the two capitals of the world), we would put a ferry there which would make the transit a pleasure in lieu of a dread. The Club train runs from London with its five millions of souls to Paris with half the number once a day, costs about six cents a mile, and is rather a petty affair for the fuss they make over it. From little provincial Boston, with its scant half-million population, you have some twenty trains a day, giving you more speed, more comfort, and vastly more elegance for two and a half cents a mile, and you are not limited to a paltry sixty pounds of impedimenta, or atrociously taxed if your wife happens to have brought along a few extra Saratogas to swell the weight. Our baggage is rarely subjected to delays or impost; English luggage is not so lucky. It takes thirty-eight hours to run from Paris to Rome, some eleven hundred miles, if my memory serves me; and you practically have no comfort whatever for the five cents a mile you pay. You run from New York to Chicago, nearly the same distance, in twenty-two hours or less, at half the cost, and in what luxury! How distinctly we lead in travelling, despite the occasional superciliousness of the Pullman nigger!

"Where'er I roam, whatever lands I see,
My heart, untravelled, fondly turns to thee,"

and I might add, my body does too, if travelling is to be synonymous with comfort.

But let us come to the Frenchman. It used to be said that there were many Church people who would not subscribe to the Thirty-nine Articles, but who had an implicit faith in the Forty Thieves; and it is a sort of fortieth article to every dweller in the bright little, tight little island that Johnny Crapaud cannot ride. But he can. In some respects, such as fine training and school-riding, he is vastly the Briton's superior. And now that he has taken a bad form of the international disease yclept Anglomania, and has begun to do some rough-and-tumble riding, he may prove still more of a rival to his neighbor across La Manche. The French military man rides well. At Saumur the equestrian education is good. I have seen a number of Saumur cadets riding over a decentish obstacle. They all showed excellent skill, though no one can judge from drill-ground or *manége* riding how a man might ride to hounds—if the latter is to be made the ultimate test, as it should not be. For the purpose for which the Saumur training is intended there is a sufficiency of leaping. There are other things in cavalry drill, or in the preparation of an officer for staff service, besides jumping obstacles, though it is hard to convince a Briton of it.

They have recently been taking riding photographs at Saumur, which are published in a series, *à la* Muybridge, but on a very limited scale. I was shown photographs of a horse in the successive positions of the trot and canter

HOW TO DO IT

as an unusual thing; and when I said that the University
of Pennsylvania had taken all animals, from men to birds,
in motion, and had published a series of plates containing
thirty thousand phototypes, I was stared at politely but
reproachfully and incredulously. We are given credit for
very little abroad. The simplest thing you tell a foreigner
runs the risk of being looked at as a gross exaggeration.
I have had intelligent people gaze at me as if I had been
spinning a monumental yarn, to put it mildly, because, *e.g.*,
I told them that Pittsburg had for years been lighted and
heated and had its factories driven by natural gas, or that
petroleum was transported by pipe-lines, over hill and dale,
from the oil-fields, several hundred miles, to the ocean.

When I was a small boy, the elevator in the Continental
Hotel in Philadelphia was already running, and it was

soon followed by elevators all over the country. After a generation or so the English caught on to the idea and began to put in timid little things of the same genus, but by no means of the same species, and called them Lifts. By-and-by the people on the Continent saw the point and put in a few still more timorous *ácenseurs:* "Etonnants, ces Anglais! Quelle invention! Voilà qui vaut la peine!" In 1854, if I remember right, George Francis Train put a horse-railroad on the Bayswater Road from the Marble Arch to Kensington Gate. I rode on the first car. The scheme failed, because it was not legally protected, and the cabbies were down on it and could not be prevented from driving at a walk on the track ahead of the cars. Horse-railroads were then as old as the hills in America. Again, after the lapse of half a generation, the English caught on and started what they improperly called trams; and later the simple Continental folk followed suit with their *Tranvays.* Not a suspicion that we Americans had ever had elevators or horse-railroads; oh no, it was the original, the wonderful, the veritable English lift and tram—"Donnerwetter, was für Kerle, die Engländer!— and so forth, and so on.

The French civilian is not, as a rule, as good a horseman as the "militaire." There are many high-school riders who are masters of the art. But there is no special sport in which to shake the average Frenchman into the saddle, unless it be those which by imitation he has taken from Albion, just as we have done at home; and these can be, or are, pursued but in a few places. As a rule, the French civilian impresses you as rather finicky in his style. When he rides in the Bois de Boulogne there is a lack of freedom in his equitation, which is well characterized by the constant use of the bit rather than the bridoon. And whatever national method he may have had in the days of

Baucher, or ought since to have built up on the foundation
laid by this great man, seems to have been swallowed up
in his craze for matters English. In dress and horse rig
and seat he closely follows the Briton, and then forsooth
rides all day long on the curb, as the Briton never would
do. This incompleteness makes me think of the portrait
of the Jam of Jamnugger, which I possess, dressed in all
the magnificence of a Hindoo maharajah, except for his
feet, which are incased in a pair of three-dollar Douglas
shoes! Please note that this also is not a paid *Ad.*.
though it ought to be. In many matters equine the
French are as admirable as in their own specialty, the
Percheron; but not so in riding. And yet, as was observed long ago, they are horsy enough to call their
mothers mares and dub their daughters fillies.

The French have done one thing which we must not
forget. The first man who showed the world that intelligent kindness was the real secret of horse breaking and
training was the Frenchman Baucher. Up to his day
colts had been broken by cruel methods, and were never
more than half trained. The tempers of the majority
were irretrievably ruined. Baucher taught an entirely
new system, and the whole world has benefited by it.
Even English breakers, though they scorn his higher education, unwittingly make use of the devices he introduced.

It has, however, been reserved for Governor Leland Stanford's farm at Palo Alto to perfect the methods of kindness. The men on the place are forbidden to speak in an
angry tone to a colt; a man who should swear at or strike
one would be instantly discharged. From the time the
foal is born, he is habituated to the presence and the gentling of man, and is taught that he receives nothing but
kindness and favors at his hands. One rule is enforced:

when the foal or colt is near his groom or his master, he must never indulge in play, but stand quiet and allow himself to be petted or handled in any fashion. In the paddock he may fool to the top of his bent; but never in the society of man. As a result the colt does not have to be broken, in our sense of the word; he is ready to be hitched up and driven when he is old enough to work. The system is perfection.

XXXV

WHAT shall be said of the German rider? That, within certain limits of his own, and these are practically confined to cavalry methods, the German rides well, no one can deny. A squadron, or a regiment, or a brigade of cavalry moves in an irreproachable manner; the troops drill like automata; their conduct in the field is worthy of their history; but when you see the men by themselves they do not always impress you as easy at their work. It may safely be assumed that the Germans know what they are about; and that they can organize and drill cavalry has been sufficiently demonstrated. Our comment can extend no further than the individual.

When, as a boy, I was in Prussia, there was nothing more revolting to the sense of propriety of the average citizen than matters English; now there is a strong proclivity to the international disease. On a number of occasions in my youth I visited school friends at their homes in the country, and there found a deal of excellent riding. In those days German was the home language, but French was universally employed in social intercourse, and the mother-tongue was interlarded with Gallic phrases. We would be comfortably talking German, perhaps even indulging in the old Berlin patois, which included in its vocabulary the "Ne!" or the soft pronunciation of "g," which gave rise to the phrase "Eene jute jebratene Jans ist eene jute Jabe Jottes," when a runaway ring at the bell would startle all of us out of, or rather into, our propriety, and we would begin to chatter French as glibly as, if not with the brogue of, denizens of Paris—for it might be company. What in those Gallo-Teutonic days they used to call the Parforce Jagd was stag or boar hunting in the saddle, during which you were compelled to ride over all kinds of country, sometimes stiff enough. This was not done at racing pace, nor were the obstacles as bad as the ox-fences in the Midland counties; but still it was fairish sport, and the game was better worth having than Reynard's brush or pads, for the pack is wont to devour Reynard, while we used to eat the stag or boar (when we got him) at the hunt-dinner in the evening, or a day or two later when he had got more tender. The run was not infrequently through heavy timber, where there were many fallen trees to clear, and a deal of thicket to get through; and I have seen excellent horsemanship in such a hunt. Horsemanship is relative. Because Buffalo Bill or Sotnik Dmitri Peshkof could not keep in the same field with the hounds over a difficult country is no proof that either falls short of being one of the best of horsemen.

I think the German military rider is a trifle stiff; and I do not like the way the soldier is taught his leaping exercises. It is rather absurd to make so much account of jumping; but the world is agog on the subject, and he that leapeth a six-foot fence is greater than he that taketh a city. No horse in cold blood leaps willingly with anything but an easy bit; and yet the German soldier is taught to use his curb exclusively. The obstacle the enlisted man leaps at squad-drill is a small affair, over which the horse could almost step if he tried hard, and of course the commonest troop horse clears it easily. But I have never seen a German soldier sit down on his horse at even such a leap; he does not curl his sitting-bones under him, as the phrase runs, but relies on the stirrups and goes out of his saddle at a two-foot hurdle. Sometimes a German soldier riding at a hurdle is the very type of how not to do it.

There is no man who sits down on his horse more admirably than the negro. He seems to settle into his seat in much the same limber way he dances a break-down. While his muscles are all in readiness to grip his horse or saddle, his joints are loose and he gets nearer to his mount than almost any man I know. While he may not always be discreet in his management of a horse, he is otherwise a capital example for the ramrod soldier to imitate; and when a darky is a good horseman he is apt to be ahead of his white competitor. He and the horse invariably understand each other. I have had negro grooms who would keep the paces of my saddle-horses pure and distinct, and whom in my absence I would trust to ride them month in, month out, when I would not let one of my white grooms —certainly no English groom I ever knew—get astride one, even to ride him to the blacksmith.

What I have said above is not all there is to German leaping. The cavalry often goes at an obstacle by troops; and horses, even on the curb, will leap vastly freer in company than singly. So far as manœuvres go one can scarcely criticise the Germans, and their squadron-drill includes riding over a wall and ditch. The men rarely lose than seats, and this leaves little to be said. It is the individual soldier who does not at all times impress us so favorably. I am not speaking of the officers; as a class they ride well, and I have known many splendid horsemen among them.

The German civilian rides *à la militaire;* every man has served his time. There is a certain set fashion throughout the German Empire in every phase of life. Things are conducted within lines which forbid their ex-

pansion into types. In America, in the Orient, you may
find numberless types, the pattern of each of which is its
own individuality ; but ever present organization, in civil
and military matters alike, all through the German structure, forbids novelty. All things are cast in one mould ;
and there may be said to be but one type of horseman.

HOW NOT TO DO IT

XXXVI

I FEAR we may not be permitted to wander together all over Europe. We must ride to orders, and seek climes more full of oddities in horsemanship. There is not much difference, after all, between any of the riders of the great military powers, barring Russia. As in Germany, they all pattern on the same model, and produce, with some questions of degree, about the same horsemen. If Austria could claim that her people were fit followers of their gallant Empress, who is noted as one of the best riders who ever led the field over Warwickshire, they would be distinctly at the top of all the horsemen of Europe; but Her Majesty is a clear exception to every rule of royalty. She is peerless in the side-saddle. The Austro-Hungarians, in the recent Berlin-Vienna ride, were ready victors, and received from the German Emperor the compliment of being called the best cavalry in Europe—a truism partly due to their pattern being at hand in the admirable light horse of their eastern dominions, which they have cleverly imitated. The Russians have, in a similar manner, patterned to a certain extent on the Cossack; but of him we shall treat when we come to the Oriental, whose ways he possesses more than those of the European.

The Italians present nothing peculiar in their equitation. They are cast in the same military mould as the rest of nations, though their method is to-day somewhat marred by the English saddle and an imperfect imitation of the English seat; and these are, I deem it, inapplicable to cavalry riding of the best order — a point on which I have elsewhere dilated.

With reference to army officers in Europe, I must say that I have always found among them not only admirable riders, but a strong spirit of appreciation of what is best in horsemanship as well. It may be assumed as an axiom that what they know and what they do is best fitted to what their respective military duties may be. To say that our own army officers could readily learn to do their work, and that they would naturally have much more to learn in order to succeed on our peculiar terrain and under our difficult conditions, while it may be praise to the adaptiveness of our men, is by no means a discredit to those whose duties savor as much of the barracks and drill-ground as the duties of our army do of what is technically known as partisan warfare.

XXXVII

Whoso, when he reaches the home of the Moor or the Bedouin, or stands where, scorning to live under a roof, the Arab of the desert pitches his camel's-hair tent and lazes away a profitless existence, eating his bread in the sweat, not of his own brow, but of that of his slaving wives and daughters; where the date-palm and the olive-tree—or at need the Barbary fig—stand between the list-less son of the prophet and annual starvation; where man is literally the dust of the field, and mixes with his native soil as constantly during life as after death; where woman has no soul, and is but a crude promise of the houri of the hoped-for paradise; where every instinct points to indo-lence, and where man has not bettered his condition one jot for fifty generations; whoso, because he is among Arabs, fondly imagines that he will find himself among better horses than surround him at home, is doomed to grievous disappointment. Good horse-flesh is as rare on the Arabian desert as it is in England or America. There are more high-grade horses in Kentucky to-day per thou-sand of population than the first home of the ancestor of all blooded stock has ever boasted. A faultless steed is a pearl of great price; it is difficult to be found; and like the scriptural jewel, a man must often sell all that he hath to buy it.

" Where are the Arabian horses?" you ask, on reaching Morocco or Algeria. " Those are Arabians, pure blood," comes the answer, with a gesture towards some diminutive equine specimens. for all the world like broncos. "But the proud, gentle, high-spirited, well-mannered, intelligent, beautiful Arabians, of which we have from youth up heard—which we have come, lo! these many thousand weary miles to worship?" "Ah, you must go to the desert for those!" You accordingly journey to the edge of the desert, perhaps Biskra way, or perchance over hill and dale of never-ending golden sands to the first oasis out beyond the limits where white men congregate; but, alas! it is always a sheik or a caliph farther on, at the next oasis, or the next, who has the perfect animal your eye longs to feast upon. Or else, as ill-luck will have it, he has just started with his pet, his choicest mare, the apple of his eye, on a visit to the second cousin of his grandmother, a hundred leagues away. I have, I believe, just missed the most peerless steed of the Orient some forty times save one.

The reason is not far to seek. Good horses come solely from selection and breeding. But, you will object, there was no breeding to produce the bronco, of whose wonderful qualities you have heretofore told us. On the contrary, there was natural selection of the very best. Starting with pure blood—*i.e.*, the Moorish horses carried by the Spaniards to America, and there, fugitive or abandoned, the survival of those fittest to flee from wolves or to search good pasture and water over immense stretches of prairie land, bred the hardiest of stock. Man, with the utmost care and skill, could in a certain sense scarcely have done better by the race in all except beauty. On the other hand, starting from the same stock, let man overwork and underfeed the horse and neglect his breeding, and in a few generations the noblest race will degenerate. It is just this which has taken place in almost all the countries which ought to possess the very highest grade of horse-

14*

flesh. We are wont to associate an Arab with the idea of
love for and gentle treatment of his steed; on the contrary, it is less than one in a hundred Arabs who treats his
horse with intelligence or with kindness, and therefore it
is less than one in a hundred which becomes anything but
a commonplace beast of burden.

There are two kinds of Arab tribes: first, those dwelling
in the cities, subsisting by the lower trades and living from
hand to mouth in crowded filth, and those dwelling in
the lesser communities, such as small towns and villages,
earning a precarious livelihood by a crude sort of agricult-
ure or by raising dates or olives, and living in mud-walled
huts roofed with thatch, sod, or tile; second, the tent-
dwellers, who rove from place to place and are purely a
pastoral people, subsisting on the yield of their flocks and
herds and the breeding and sale of the camel, horse, and ass.
Among the first, when they have any, as is rare enough,
the horse has become a sumpter animal, a means of transportation or an item in husbandry, and has, as a matter
of course, fallen from his high estate. Among the latter
he has kept some of his better qualities; among some of
the wealthy he has retained all his attributes. It goes
without saying that in the cities it is the rich who own
the finest stock; on the desert this is not always true.
Unless ground into the very dust by poverty, many a man
who owns no other earthly possessions may have as fine a
mare as the noblest sheik; and he will starve his own flesh
and blood to keep her sleek and hearty. In fact, it is she
whose foal will annually fill the empty exchequer.

An Arab, meaning a tent-dweller, for in an equine sense
the town-dweller is no Arab, loves first and above all his
mare. No need to recite the oft-sung affection he will
lavish upon her, the care he will take of his glossy favorite, for whose preservation he will gladly pinch his own

belly. Next to his steed he loves his fire-arm. This, po-etically speaking, ought to be a six-foot, gold and jade in-laid, muzzle-loading horror of a matchlock, which would kick any man but an Arab flat on his back at every shot; but actually, in Algeria and Tunis, when he lives near a city and is allowed by the French authorities to own one at all, it is rather more apt to be a modern English breach-loader of approved pattern, with plenty of ammunition handy. You must fly from the busy haunts of men in these days of ours to find the ancient matchlock. Next to his fire-arm the Arab loves his oldest son, in whom he really harbors a worthy pride. Last comes his wife—or one of his wives. If he is a man by nature faithful, his first wife may always remain his favorite; if inconstant, it will be his last. Daughters do not even count; I mean the Arab scarcely takes the trouble to count them, unless in so far as they can minister to his comfort, dietetic or otherwise. Until some neighbor comes along and proposes to marry, in other words to make a still worse slave of one of them, she is only a chattel, a soulless thing. And yet she is said to be a pretty, amiable, helpful being; said to be, for no one by any hap casts his eye on one worth seeing. I have made every effort, within and without the bounds of Arab propriety. I might say safety, to investi-gate the Arabian maiden—but to no avail. This disre-gard of women, be it said to their honor, does not always apply to the wilder, but more intelligent, independent, and manly Bedouin of the Syrian and Arabian deserts. But of this when we get so far upon our travels.

Let me premise, in this screed anent the horses on the south and east of the Mediterranean basin, that it is not my purpose to descant solely upon the choice steeds which may be classed as Arabians. This is the burden of the song of nearly all who tell us of the horse of the Orient.

The Anazeh mares are claimed by the best judges to be the only royal stock of the eldest branch; but this information does one no good; for by no chance whatsoever does a Frank ever come within a distance of winning such a prize. In America, a long purse will buy a "Sunol" or an "Arion," a "St. Julien" or a "Nancy Hanks;" but his Imperial Majesty the Sultan himself has neither money nor wit nor power to purchase or take one of the best or even one of the second best Anazeh mares. They are, so far as we are concerned, out of the race. I purpose to tell you of the average Arabian, the horse that a Frank may buy; one who is of as good lineage as the animal a well-to-do citizen rides in our part of the world. Few of us throw our legs across a pure descendant of "Lexington," or even of "Justin Morgan," and it seems to me that there is more interest in the steed of every day than in the mystery surrounding the horse one sees as rarely as we see a Derby winner; a horse we must pursue as one does the *ignis fatuus*, and who is equally evanescent.

The true Arab's undoubted love for his steed has kept up, in some few places over the entire area where the Arabian horse flourishes, a more or less pure strain of the wonderful old stock. The wealthy or princely have no doubt improved on the original, but not in any great measure; certainly not by any means as we Anglo-Saxons have done. The heritage of the Arabian or the Barb— there is only a difference in nomenclature and habitat between them; they are otherwise, barring some equine points, very nearly the same animal—is the power of transmitting his qualities in undiminished measure to his offspring, and the power of extraordinary endurance at speed. What the latter means I can only explain illustratively. It is not distance that kills, but speed. Any decent horse can go thirty miles a day with a reasonable load over good roads at a walk, and keep on doing it day in day out for years, fat and hearty No horse that was ever foaled could run or trot, at the top of his speed (say a 1.42 or a 2.15 gait), three one-mile dashes every day for a season without breaking down. In other words, at speed a horse cannot do one-tenth of the distance he can at a slow gait. It is only the occasional coarse-bred horse who has speed; and when one has it, still he cannot stay at speed. But this is just what the old desert blood enables a horse to do; and it is this wonderful quality which, through the English thorough-bred, we have got at home in our runners and trotters and saddle-beasts, and by a principle of natural selection in the bronco. And this same quality we Occidentals, by more intelligent and careful breeding and training and racing than the horse has ever undergone elsewhere, may fairly claim to have improved.

WHERE this wonderful creature, the Arabian horse, originally came from will never be known. It seems to have been shown by geologists that remains of the horse are found in older strata, or associated with more ancient races of men, in Europe than in any part of Asia. Whether this proves that the horse had his origin in Europe, or merely that research has been pushed further on European soil than it has been in Asia, it is not within our province to inquire. So far as concerns good equine stock —*i.e.*, the horses impregnated more or less by thorough blood—we need go no further back than what we know of them in the Syrian or Arabian desert; the horses of the Libyan desert came from these; the Spanish horses came from the Libyan desert, and our broncos came from the Spanish; while the English thorough-bred has descended from sires of either the one or the other, imported into England under the Stuarts. Whatever the history of the horse from a geological stand-point, it is not worth while to search beyond what we can glean from the early history of the steed of the Bedouin. In some manner the Arabian came of a common native race of horses which man had intelligence and patience enough to seek to improve by breeding them in a congenial climate for many generations; or rather he came of a common strain which first got improved because the man of the desert found his profit and his safety in the superior speed and endurance of his steeds, and naturally bred from these. This is the summary of all we know.

In what is modern Algeria, the Mauretania of the Romans, where Carthage was a great city long before disdainful Remus hopped over Romulus's wall, there is little doubt that the nimble, intelligent runt of a steppes pony, which furnished the mounts for the Numidian cavalry that later all but destroyed Rome in the Second Punic War, which had no bridle but was guided by a stick or by the legs and voice, and whose endurance knew no bounds, was the ancestor of the native horse of to-day. The same thing applies to Morocco. There were other similar breeds in other parts of the East, some of which had been earlier perfected ; but the horse of the Algerian country no doubt descended from the Numidian pony as he is known in history. The steppes horse, of whatever country, is generally a stayer and a good progenitor. All others get weeded out from the herds by wild animals or by scant forage. Just as the modern thorough-bred comes of the native British mares impregnated by Barb or Arabian sires, so with the Numidian pony. Upon this animal an impress must have been made from time to time by importations of markedly good individuals from farther east, for the horse, like civilization, has uniformly travelled westward, until now, the Californian claims, it has reached its highest development on the Pacific slope; but when the French conquered Algeria in 1830 they found the country horse on a decidedly low level. That the Barb had theretofore been a noble creature is sufficiently shown by the history of the Moors in Spain ; but neglect had sapped his quality.

There was not much done by the French for some time to improve the stock, but later the best grade of stallions were bought by the Government for public use; a number of fine ones were purchased from the trans-Jordan Bedouins of Syria; breeding for the army was carefully attended to, and now the cavalry of the entire Nineteenth

Corps d'Armée is mounted on what may be called Arabian horses, while numbers go to France. The corps has about fifteen thousand such animals. Only stallions are used. Mares out on the desert are kept for breeding; within the limits of civilization the few there are have been put to work in the fields. One almost never sees a gelding.

The Algerian horse may in every sense be highly commended. He is docile from inherited kind treatment, is readily broken, and is, as a rule, without tricks. He has the kind eye and gentle manner of the Barb, a small but not very bony head, a short, light, but round barrel and perfect legs and feet. He is often leggy, but has good lung-power. He has not quite enough body to suit my ideas. That roundness which we all like behind the girths, and which we consider essential to good qualities of endurance, does not often exist. An old-fashioned horseman would say that, to all appearances, he did not carry his feed well. Perhaps he is not fed as much hay as our stock has to have for mere warmth. He is neat-turned and averages good-looking, but he does not carry an extra-high head, and rarely carries a decent tail. They hog his mane not infrequently, a habit which is generally bred of Anglomania among the French, though it is not unknown even among the Bedouins of the desert. The drawing-book or lady's-album Arabian one may go many a Sabbath-day's journey to find—and then fail to find him. There do exist Arabians with the wonderful head, speaking eye, nervous ear, teacup muzzle, delicate throttle, powerful shoulder, wrought steel legs, high croup, and tail a poem; but they are very much like black pearls; we know that there exist such jewels, we occasionally see one in Tiffany's or on the neck of some *décolletée* lady, but they are beyond our reach. Two Arabians were sent over to General Grant as a present. They were good specimens, but not the very

FRENCH ALGERIAN CAVALRYMAN ON BARB

best of their kind, according to the Anazeh standard. Some French officers in Algeria have picked up fine Arabians from sheiks in the desert, for which they have paid, I was told, from two thousand francs and upwards — a cheap enough price in any event, for, like trotters in the 2.20 class, the number of good ones is extremely limited. You or I would have to pay thrice the sum.

One thing you will be very sure to find in every part of the world, and that is that work and show do not go together—your every-day utility-horse does not carry about his patent of nobility with him, however high-bred he may be. He proves his lineage by what he can do, not by his simple looks. If you want to have a show horse you must keep him for show. You will find him standing in every part of the country, from Palo Alto to Bangor, in all of our Eastern racing-stables, in every great breeding establishment at home or abroad. He bears his pedigree in his fervid eye, his grand arched crest, his perfect form, his noble bearing, his high switching tail, and his bold, free step. He points to the performances of his get to prove what he himself might accomplish, and often to a past record as fine as theirs. The show horse is not the worker, nor is he to be easily found, even in Arabia. And I doubt whether the entire area of the Libyan and Syrian deserts boasts as splendid a specimen of horse-flesh as— say old " Longfellow " or " Electioneer."

XXXIX

THE Algerian cavalry horse is a very attractive fellow. He stands from fourteen and a half to fifteen and a half hands, not often higher; weighs, as I gauge him, eight to nine hundred pounds—though they claim that he actually weighs one-fifth less than this—and is able to carry his man with sixty pounds of baggage, say two hundred and ten to twenty pounds in all, a strong day's journey and repeat. I have been unable to find good proof of many wonderful performances, such as our cavalry on the plains with American horses, or cowboys on broncos often enough exhibit; but there is not the same call for exceptional performances in Algeria; and if one were to believe the Arab when he is boasting of his pet's ability to go, one would set the average Arabian down as equal to a trifle more than a Baldwin locomotive. Great tests of distance and speed have to be called out by trying circumstances; they are rarely needed among a people to whom time is absolutely nothing.

More can be told about camels. There is one desert postal route that I heard of in Algeria, but that, though I have no reason to doubt its accuracy, I cannot vouch for, which a camel covers between sunup and sundown, one hundred and seventy-five kilometres or one hundred and eight miles, and back again next day, month in month out, carrying not exceeding two hundred and fifty pounds, or half its full load. I have found but one record of what I call great work by horses. About eighty miles a day, act-

CAVALRY LEAPING DRILL IN ALGERIA

ually measured, is quoted as very great going—to pay no heed to manifest exaggerations. This distance is in truth excellent, but far from great; it has been more than doubled up on at home. One cannot, as a rule, measure the ground covered by the horse on the desert, for lack of statistics or of any sort of reliable testimony.

It may be assumed, I suppose, that every one is permitted to prevaricate (is that the proper word?) when narrating successful tramps after fish; but it is a curious fact that the larger the game the smaller the prevarication is apt to be. Horse talk is wont to be interlarded with occasional suspicious statements, or at least with statements which will bear a bit of checking off. The Arab is no exception to the rule; he is quite untrustworthy when telling of his steed's performances. There is only one thing in which he is uniformly truthful, and that is pedigree. This is because he cannot hide it; it is a matter of public notoriety in his tribe, and though he may cheat a stranger, it is futile for him to seek to impose on an Arab. In this pedigree matter he is forced to be more reliable

than our own horse-dealers. The manufacture of pedigrees, when they cannot be traced in the stud-book, is an
art much in vogue.   In most American horse-markets
there is a steady manufacture of pedigrees going on; and
the practice thrives because a man who is cheated is
wont to hide the fact, of which he is heartily ashamed,
rather than seek legal redress and get laughed at for his
pains. This unwillingness to perform one's duty to the
public is a distinct American failing.

A very well-vouched-for performance of which I have
heard in the Orient is the one already given, viz.: fifteen
hundred kilometres, say nine hundred and fifty miles, on
one horse in forty-five days, of which twenty-eight days'
actual travelling—or thirty-three miles a day. This is a
creditable ride, to be sure, but far from a noteworthy one.
And the feat was performed, not by an Arabian, but by
a Kurd horse, bred on a Persian dam by an Arabian sire.
This was a single rider with a small escort. Many of our
cavalry regiments have discounted this speed for long distances, and groups of from six to twenty have beaten it
out of sight.

A very excellent performance by Arabians has recently
been given me by Colonel Colvile of the British Army, who
has permitted me to quote him. "A party of Towasi
Arabs, mounted on Egyptian cavalry horses and accompanied by two hundred and fifty baggage camels carrying
water and supplies, left Assiut, on the Nile, at 6 P.M. on
June 28, 1884, under command of Lieut.-Col. Colvile,
Grenadier Guards, and Lieut. Stuart Wortby, Sixtieth
Rifles, and arrived at Khargeh, in the Great Oasis, at 4
P.M. on June 30th, a distance of one hundred and twenty
miles, in forty-six hours. One long halt was made from
11 A.M. to 4 P.M. on June 29th; and the horses being
allowed to go their own pace, frequent short halts were

made to allow the camels to catch them up. No water
was obtainable on the way, and the horses were only
watered once — *i.e.*, during the long halt on the 29th.
After fourteen hours' rest at Khargeh, the party proceeded to Beris, distant sixty miles, which they reached
at 2 P.M. on the 2d of July. No horses were lost. Here
four hundred men and all the horses were left, and after-
wards made their way to the Nile at Esneh, distant about
one hundred and twenty miles. I am not in possession of
any details of the march, but as the party was unaccom-
panied by camels and no water is obtainable on the way,
it was probably more rapid than that from the Nile to
Khargeh."

This march, especially in view of the want of water, is
of great interest. It ranks well with some of our own
cavalry marches, but does not quite approach the best.

The Arabian's gait is usually pure; you meet many
trappy goers who have what one is apt to call a peculiarly
Arabian style of picking up their feet, neat and rapid, but
not too high, and very attractive. I have come across
more shying Arabians than I expected, no more, perhaps,
than there are with us; but a horse which is so docile
ought not to shy at all. You see many stylish ones when
they go out fresh or are feeling particularly well; but I
have never met one who showed vice or stubborn temper.
There are some, but they are few; the Arabian seems
easy to manage and easy to sit when putting on airs.
Taken as a race, his manners are irreproachable.

One finds in Algiers quite a number of Percherons at
draught; occasionally a mixture between Percheron and
Arab. Now and then a cob, stranded by some swell from
London or Paris, disconsolately seeks his kind on the
streets of this delightful city. A few ponies, and from
time to time a fine English-hunter type of imported

horse for a heavy-weight officer or a winter resident, may
be observed. There are many heavy French officers.
The Frenchman has a habit of putting on fat which is
quite noticeable, and, though small, he needs a weight-
carrier. There are some imported carriage pairs. But as
a rule, whether under saddle, or in the cabs, or drawing
wagons, or harnessed to pleasure carriages, every city
horse bears some mark of the fine old blood. Either the
face or the throttle, or the clean leg and mule hoof, or the
flea-bitten gray—a distinctive Arabian color—will tell the
story. The impress is as strong as it is beautiful, and will
always remain.

The Morocco and Algeria type of horse is rounder than
the type east of the Libyan desert; he impresses you as
having a bigger barrel. Except for a few points which
are more distinguished, more blood-like in appearance
than our own native strains, and for the fact that he
stands with a bit more daylight under him as a rule, the
Barb is not unlike what we call a "Morgan." But he lacks
the enormous girth of the latter, and for his inches will
not weigh more than three-quarters as much. Nor do I
think he can boast any more grit and capacity to do a distance and repeat; while in speed, at any gait, I should
put him on a distinctly lower scale than the descendants
of old "Justin." He cannot run a heat race any better,
and he can rarely trot a four-minute gait. When it comes
to traction, for which the "Morgans" were always remarkable animals, the Arabian is simply nowhere.

XL

THREE of the regiments of light cavalry in the French army in Algeria are recruited solely from the Arab population. The men are called Spahis, and are said to be excellent in their place, amenable to discipline, and apt to prove effective within their limits when called upon. The Berbers, or aborigines, who were in the land prior to the Arab conquest, do not appear as a distinct type in the army. They have been ground down by many generations of poverty, and seem to have lost the notable old Punic trick of fighting. As a military material they are inferior. Most Arabs—all the pastoral or nomad Arabs, in fact—are stanch French haters. They are held down with the strong hand alone. Only the exceptional Arab, who has given in his submission and is deemed quite trustworthy, is ever allowed to have powder and lead in his possession. All others are deprived of fire-arms and ammunition of every nature. But an Arab who has once accepted the situation, as does the Spahi who enlists, may be trusted, they say, implicitly.

The Spahi retains his national dress, furbished up to make him feel proud. He rides in a saddle which is all but as bad as the one the Indian used to make with straight up and down pommel and cantle, and has by no means the latter's *raison d'être*. The tree and bearings are long. The pommel is coarsely finished, and rises with scarcely a slope to about the waistband when the man sits down in his seat. The cantle rises almost perpendicularly, and is two inches higher than the pommel, really above the small of the back. Saddle-cloths are used by the Spahi *ad libitum*, and woven girths and leathern fittings finish this singular saddle. The stirrup-leather hangs from the middle of the tree, and the foot is thrust way into a huge metal stirrup with a foot-piece square and big as a platter. A breast-strap holds the saddle in place for lack of ribs to keep it where it belongs, and the horse is bitted with a gag hung in a peculiar bridle with large square blinders. The Spahi's sword rides under his left leg, like the Mexican swell's; his carbine he carries in his hand or slings from the shoulder or saddle; he has revolvers in his holsters, and all his weapons are of the best make and pattern.

He is quite a stunning fellow this same Spahi, with his turbaned head and flowing red, white-lined burnoose, his light-blue baggy leg-gear, dark-blue jacket, and generally dramatic manner. That he feels his own importance is manifest. His face is bronzed, his eye flashing, and his manner quick and decisive. He is deferential to his superiors, haughty to all he considers beneath him. From a glance at his saddle one may readily see how it is that he can stand so high in his stirrups as he sometimes does when he gallops past you. He mounts as we do, though one would scarcely imagine that he could get his foot up to his short-hung stirrup, or throw his leg across his extraordinary peaked cantle; but he mounts indifferently from either side. The fact that his tall-appearing horse averages barely fourteen-two accounts for his mounting so easily. The Arabian is very deceptive in looks. One feels tempted when you know him to refer to him as a pony— a term, indeed, commonly employed in Egypt—though at a distance he looks tall.

The Spahi's seat is peculiar. It is, from the side view,

A SPAHI AND HIS BARB, ALGERIA

much like the type of the aboriginal Indian of our plains. When he sits in the saddle he is apt to lean forward; from hip down to knee the leg is almost perpendicular; and from knee down it is thrust back at what we civilized folk deem a most unhorsemanlike angle. He hates spurs because they prevent his drubbing his horse's flanks with his heels, as well as clutching on by them. Still, after a certain period of association with the French, fashion will sometimes claim him for her own; he will put on spurs and try to keep his heels where they belong. But he is then no longer Spahi *à la nature*. He is very expert in the saddle, both in the way of tricks and drill. His Arabian may look sleepy while he stands, but he will wake up to astonishing activity so soon as mounted. He quickly catches his rider's mood, and can be either steady or gay as you may ask.

Most Arab saddles have such an abnormal breadth between the knees that they oblige you most uncomfortably to spread your legs. This does not peculiarly apply to the Spahi's saddle, which has been cut, on a sort of a military plan, to the Arab pattern. But if you want to try the way Orientals usually sit in the saddle, get an extra wide cane-seat chair, sit astride it facing the back, and then put your heels up on the side rounds. Don't lean on the chairback; imagine a cantle behind you about two inches above the buttons on the back of your coat, and you have it exactly. If you propose to ride this way, make up your mind to the *acme* of discomfort until you are used to it. Your feet will go to sleep, and your hips will get tired enough to make you howl before you have covered ten miles. Even an old horseman who is used to an English or to our military saddle must undergo the same trial. We should call it an impossible seat for all-day riding; but the Oriental habit of sitting cross-legged, or on a squat, gets the muscles of the legs and hips used to the confined position, and the Arab will stay in the saddle all but as long as the cowboy or one of Uncle Sam's soldiers.

All Arabs ride with a severe gag-bit, just as all bronco riders are wont to do. The bit of the country is like one style of Mexican bit—to wit, a ring in the horse's mouth held in place by the cheek-straps, and with a single branch projecting down from the back of it; and it is to this that the reins are attached. Of course the horse guides by the neck, as all but hyper-English horses do, and as all horses should. The rein is held slack, but the least tightening of it on the severe gag-bit compels the horse to jerk up his head. The nice use of the curb as taught by the school is quite unknown. Each nation has its own peculiar style. The Englishman and his imitators like to ride a gentle, easy-mouthed horse on a snaffle-bit, and to let him carry his head in a natural way, without seeking by suppling to improve on what nature has done for him. This method acts well enough with the average good-mannered horse. With any other he must resort to a harsh bit, and the horse will take hold of it and worry himself while annoying his rider, because he has been taught no better. The school-taught horse is an abomination to the Briton; but not so to him who knows his ways. He has a well-trained mouth, and a neck whose muscles bend without effort; he brings his head in to either curb or snaffle with that delightful give and take of the rein which is the height of comfort to man and beast, and which is indicative of an ability in each to understand the other that exists in no other method. The cowboy *et id genus omne*, and the Arab, use a severe bit that hurts the horse's mouth whenever the rein is in any degree tightened; it throws up his head with an uneasy motion which appears to interrupt communication between hand and mouth. And yet the

REMOUNT BARB FOR ALGERIAN CAVALRY

proof of the pudding is in the eating; these natural riders care little for the refinements of horsemanship, despite which both cowboy and Spahi are, each in his way, inimitable.

But this nervous dread of the bit distresses me. I have a photograph of a line of Spahis coming to a sharp "Halt!" and every single horse in the line has his nose in the air. A line of school-taught horses would, on the contrary, probably show not one whose head had not been brought in quietly to the bit; still they would have stopped just as short, and vastly more comfortably to man and beast. In the one case the horse has no dread of the bit, and the neck is supple; in the other he fears it, and his neck is generally stiff. Artists have a trick of painting Arabians with the neck finely arched, but this is just what the gag-bit prevents. It is the rarest thing to see an Arabian carry what schoolmen call a good head. His nose is uniformly in the air when his head is up; only when fretting on the bit does he arch his neck, and then he gets his head way down. That nature has given him a peculiarly fine neck is true; the lines of the crest and throttle are exquisite; that he almost never arches it is equally so. The three-year-old illustrated brings his head in because he is being broken with a bit and bridoon. It is not uncommon to see the Arabian, properly bitted by a European owner, carry a perfect head. He could not be made on a better model; but the Arab's method does not utilize what nature has given him.

It does not seem to me that the method of the cowboy or that of the Arab makes a good mouth. Neither bronco nor Arabian, except under abnormal conditions, ever pulls; he never even tightens the rein. This is no doubt better than the common run of English-broken horses on a snaffle, who will take hold of you, and bore and bore

until your arms ache; but, on the other hand, it is far from
being the delightful feel of the school method, where there
is a fine and delicate but constant appreciation by the
man of the horse's mouth, and by the horse of his master's mood and wishes. It is certain that no school airs
could be taught with a bit of which the horse is as shy as
he is of the cowboy's and the Arab's; and I have noticed
that in the *fantasiyas*—of which anon—the Arab is wont
to make his bit less severe, if it is of the kind he can alter,
or else to use an easier one. Nor could school airs be
taught to a horse capable of boring on your hand.

While speaking of guiding by the neck, I will mention
a very queer way the Arabs have of driving with a single
rope, one almost as peculiar as our own way of driving an
army mule-team. The horse or mule so driven wears only
a rope-halter, from which the rein-rope passes back to the
cart on the nigh side of the neck. He has a very high,
round saddle to bear the cart-shafts. If the driver desires
to turn to the left, he simply pulls the rope. If to the
right, he tosses the rope over to the off side of the saddle
and then pulls. This pull bears the rope against the nigh
side of the horse's neck, and thus turns him to the right.
In other words, the horse is taught to guide one way by
the neck and the other by the rein. This is common
enough under saddle, but the method of driving seems
original.

In our old Civil War times the method of teaching mules
to turn to right or left was wont to be more speedily effi-
cacious than reasonable. The nigh mule of the pair of
leaders had a single rein buckled in the nigh ring of the
bit. The off mule had a bar from the front of the nigh
mule's collar to his own bit, so that he must turn, nilly
willy, with his mate. To turn the pair to the left the rein
was steadily pulled; the near mule had his head brought

SPAHI RACKING ALONG THE ROAD

round to the left by the pull; he was apt to follow his nose; the off mule was pulled over in the same direction by the bar, and presto! the trick was done. The mule soon caught on to this thing. But to turn to the right was quite a different matter. The only other thing the driver could do with the rein was to jerk it; but this conveyed no special idea to the mule—he must be taught the jerk as an arbitrary symbol. So, when drilling the mule to go over to the right, the driver had with him an assistant with a stick, who walked along close to the nigh mule's head. When the driver pulled the rein, he did nothing; when he jerked it, the assistant gave the mule a lusty whack on the near side of the head. The mule very naturally sought refuge away from the blow, turned his mate with him, and presto! that trick, too, was done. The mule lacks not intelligence, and he very speedily learned that a jerked rein was very apt to be followed by a blow on the near side of the head, and made haste to get away from it. The plan was crude but effective.

The same method *in petto* has for generations been a favorite with the school-master, who has thumped the alphabet into his pupils' heads with his knuckles. How much happier is the child of to-day with his Reading Without Tears, than the child of sixty years ago, when the vowels were not recited a-e-i-o-u, but a by itself a, e by itself e, i by itself i, etc. Fancy spelling "puzzle" p-u by itself u-izzard-puz; izzard-l-e by itself e-izzle-puzzle. Yet I have known a man who, in New England, was taught to spell that way early in this century.

One of the Spahis in the illustrations is racking along in a very horsemanlike manner, except that one cannot become reconciled to the nose in the air—it constantly suggests a bit which the horse fears. The other, at first blush, is riding a brute. But a look at him shows that the

16

SPAHI, EQUIPPED FOR "FANTASĪYA," MAKING HIS HORSE REAR

rise is not horse-play or ugliness; the rider is forcing the animal to rear as an exhibition of horsemanship. This is by no means the fine performance which the school requires, but rather a crude and shallow trick, common at the *fantasīyas* or horse-parties, where all the riders of the neighborhood meet to show off their steeds and to let off superfluous steam. The shawl hanging over the croup is the drapery usual at this ceremony. All ceremonials, ancient and modern, appear to have demanded draping, more or less extensive, of the horses. Pictures of the ancient tournament always show the horses draped to the ground.

As in the case of every people, one may pick flaws in the Spahi's horsemanship; but despite his want of delicate handling, he is clearly one of the best of horsemen, as he understands the art, and is as devoted to his beast as is the most traditional of Arabs.

XLI

THE French cavalryman rides well, as all mounted men serving a long enlistment do. In Algeria he interests us because of his horse. His saddle is much like our old-fashioned artillery pattern; his equipments vary little from the usual. But he has some objectionable ways. In order to make his horse walk fast, which he accomplishes well enough, he is, like his congener in France, continually drubbing his flanks with his heels. This habit tends to make him grip too much with the calf of the leg, and to turn out his toes in an ungainly fashion. A man ought to ride close and be ready to grip with all the legs he has got; but one does not like to see the heels constantly held too close. The leg, from the knee down, should be nearly or quite perpendicular—in fact, naturally pendent—a habit which will keep the feet where they properly belong. One finds lamentably unmilitary riding among soldiers in this generation: the habit is marked, even in Berlin or Paris, where a cuirassier or a Uhlan is often seen trotting along, trying to rise and leaning forward for the purpose, when his stirrups are too long to enable him to do so otherwise than with an awkward bump. You never see one of our cavalrymen do this. After observing modern army-riding in most of the countries of the accessible world, I am inclined to prefer a thoroughly good West Point seat to any; not the tongs-on-the-wall seat which sometimes obtains, but that which most nearly approaches the natural in our usual army-saddle. And be it noted that even the Briton of to-day is coming back from the very short stirrups he used to consider essential to fox-hunting, to a seat much more like the bareback.

Talking of sticking out the toes, since the abolition of the old style, every rider is subject to the habit. I can remember when the rule was to keep the feet parallel with the horse—a thing never now done, and, be it acknowledged, rarely kept to then. We Americans have the only cavalry which rides with hooded wooden stirrups. Perhaps these are not handsome *per se;* but any soldier who has ridden day after day with the thermometer ever so far below zero will bless the man who first invented this protection against frozen feet. And, moreover, if a man is going to turn out his toes, our hooded stirrup quite hides the trick which a brass stirrup makes unduly prominent.

The French officers have, of late years, all taken to the English saddle, and ride ostentatiously *à l'Anglaise*, a regular "to cover" gait. There is, all the travelled world over nowadays, nothing more marked than the influence of all things British. In my early European tours in the fifties, the Englishman, and especially the English maiden, were outrageously caricatured. The Briton was the butt of all comic stories; he was the stock-in-trade of the *raconteur;* proverbial philosophy was fairly shot at him; nothing about him was acceptable but that universal panacea, the £ sterling. But now the tide has set in his favor; everything everywhere is so English, you know: not only his beefsteaks and his tweed suits, but his manners and his horsemanship are in every section of the habitable globe; you are even invited in France to *five o'cloquer* with your lady friends. The countries the Briton has overrun have found that he possesses other sterling qualities besides the £ *s. d.* And well it is. An infusion of good

Anglo-Saxon common-sense has been a distinct benefit all
over the Continent; and the sublimity of British egoism
in accepting the change is truly delightful. Were I not a
Yankee of the Yankees, might I be a Briton! He feels
that he may seize the best of everything as a right, and
takes umbrage if some one has got ahead of him. As a
cowboy divides all mankind into ranchmen (the sheep)
and tenderfoots (the goats), so the Briton knows but two
classes: subjects of her Majesty or—what is the modern
equivalent of the βάρβαροι of the ancient world? Philis-
tines? He is monumental, your Briton. I love him for
his magnificence of self-assertion, his unlimited "side;" I
am disposed to hate him when he treads on my traveller's
toes, as now and then he happens to do.

Among his imitators are the army men. No doubt
Continental officers have profited by the bit of English
rough-riding they have learned of late years, but their
self-assumed British style looks like overdoing the practical. When smokeless powder shall have brought all uni-
forms down to butternut or some other humdrum color,
this style will be eminently proper; but so long as the
gay and gaudy is *de rigueur* in the uniform, the method of
riding ought to correspond. Not that there is the least
objection to English horsemanship or English tweed suits.
On the contrary, both are practical, admirable. But to
see an officer with red peg-top trousers, gold-laced red cap,
a light-blue jacket trimmed "with ribbons and bibbons
and loops and lace," and a dangling sabre, on a flat English saddle, and rising to a swinging trot as if he were
astride a cover-hack, is too much like serving you *Veuve
Cliquot* in a pewter mug to suit my ideas of the appropriate. *Veuve Cliquot* is good; so is a pewter mug; but the
twain do not match. Moreover, if a soldier uses his two
hands to guide his horse, as these French Anglomaniacs

do, how, forsooth, shall he use his sabre or his carbine? I must not be construed as objecting to the trot. It is an essential gait, and the one our own army men most constantly use as an alternate with the walk. But a soldier should ride a soldier's trot, not a cross-country rider's—at least, when in uniform. Else why the uniform? This being but an outward and visible sign of the inward and spiritual discipline, why not preserve the other elements which go to show the soldier? Pipe-clay is disappearing. It was only a manifestation of discipline at any time; and as a uniform is exactly this and no more, the soldier's ways should be in keeping with the dress.

I am solicitous to avoid the imputation that may be cast upon me of being an Anglophobist. Like Artemas Ward, I scorn the allegation and defy the allegator. What I have heretofore said ought to suffice to prove that no one has a more sincere regard and admiration for most things English than I. Her Gracious Majesty the Queen-Empress has scarce a more loyal subject. Why, I can remember her way back in 1851, in the Great Exhibition year, when she was still a young queen, and used still not infrequently to be seen in the saddle in the Park. My loyalty to her has never swerved, and my six or seven years in England have made me almost a Briton, in fact, as my old Salem ancestry truly was up to 1776, of glorious memory. But may I not criticise withal? Is my loyalty the less because, when I get wrathy, I "write to the *Times?*" In horse sports, as a nation, the English are easily first. I grant it with pleasure, and whenever I take down Whyte Melville or some other charming chronicler of the hunting-field, I fall in love anew with this splendid people and their ever-green land. But—well, the buts have already been put in. Let us change the subject as radically as we can. God save the Queen!

XLII

Of all horse-flesh, so to speak, the patient little commonplace every-day ass takes the lead. There is no denying him the palm. Were I a Homer or a Dante, or eke
a Holmes, I would indite an epic, or at least pen an heroic
rhyme to the character, strength, and courage of this
noblest of the equine race. In every country where severe economics are thrust upon the people, the ass comes
to the rescue and does the work which no other creature
alive can do. He lives on nothing; he is rarely fed—in
times of drought or extra hard work a pittance of barley
—but is turned loose to find what he may. He is never
vicious or obstinate, but works on hard and faithfully
till his poor old ears flop downward from age, his head
droops from weariness, and he literally falls under his load
and dies in his tracks, after serving his often cruel master
some score or more of years. When he is put to work as
a yearling—for he often is—he does not last so long. I
have ridden one at eighteen months which had been
trained but two weeks, and yet was gentle, bridle-wise,
and well-gaited. Where is there such a horse?

The habit of cruelty to the ass, though universal, is
sometimes only thoughtlessness. It is bred in the bone.
You will see a child cuffing and beating a donkey which
is standing under its load at the door, "just to learn how."
The utility of the ass is always recognized. Æsop, who
tells us that to the ass's prayer for a less cruel master Jove
replied that it was beyond even his power to change the

human heart, but that he would do the next best thing and give his supplicant a tough hide, unquestionably knew both men and donkeys. In Mexico, when two Indian farmers meet, they pass the time of day, inquire for each other's wives and children, and then always comes the question, "How is the burro?" Indeed, as the burro earns the daily bread for the family, this is natural enough. No doubt the h'mar of the East is equally considered; but he is the victim of man's heedlessness and capacity for cruelty and experimenting.

There is one queer asinine trick the Arabs have. With the notion that the Lord did not know how to make the donkey's nostril, they slit it upward two or three inches "to give him more room to breathe." They say, too, that it improves the tone of his bray, though this may be questioned by all who have listened to his delectable song. Still, the Arab is fairly generous to the little toiler; there are comparatively few sore-backed donkeys in Algeria, Tunis, and Egypt, which speaks more for the people than can be said of Italy or Spain or Mexico.

There is no question that, feeding quite apart, the ass will kill any horse or mule; and it is clear that, weight for weight and load for load, he daily outdoes the camel. The latter, weighing fifteen hundred pounds, carries five hundred; the ass weighs two hundred and fifty to four hundred pounds, and carrying one hundred and fifty to three hundred, outwalks the camel by a mile an hour. In the Mexican mines, a donkey which weighs not over five hundred pounds at the outside, will carry a load of ore equal to his own weight out of the mine, go back empty, and work all day. He is fed high to enable him to do this, and does not live long; but what other mammal can equal this feat for even a week?

The donkey is guided by the voice, a stick, or a rope-

halter. The halter-rope lies on the left side, and is pulled
to turn him to the left, or borne across the neck to turn
him to the right. The stick is used to touch his neck on
either side if you desire him to turn to the other. Or the
least raising of the stick suffices; while, if you are walking behind him, a mere touch on either flank will turn him
quickly and surely. It is most commonly the stick which
is used, and this serves the double purpose of guiding and
striking. But, Lord save the mark! it is wont to be the
man who needs the stick, not the beast. No more patient
creature exists; it is not he who is obstinate or treacherous, it is his master. Dear, patient ass! did we but recognize the half of thy virtues, we should glory in being
called by thy name, not resent the appellation!

The donkey in the Orient is often very small. I have
measured them, full-grown, only thirty-two inches high—
no bigger than a St. Bernard; not so big as some of the
prize-winners. I rode one last winter to Abraham's Oak
from Hebron, on which my toes touched the ground though
I was on a pad; and I measure but five feet seven. The
little fellow seemed to make nothing of my one hundred
and fifty pounds, but racked away at a good four and a
half miles an hour. On a creature like this a load equal to
half his own weight will habitually be put; his owner will
ride atop of the load, and the little hero will go off at a
sharpish running-walk and do his twenty-five miles a day.
This sounds incredible, but it is literally true. The ass in
Algeria often carries three-fourths of his own weight all
day long. One sees two men on a donkey which weighs
a bare four hundred pounds—a load and a man on a
donkey they claim to weigh only two hundred and fifty
pounds. The little creature can be bought for seven or
eight francs, does during his life the work of a dozen men,
and exhibits the virtues of a score of saints. I was tempted

COUNTRYMAN ON AN ASS

to buy a hundred to send to the Columbian Fair, and a contractor offered to deliver them on board the Marseilles packet at Tunis for seven hundred francs. This is barely half a cent a pound, not counting the virtues. One sees Arabs coming into Constantine with a donkey-load of wood, which they sell for three francs. They have come twenty-five miles with it; they sell it, and next day ride the donkey back. As a meal costs them but two cents, the wood nothing, and the donkey does all the work, what seems a small profit for a two or three days' trip is really a good one. And who is it that earns it?

As I have previously observed, all saddle-beasts in the East go what those who would limit the horse to the English standard are pleased to call "artificial" gaits. In fact, three-quarters of all the animals in the world which are used for riding do so. Mules broken to saddle always what they call "sidle" or amble; all donkeys running-walk, rack, or amble. They scarcely have to be taught. Little ass-colts often rack alongside of their dams as if there were no other method of progression. I have seen bullocks amble or rack. Why, then, are these paces artificial? They are in reality natural to every member of the equine race—I might say to all four-footed animals. But it is chiefly in our Southern States that these gaits have been studied as an art, and have been improved upon and bred from.

The donkey in Algeria is not used for riding by all classes, rich and poor, as he is in Egypt and Syria. In fact, he is rarely seen with a saddle. He has a pad, very similar to the pad on which the bespangled queens of the sawdust ring dance their short hour to delighted boys and rustics, only more crude and better suited to his diminutive proportions. This pad has no stirrups, and is so wide as to make a seat on it extremely tiring to the uninitiated.

The Arab sits astride or sidewise, and as the pad is rarely girthed at all, or at best by a slender cord, it is much like walking on a tight-rope or managing a birch-bark canoe to sit on it, until you "catch on." It is the reverse of our trick of girthing a horse well and then sticking to the saddle. The horse, when in the service of a native, is not uncommonly equipped in the same way. Between this pad, which serves equally for riding and loading, and the saddle of the Spahi, there is a vast category of sizes and styles; all, however, much too wide. I have often seen a pair of stirrups improvised by tying two bags together, slinging them across the pad, turning in one corner of each, and thrusting the foot into the pocket thus made. This sounds ingenious, and is really so, but such a flimsy pretext for a saddle, or, in fact, all the gear used for saddle or harness all over the Orient, would be cast on the dump-heap by the poorest American farmer. He would not risk his bones with it.

The life of a saddle or a harness is much like that of a fine city vehicle. A swell, for instance, buys a five-hundred-dollar buggy, and uses it three or four years. It then goes to auction, and is bought by some one who runs it in the suburbs for six or eight more. Thence it goes, by another auction sale, to a countryman, who will run it twenty years, unless it sooner meets with the fate of the one-hoss shay. In the Orient you never see saddle or harness in any but the latter state. They always look as if they had never been new.

XLIII

THE Arab is a tall, straight-featured, well-shaped man, varying in color from a dark bronze to a tone quite as white as some Europeans. He is decidedly handsome. Women are apt to be struck by the manly beauty of the Tunisian, and he is indeed a fine specimen. Men have less chance to be struck by the good looks of the Tunisian women, for only the veriest apologies for women are ever allowed outside the harem walls unless closely veiled. I must, however, except the pretty young Jewess —bless her heart!—who goes freely about in a sack-coat and tight trousers, and showing her face—bar powder—just as the Lord made it.

The Arab is, in his way, cleanly. He is supposed to wash his feet before praying, and his hands and face before and after eating—many, in fact, do so; and he is apt to bathe in streams at not infrequent intervals, unless the weather be too cold. But—and there is in the Orient always a *but* on this subject—he can scarcely be gauged as up to our standard of what is next akin to godliness. One sees at the hut doors all too many instances of cerebral insecticide to be reconciled to the Arab as a clean mortal. No odor of nationality is, however, apt to exist in a dry climate, so that he is, *quoad* the nostril, unobjectionable.

I am not so sure, by-the-way, that cleanliness is next akin to godliness; I should be tempted to reverse the terms. If you want to convert a heathen, it is, despite the precedent, clearly a blunder to begin by telling him

that all his ancestors are in sheol, whether you yourself believe the statement or not.   The more natural process, it
seems to me, would be first to dump him into a bath-tub,
or the equivalent most handy ; then to fill his stomach ;
last, to bring up the religious question.   The word bath-
tub is generic; it denotes every physical means of cleanliness.   Unquestionably, a well-scrubbed, well-fed savage
would be more apt to take to the truths of theology than
a hungry one grovelling in his native filth.   But let us
taboo religious discussion as well as political.   I may be
treading on some good horse friend's toes, though I have
found most horsemen liberal in their dogmas, even if old-
fashioned in their faith.

Despite his good looks and well-knit frame, the value of
the Arab as a laborer is not great.   He works by fits and
starts, and the intervals between fits are long.   He can
and does at times work hard and fast, but it is only to
indulge the longer in laziness by-and-by.   Many of the
pastoral Arabs who own flocks gauge his value closely ;
they hire herdsmen for their food, three dollars, and two
sheep a year.   Lodging is *al fresco* most of the time.   The
shepherd is expected to get along in any weather which
will not kill off his herd ; and as to clothing, an Arab
herdsman can get on with a minimum.   So long as the
warp and weft of a bit of cotton cloth will hold together,
he can, with the use of thorns for pins, fashion a garment
which meets all his requirements.   In cold weather he and
his sheep or goats herd together in any convenient shelter
—under the brow of a hill or behind a clump of rocks, or
in one of the natural caverns which abound in a slaty
country—and he gets a great part of his warmth from
them.   Most of the year he can bask in more sunshine
than we should like.

One can have a deal too much of a good thing, even of

old Sol's company. A story is told of a British tar of the
ancient order of things who had been cruising on the
coast of Africa for several years and was finally ordered
home. As his ship sailed up the English Channel, in a
fine hearty yellow fog, out of which one could cut chunks
with a hatchet, the hard-baked old tar, coming up from
below, drew big inspirations of the home air into his
lungs, and " Ah, shipmate," said he, " 'ere's weather for
you. None of your blasted sunshine !" He had had too
much of a good thing.

In what I say of the people I am, of course, not referring
to the educated, intelligent Arab. He is what well-to-do
folk are everywhere. I passed some days with the Caliph
of K'sar Il'lal, and can truthfully say that I have never
met a man with finer instincts, nobler presence, or more
abundant courtesy, no part of which came from any source
but his own deep character and native training. There are
also sheiks in the same vicinity who would murder you
for your money until you had broken bread with them ;
but so there are in America, and breaking bread with these
will by no means serve you.

There are rich and well-bred city Arabs who have
learned many ways from the Franks with whom they
come in contact ; but I prefer their own native customs.
The unspoiled, well-mannered, educated Arab can scarcely
be improved on—save in what we are vain enough to call
intelligence. But who shall measure intelligence? Theirs
suffices for them, and ours appears to them heathenish.
To learn a few thousand texts from the Koran affords
them an altogether better culture than all our science and
art and letters—so they claim.

They all dress alike—Arabs, Berbers, Moors, and the rest.
Item : one " b'iled rag," not the b'iled rag of the wild and
woolly West, but a yard or two of cotton cloth, cut off a
17

piece and sewed up bag-fashion, with holes made in it
for the head and arms, now and then affording the luxury
of short sleeves ; and which under no circumstances whatsoever is b'iled until age has withered and custom staled it
into actual rags.   Item : if well off, a sleeveless buttoned
vest.   Item : real "bags," to adopt our young hunting
swell's term, for trousers.   Sartorially speaking, these are
made of cotton, and are literally like a bag whose depth
is equal to a little more than the distance from waist
to knee, and whose width equals thrice or more times the
distance a man can stretch apart his legs.   Cut out the
two corners of the bottom of the bag, step through the
holes, and tie the stuff—hemmed or not according to fancy
—around the knees ; then gather up the mouth around
the waist, and you have the Plymouth Rock pants *du
pays*.   There is thus left pendent between the Arab's legs
a bag big enough to hide himself in.   Less stuff will suffice
if there be not enough on hand.   The origin and utility of
this leg-gear it were vain to inquire.   Item : one scarf to go
a number of times round the waist.   Item : if cold, an additional shirt-like garment of woollen goods coming down
below the knees.   Item : one burnoose, or peculiarly-cut
cloak of white or, in Tunis, blue woollen stuff, with a
very roomy hood, exceeding loose, so as to wrap about
one and throw over the shoulder.   Item : one fez, with
some cotton cloth twisted up rope-fashion to wrap around
it in the guise of a turban.   Item : one pair of shoes (or
not, as the case may be), made of anything from woven
rushes to Morocco leather.

There are some variations to all this, but they are slight.
The Arab is everywhere clothed in bags, right or wrong
side up.   In this dress, or so much of it as he can afford,
the native lives day and night, from early manhood to
old age, and when he dies he is buried in it, or the gar-

ments go to his son and heir. A very few working city
Arabs wear ready-made clothing from France, England,
or perchance even America. More's the pity! It sounds
the death-knell to national costume.

Where shall we go next to find an unspoiled nation, except away to the interior of Asia or Africa? The very
remotest corners of the earth are invaded by ready-made
clothes. If the Bible could be introduced with half the
ease of these abominations, this generation would see the
millennium with its own eyes. When I say Bible, by-the-
way, I mean the Sermon on the Mount, and not Jonah
and the Whale, as an article of faith. Far beyond the
reach of the railroad you see graceful national costumes
supplanted by cheap European clothing. Now, I maintain
that national character resides largely in legs. Years ago
you needed only to look as high as a man's knees to tell his
nationality. Think of the delicious legs of the old-time
Italian peasant--real stage-brigand legs, pure and unde-
filed—now chased into inaccessible mountain recesses!
Think of the legs of the Russian peasant of to-day, all
boots and padding, no more to be unwrapped than an
Egyptian mummy! But all *fin de siècle* legs look alike.
It is only when you get way beyond the path of Cook's
Tours that you find either a type of clothing or the graceful looseness of garment which ignorance of civilization
breeds.

I believe that no trouser-wearing human being, unless
he be a much-travelled man, can have any idea of the
horrible perversity of the cut of the Oriental home-made
pants; it is atrocious, heart-rending. The variety of badness in style must be imagined; it cannot be described,
but—well, it reminds me of an incident, the real origin of
the story as since sometimes narrated. It was very many
years ago, when the now godlike Poole was struggling

into celebrity. A friend of mine, Mr. Hand, a city solic-
itor, had all through life hated his legs, principally because
his trousers bagged at the knees with that pertinacity
which, among inanimate objects, only trousers can exhibit.
"Why don't you go to Poole's?" said a peripatetic, *flâ-
neur* club friend; "his trousers never bag; look at mine!"
So off goes Hand to Poole's, states his case, and, under the
assurance that the forthcoming garments shall not bag at
the knees, orders several pairs at three times the custom-
ary price. They by-and-by came home, and were delightful to look upon, to incase one's legs in; but alas, in
a se'nnight or so, the telltale bagginess began to be seen.
In a rage, off marched Hand to his Sartorial Highness, determined to have the law of him. "It is not necessary to
look at them, Mr. Hand," calmly replied the self-satisfied
ninth to Hand's aggressive salutation; "our trousers never
bag at the knees." "But there they are—as bad as any
eight-and-sixpenny pair made in the city!" screamed irate
Hand. Adjusting his eye-glass, the apparently surprised
but none the less confident tailor condescendingly stooped,
smoothed his hand down the front of the garment in dispute, gazed at the knees a moment, and then, taking from
a distance a side view of the same, and dropping his glass
with a half-supercilious, half-pitying smile: "Why, Mr.
Hand," quoth he, "you have been sitting down in those
trousers!" They were park trousers, to be promenaded
in, no more.

The Arab in Algeria and Tunis may be dressed in rags
and tatters, but he is no beggar. Only the blind beg. This
is really a point in his favor, and it is a great relief from
the mendicancy of many other countries to find a poor
population which does not hang on your skirts for alms.
So much can, however, not be said of his brother beyond
the desert, nor can it be said of any country where, owing

to the folly of tourists, the word *backsheesh* is current coin.

The rich man among the Arabs dresses richly. His shirt is of fine linen. His inside vest is buttoned, the outside one is worn loose. A long paletot often takes the place of the latter. It is cut part way down from the throat, and the loose armholes allow the arms to be held in or outside. The wide trousers are bound about the waist by a costly scarf. Over all is frequently worn the long, loose tunic, cut V shape at the neck, and with short sleeves set on low down. The hands are as frequently kept inside as out—in winter for warmth, in summer from habit; and an Arab reaches out from the V at the neck for anything he wants handed him with a peculiarly limited motion, which at first you fail to comprehend. The burnoose is an out-of-doors garment, and the fez may or may not have the turban-cloth. The swell wears what look like European socks, and his slippers, usually trodden down at heel by the common or careless, are handsomely embroidered, or else of fine morocco, red or yellow. The calf of the leg is naked. Parts of this dress are dropped at intervals according to the season. There are few persons more really magnificent than a well-dressed Arab sheik, or a man of wealth. In our days of business suits which clothe all kinds and conditions of men, the dress is uncommonly attractive—on an Arab. That it would work in with our habits one would hardly allege. But the trousers, of whatever cut, have one manifest advantage—they do not, cannot, bag at the knee, whether you sit or stand.

XLIV

To come back to our quadrupeds. This dress is, of all clothing, the one you and I would select as being most illy adapted to horseback work; and yet the Arab is equally at home in the saddle or sitting with his legs crossed under him. Like all every-day and all-day horsemen, he is perfect within his lines. Some people yield him the palm among all riders, an opinion which I do not share. He might perhaps be said to occupy the highest position among horsemen, in that he has bred and educated the most docile race of horses known to man, and the one which has given the civilized world the impress of thorough blood. But as a rider I am inclined to think that our own skilful equestrian could beat him in riding over a country, in rounding-up a big bunch of ugly, stampeded cattle, in the twists and brushes of polo, in school-riding, or in almost any duty or pleasure requiring in its kind horsemanship of the highest order. This has really been demonstrated in some things; but, *ex uno*, we must not fall into the error of *discere omnes*. The Arab, when he is a horseman, is a superb one, even though he does not come within our canons of the art. When the horse is only a beast of burden or a means of transportation, the Arab is no better than his ilk elsewhere. When, as in the desert, the horse is his pet, his companion by day, his dream by night, the Arab is, in a sense, incomparable. No master can be more kind. No dog is more intelligent than the dark, liquid-eyed mare he has bred and trained, whose

ancestresses a hundred generations back his ancestors
have loved and trusted. This mare—would that we human beings had not been civilized out of so many of
our animal qualities!—will follow him day and night. She
would fret her soul out at being hitched to a post, and her
master would scorn to tie her. She will stand immov-
able in the midst of danger and fright which would make
any of our horses frantic. She will carry her master
through fire and water. She will unflinchingly face
wounds and death so long as the hand which has fed her
is laid upon her neck. She will stand over her disabled
lord till help arrives, or she will go alone to seek it and
return with it to find him. She will kneel for him to
mount, and she will bear him bravely home, if she falls a
sacrifice to her devotion at the door of her master's tent.
These are not always fables. The horse, treated as he
should be, generation after generation, develops a rare intelligence, and shows as noble an affection as the dog.
But, as above said, even in Arabia, this horse is the pearl
of great price. Thrice happy the sheik or caliph who
truly claims to own one!

In the desert proper the horse is not always shod; in
the stony localities he must be. The Frank shoe in Algerian cities, owing to the European influence, is driving
out the old Arabian plate. The foot of the unshod horse
is everywhere and always strong and healthy. The Arabian foot is, in fact, uniformly good. I have scarcely
seen a horse point, even on the pavement. There are few
interferers; some overreach in harness, but not of course
in the saddle, as no unspoiled Arab can be persuaded to
ride a trot, and this is the only gait in which the habit
can prevail.

XLV

ONE of the great events of the year in Algerian matters equine are the races at Biskra, on the edge of the desert, or in what one might more properly call the first oasis. In Tunis the *fantasīya* is the fad. One can scarcely compare the Biskra races to our own, but they bring out some rather fine specimens of horse-flesh, and have some curious features. Among these are camel-races, at which some of the best running camels compete, not at long distance, which is their great power, but at short distances for speed—a thing they are not remarkable for, according to the creed of these modern days.

The running camel is to the porter camel as the thorough-bred to the mongrel cart-horse—the one has speed in a certain sense and vast endurance at speed; the latter has no speed, but simply great endurance under weight or at traction. I saw a couple of laboring camels, worth about a hundred and twenty-five dollars apiece, each doing quite the work of a pair of horses, which were running an olive-crushing mill belonging to my friend, the caliph, on three-hour shifts, day and night, and had been doing it for a number of months. Such a camel will carry five hundred pounds a great many consecutive hours. They eat little and drink less—actually considerably less —than a horse; and their excretions are correspondingly small.

The Biskra races are got up mainly by the Europeans, but the great delight of the Arab horseman is the *fanta-*

BICHARI CAMEL-RIDERS, UPPER EGYPT

siya, and they always have one or more such events. The entries to these number all manner of horsemen, armed and unarmed, who ride more or less wild figures to more or less monotonous drumming music, and who end by a most excited and exciting *pot-pourri* of feat riding. They stand in their stirrups and throw their guns in the air, whirl them about in the most approved warlike style, and fire them at intervals in what seems an uncalled for and dangerous fashion until you know that they are loaded only with blank-cartridge. The horses for the moment partake the enthusiastic bedevilment of their masters, and rear, wheel, kick, buck, rush, stop, turn, and twist for all the world like a bunch of broncos after a winter's rest,

the men shouting meanwhile, yelling, screaming like so
many demons. No picture can do justice to the kaleido-
scopic fervor and wildness of the scene, if many riders are
engaged in it. It is a seething whirlpool of wild, unmean-
ing, half-merry, half-fanatical excitement, in which no end
of excellent horsemanship comes to the fore. From time
to time the riders stop and rank themselves for a rest on
one side; then out come individuals to show what their
steeds can do. They pirouette and dance a while, and
then make a rush at full gallop to one or other side, stop
suddenly, and wheel about. There is no specific art in
what they do; each man has trained his horse on his own
untrained ideas. They have a close seat, clinging with
their heels, and exhibit a great deal of skill, in their gy-
ratory exercises; but once seen, the *fantasiya*, like a
circus, loses its interest. All semi-wild nations do about
the same tricks on horseback. I think our Indian, or a
Cossack, will easily excel them all, while nothing I have
ever seen in *fantasīyas* in the faintest degree approaches
the fine work of the school-trained horse in the hands of
a master of the art. The one depends on speed and
violent motion; the other on slow and rhythmic movements, vastly more difficult to execute, and requiring a
system of education which the *fantasīya* work quite lacks.
The one is a sailors' hornpipe rapidly played on a fiddle;
the other is an adagio of Schumann on an Amati.

Here is one of the Arabian horsemen, ready to take part
in the *fantasiya*. His seat and steed show the type well;
man and horse are what you are wont to see. In action
this horse will show to decidedly better advantage. The
docile nature of the Arabian robs him of much of his
beauty in a picture at rest. Yet if you examine him standing, you will find many points to commend, few to condemn.

READY FOR THE "FANTASIA"

As you perceive, from this man's seat, a spur would be of no use to him, and a decided irritation to his well-mannered mount; for an Arab of the people can no more forego the luxury of beating time on his horse's ribs than an Indian. Even when riding with counterless slippers and without stirrups, he manages to keep up the swinging of his legs, and yet he never loses a slipper. An occasional stirrup is made with a sharp point on the inside to use in lieu of a spur on the heel. This wide, flat stirrup is not uncomfortable. It is curved upward, and affords a means of resting the foot by constant change of position. The Arab usually thrusts his foot home in it. In fact, nearly all horsemen do "ride home." The cowboy, unless he has them hooded, wears the big wooden stirrups against his ankle. Our trooper, with the hooded stirrup, cannot thrust his foot beyond the point where his toe touches the hood; but if perchance he has a pair of hoodless wooden stirrups he is apt to get his foot well in. It is a natural thing to do, and all natural riders do it. The military man who uses a brass stirrup, and the riding-school man or those who take him as a model, are the only ones who hold the stirrup under the toe or the ball of the foot.

XLVI

THE enormous hat sometimes worn by the village Arab is an outgrowth of a heat and sunshine which even the natives cannot endure without protecting their heads. The turban has come from the same cause. In all tropical countries some means of avoiding the danger of sunstroke is universal, though the natives can stand a sun which would be fatal to a Frank. In India, Europeans who have to be much in the sun often wear a cork or quilted cushion inside the coat down the spine from neck to waist; for any part of the vertebral column is sensitive to excessive heat. The top or front of the head is much less so than the base of the brain; whence the wearing of the turban on the back of the head or the helmet, or the pugree or its equivalent. Animals, from inherited ability to resist its dangers, do not often suffer from the intense heat, which, in summer, registers, they say, 110° Fahrenheit and upwards in the shade, while in the sun one may almost do the family cooking. Still, in many places, horses, especially if imported from a temperate climate (as the Australian waler in India), are better for a hood over the head.

This big hat is quite common in Tunis, is made of plaited straw, and is heavier even than a Mexican sombrero. The heavier the head-gear the safer the man from sunstroke and really the more comfortable.

The Tunisian countryman rides not a saddle but a pad, and this is more generally useful, as it can be employed

"FANTASIYA" RIDERS, ALGERIA

for a pack better than for riding, but it will serve a turn at that. An Arab saddle is uncomfortable enough; to ride a pad is the height of misery. As a rule, it has no stirrups, but they are occasionally present, and then not fastened but thrown loosely across the pad, which is very thick, extremely wide, and frequently has no girth whatever. It runs up over the withers and back beyond the coupling. A habit of balancing keeps the rider and pad both in place. With a horse of any spirit girths are indispensable; still, a horse will give a good deal of a shy without throwing either man or pad, if the man has caught the balance-trick.

Since the French assumed what they call "financial control" of Tunis, the roads have been improved *pari passu* with the rest of matters. Most of the roads before they came were only worn saddle or camel paths; in the interior there is still nothing else. On the coast were a few mud roads, able to accommodate the rough vehicles occasionally owned by the natives. Along the road there is uniformly a mud-bank thrown up from the ditch dug on either side to drain it; a similar bank, for irrigating purposes, is put around every enclosed field, and each one is crowned by the Barbary fig or prickly-pear cactus. This plant grows everywhere, is killed only by frost which almost never comes, and bears in abundance a watery fruit almost as big as an apple. This is the one means of staving off starvation which the Arab possesses when his crops fail, as they sometimes do in seasons of drought. No care need be given to the plant, which often grows to be ten feet high.

The Arab's cultivation is the barest apology. All he does is to sow his seed in December or January on the untouched soil, in among the stubble of last crop, then scratch it in with what he calls a plough, but what is only

18

a curved iron-pointed forked stick, and leave the rest to
Allah. His crops are not unapt to fail unless there be
goodly rains. If there is enough, the soil yields plentifully
by April or May. In the summer there is no rain; the
earth is like a furnace seven times heated, and nothing
can grow. The Barbary fig is then the saving clause in

TUNISIAN HAT

the Arab's existence. It is lucky for him that generations
of scant rations have got him used to eating sparsely. It
is amazing how little the people of hot climates—unless
they are of European stock—can get along with. A handful of rice three times a day enables the Japanese coolie
to drag you in his jinrikisha a good forty miles; or the
same food will carry the Calcutta coal-heaver through a

long day's toil. He needs little ; but when he can get it he will eat heavily, they say.

Northern people have the trick of eating for two purposes—warmth and aliment. The Eskimo consumes enormous quantities of blubber, but the bulk of it goes to keep alive the fire in the human stove, without which he would freeze to death. The good half or more of what we Northern Europeans eat is from an inherited tendency to "shovel in coal ;" only a small part is assimilated for nourishment ; and we carry the trick of eating wherever we go—liver or no liver. But so much is not essential in a hot climate, and the native population learns to live on a quantity (to say nothing of quality) which to us would be the shortest of commons. I have never been able to reduce the average food consumed by the Oriental to ounces ; but compared, say with our army ration, I fancy it would be less than half the weight, perhaps less than a third. At the same time, when food can be had, the Oriental will vie with his Occidental brother in eating ; and the rich are often notorious gluttons. The poor make a virtue of necessity.

There is a curious fact bearing on this stoking theory which is well known among the lumbermen in our Eastern States. The capacity of the horses they use out in camp to keep warm is gauged by the amount they can eat and digest. They are mostly small horses, but tough and rugged creatures, of "Morgan" pattern. Unless a horse will eat up clean a full bucket of oats three times a day, he is considered useless for this work. He will "starve with cold," and they send him back to the settlements where he can be blanketed. More than half he consumes goes through his system merely to supply carbon to warm him ; his digestive apparatus assimilates such part as is needed for alimentation. The Indian pony worries through the winter because he is not worked, so that the little he gets goes for fuel, and not to replace tissue lost by labor; and also because his ancestry has worried through the same trials, and he is their fittest survivor. But the lumberman's horse comes of stabled stock—a very different creature— and must be kept warm by artificial means, or extra food.

The Oriental horse partakes of this hot-climate quality to a certain extent, and is fed much less than ours; but, as with men, I have been unable to gauge his relative pounds of consumption to my satisfaction. In the country you can get no reliable information, nor do they feed by measure or by rule; in the cities and in the army they fall partially into Frank ways, and feed more according to our measure.

XLVII

WHEN you get far enough away from the every-day traveller and come in contact with the "sure-enough," simon-pure Arab caliph or sheik, you often find a character above reproach, a personal bearing graceful, high-toned, and nobly simple, and a courtesy, truth, and kindness which are a revelation to us prosaic Anglo-Saxons. I am proud to possess the friendship of such a man. He was my host —Si Nassour ben El Hadj Salem, Caliph of K'sar Il'lal. With this gentleman—and a gentle man he was in every sense—I spent some days not far from the ruins of ancient Thapsus. I had a neat and artistic-looking Arabic letter from the French authorities, who, by reason of their financial control, will soon transform Tunis, like Algeria, into a French province. And it is, no doubt, better for the land, save only for the loss of its picturesqueness, and this is a loss indeed. The Bey of Tunis has but little real authority left, and can devote his abundant leisure to the society of his four hundred wives, to whom (or should I say to which?) a new one, usually a Circassian girl, is added by each incoming by-monthly steamer from the East. He holds court once a week in the old city palace, amuses himself by chopping off a few criminals' heads, and again retires to his country palace near La Marsa.

I could not read the letter which was my safe-conduct, but some time after a scribe translated it to me in French. Here it is in English

"Praise to God, the Only.

"To the honorable, the bous and sheiks of the township of M'Kalta, whom may God replenish with happiness! After the salutation and the mercy of God, the respectable the Colonel, bearer of these presents, comes among you, into your township, to make a trip for his gratification. We recommend him to you most particularly. He will be your welcome guest.

"Written by the humble after-named, under God, Tauchon, Civil Controller at Sousa, the 22d Djoumada 2d, 1309.

"(Sig.) C. Tauchon," and an official seal.

The date is that of the Hegira.

Armed with this screed and accompanied by an escort of Spahis and an interpreter, I started for the interior. As luck would have it, there are two M'Kaltas, one being within the jurisdiction of K'sar H'lal. I reached this M'Kalta, and presented my letter to the wrong man, as I had intended to go to the other M'Kalta; but the wrong man proved to be distinctly the right one, for he was the most noted chief in that part of the country, and my safe-conduct was of a nature to be respected by every one.

The caliph received me with literally open arms. He was sitting in receipt of custom—the Arabs coming in to pay their annual tax on olive-trees, which, though but a part of a cent per tree, amounted as a total to a very large sum—and gave himself up to me at once, adjourning all other business, and bidding several supplicants come on the morrow. This struck me as an interruption to business; but as time is by far the least valuable of the possessions of an Arab, and every one was doubly compensated for any delay by the sight of a Frank—about one of whom turned up there every two or three years—the act was by no means strained. Coffee was at once served—such an aroma of pure Mocha I had never tasted before—and we sat down, he and I and some of the sheiks who remained, cross-legged or upright, as far as to each was comfortable. Through the medium of my interpreter's Frenche of Stratteforde atte. Bowe, and still worse Arabic — which, curiously, he could speak, but neither read nor write — we talked hour after hour, as other guests, lured by the stranger, dropped in to swell the circle. I soon saw that I must not expect to regain Sousa and catch the steamer I aimed for, and I was correct. But it was better so. The whole experience was a rare treat. In all my travels I have never met a man more fit for the society of princes than Si Nassour ben El Hadj Salem. Of tall, full growth, he had a face of great dignity and beauty, a smile any woman might envy or fall a victim to, manners gracious and courteous and anticipating as we Teutonic rustics — more's the pity — so rarely see in our *soi-disant* civilized intercourse, and a bearing every inch a—caliph. He had inherited his caliphate from an uncle, and was highly considered by the French.

I spent some days under his care, eating out of the same dish—and with my fingers at that, for though my interpreter and I had provided ourselves with forks and spoons I preferred to imitate my host—sleeping in his own soft, hand-made blankets, and journeying to and fro with him in the neighborhood to all the places I wished to visit in the footsteps of Cæsar. He would not let me out of his sight, and yet his presence was not for a moment *de trop*, nor his courtesy overmuch. He furnished me with his best steed, and a fine fellow he was, and rode with me wherever I went or came.

I had all too numerous opportunities of judging how little heed Orientals pay to their own or any one else's time. Whenever we would pass through a village, or near by some friendly sheik, we were constrained by polite insistence to come in and break bread. This was not

a ceremony to be lightly thrust aside, nor indeed easy so
frequently to go through. These simple folk saw a Frank
so rarely that I was like an odd specimen of *feræ naturæ*.
So little did they know of what lay beyond their horizon
that even my host had once only been in the City of
Tunis; scarce another in the country round had even
been to Sousa. The word Frank had no definite meaning, except that the Franks dwelt beyond the only sea of
which they knew—the Mediterranean; and they recognized no difference in the French, Germans, Italians, Spaniards, English. They had never heard of the Atlantic,
nor of America. I identified myself by telling them that
I lived in the land where the cotton-plant grew; and as
they all wore cotton goods of English manufacture, this
was to them a pleasure to know. When I told them, in
days' journeys of a horse, how far off my country was,
they "Allahed!" in a marvellous fashion. My watch and
chain were a great charm to them, and they never tired
of examining a pair of gossamer rubber shoes I wore, and
every one wanted to see me stand in a pan of water, and
then show my dry feet within. The elasticity of a few
rubber bands I had in my pocket was again a wonder.
A gross of such would have bought out half M'Kalta.
They were very children, and yet delightful in their grace,
dignity, and politeness. The usual repast was seethed
kid's flesh (not bad eating by-the-way), or lamb, and the
national dish, koosh-koosh, a sort of wheaten preparation
which resembles cooked rice, and is eaten with a pepper-
sauce, was a truly delicious species of curry. The dexter-
ity in tearing the meat apart with the fingers of one hand
was marvellous. Once I was offered some native wine
(vile is no word for it), and when I asked how it came
that, among sons of the Prophet, there was wine made,
they laughingly said that, of course, no one drank it; and

MY FRIEND THE CALIPH

yet there was a good deal made and sold. When they learned that their guest had lost his leg in battle, and could not sit cross-legged, they absolved me with great unction from the position usually demanded by polite rules, and made me very comfortable, though I thought I was narrowly watched to ascertain that I was not prevaricating, as the fact seemed inexplicable to them.

I could write a book anent my Arab friends, but must refrain. Suffice it that I was entertained like a prince, and that I grew fond of my courtly host as I sincerely believe he grew of me. On parting he kissed me on both cheeks, called me brother, bent his forehead to the ground, and told me that his head was at my lifelong service; conjured Allah to see me back to my own roof-tree (ridge-pole he called it in Arabic), and placing his right hand first on his heart and then to his lips, bade me what I think was an honestly regretted farewell. We had become good friends, and I hope to welcome him some day at home—for Si Nassour ben El Hadj Salem, little travelled as he is, thinks of coming to America in this year of grace, on an errand too long to detail, but which proves both his enterprise and intelligence, and his care for his people's welfare.

I would have given much to get a picture of this caliph as he sat his fine Arabian. I can but give a distant approach to it, in the photograph of another man of that ilk.

As it happened, my friend had several good horses; but it does not follow because a man is an Arab and a caliph, and rich besides, that he has any at all—except for ordinary transportation or the use of his servants. He may prefer camels or asses. Some sheiks never leave the place where they hold sway, never move about, and need horses as little as a knowledge of Greek. My caliph, to tell the

truth, rarely rode; but he could ride and did know a good
horse.

One day the caliph asked me to sit beside him while
he held court. I did so, and was witness to a number of
Oriental scenes of strongly dramatic interest. The usual
litigants were at odds about land or money matters, but
the decision of the caliph, after a hearing, generally
about a half-hour long, seemed to be readily accepted—as
of course it had to be. The quiet, earnest attention and
final summing up of the caliph were in striking contrast to the voluble fervor of the applicants; I could
see whence came his very great influence.

One case was that of a father, whom his son, some
seventeen or eighteen years old, obstinately refused to
obey. The father besought the caliph to compel his son
to do his bidding, the son complained of his father's treatment. The father opened his case with apparent violence
(Oriental fury, however, often goes for naught), and the son
was equally angry, but sullen withal. The caliph had the
right to punish the son in any way, by imprisonment in
chains or stripes; but after listening attentively to all each
had to say, he held up his hand to end the evidence, and
everything in the room at once was still. His face was a
beautiful picture. He began in a low, sweet, but rapid
voice—all Orientals speak rapidly—dwelling on some of
the long vowels in a musical tone as delicious as Salvini's
Italian, and with an utterance which ran from a deep,
rich base to the high soprano, yet perfectly natural withal.
The son, I was told, had been extremely guilty, according
to Tunisian notions; but the caliph sought other means
than severity to accomplish his end. His words were
addressed alternately to father and son, and the effect
on each as he proceeded was marked. He spoke with
evident authority, and yet with a persuasive tone, which

at times was pleading, at times convincing. As he went on I could see the lad's face soften—a quiver flew at times across his mouth; as he had come in I thought him ill-looking—I found he was really a handsome lad.

The caliph went on, plainly telling the youth how he had failed in duty and common-sense alike, and explaining to him that where lay his filial piety there lay also his present and future happiness. I turned from one to the other, for each was a study of character of extreme interest. Not a word of all the judge said could I understand; but the tone was such as to yield the hearer its closest import. In a moment more came the climax. The lad had been swallowing his emotion in great gulps, and now, with an outburst of sobs, he broke into a flood of tears, threw his arms around his expectant father's neck, and wept audibly. Recovering himself he turned to the caliph, said a few low-spoken words, and waited for what more he had to say. Bidding him continue on his good resolution, the caliph waved an end to the matter, and father and son left the court-room with arms around each other's shoulders. I have rarely been witness to a more impressive scene, and the dignity, graceful diction, and beautiful voice of the caliph have lingered with me ever since.

But I am afraid that the title to this volume has been given amiss. It should have been "Yarns of a Globe-trotter, and, Incidentally, Horseflesh." I must strive to keep to my subject.

XLVIII

Horses must be averaged. It will not do to select the exceptional horse for description lest the reader fall into the assumption that all other horses resemble him, or, at least, that the majority do so. This is, indeed, not entirely an error. In the Orient all horses have some of the marks of Arabian blood. There is a singular beauty to some of the points of the Arabian which, even in the commonest stock, never gets quite lost. You rarely see a horse without one or more of these, and an odd specimen will now and then crop out among the lowly bred country horses which has all the points of some noble ancestor. Heredity is an obstreperous thing to deal with. In families which, ever so far back, have had some trace of negro blood, perhaps quite forgotten, it is said that a Guinea-black baby will occasionally turn up, to the great distress of all concerned and the suspicion of many.

Among the Arabs, barring the desert tribes, it is, as elsewhere, the rule that only swells have fine beasts. So it is with us; and after seeing many horses in many lands, I must give it as my opinion that the "Kentucky farmer" rides, on the average, a far finer, better trained, and abler horse than the Arab sheik. Moreover, there are — as I have before observed—more splendid specimens of horse-flesh on the breeding-farms of America than there are in any Oriental studs, quite apart from the greater size of our thorough-bred.

By-the-way, this same Kentucky farmer is an odd type

of soil toiler. He owns a fine old homestead (a country gentleman's "place" or "estate" in reality, but he calls it a "farm"), perhaps inherited for generations, and boasts acres as broad and beautiful as an English park. He gets into the saddle after a decidedly late breakfast for a farmer, rides around to visit his crops and the stock, gives a few directions to his headmen, and then canters off into—let us say Lexington, for a drink and a chat and billiards, or some other amusement with similar farmers, and God gives the increase. On work of the easiest the Kentucky Blue Grass farmer grows rich. Just think of the toil and moil of our poor New England farmers, your ancestors and mine, good friend, and for what? Well, for

TUNISIAN WITH TWO-YEAR-OLD BARB

the strength of loin, the unclouded brain, and the iron will which has begotten and bred the sturdiest, most intelligent, and most enterprising race the sun has ever shone upon! The New England farmer has raised men and women; as for crops—why, they are crop enough.

Some well-qualified judges maintain that the English thorough-bred, by generations of breeding exclusively for speed has lost bone and structural strength, and it is suggested that a cross with the old Arabian desert blood would be a benefit. It is true that the one-mile speed has grown relatively beyond the five, ten, or twenty mile speed; but this does not necessarily mean that the endurance of the thorough-bred has decreased. It takes—*teste* "Ten Broeck"—as much endurance, in a certain fashion, for a horse to run a mile in 1.39¾, as it does for him to run four miles in 7.15¾, the average of the latter per mile being 1.49; but to breed for short bursts of very high speed has perhaps a tendency to overdevelop the greyhound type. And no doubt there is a certain weediness in some families of racers. Be this as it may, it cannot be claimed that the Southern saddle-horse lacks bone. Many fine-bred ones are up to great weight, and most have large round barrels, and by no means too slender a skeleton. They are as nearly perfect as may be for saddle (not racing) speed, for carrying ability, and for gaits and endurance. The racer is quite another horse, but he, too, has more framework than his English cousin.

There are a number of points which must be granted to the Arabian. Eliminating the wretched little country horse, of small value because overworked and underfed, the average horse of good stock has excellent bone and an exceptionally well-built structure. The shoulder has a peculiarly fine slope; the back is very short above, and the line is very long below; the reach from top of rump to hough is extra long; the neck rises just as it should from the withers; the head is put on just right; the legs and feet cannot be criticised. The superlatives are purposely employed. Moreover, there is a certain ease and grace of movement that is essentially Arabian, which comes of a skeleton put together on good principles, and then well clad with muscle and sinew. On the other hand, while our long, lanky, bony, often somewhat ungainly performer lacks the Arabian's symmetry of looks and movement, he impresses you with the ability to run and repeat, to carry you through to the death, which even the best horse in the Orient does not convey. The fine Arabian is singularly handsome; there is no form of words which will explain the effect he has on the horse-lover who is attracted by the artistic as well as the "horsy" points. He unquestionably possesses grit and endurance, but I believe that in losing some of his grace we have gained in stamina in stock of equal grades, while our every-day teamster, coacher, and business horse can readily discount him by his superior weight; and this weight, while it may, coupled to our hard roads, be more trying to legs and feet, does not appear to have deteriorated the useful qualities of our animal.

The illustration shows the size of no end of colts in daily use in the East. This was a two-year old—we should call it a yearling from its looks, and weedy at that. Still the colt was able to do a good day's work; and though such a little creature may be much abused, his legs and feet will stand up under it in a marvellous manner, explicable only by the fact that his ancestors, for a thousand generations, have stood on the ground out-of-doors instead of in ammonia-soaked stalls. The rider appears tall; in truth, he was but about five feet eight. The colt was little above thirteen hands.

The term sheik in the Orient is about as universal as

19

A TUNISIAN SHEIK

cap'n or jedge in most country districts in our part of
the world, though military distinction is not colloquially
conferred on account of the number of chimneys a man's
house may have, as it is said to be south of Mason and
Dixon's line; there are few chimneys. The sheik before
us boasts no such architectural luxuries. But though he
may live in a hut of rushes and his women may do the
cooking *al fresco*, rain or shine, he is wont to own a good
horse. And he is a proud fellow, this penniless sheik;
proud of his religion, proud of his nationality, proud of his
lineage—almost as proud as he is of the lineage of his high-

bred mare, on the feats of whose forebears he will descant
by the hour and multiply by three the miles they may have
done between sun and sun. He is rarely separated from
his old flintlock, perhaps the most harmless fire-arm which
exists—to the enemy. He does nothing for a living except to loaf; his inherited dignity—for was not his great-
uncle a sheik before him?—forbids him to work. He
owns a few olive-trees, some little flocks and herds, an
ass, and a horse or two, his women cultivate a small gar-
den-patch and an acre or so of wheat; the prickly-pear
and date-palm are there at need; and if he can worry
through the distress of the few rainy weeks without soak-
ing into pulp, God's sunshine and fresh air are his for the
rest of the year. He is content with little to eat; generations of sparse food have robbed the poor Arab of any
semblance of gluttony; strong drink is prohibited by
the Koran, and, curiously, the injunction is wont to be
obeyed; but give him the long daylight for loafing, and
anything on four legs to carry him, and he is happy. He
little reeks what his wives and daughters are. They, poor
souls—stay! they have no souls according to his belief,
and may not even go into the mosque to pray. "Why
should they pray, forsooth, having no souls to pray for?"
he will ask you; they, poor creatures! live in the reflect-
ed happiness of their lord.

XLIX

When we cross the Libyan desert—which from its westerly limits is usually done by a prosaic Mediterranean trip back to Malta or Italy, and thence to Alexandria, rather than aboard a "ship of the desert," for it is easy to go around and all but impossible to go across this merciless waste—we come to a more marked type of the so-called Arabian than we find in either Morocco, Algeria, Tunis, or Tripoli. The first thing which strikes the horseman on reaching Egypt is the high-carried tail. The close-hugged tail which to such a degree disfigures the otherwise admirable mount on the west of the Libyan desert is here replaced by the fine upright haunch and high-set tail which we have so long admired in art. The whole bearing of the animal is altered by this single feature. One would scarcely credit the change. It is not the artificial tail of commerce, produced among civilized (?) nations at such a cost in pain and sacrifice in looks for the delectation of ultra-fashionables; it is the same fine tail you see bred for in Kentucky, set on a haunch which none but the Arabian can boast. The reason why the tail of the Spanish horse is carried so close is that he is of Moorish origin. It is, perhaps, impossible to determine the exact line of demarcation in race or breeding which separates the close-carried from the high-set tail, or to give the *rationale* of either; at the Libyan desert is the geographical line of separation. It suffices to call the horses on the west of the desert Barbs; those on the east Ara-

ARABIAN POLO-PONIES, CAIRO

bians. The so-called Godolphin Arabian, one of the
progenitors of the English thorough-bred, was really a
Barb, and his pictures show this low round croup and
tail. He could not have come from the Syrian desert.
The tail dates back many hundred equine generations.
In his day an "Arabian" or a "Turk" meant any Oriental horse.

A low-carried tail is sometimes climatic. I have been
told by horse-breeders on our Western plains that if for
two or three generations the horses have been compelled
to turn their backs to the winter blizzards and hug their
tails from cold the best of natural tails will droop. As
a rule, a severe climate produces a low tail, a hot climate
a high one. But this does not quite meet the case of the
Barb. Perhaps the Arabian sires which went originally
from the Syrian desert to the Barbary States were too few
to eradicate in the native race they impregnated the low
tail it had, and which most "horses of the country" have;
they were unable radically to change horses for which as
a race nothing had been done in the way of breeding,

and which during some months each year had been obliged
for centuries in the uplands or in the foot-hills of the Atlas
range to turn their tails to the chill blasts of the rainy
season.

The horse came into Egypt with the Hyksos, or Shepherd Kings, less than seventeen hundred years before our
era. Previous to that time asses were the only specimens
of the *genus equus*. No horse figures on the earlier mon-
uments of Egypt. The modern horse of Egypt is a different animal, of more recent importation, but also from
the Shepherd Kings of to-day, the pastoral princes of the
desert. This modern breed has a curiously uniform type.
You see them of all sizes, from the polo-pony to the heavy
wheeler, but the type remains. If mixed, the strong Arabian blood predominates in the look of the offspring. In
other countries horses vary both in size and type. You
have everything, from a Sheltie to a Percheron, each distinct in kind as well as size; there are several distinct
races. In Egypt the type is constant; there is but one
race. The head is small, the face intelligent and mild,
but not generally as fine and bony as one anticipates.
The perfect head is as rare as the perfect horse. The
neck is rather short and full in front, with good crest and
distinctly fine throttle; by no means as clean as the thorough-bred's, but much more neatly turned. The crest is
full, the withers low, but the shoulders sloping; the barrel
not quite as round as one would like, but well coupled to
a nearly perfect haunch. Looked at from front or rear,
the horse has not as much breadth as fills the eye, but one
sees far fewer weedy-looking horses than west of the
desert. The legs and feet are as good as can be. Even
the old broken-down hacks have no windgalls. Nor does
one often see a lame horse. Infinite stress is, among the
Arabs, laid on good legs. As the Arabian legs are uni-

ENGLISH OFFICER ON ARABIAN, CAIRO

formly good, whenever a horse shows blemishes or strains
in them he is considered unsafe to buy. With us a horse
with a few wind-puffs or a splint or two is by no means
to be condemned. The Arabians rarely interfere, but
often overreach when taught to trot, as they now are by
the English, or for the English by the Arabs. The foot is
neither too much like the mule's nor too flat. It is round,
rather high, and with naturally a good wide frog. That
horror of our climate, scratches, are not often seen in the
dry air of Egypt, but the practice of hobbling often scores
the fetlocks permanently. The shoe of the Arab horse in
Egypt is the plate with a small hole in the middle—a
bungling apology for a shoe. In Cairo the European shoe
is gaining in use; among the Arabs the old plate still prevails, but it is less bad than among the Syrian Bedouins.
The cut shows a very fair type of the average Arabian
bought by the English officers or residents in Cairo. For
his inches he is hard to beat. The officer's seat is just a
trifle long, but excellent. It is a hunting rather than a
military seat, bar toes.

The Arabian is unquestionably good as a goer; but in
a country where there is neither fence, hedge, ditch, nor
other division of the fields, we can scarcely expect a horse
to jump. There is, however, a leap recorded to have been
taken by one Ragh-Ap (*alias* Amin Bey) at the time of
the massacre of the Mamelukes, which in these days of
prize-jumping is certainly worth a notice, whether credited
or not. In order to escape from the massacre, this man
headed his Arabian for the edge of the cliff where now
stands the Citadel of Cairo. The noble animal never
paused, but conscious of his master's peril took the leap, a
most prodigious one, and landed—the fact is well authen-
ticated by the footprints in the stone shown by the pious
and horse-loving Moslem of to-day—eighty feet below,

and something over a quarter of a mile distant. What, after that, becomes of our paltry seven feet three of horse-show timbre?

By-the-way, speaking of the fenceless condition of the country, did it ever occur to you what a queerly shaped land Egypt is? Fancy a country one thousand miles long by scarcely ten miles wide. And yet this is the shape of agricultural Egypt from Cairo to the first cataract. The rest of the land is mere desert. The whole country is likened to an open lotus (the Delta) with a long stem and one single bud, the Fayum.

The Egyptian Arabian is fed on barley, beans, and clover-hay—which is sweet and abundant in the Nile region—or the green clover for the early two or three months of the year. The first growth is cut down and fed green; it is a sort of "spring medicine," our Hood's Sarsaparilla; the second is allowed to grow up for hay.

The average of the Arabian saddle-beasts here as elsewhere is undeniably high. The variety of type which we see in the well-bred saddle-horse at home cannot be found; but that the Arabian is serviceable and satisfactory as a mount is not to be questioned. His good-nature is uniform, his gaits are fair, and he can stay. I have heard it said by English people that you cannot run him as far and fast as a good hack at home; but this is, I take it, a matter of feed rather than endurance. The saddle-beast held by a saïs, or outrunner, is the type of a lighter kind of horse, not up to quite so much weight. And yet he will surprise you by his activity under two hundred pounds. But while, in the streets of Cairo, or on the Gezireh drive, one sees plenty of neat-turned saddle-beasts whose lines and action are very taking, it is rare that one is attracted by a "stunner"—by a horse all life, all action, all ambition. I have seen vastly more splendid

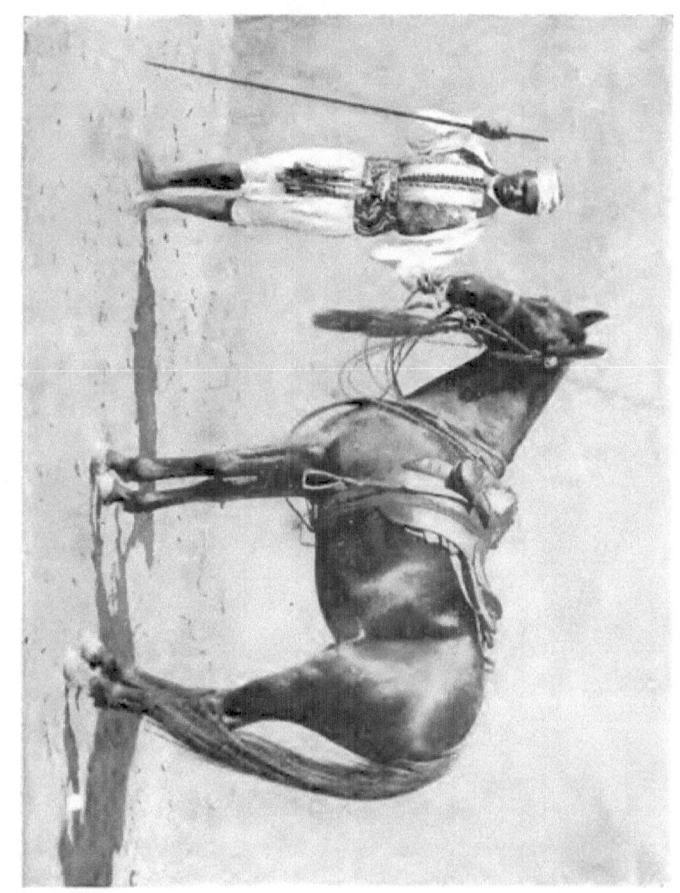

SAÏS HOLDING ARABIAN, CAIRO

saddle-beasts in Lexington than in Cairo, though the latter is a capital with a splendid court and a large garrison, and many times the size of the little Kentucky city. I have owned more than one horse who could, in gait, style, and all saddle qualities, outshine anything I have seen in the Orient. This sounds like boasting; but I do not intend to exaggerate. My "Jewell," when he was at his best, was not only as handsome as anything I have seen in the Orient, but he looked as if he had the pluck and ability to go over a house—an appearance which most Arabians lack. Relative endurance is hard to determine. Each class of horse has enough. One never sees the long, fine thorough-bred in Egypt. It is more of a chunk, with perfect legs and feet and all-round good points. The type of "Longfellow," "Ten Broeck," "Saunterer," "Fisherman" is never seen among the Arabians. The latter has stouter bone and more flesh, but less size, less accentuated points, less "do and die" look.

Stallions alone are in use—though the Bedouins prize their mares. One wonders what becomes of the mares. In Algeria and Tunis one sees them working in the fields; in Egypt one does not see them at all. As the habit of gelding is unknown—or has been until the English occupation, and is rare to-day—it is not convenient to work both sexes together; and though I have been told that the Libyan Arab prefers the horse, it is much more probable that the mares are kept for breeding and the stallions mostly sent to the cities for sale, as is the case in Syria. I found it so—at least, wherever I went. If a man wants to raise horses he must not sell his mares. And all nomad Arabs breed. No doubt if one went out among the breeders in Egypt he would find nothing but mares and an occasional stud.

The saddle is much less marked in its make-up than

west of the Libyan desert. It has but a slight pommel
and cantle, and it is by no means uncouth. Many of
them are less individual than the saddles on our plains. It
is evident that the Great Desert is a distinct boundary in
many matters equine.

L

AN Arab for his own use trains his horse to rack or amble, canter or gallop. He abhors the trot—which to him is the mark of the slavery of wheels. If a colt shows an inclination to trot, he hobbles him with a rope from his fore to his hind fetlock on either side, to force him to pace. But the Arab does not know the fast rack, or single-foot. The only people I am acquainted with who have developed the so-called artificial paces of the horse in a scientific way are our Southerners, though the Cretans have the gait beyond any other Orientals. In Kentucky a horse will often running-walk, rack, and trot perfectly, and of course canter and gallop, with a crisp performance of each gait. The Arabian has but an amble or a slow rack—never more than one of these gaits. When taught to trot, in which he never excels, his other gaits appear to be lost. I once examined a number of horses for sale in Cairo, averaging thirty to fifty pounds sterling each in value, which price would be the equivalent of four to six hundred dollars here. I was looked on as a *bona fide* purchaser, and the traders were very eager to sell me an animal. The horses were all led out, mounted, and, to my surprise, shown me on the trot. When I asked for a canter, or a rack, they stared at me as a *rara avis*. Here was a white man—a Frank—who did not want a trotter for the saddle! Allah be praised! But I also found that the training of each beast to trot had utterly ruined his other gaits. He was all mixed up. Even his trot was not

true, and he was uncertain in his rack or amble, and hard
to start into a canter. It would be a ticklish thing to bring
him back to his fine saddle paces. All those that I saw
and tried were what you might call a very likely-looking
but poor lot of a good type. For the saddle each was
spoiled—except to sell to an Englishman, or to some
imitator of the English style. And of these Cairo to-day is
full. The Arab or Turkish swells who are thrown in with
the English have taken to their ways. The native official
will ride his horse on an overreaching trot which makes
one's teeth grit, when if left to his natural gaits the horse
would move as smoothly as a meadow brook.

It is common to use the term "artificial gaits" in referring to the running-walk or rack. I have employed
it because it is generally understood. A new word ought
to be coined. Suppose we say Southern gaits. It is
absurd to talk of artificial gaits when, as I have before
pointed out, nine-tenths of all animals belonging to the
horse tribe in the world thus travel, and that without
training. The rack was understood generations ago in
England. One of the earliest writers on the horse, old
Blundeville to wit, speaks of the Spanish jennet, of which
there were many brought to England especially for ladies'
use, as going "neither trot nor amble, but a comelie kind
of going like the Turke" (Arab)—*i.e.*, as going something midway between trot and amble, either a rack or
a running-walk. It is more natural for a horse to rack
than to trot. Don't smile. This dictum is sound. I am
referring, of course, solely to saddle-beasts. When one
puts a load after a horse the trot is no doubt a better
gait, but it has to come by training or inheritance.
The wild horse everywhere gallops, or slows down into
what we call a canter, which is, however, not the real
canter, but a short, broken gallop. The park canter is

quite another thing. A wild horse may now and then jog—*i.e.*, go a short trot; but he will be quite as apt to pace, and if he is slowing down from a gallop to a walk he is much more apt to rack, because the rack is more nearly intermediate, in the sequence of feet, between gallop and walk than is the trot. This fact is not generally known, because most people do not recognize a rack when they see it.

I refrain for the moment from going into the technicalities of the sequence of the horse's feet in the various gaits; but if any one will study this thing from practice and from instantaneous photography, he will see that the true trot is less allied to the one gait every one acknowledges to be natural—the gallop—than the rack.

As I said, for drawing loads the trot is the thing, because a horse is using two feet at a time, and is by so much stronger; but if you want the neat, quick, crisp action which alone makes the highest saddle qualities, you call for a style of going to which the rack is naturally adapted, while the trot is not. A single illustration will serve to show my point. If you are cantering at a good rate along the highway and want to slacken speed—as to allow a carriage to pass across your path, or for any other purpose—you cannot pull down to a trot and start into a canter again without a distinct interruption of gaits—a bumping, to be plain about it. But you can pull down to a rack, and bound out again into a canter, without the slightest perceptible change of the horse's rhythmic movement. Or, again, if from a lively canter you pull down to a walk *through a trot*, you have a certain amount of bumping while the horse is jogging; but if you teach your nag to come back to a walk through a rack—*i.e.*, from canter to rack, and from rack to walk, you have not the remotest

20

semblance of irregularity. No argument is needed to show
why; the gaits themselves prove the case.

I maintain that the rack—or, to employ our new coinage—all Southern gaits are natural. You will pardon my
recurrence to this subject, but it is a part of my text, you
see, and I like to ring the changes on it. When one is in
the pulpit, he has the right, I believe, to go back to his
text, even at the risk of occasional repetitions. You will
find that I only partially repeat myself, and I propose
that no equine sinner shall remain immersed in his iniqui-
ty for lack of proper instruction. I say the rack is natural. Every donkey in the East, and in all European countries where he is used, racks as a matter of course; so does
every horse that is ridden in the Orient—a fact I have already pointed out. You may say that this does not prove
the case. Strike, but listen!

No one will deny that the walk is the first of the natural gaits. Now, if you take a young horse, who does not
come of strict trotting ancestry, and has not been broken
to harness, and after training him to a light, elastic, fast
walk, will push him on to a sharper gait, he will not fall
into a jog-trot; he will amble or rack. If you let him go
a careless, humdrum, snaffle-bridle gait, unworthy of a
saddle-beast, he may perhaps fall into a jog; but that is
not my point; I am talking of a well-poised horse, not a
wheeler. Again, even if your horse is on a jog-trot, if
you will use whip or spur to unsettle him, and at the
same time not allow him head enough to gallop, he will
fall into an amble or rack. Even a horse trotting in harness, if frightened, or struck with the whip, or jerked up
with the reins, will fall into a rack. Why, then, is the
rack artificial? It will not do to call it so. If the English made as good saddle-beasts as they make hunters or
racers, we might subscribe to their opinion, and allow the

rack to be called artificial.   But the truth is that, all over
the world, riders who excel in pure saddle-work not specially diverted to some one object—as hunting is to galloping and jumping obstacles, or racing to pure speed—but
with whom the mere riding for business or pleasure is the
object, and who aim at the greatest ease, handiness, and
ability in their horses, employ the amble or rack as the prin-
cipal gait, the canter next.   Unquestionably, *quoad* the
saddle-horse, the rack must be called natural, the trot the
artificial gait.   If I die before I have converted the world
to this my opinion, let it be written on my tombstone—
but that is another story.

LI

To prose for a paragraph on the technical part of the case. You may skip this if you like; it is technical, not chatty. But if you will study it out it will repay you. The gaits of the horse are:

1. The simple walk, in which to the eye one hind-foot moves out first, followed by the alternate fore-foot; then the other hind-foot followed by its alternate, not at exactly equal intervals. If you listen to a walking-horse's hoof-beats, you will find the four beats to be rather in sets of twos. This gait varies from two and a half to four and a half miles an hour, and gives a very slight forward and back swaying to the saddle.

2. The running-walk. The sequence of the steps in this is the same as in the simple walk, but the horse has a brisker, more elastic motion, and appears to put more life into his gait; each foot is put down and taken up quicker; he will go up to five and a half or six miles an hour on it, and the saddle has a slight up and down, but very easy, feel to it.

3. The amble, which is a slow pace, in which the feet on the near side come down exactly together, followed by those on the off side at equal intervals. The saddle feels very easy, with a slight swaying motion from side to side.

4. The trot, in which the diagonal feet come down exactly together—i.e., the near fore and off hind, and the off fore and near hind at equal intervals. When slow, this is

a jog; when fast, a flying trot. They only differ in degree; but on the flying trot the horse is propelled so vigorously that between steps he is sometimes in the air, while in the jog and slow trot one set of feet is always on the ground. The feel of the saddle is a bump up and down, to avoid which on a five-mile trot and upwards one rises to each alternate step. On a jog you cannot rise; to a very rapid trot one need not always do so. Owing to a difference in conformation or strength of the hind-legs, some horses are easier when you rise to one rather than the other leg.

5. The pace, which is a fast amble. When at speed at a pace, as in the flying trot, the horse is often in the air between steps. The feel of the saddle is sometimes a bump, sometimes a sway from side to side, differing in individuals.

6. The rack, which is a gait half-way between the trot and pace. Here the feet follow each other at half intervals, each one coming down separately. In the trot and pace the hoof-beats sound "one, two! one, two!" In the rack they sound "one, two, three, four! one, two, three, four!" in the same length of time—four beats instead of two for the same speed, each hind-foot following its fore-foot at a half interval, instead of coming down with it. The saddle is perfectly quiet under you; the gait is the very poetry of comfort. Speed, six to fifteen miles an hour; or, as a rarity, a three-minute gait.

7. The canter is an irregular gait, by most people described as a slow gallop; but it has, mechanically speaking, not much in common with the latter gait. An Englishman will describe his thorough-bred as cantering twelve miles an hour, but he is really going a three-beat, or hand-gallop. If you call a five or six mile gait a canter you cannot call a twelve-mile gait a canter, for the progression of the animal is mechanically different. I am not seeking

a quarrel with the nomenclature, for in many places a canter is called a " lope," and a running-walk a " run," or a fast rack a " single-foot." Localized epithets always exist. What I mean is that the slow and fast gaits are not alike, and should have different names; and "canter" has for ages been applied to the slower gait. I am inclined to wander a bit here, but—

Well, the " canter " (which is of Canterbury origin, and perchance the " Wel nyne-and-twenty in a companye " fell into a canter at the end of each tale) is a gait much more "artificial" than the rack. The gallop is natural. The canter proper must be produced by training in every individual. A horse will naturally fall to racking; he never will fall into a canter untaught—fresh proof that the slur on Southern gaits is incorrect. The " Kentucky wriggle " is a pure gait.

The canter is produced by reining a horse back from a three-beat gallop. Individuals differ much, and the same horse differs often in the performance of the canter. But every one who has ridden it remembers the feel as of a sort of pause at one period of the stride. Well, at that moment three feet are on the ground, say, if leading with the right shoulder, the off hind, and the near and off fore-feet, while the near hind one has just left it. The off fore-foot is the last to come down, and is thrown forward where you can see it over the horse's shoulder; and because its action is more pronounced than that of the other feet, the horse is said to be leading with that foot. This hoof-beat is the very pronounced *three* of the " one, two, *three!* " sound of the canter. Just before the time this leading-off fore-foot comes down, the near hind-foot goes up; then the off hind and near fore, quite or nearly together; and then from the leading-off fore-foot the horse goes into the air, and you feel the rise in the gait. This is followed by the near hind-foot coming down, again to be followed by the off hind and near fore feet, which completes the stride to our beginning. Many photographs of cantering horses do not look like a canter at all. The most common one shows all but the leading foot on the ground at the same moment.

8. The three-beat, or hand-gallop, in which the hoof-beats sound "one, two, three, pause; one, two, three, pause." Assuming the horse to lead with the off shoulder, the *one* is from the near hind-foot, the *two* from the off hind and near fore, which come down together, and the *three* from the off fore-foot. But the gait is too rapid for the horse ever to be at any one time on three legs; hence the difference from the canter.

9. The run, or four-beat gallop. This sounds like " one, two, three, four, pause; one, two, three, four, pause." When the pause occurs the horse is in the air at the end of his stride and is gathering all his legs under him for the next one. His four legs come down exactly like four spokes of a wheel; but as there is not, after the four spokes have done their work, a continuous succession of spokes to sustain the weight of the body and propel it, the horse pauses from leg action and gathers them under him for four new propulsions, or rather has been gradually doing so with each leg after it has completed its *quasi* spoke-work. The hoof-beats, after the pause, come (if the right shoulder be leading) near hind, off hind, near fore, off fore, at exactly equal intervals; then, during the next pause, the horse, which has risen into the air from his off fore-foot, reaches out his near hind-foot and puts it to the ground for a new stride. Nothing so well describes his action as four spokes of a wheel. If you think a moment, you will see that the horse *must* first plant the hind-foot, or rear-most spoke, and *must* end with the fore, or foremost spoke.

By-the-way, talking of nomenclature, did you ever reflect, after you and your best friend had been at loggerheads for an hour or two over some political or social or theological or personal problem, and had been about ready to order pistols for two and coffee for one, that, after all, you were of the same opinion, but that you had been misunderstanding each other's terms and thus misinterpreting each other's ideas; in other words, that when he said A and you said X, you really meant the same thing, but had a different term to describe it? Unless you have both been taught in the same school, you must first sit down and find out what you mean by the phrases or words you use, before you know whether you have anything to discuss or not.

LII

LET us again, for a moment, leave the proud horse of the desert, the favorite of the sheik, the pampered but noble companion of the Arab, and turn to his patient, pathetic cousin, the ass. Oh for the pen of a ready writer to draw up an eulogium on this humble martyr! What panegyric shall do him justice? There is nothing of his breed—there is no animal in the service of man—that so nearly personifies the cardinal virtues. He has positively but one weakness, and that is a failure to understand music as we do. He cannot sing to the contentment of our classical ear. But, despite even this, the more I see of the ass the more sincere is my respect for him. I would fain erect an altar to him and burn incense at his shrine. He may not bear his master company to an equal sky, but surely he deserves a heaven of his own. Why, when he does such uncomplaining, never-ending work, impious man should not hold him at his true value it is hard to conceive. His toil is remunerated with the meanest food; his truly heroic efforts are rewarded by a constant shower of blows, by a constant call for greater effort. In Egypt a camel-load of green clover—a quarter-ton—sells for almost a dollar of our money; a donkey-load for forty cents; and the camel weighs five or six times as much as the donkey. In other words, the "marvellous" camel bears but one-third his own weight, the donkey four-fifths of his. If you overload the camel he will growl his protest; he will refuse to rise. Whoever heard of the ass re-

fusing the heaviest of burdens, even twice in proportion
that of the camel? To whom shall we award the palm?
Unreasoning master, it is thine own turgid soul that is
burdened with the vices thou imputest to thy humble, dili-
gent, uncomplaining servant! Talk not of thy Ten Com-
mandments, miserable man! Thy ass heedeth thy law as
thou never obeyest the Decalogue!

Every one remembers the curious, protesting cry of the
ass-driver in Italy. Its tone—"Āāh !"—is a constant reproach: "Do, for Heaven's sake, go faster, you poky, lazy
beast !" when the brave little fellow is struggling on with
a load under which no other animal God ever made could
possibly stagger. That for ages untold the ass has been
thus under the ban is oddly shown in the tomb of Tï, in
ancient Memphis. In one of the queer but curiously natural processions of the servants of Tï, which are cut on
the walls of the funeral chamber, is a man with uplifted
stick driving a donkey. The hieroglyphs make him say,
no doubt with the same protesting tone : " Men love those
who go swiftly, but they beat the lazy ; *if* thou couldst
but see thine own conduct !" The tone of the modern
Egyptian is, however, not so protesting as that of the
Italian, though he has the same cry, "Āāh !" to hurry on
his beast. One now and then hears our cluck in lieu of
the " Ā-āh !"

It is truly a marvel how this tiny creature can perform
such labor. I have studied him carefully. It is well
known that a man can outlast, outwork, and outcarry a
horse. But the ass can do more than man, the most enduring of living creatures. He is able to carry his own
weight and work all day. What man can stagger an
hour under from one hundred and fifty to two hundred
pounds?

They have some queer habits with the donkeys in Egypt.

EGYPTIAN WOMAN'S STYLE

One who trespasses on a neighbor's land—in innocent search of his natural food, poor fellow!—is dubbed a thief, and has a piece of his ear snipped off for each offence. Being hobbled when "at liberty"—by tying the fore-legs together—the donkey cannot go far, and luckily for him is not often proven guilty. The so-called thief would else soon have no ears to clip. To quote a pretty custom as a foil to this cruel one: the ass-colts have ribbons tied around their legs above the knees and hocks, and I have seen them with ears bored at the tips and tied together—as if to cultivate a habit of carrying them erect. An ass-colt is one of the prettiest of creatures.

Place aux dames! While on the subject of the patient ass, we may glance at one of his constant patrons, perhaps the most peculiar rider that exists—the Arab woman. No such curious seat can be found elsewhere. The donkey-saddle of the East has no cantle whatsoever, but in Egypt a pommel—high, round, and full. The seat is so short that unless you use very long stirrups only a part of your riding surface rests on the saddle; the balance hangs over the rear of the tree where the cantle should properly be. It is a most uncomfortable seat for a big man, who must overhang a good deal. For a small man it will do. The Egyptian female uses the man's rig and sits astraddle; but she does not ride with her legs hanging down; this would not suit her ideas of propriety, though her Syrian cousin does not agree with her in this, but rides exactly like a man. Our Egyptian rider shortens her stirrups until the leathers are but a couple of inches long, mounts from a block, sits on the saddle as far forward as she can, throws her feet to the rear so that they are right under her thighs, and rides solely by balance. Her knees are on either side of the padded pommel, and she might well get some kind of a hold on it; but she attempts nothing but a balance seat, and her knees wobble in and out as she progresses along the street in charge of her black attendant. She is a sight to behold, and unquestionably the oddest Amazon there is. She cannot properly be said to have any seat at all; but as the ass never shies or acts otherwise than as should a well-behaved little fellow to whose care is confided so precious a burden, and as his gait—a rack or amble—is ease itself, the lady's seat on her saddle is secure enough. Under the saddle is an indefinite array of blankets, which raise her far above his back.

I desire to suggest to those of our lady friends who wish to startle the community, and to grasp such additional public attention as their natural charms do not entice, that in lieu of riding *à la militaire*, they adopt the Egyptian lady's seat. That such a rider would be the cynosure of neighboring eyes cannot for a moment be doubted. But I should not like to insure her a long *promenade*.

Her Egyptian ladyship's little mount is often clipped in fancy patterns all over his body. Around the hind-legs, just above the hocks, are bands of zigzags alternating with straight lines; on the buttocks are various neat devices produced by the scissors. Around the neck hang some chains of brass or gilt coins, or blue and yellow beads, and the bit has a row of jangling rings—all of which make merry music to the fair one's progress. This seems appropriate enough. But when you see a selfish Moslem comfortably bestriding his ass, while his pretty, young, only half-veiled wife trudges in the mud behind him, with much ado keeping up with the donkey's rapid gait, one wonders which is the brute of the twain who go in front. The four-footed one would never be so selfish.

LIII

THE Arab donkey-boys are not often cruel to their little charges, or, at least, cruelty has been much checked. There has been a considerable change for the better in Egypt since the English have been in the land. The soldiers of the English garrisons have been forbidden to ride any donkey which shows signs of ill-treatment or saddle-galls, and the effect has been astonishing. Even the Arab can catch the true commercial idea up to a certain point. They are wonderful barterers, these Arabs, but they have not, as a rule, a very clear conception of what commerce means. So with all semi-civilized peoples. In Mexico, once, at Guadalajara, I think, where we could buy a dozen oranges for about five cents, the caterer of our dining-car was unable to buy two hundred dozen at any reduction whatever; the people did not understand wholesale dealings, though oranges were rotting by the cart-load. Nor would they sell him more than a certain amount of mutton at a time, though they had flocks in abundance, nor at any discount from the price demanded by the pound. They failed to see the difference between wholesale and retail. The Arab is much like this. He will haggle over the price of a carpet for days, and beat you out and out; but he is a poor business-man, after all. Still, he soon saw his profit in treating his donkey well, when he could not let him if he looked neglected. The city asses are in good condition (in Cairo there are many fine ones), and it seems to me that the instinct of cruelty

is less marked in Africa than in Southern Europe. The
Oriental is indolent even in his neglect or abuse, and he is
better-natured.   On the Bulak bridge, one day, I saw an
Arab brushed off his donkey by the load of a passing
camel.   He fell into deep mud, and with an aggravating
thump.   An Italian or a Spaniard would have got up and
instantly taken to beating the donkey, though it was in
nowise the little fellow's fault.   But the Arab merely
pulled himself together, expended a voluble Arabic ob-
jurgation on the owner of the camel, mounted his ass, and
went on with a laugh.   I longed for a phonograph ; the
rattle of the words was so catching.

The donkey-boys have one habit, however, which is
thoroughly bad.   Whenever the donkey is not at work his
head is tied back to the saddle, and is kept there hours at a
time.   The result is that the poor little fellow bores upon
the tight rein, and suffers acutely from the unchanging
pressure on the mouth.   If he can get near a wall or a
tree, he will lean his poor nose hard against it as a relief
to the cruel pain.   It is said that the practice is necessary
to keep him and the others about him from going on a
stampede, especially near water ; but the thing is overdone.   Hobbling would be equally easy and more effective.   All donkeys have hard mouths as a consequence of
this habit.   You can ride them on a loose rein, but if he
were determined to go you could not pull one up with a
windlass.

I once had a really narrow escape with a hard-mouthed
ass.   I was riding on the side of the hill which, opposite
Jerusalem, makes one slope of the valley of Kedron, near
the village of Siloah.   The hill is as steep as the roof of
a house, and is formed of huge masses of protruding
rock and gigantic bowlders, on and against which the village is built.   So marked is the rocky nature of the hill-

TIRED DONKEY-BOY

side that from the other side of the valley, half a mile
away, you can scarcely see that there is a village nestling
in the rocks. Well, my son on foot, and I on an ass,
followed by the usual ass-driver, were winding our way
among and around the rocks and bowlders, along tortuous
foot-paths so narrow that my knees were being constantly
excoriated though the ass kept the middle of the path.
when, to my disgust, Mr. Jack lifted his nose and his
voice in a " he-haw " of delight, and began to gambol forward ; and, to my horror, I perceived ahead of us, on a
lower path, to which a sane goat would hardly have ventured to seek its way, so rugged was the ground, the
Jenny who had moved my mount to such unusual excitement. Before I could gather the reins—for I had been
letting the imperturbable and surefooted little Jack take
his own course—the villain was on a gallop towards his
Delilah. I tried to pull him up; I sawed his mouth, I
jerked, I strove ; as well pull on a hitching-post. I re-
alized my situation at once. There was no danger of
Jack's going down—an ass will clamber up or jump down
unheard-of obstacles — but the question was whether I
should not get brushed off, or the ill-girthed saddle turn in
this novel race. On we went, and on started Jenny, as if
it were royal sport. My stupid ass-driver, with a pious
but unhelpful "Allah !" sat him down to watch the event.
His only stake was a little backsheesh which he would
forfeit if I was shot down the precipice to the Kedron,
three hundred feet below. My son unluckily was behind,
and could not get past us on the narrow pathway so as to
seize Jack by the head. With a clear road he could safely
have outstripped the ass, for the pace was not fast ; but I
never rode so determined a creature. I have repeatedly
been run away with by horses, but I never felt such an
absolutely cast-iron mouth. Finally, Jack reached Jenny,

and I flattered myself that I could pull him up. Not so;
on went Jenny, on followed Jack, "he-hawing" with horrible persistence. Up went Jenny's heels, smartly cuffing
Jack's nose and chest; but this was mere play. Jack
kept biting at her rump, and she let fly her heels at every
alternate stride. All my efforts were now pointed at
avoiding these kicks, which several times struck my stirrup and my stirrup-leather, luckily a broad one, and Jenny
was unshod. I have since childhood felt an ambition to
visit the brook Kedron; but it now looked as if my ambition were to be all too summarily gratified. My son
was posting on behind; he could at any time have seized
Jack by the tail, but his tail was presumably almost as
tough as his mouth. Finally, the ass-driver's appeal to
Allah prevailed. By a bold scramble up a rock and a
ten-foot jump on the other side, my son headed off Master
Jack, whom Miss Jenny's dalliance had for an instant
delayed, and, by a smart blow across his face and a grab
at the reins, helped me stop the brute and drive off his
temptress. Why Jack's jaw did not break with my jerks
or the severe curb he had I cannot explain, all I know
is that I was powerless. Give me a frightened horse
every time rather than an amorous Jack. On a broad
highway it would have been fun; but any one who has
ever clambered up to Siloah will understand the uncer-
tainties of the case during this far from interesting race.
Finally, as a wind-up, the ass-driver reached us and—amazing to relate, but comprehensible to all who have seen
him in his native haunts—actually extended his hand for
backsheesh; no doubt fervently believing that his cry
to Allah had saved me rather than my son's breakneck
jump.

The loads the little ass bears are often as peculiar as
they are heavy. I have seen him carrying a bulky load

of cane which trailed along the ground on either side and
behind him. The butts protruded beyond his head, so
that only from the front could you perceive the motive
power of the curious mass. From the side naught was to
be seen but an occasional ear thrust out from the
moving bulk; the rest of the donkey was lost. About
dark, one day near the Damascus gate at Jerusalem, I saw
a still more curious one. While musing on the mutability
of human, the degradation of Semitic affairs, and seeking to decide the pros and cons of Gordon's New Calvary,
a donkey suddenly appeared to me, coming from the
slaughtering ground opposite the Mount of Olives, laden
with fresh sheep-hides, wool side out. The little beast had
but his head protruding from the quivering, bloody mass;
you could just catch sight of his pattering feet. In the
gloaming he was actually a startling creature, and all but
gave me a tumble from the wall on which I sat. Even
Cuvier, father of naturalists, could scarce have classified
and might properly have fled from him as a truly supernat-
ural entity—though, indeed, Cuvier is credited with once
readily classifying the devil. It was thus: His pupils, in-
credulous as to their master's alleged contempt of his
Satanic Majesty, had dressed up one of their number as
like him as they could, had phosphorus-streaked and armed
him with the proper sheol pitchfork and other properties,
and had sent him into the philosopher's garden one night to
scare him. " Who are you ?" quoth Cuvier, as the appari-
tion leaped out from behind a bush. " I'm the devil and
I've come to eat you !" howled the fiend, with a dreadful
stage-caper. Startled for an instant, Cuvier quickly re-
covered himself, and contemptuously looking the *soi disant*
devil over from head to foot : " Horns, tail, hoofs—grami-
nivorous; you can't do it !" said he, and turned upon his
heel. Unlike Cuvier, with me it became a perceptible case

of demoralization before I classified my strange intruder. My musing had prevented my noticing the unmistakable sound of his gait.

Why the above should suggest it, I wot not ; but here is a terse and characteristic Arab proverb, which I pray you to read, learn, mark, and inwardly digest.

" Mankind is of four classes :

" He who knows not, and knows not that he knows not, is a fool.   Shun him.

" He who knows not, and knows that he knows not, is simple.   Teach him.

" He who knows, and knows not that he knows, is asleep. Wake him.

" He who knows, and knows that he knows, is wise. Follow him."

LIV

"SPEAK, ye that ride on white asses, ye that sit in judgment and walk by the way," sang Deborah of old; and to-day the white ass bred by the sheiks of the desert is a noble animal and highly prized. Such a one is shown in the illustration. The rider of such an animal might well sit in judgment, though to walk by the way is not often the habit of the dignified Arab of our times. He will let his wife walk, he himself prefers the comfort of a horse or ass; and the latter is not infrequently chosen as the better mount. The white ass of high quality commands, as asses go, a long price; and for comfort on a journey is almost unequalled—for speed unexcelled. On rough ground he is more surefooted than any horse, and a very goat for climbing. The specimen illustrated shows signs of knees roughened by kneeling down in stony places, and the marks of hobbling on his fore fetlocks. Many are better cared for and have no such blemishes. But, as a rule, all asses show scored knees, not from falling, but from lying down where the ground is rough. There are asses which are not surefooted—generally from age or overwork—but the ass is wont to be so.

Perhaps as wonderful as the donkey, almost, is the donkey-boy. He always accompanies his fare—you have to give him unusual backsheesh to induce him to remain behind; and however fast the donkey goes, the boy is always up. In fact, he tries to hurry the donkey all he can, the sooner to finger his backsheesh. He trots along, carries

a bundle of clover for the donkey, the bundles of his rider.
and sundry other things, and seems to care naught for distance or speed.   He has no particular style of going, but
he gets there.   He often breathes hard, but seems to mind
it not a whit.   The farthest on a stretch I ever rode a
donkey at a sharp gait was to the Pyramids from Cairo,
eight good miles.   This distance in an hour and a quarter
was child's play to the lad, who had wind enough to keep
after his donkey in both senses; and on the way home
was yet more lively.   I have often wondered whether
they live long or not; you see them unnumbered years
old; but were these old men ever real donkey-*boys?*   It is
no sin to prevaricate to a dog of a Christian; so that the
old man's assurance that he has worked at the trade for
anywhere from fifty to eighty years goes for nothing.

Another great footman is the saïs, or outrunner.   This
man is often the finest type of a running animal.   He is
clad in purple and fine linen.   His nether garments are of
light thin white goods, loose and gathered at the knee,
and so made as not to hamper his movements.   He wears
a shirt often trimmed with the finest laces; a sleeveless
zouave jacket of velvet, fairly glistening with gold embroidery, covers his body, and a gorgeous sash binds his
waist.   He wears a snug fancy fez-like embroidered cap,
or sometimes a light turban.   In this gay and costly dress
he precedes his master's carriage, ostensibly to make room
through the crowd, really for show; and on the road will
run at a seven or eight mile an hour gait as long as the
horses.   Two saïs running together is the proper thing
for a swell; but the carriage to our eye is not always as
neatly turned as the saïs.

The Arabs are a light, lithe, strong, and nimble race, as
well as handsome beyond cavil.   They have many fine
physical qualities.   The Arab's feet are wont to be large,

but that is because he walks barefoot; his hands are often made coarse by labor and neglect; but his joints are neatly turned, and his bone is small and dense; his muscular structure, while lacking the fulness of fatter nations, gives him considerable strength, and he has rather exceptional endurance. The same climate which produced the Arabian horse has produced the Arabian runner. He lives under skies where simple food and little of it will keep the human animal in good health and strong. He has to eat purely for alimentation; he does not raise enough to enable him to overeat; his stomach remains in better condition, and if reduced to slender rations he does not so soon become a starveling.

LV

THE saddles in Egypt have no special type, though all partake of the general Oriental features. You see everything from a donkey's to an English saddle on the horses. One common type has the sitting-place round like the outside of a huge water-pipe. From the front projects an upright two-inch square perpendicular piece to serve as pommel; the high and slanting cantle is scooped out much after the fashion of a giant oyster-shell. The flaps are long and square, and the stirrups hang inside them. In the country well up the Nile the saddle-tree is simple, the bearings made much like those of the old-type Indian, but with a pommel and cantle less prominent than even a McClellan. The two bearing-pieces are whittled out crudely, and shrunk in place by covering the whole with rawhide, leaving the saddle open down the back, like a very illy-made, unfinished Whitman tree. Under it goes a folded blanket; over it no end of rugs, all in picturesque·disarray. The stirrup-leathers are hung well forward, and the girth is kept so loose that it is often fastened only by a packthread. I have not seen a single well-girthed horse in Egypt ridden by a native. To us, who believe in keeping a saddle in place and then sticking to it, this seems odd; but the natives do not appear to heed the matter, and their saddles do not slip, even in violent turns and twists. The bit is, of course, a gag, and the trappings are as gaudy as they are apt to be dirty and rotten.

I have often wondered at this insecure girthing, but the secret seems to lie in the man's holding on bodily with his heels just below the semicircle of the horse's barrel. As you could not pull off from a cylinder a steel rod bent around it, and open less than a semicircle, so, if his muscles are rigid enough to keep his heels well pinned into the steed's flanks, will the Arab remain firmly fixed in place, girths or no girths. He does no more than half of the rest of us, who often wear dulled spurs so as more conveniently to hold on, or who else bring our horse in with bloody flanks when we have not consciously used our persuaders at all.

There is a good deal in the nice balance of horsemanship, and a strong grip will often hold the saddle in place. One day, many years ago, I was being shown the paces of a famous stallion at Mount Sterling, Kentucky. Just as the rider started out his one girth broke; but far from stopping, he only bent down, seized the dangling girth, threw it across the horse's withers and went on quite unconcernedly, showing the fine gait of his mount to perfect advantage, and keeping his saddle in place merely by grip and balance.

The lack of the graceful burnoose makes the Egyptian Arab a less attractive horseman than his kin of Algeria and Tunis. But I have seen some very neat-turned horses in Upper Egypt. I remember in particular a fine four-year-old I saw ridden by an Arab at Belianeh. I was prosaically plodding along on my donkey towards the temple, at Abydos, of old Seti of blessed artistic memory, when I ran across this man. A friendly nod, an approving glance at his handsome iron-gray, and a couple of cigarettes, quickly induced him to exhibit his horse at his best. He was almost the only Arabian I have seen whose head was properly in hand, who was well-gathered,

and who did not constantly throw up his nose. The colt
could piaffer, gallop in place, traverse and pirouette very
handily, and possessed the highest grace. His owner had
a light hand and a fine seat, and seemed very fond and
proud of his mount. I talked with him in signs sufficiently for him to see that I understood what he was
doing, and he seemed equally surprised and glad to find a
Frank who did so. After a few moments I managed to
make him understand by signs what I wanted him to
have his horse do; and for a mile or two my companions
and I enjoyed a real treat. I think, however, that I had
the best of it, as they were admiring the rhythmic movements of the steed, and I was appreciative of both these
and his own and his master's intelligence. But the performance was only individual cleverness; there was apparently no teachable method in it. Some things were
manifestly done the wrong way, and at times it was the
good spirits and light feet of his Arabian which were in-
ducing the performance rather than the indication given
by the rider.

We must not leave Egypt without a glance at one of
the camel-riders. The stories about the performances of
camels are conflicting. I can vouch for some of the crack
performances of horses; I can only quote what I hear
about camels. There is, both in looks and action, as much
difference between a running and a porter camel as between a cart-horse and a thorough-bred. The porter-
camel is a thorough *lourdeau*. His body is a misshapen,
bulky mass; his hair is coarse; his limbs are big-boned
and awkwardly turned; his neck is more ungainly than
need be; his head unintelligent or vicious, though often
patient or pathetic. If aged, his under-lip hangs down
and flops in a most distressing manner. He is strong and
able, and it is from this that proceeds his endurance, for

CAMEL-RIDERS ON THE DESERT

he lacks grit, and if overloaded will sullenly refuse to rise.
The running-camel, on the other hand, shows blood in
every point. Though the outlines of the camel cannot
be said to be attractive, this creature, if you examine him,
has precisely the same points as a greyhound or a racer.
A fine, bony head, full nostril and throttle, no extra meat,
enormous thorax, which girths even bigger than the porter's, slender abdomen, almost suggesting a lack of muscle in the loins, fine shapely limbs, with shin-bones and
sinews as clean cut as a two-year-old in training; higher-
standing feet, but with greater power to spread, so as to
get a proper footing on the sand; and, above all, a look of
gentleness and yet courage, which is unmistakable in all
high-bred mammals. His saddle qualities correspond to
his physical. To ride a porter-camel is a task requiring
as much stomach as to fish for cod in a ground-swell.
To ride a runner is, when you learn the trick, not disagreeable, but, like riding a horse, the trick must be learned. The camel-riders have a way of putting on a sort of
overhead check, and attaching it to the runner's nose-ring,
which shortens his gait down into a comparatively easy
amble. As to speed and endurance I can testify solely
from hearsay. The specimens illustrated are from Upper
Egypt. You can plainly see the running animal.

I have sought no special opportunities of testing camels
on long journeys. My taste does not lie that way. My
riding of camels has been Philistinic, not professional.
But in lands where all your food comes in to market
a-camel-back; where, whenever you go out riding or driving, you must make way for, or at least give half the road
to, a string of a dozen or twenty camels every half mile;
where these beasts are the railroad, the steamboat, and
almost the electric cars — hold, it is our little friend, the
ass, who is this, and better than the electric car he is:

where the camel is all things to all men, except only as an article of food, one has to take a species of interest in even him.   I have been able, I think, to gauge the horse fairly well; I cannot say that I know more about camels than the superficial and apt-to-be unreliable hearsay of his fellow-man, so to speak, has given me.   But I have been told by English army officers in Egypt, who have become familiar with what camels can do, that the performance heretofore quoted, of over one hundred miles a day, kept up for a long period, is not beyond belief.

LVI

Though in my journeys through the Orient I have had the good-fortune to see somewhat of fancy stock, I have not purposed to pay much heed to the studs of the great princes; the horse of the people interests me more. One could scarcely expect a man to gain much of a knowledge of the horse of North America by taking him through the stables of Leland Stanford or over the Alexander farm; by driving him out to Milton to see "Arion" and "Nancy Hanks;" or by personally conducting him through the great training stables of the men who carry off the big racing events of the year. Nor does a man who describes the choicest specimens of the Arabian world convey to you any idea of the Arabian as most of us would see him. To pass in review the inmates of the imperial stables, or the stud of the Khedive, or even to tell about an exceptional specimen found in the tents of a Bedouin sheik out in the Arabian desert, is to portray a faultless creature—a sort of equine Thaddeus of Warsaw. A man may fall down and worship some of the beautiful Arabians, like the one in the illustration, for instance, who belongs to the Sultan, and whose lines, standing, are as perfect as his grace in motion. He is fleet and able; he is gentle and intelligent, and he possesses the rare artistic beauty all must delight in except those who reduce the horse down to the level of a sumpter-animal or a gambling-tool. He is deservedly an object of our admiration. But so we may go into ecstasies over many of our own noble sires or great prize-winners.

This exceptional creature is not, however, the horse we want to know; it is the average horse and rider all over the world which most appeals to us—the horse we ourselves might own. At all events, the latter is the horse I have proposed to chat with you about. You can find out the merits of the famous Arabians from other writers, for there are many such.

It has been habitual to give us accounts of only the splendid horse of the sheiks and emirs; and many, indeed, of those who have painted them have not been students of the race. While there is a color of truth in all that we have heard about the Arabian, while the exception is as marvellous in his way as a " Flora Temple" or a " Black Maria," the average Arabian is by no means superior to our own average horse—scarcely his equal. He is, moreover, so small as to be useless for any but light performance—an ordinary carriage to go a distance must have three or even four horses ; he would not do our work at all.

The exceptional Arabian is unquestionably a fine fellow ; but—and I think I may claim some experience, as I have seen and used horses in a great many parts of the world—apart from a certain attractiveness we readily grant him, I do not think that the best Arabian is nearly as good as the best hunter, the best trotter, the best racer, or the best saddle-horse of England or America ; and I am quite sure that I would stake my money on a hundred broncos of the Western plains, ridden in their own way by cowboys, against a hundred Arabians of the Syrian desert, ridden by Bedouins—for a pull of one to five hundred miles under conditions fair to each. This may be a strong statement, but I believe it to be a just one.

I by no means underrate the Arabian. In addition to his beauty he possesses many sterling qualities, and has

AN ARABIAN SIRE

retained in full measure that wonderful power of transmitting his virtues which has made his impress so strong on all the stock we most prize at home. But he has never been intelligently bred by the Arab world at large. We may not, perhaps, deny that a few of the Arabs of the Syrian desert have kept his qualities unsoiled ; but there is no proof that he is any better to-day than he ever was. We know that our thorough-bred stock is better than it used to be, better than its desert ancestry. We know that whenever our second-raters have met the best Arabians they have conquered them even on their own soil, in their own climate, and at their own distances. So far as such things can be measured, we know that our performances in England and America are quite unequalled by the Arabian ; and we have good cause to believe that, for our purposes, our common run of horses as much excel in usefulness the common run of Arabians as they do in size. Moreover, I do not believe that there was ever an Arabian foaled which could perform the feat of the little El Paso-Chihuahua express pony. I am quite ready to be corrected—by a proper record.

Right here let me disclaim any value which may be placed on the recent so-called Cowboy Race from Nebraska to Chicago. It was not a cowboy race, but a S. P. C. A. race. Fancy sixty miles a day being the winning gait! Why, a decent cavalry brigade can march sixty miles a day for a month. I speak on behalf of those men who know the real value of broncos and plains horses, and the real capacity of the cowboy to ride. For a man to ride a distance race with an agent of the S. P. C. A. at his elbow to keep him from committing Berghlary savors keenly of the ridiculous.

LVII

WHEN we reach Syria we approach as near the home
of the best type of the Arabian horse as the traveller is
apt to get. The nomad Bedouins or Kabyle tribes beyond
the Jordan, who winter in the Arabian desert and wander
northward to escape its summer heat and droughts, probably own the best blood that exists. It is here that the
French have found the fine stallions they are using to re-
trieve the failing stock of Algeria. These Bedouins are
not numerous; twenty-five thousand souls will cover all
the tribes.

I believe that these Bedouins have kept nearer than
any other people to the purest strain of Arabian blood.
You must ride for many days, and put up with a good
deal of privation, heat, and dirt to reach the habitat of
this truly noble beast, but it is worth your while. The
Arabs beyond the Jordan are practically not subject to
the Turkish rule. They are strictly nomads, and for sub-
sistence raise camels, asses, and horses, beeves, sheep, and
goats. They come and go at will; they bulldoze the
agricultural peasantry into giving them a large modicum
of their crops as tribute, and the poor soil-tillers find it a
far safer means of securing quiet than to rely on the Sultan's shallow pretence of protection; they demand backsheesh even from those who only go down from Jerusalem to Jericho, lest they, too, should fall among thieves;
they make war on each other at will; they are as free as
the Sioux of 1840. The simple trip to the Dead Sea has

to be made under escort of a Bedouin, as a species of
backsheesh to these wild tribes, while to go beyond the
Jordan necessitates as complicated a previous diplomatic
negotiation with the sheiks through whose territory you
desire to pass as the transfer of a European province.
You cannot deal with one; all the tribes are at war, or,
at least, in a state of armed neutrality; but you may deal
through one with the rest. After you get into their
midst you are handed from one tribal limit to another
with as much ceremony as if you were a distinguished
State prisoner—which, indeed, you are. There is no risk
to your life, unless you should fall in with warring tribes,
and then little; but you do well to carry no valuables.
Having made your trade and agreed as to backsheesh,
the payment of the half of which you are generally ad-
vised to reserve to the end, you may commit yourself con-
fidently to your swarthy-skinned guides. Particularly if
you are fond of horses will you excite their sympathy.
Many is the suspicious-looking Arab who has hailed me
as a brother, because out of two horses I instinctively
picked one with the better points. Many is the fraternal
embrace I have been fain to submit to. But all this apart.
I am not writing a book of travels.

The Syrian Bedouin is in some respects a better type
of man than the Arab of Africa. To begin with, he has
more respect for his women. No traveller sees anything
of an Arab's household; it is discourteous, and not always
safe to refer to his wives. When I was visiting my friend
the caliph—not of Bagdad, but of M'Kalta—I was much
tempted to ask some questions as to his family. The Koran allows him four wives—how many he has I know not.
His two sons, one fourteen and one eight years old, I
saw a number of times; he was proud to introduce them
to me. On several occasions a couple of little girls, who

had escaped from the women's end of the khan, came running out into the enclosure. I beckoned to them, and they
came to me; but my conversation with them was as limited as it would have been with a French dog or cat.
By-the-way, do you know the French, or German, or Italian, or Spanish equivalent of "Pussy, pussy, pussy?" I
have frequently been stumped in my attempted conversa-
tions with foreign animals by lack of knowledge of their
patois. And they resent the foreign tone or words more
than children. Well, as I said, the little girls came to me
and were soon reconciled by a bit of chocolate. I always
carry chocolate in my pocket on a tramp. Half a cubic
inch of good chocolate — I like Menier the best, though
this is not a paid advertisement—will stay the stomach
better than anything I know. The little girls, despite
their odd garments, were just like children anywhere; but
soon a serving-man came and lugged them away. There
were, I have no doubt, a number of women in the khan,
but while I was there not a sight of them could I get.
All the service was by men. I dare say I was wise not
to make inquiries. I might have offended the sense of
propriety of my delightful host.

To return to the Bedouin, I am told that he pays considerable heed to his wives and daughters; his first wife
is held in special honor, and really rules his house—or, as
he lives in tents, one might say, his outfit. With the Syrian Bedouin the woman has the same soul that Allah gave
the man. She works, but is not degraded to a state of
slavery. Her toil is mostly within the tent, but it may be
with the herds. In any event, the man does the heavy
work, the woman merely helps.

LVIII

THERE is, as I have been told and have already stated, a curious equine distinction between the African and Asiatic Arabs, in that the latter ride mares, while the former use stallions for saddle-work. I have reason to believe that far out on the Libyan Desert proper the same rule as to the preference for mares prevails; but on the edge of the desert the stallion is apparently the most used. Among the Syrian Bedouins the stallion is an altogether secondary animal. The mare is the darling of the sheik, the pet of the family. She is treated as a child, far better really than the children. One or two of the most promising of the stallions are kept, the rest are sent into the cities for sale. A mare is never sold. This accounts for the fact that the tourist, who never gets far beyond the cities, sees only stallions. The price paid for a good average four-year-old horse delivered in Damascus or Jerusalem runs from thirty to fifty dollars; a fine horse costs seventy to one hundred dollars; there is no price put on a "stunner;" you must negotiate for him as for a homestead —perhaps as you would for a wife.

The high-bred Arabian Desert mares seem always to be kept in condition. They are spare, and their naturally small frame makes them appear more so. "You raise buffaloes, not horses!" an Arab of the desert will sneeringly say to the owner of a fine, well-rounded, picture-book stallion. The splendid beauty of the Arabian, as we understand it, is to him an utter delusion. He has but one test — race, and the speed, gentleness, and courage which ought to come of race. The Arabians which the ordinary traveller picks out as the finest are those which fill the eye; the best mare in the desert may be far from a beauty; she is "a rum 'un to look at, but a devil to go."

The Bedouin cannot be induced to sell a mare. It is in her that he takes chief pride; through her he keeps the pedigree. If forced by debt or distress to part with her, he has the right to stipulate that she shall be bred to such and such a horse, and that he shall have the first mare-foal. He will never ride a horse when he can ride a mare. Most of the Bedouins who are put on escort duty ride horses, but this is because all the travellers do the same, and it is not convenient to mix the sexes; but let him get beyond the reach of the current of tourists and it is his mare he bestrides; it is to her that he trusts his life. Geldings exist, but they are rare. I remember to have seen but two or three in Syria.

It will, I fear, be a disappointment to the reader for me to say that the common Arabian of Syria is so nearly like the bronco that the Bedouin might be set down as a cowboy—bar clothes and seat and intelligence. So far as the horse goes you might mix a hundred of each in a big corral, leave them alone a month, and it would be hard for any but an expert to pick out either kind. By common Arabian I mean the saddle-horse that is used in every-day life, the equine *vin du pays*. Take a hundred of the average of these horses, and seventy of them will be broncos; the rest will show some marks of what we Occidentals call better blood. There are two or three points of difference: the Arabian croup is higher, the barrel back of the girths less swollen, the withers less prominent, the ewe neck by a shade less pronounced. But the work-a-day Arabian of Syria plainly shows his cousinship with

BEDOUIN ESCORT FROM JERUSALEM TO JERICHO

the cow-pony of our plains. He shows, too, the old steppes type to which all horses tend to revert, as the dog does to the jackal type, unless bred by man. The fact is by no means so prominent in Africa. There you are less wont to travel on horseback; in Syria you must do it, and the country is so full of saddle-beasts — among them multitudes of poor ones—that you cannot fail to observe the fact.

For the common Syrian hack it must, however, be said that he is tractable. His long acquaintance with an easygoing and kindly race of men has vastly improved him. His manners are just what the bronco's are not. He will not buck, or bite, or strike, or "fool." In all this he is vastly the superior of the wild horse, whose natural want of manners has been increased manifold by the naturally cruel Indian and by the cowboy, who is too busy to devote time to gentling him. Like Artemus Ward with the tiger, he is apt to fondle him with a club. To the Arab, however, time is nothing; his climatic indolence leads to innate kindness. So far as capacity to go is concerned, I have already pronounced in favor of the bronco. But for a pleasant mount commend me to the placid-eyed, sweet-willed Arabian, whose ample courage is tempered with moderation, and whose desire to do your will is shown in his every act. If there is anything which I as heartily despise as I honestly admire, it is a bronco.

And I find that I am not alone in this. Out on the ranches, old settlers "hate a bronk," and you cannot hire one to ride an "outlaw," as they call a bronco who is so tricky as to be really dangerous. On the old-fashioned ranges a cowboy is expected to take one or two questionable ponies among the six or eight he rides; but he won't take any more than his quota. A man who doesn't object to an over-allowance of "bronk" can get a job any day anywhere. But there are few of them, except on the newer ranges.

Unless for the saddle, the Arabian is not worth his salt. He is too light for draught. For the saddle, the Kentucky type is better; as to gaits, infinitely to be preferred. When I say Kentucky, I mean the best class of Southern-bred saddle-horses everywhere. I am naturally led to speak of Kentucky as I am more familiar with that State than the others. The gaits of the Arabian horse are not as pure as those of the Southern. He has but two which may be called perfect—the walk and gallop. His flat-footed walk is undeniably good; on the whole, better than the average in the South, and that is saying a great deal. His amble or rack is good, but neither rapid nor even and reliable in individuals. He has rarely a canter proper; he always gallops. To "canter all day in the shade of an apple-tree" is an unknown art to him; he must go a given speed. I have not seen a single slow, easy, rhythmical canter in Asia or Africa, though I have seen a Bedouin at a *fantasiya* plant his spear, and canter around it without quitting his hold. This was, however, at great exertion to man and beast, not performed as my "Patroclus" used to do it—quietly, well-collected, and without strain. The Arabian's gallop is rapid and neatly poised; he gathers handily and quickly; but he has not the true racing stride. Still, for saddle-work, his gallop is good. Except these two, the Arabian has no gait worth mention. His amble or rack is slow; he cannot start out into a sharp, fast, twelve-mile rack. The running-walk as a steady, trained, uniform gait, is unknown, though some individual horses happen to blunder into it. Nor has the Arabian saddle-beast a trot, unless trained for a Frank.

Saddle-gaits are a matter of intelligent education. Unquestionably, in his sharp and sudden manoeuvres in the *fantasiya*, the Arabian is an expert. But a good polo-rider will beat him even at this game, and in any event it is not pure saddle-work. It is like any other specialty, as hunting or racing. For unadulterated saddle-work I have owned Kentucky horses far and away ahead of anything I have seen among Arabs, and I do not claim to have had princely horses, but only the best of the average run, well-trained.

There is one exception to the rule I have given. The Cretan horse often has a fast rack. He goes the gait in perfect purity, and is said to be able to carry a man twelve miles and over within the hour. When the ordinary good horse brings ten or twelve pounds sterling, this little fellow, who differs only in ability to go from his cousins, and is otherwise a mean-looking, low-headed runt, will always find a purchaser at forty pounds and upwards. I could learn nothing of his ancestry. ·

The Syrian saddle has many varieties, none very marked. From what resembles a high-cantled, leather-covered English saddle to one of modified Oriental type, you find all kinds and sizes. The saddle is rather apt to be covered with a sheepskin, so as to conceal its peculiarities. The man's seat is the same as in Africa, with very short stirrups, knees thrust way forward, and heels dug into the horse's flanks. There is no pretence to hold on by the knees; the grip is solely with calf and heel. Most saddles, if you will use long stirrups, can be made fairly comfortable to a small man; but no one, not used to it, can ride *à l'Arabe*. There is no chance to move in an Arab's saddle, and a sudden jerk. if it unseats you, does so effectually; in an English saddle there is much room for readjusting your seat after a sudden jerk. In the one you are fairly kicked out of the saddle; in the other you may recover yourself. The saddle in Asia Minor has a leather-

23

covered, half-military seat, semicircular on side-view, with
a pommel very full and wide between the knees, and more
uncomfortable, if possible, than the Syrian.

The Syrian bit is the curious gag used in many places
in the Orient. It has two branches; the curb - chain is a
ring permanently jointed to the top of the tongue - arch.
In putting the bit in the horse's mouth, you slip this ring
over his chin. One size does for all horses; but as the
Arab is not a three-legged rider, leaving his reins loose at
all times, the kind of bit is of not great importance; it
will not gall. But it is a bit a heavy jerk of which may
break the bone at the back of the horse's jaw. The bridle
is always a fancy one, often trimmed with shell-work, and
the breast - strap and saddle - trappings are wonderful in
their tawdry picturesqueness. Many a Bedouin, however,
even if he owns a noble mare, is too poor to boast a bridle.
He rides with a rope-halter only. The intelligent creature
does not even need that, the voice is enough. Colts are
broken to saddle and taught their gaits with halter alone.
If, as rarely happens, a colt is fractious, the rope is passed
through his mouth. A Southerner, whose children ride
the colts at pasture with a mere stick, understands this
well. It is half docility, half daily familiarity of the horse
with his master. This habit of docile breaking is thousands of years old in the Orient. Light native cavalry of
all ancient countries used to ride without bridles, guiding
solely by voice and legs. Such was Hannibal's famous
Numidian horse, and we know how wonderfully they
could gallop around the enemy. Their favorite tactics
was to make a sudden attack, fly at the first bold resistance, and attack and fly again, until they had wearied
their opponents and laid them open to real assault. This
argues immense tractability in their steppes ponies. It is
a similar tactics to that in which the Cossack is an adept.

The rich coloring of the Bedouin's clothes and trappings is a never-ending source of delight to the eye. Under our own less sunny skies the showy rags would wear upon the artistic fancy. Not so in the Orient; and when a man is rich and well-mounted, and clothes himself and his horse with purple and fine linen, he is gude for sair e'en. One never tires of looking at him.

We are apt to imagine that the Arab leaves his horse as Allah made him; that he would scorn to cut his mane or tail. This is far from the truth. The Arab hogs his horse's mane quite often; he bangs his tail; he squares it short with a small switch hanging down from the centre —and a ridiculous looking tail it is, confined mostly to Jerusalem and vicinity; and, worse than all, he sometimes trims the tail short like a foal's tail not yet grown, to give his horse a youthful appearance, and under the mistaken impression as well that the hair by this trimming will grow longer and fuller. Fashion is as marked a tyrant among the Bedouins as in Rotten Row or in Central Park.

LIX

THE Bedouin is full of horse superstitions. His horse-lore is much like that of our old-fashioned liveryman of a past generation. I don't refer to the intelligent Yankee breeder; I mean the humdrum, half-*vet*, half-trader, who knew of but one cure for the staggers, and that was to sell the horse. The Bedouin, like this happily extinct horse-man, knows a horse's habits and diseases by observation solely; he has no idea of anatomy. Every species of wind trouble to which the horse is subject he merely describes as "having something wrong inside him." He treats a horse on a system of old saws. For lameness he has but one remedy, the hot iron. His horse will work to twenty or even twenty-five years old, but he thinks that he "grows weaker" after twelve. In buying he looks more at marks than points. I have never yet seen an Arab critically examine a horse from head to heel as we do, each point in proper succession. Probably they satisfy themselves as to a horse's race and general soundness, and then only give heed to marks. But they talk marks more than points. Soundness is assumed, and as a rule exists in this exceptionally hardy race.

One very intelligent Arab sheik with whom I sat down at the old, old Jordan ford east of Jericho, where all the pilgrims bathe, and with whom I conversed for hours during the mid-day heat, when I asked him what he looked for first in a horse he was going to buy, told me with the utmost gravity the "color of his feet." He

probably meant providing the horse was otherwise all
right, but I could not get him to say so. I stood beside
his horse, and laid my hand on his several points one by
one; but the old man would not even nod an assent as if
he understood me; he kept to his text. "Four white
feet," said he, "are good; with a star, very good." What,
thought I, becomes of our old proverb anent the crows?
"If he has the two fore-feet and the near hind-foot white,
it is good," he went on, rolling a fresh cigarette between
every two sentences; "but if it is the off hind-foot which
is white, he is a bad horse—never buy him. He will cost
you your life; your enemy will overtake and slay you, your
son will be an orphan." Here came in a pause awful in
its length and intensity, as if I were to be myself visited
by this dire calamity. "Two hind-feet white and a star
are good; so is the near hind-foot white; but beware
of the off hind-foot alone white!" Again an awful pause.
"To have the two near feet white is excellent, because
then you must mount and dismount 'over the white.'
And a dark horse with dark legs is good." Not a word
could I get out of this old sheik about points; on marks
he was strong. I was told that he was highly respected
by the Arabs for his knowledge of horses. I could not see
why. No judge on the woolsack was ever more reverend
or more positive; but his dignity seemed to me to be in
inverse ratio to his horse wisdom.

It is, by-the-way, curious that this white foot business
was well known in England, and, to a certain extent, was
an article of faith, some three hundred years ago. It most
probably came over with the early Turkish importations
—"Turkish" being a broad term, and covering a vast
territory.

I asked the old sheik what his horse weighed. "A
horse weighs one hundred rot'l," said he, after a prolonged
23*

pause; not his horse particularly, but any horse, he meant.
A rot'l is about five pounds. "But why?" I asked. "Oh,
because a horse weighs as much as two men," was his long
cogitated reply. "But," I quickly objected, "this horse
weighs as much as four or five or six men!" "Yes," he
gravely agreed, after waiting an exceptional time to make
up for my hasty interpellation, "but I mean a very big
man." His ideas on all points relating to a horse were
about as definite as this. In treating a horse for sickness,
the Arabs are very children. But their horses, out of
doors, and standing on the earth at all times, are as hardy
as the bronco, and need scant medical treatment.

The Arab keenly enjoys conversation, but it must be
deliberate and long drawn out. Our Occidental haste, in
talk and trade alike, they deem objectionable in a high
degree — almost insulting. You may go into a carpet-
store and haggle and haggle by the half-day, drink the
coffee invariably offered you, and even if you do not buy,
providing always you are very slow and familiar and
chatty, your visit will be deemed a courtesy, and all the
trouble the store-keeper and his men have taken to spread
out a hundred rugs for your inspection will be quite compensated for by your kind words and pleasant smiles.
But if you just go in, look at a few, and hastily purchase,
or bid on one or more, he deems you almost an intruder
on his privacy. He wants the fun of haggling and talking. The profit is a mere incident — though it be his
daily bread. In those bazaars which are kept by Greeks
or by other non-Orientals, this rule does not apply; but
it does with all self-respecting Eastern merchants. This
is of a part with their extreme slowness in coming to a
point in conversation.

Color, in the Bedouin's estimation, ranks: bay, chestnut
or sorrel, blue (comprising iron-gray, blue-roan, gray, and

white), brown, black, dun. The last is considered soft. An old weazened sheik, on escort duty with me, once recited to me the following verse, which, not knowing Arabic, I must assume the Gallic privilege of misspelling in English letters. I wrote it down according to the sound, and got a dragoman who knew a little Arabic, and spoke French with a most un-Parisian brogue, to translate it for me. The sheik said it was the production of Antar, a celebrated Bedouin emir—a prince and poet—of many ages ago:

> "El zourk merkoub ilamahrah
> Blue horses are steeds for the Emirs,
> Ouar kabham koul ameer ouakoul oali
> And princes and governors ride them;
> Amma elshougre lantarou besedig
> The sorrel, if they fly, I believe it;
> Bennat elreeh maahn hum zalaly
> The daughters of the wind fly less fast.
> Amma eldouhm zidouhoum aliga
> To the black horses you must give more food;
> Kalouhoum la itmat elliali
> Use them for ambuscades on dark nights.
> Koul elkhaïl lilhamra t'baha
> All horses trail behind the bay,
> Mit'l el sit tik dimha el gouari
> Like the Lady the servants serve her."

Of such equine notions the Arab mind is full. Before giving me the rhyme the sheik solemnly informed me that the horse wisdom of ages lay concealed therein. The concealment I believe. I told this sheik one of our own time-worn driving rhymes; but with the dragoman's small Latin and less Greek, he did not seem to catch its meaning:

> "Uphill hurry me not,
> Downhill flurry me not,
> On the level spare me not,
> In the stable forget me not."

He may or may not have got the translation correctly;
at all events he faintly smiled as if the exchange of verse
for verse had been an unfair one; but he was generously
inclined for the moment and did not claim the balance in
backsheesh. Next day, however, he did so. That verse
of his cost me many shekels. And it was apparently with
a clear conscience that the old sheik took his "present."
He evidently felt that he had given me a vast deal of
horse-lore, which in my own country would stand me in
good stead.

The Oriental is not necessarily a beggar. If you get
out into the interior you see little of it—not enough at
least to be annoying. The cry for backsheesh was created
and is generally stimulated by the European tourists; the
new-comers like to see the native's excitement, as they
elbow each other to reach the backsheesh-distributing
"personally conducted" Cookie or Gazer. While the
Bedouin by no means objects to a "present," he does not
naturally ask for it by annoying means. But short contact with the average globe-trotter will spoil any people
among whom coin is rare.

One of my friends told me an amusing case of backsheesh to which he fell a victim in Constantinople. He
went into a tobacco-bazaar to get a package of tobacco
for smoking. Its value was ten piasters (a piaster is five
cents or a "nickel"). As he entered he found a solemn
conclave of Turks sitting cross-legged in a semicircle
enjoying their coffee and water-pipes. He had been in
the bazaar before, and thinking he recognized the owner,
strode up to him and handing him a half-medjidji piece,
uttered the mystic word which conveyed the idea of the
article he sought, which, not being a Turk or a smoker, I
cannot quote. The Moslem calmly received the piece,
which summarily disappeared in the folds of his volumi-

nous skirts, and then quietly removed his pipe-stem from
his mouth and pointed with it to another man, who was
the real owner of the bazaar, and to him my friend repeated the mystic monosyllable. The owner slowly arose,
got the article and handed it to the purchaser with a
salaam, and then extended his hand for pay. My friend
pointed to the Turk to whom he had given the half-
medjidji and prepared to leave. This individual sat im-
perturbably there, as if unconscious of what was going
on. The bazaar owner shook his head and went and
stood athwart the door. My friend strode upon the de-
linquent to make him disgorge; but the Turk quietly
looked up, again removed his pipe-stem from his mouth,
and calmly enunciated "backsheesh." "You have made
me a present; Allah will reward you!" he meant. My
friend stood for a moment in doubt whether or not to
clean out the whole crowd, as, being a big fellow rather
handy with his mawleys, he might easily have done.
Then the ludicrousness of the whole affair came over him,
he burst into a loud laugh, gave the bazaar-owner another
half-medjidji, and retired, the wiser by quite as much as
he had lost. Like the open-sesame of the shilling in England, coin as backsheesh is acceptable and accepted in
every part of the Orient.

LX

In feeding and watering the horse the Bedouins seem to us to be equally unreasoning as in their veterinary practice, unless it be agreed that a horse can stand anything he is used to, and that it is well to get him used to irregular habits. The fact that the Arabian is often compelled to go an indefinite time without food or drink unquestionably makes him hardy and less apt to suffer than any regularly treated animal. In every nation there exists peculiar habits. In Switzerland many drivers will not water on the road at all, even if the horses have thirty or forty miles to do on a stretch. They are "afraid of the colic," as they say.

It is deprivation which hardens a man to deprivation. I do not mean that irregular habits will tend to prolong life or give uniform good health. Neither will athletics. On the contrary, the man who never overdoes anything, be it in exercise or in diet, is the man who is apt to live the longest and suffer the least from disease. It is professors in colleges and clergymen who stand at the head of the longevity tables. But what will kill the professor or the clergyman is child's play to the Indian, who starves for two or three days and then gorges like an anaconda. The Arabian for this same reason will go all day in the hot sun and never ask for water—impatiently, at least—even in crossing a brook. He is fed and watered —apparently regardless of the fact that he is hot or tired— in a fashion which would inevitably founder any horse in

RICH BEDOUIN SHEIK

America. He is given his pail of water and his trough full of dry or green food, or whatever else is available, so soon as he stops on a journey, or else he is ridden off immediately after. Quite as often he gets nothing at all. I have seen horses ridden all day, and have camped at noon with them near by a stream, without any one trying to water them, because they had no bucket and the banks were high. It would never occur to a Bedouin to carry a skin-pail with him. But the horses seemed used to such neglect, and never even whinnied for the water gurgling past them. At other times I have seen horses fed at very short intervals—at almost every stop. This sort of thing in civilized regions sounds quite foolish; but what is one horse's food is another horse's poison.

As a rule the Arabian has a sound appetite. When it fails after a hard pull, his master resorts to all kinds of queer devices to make him eat. He does not rub his ears and legs to restore his disturbed circulation as we would do, but tweaks and twists his ears pretty roughly, and cuffs him about the head; he ties knots in his forelock, and pulls him about by it; he pulls out and twists his tongue, and rubs a handful of feed over it. The *rationale* of all this is as hard to decipher as the whipping a Russian horse gets if he refuses to eat. But then the knout is a cure-all in Russia; there is no knout among the Arabs.

The food is much as in the rest of the Orient. Barley is the bulk of the dry food; beans, of which Cyprus exports vast quantities; oats, cut up, straw and all; plain straw cut up; clover-hay; green clover of the first crop. Barley, fed all over the East, gives a distinctly disagreeable odor to the droppings, but it is a hardy food. It is much used in California.

The Syrian horse has the same peculiarities as his broth-

ers in Africa. He weighs little for his height, and yet
without appearing over leggy. Officials in the East are
so very unreliable that I do not feel that I have arrived
at a just estimate of the weight of the Arabian horse. I
have had several put on the scales; but when a horse of
more than fifteen hands, which I should gauge at over
eight hundred pounds, is said to weigh only four hundred
and eighty-eight, as was declared to me on one occasion, I am disinclined to credit the accuracy of the scales
or weigher, or of both. The Arabian has a round, well-
coupled, but exceedingly small barrel, no breadth of shoulder or haunch, and in Syria has smaller bone than in
Egypt. From behind he is knife-blady. Still, thorough-
bred bone weighs heavy; a cubic inch of a racer's shin-
bone weighs three or four times as much as a cubic inch
of the more porous bone of the bulky brewer's dray-horse.
In most respects the Arabian is built to weigh little and
do much for his weight; but I must still hold him to
four-fifths or over the weight of a similar animal at home.
The same applies to donkeys. I have been told that a
certain donkey weighed only two hundred pounds when
I was certain he weighed two hundred and seventy-five to
three hundred pounds.

The Arabian is generally in good flesh. He more rarely
loses his roundness than our horses do. This comes in
part from his having so small a framework to fill out. It
is easy to keep a narrow-hipped horse fat. His legs and
feet are as near perfect as may be. The reason has already been given—that he stands day and night on the
ground. No Oriental stable has a floor, unless rarely
that of a pacha or an emir, so that the diseases of the
hoof from which we suffer are not apt to be found. He
is, moreover, not generally called on all day and every
day to 'ammer, 'ammer, 'ammer on the 'ard, 'igh road,

SYRIAN WOMAN ON AN ASS

so that his legs remain sound; and his weight saves him when he does have to do such work. His life out of doors or in open stables gives him fresh air at all times, and his lungs remain good. He has been kept under natural conditions for generations, and the result is a naturally sound beast. He is shod with the Arabian plate. In Syria the Frank shoe is very rarely seen. The plate is the clumsiest device imaginable—thick, heavy, and awkward. Except for a hole about an inch in diameter in the centre, it covers the entire foot. The toe is curved upward, and by wear grows more curved; the heel likewise curves upward so as to cover the entire frog almost up to the coronet. We like to see the foot rest flat on the ground, and the frog, if not touching the ground, at least close to it. The Syrian horse has the plate curved upward at the back so that the frog, though resting on the plate, is high off the ground, and the animal looks as if he were treading on tiptoe. I at first mistook the tiptoe step behind as an indication of spavin. We should consider such shoeing as bad for the sinews. After the shoe has been on six or eight weeks, the horse travels very much as if his feet were balled with snow. He is stepping on a sort of curved surface, and on less than one-third of the face of the shoe at all times. It is not a natural position for the foot. The hind toes are generally worn off square. You may always assume the foot to be good; but you can see nothing of it except the outside wall without taking off the plate. This horror of a shoe the Arabian carries from four to six months! To shoe a horse every month seems absurd enough to a Bedouin. The shoe is held in place by six enormous hand-made nails driven near together, three on either side, about half-way back from the toe. The nails are driven so that the clinches are in a group, so close that a quarter-

24

dollar piece will cover them, and generally protrude. Despite this clumsy device, the little fellow rarely cuts, and
the texture of the wall is so tough that the nails never break it away, even after months.   In the desert the
horse is supposed to be generally unshod; but enormous
stretches of the desert, so-called, are a mass of broken
stone, like a badly-laid and unrolled macadamized road,
only ten times worse; for such places he must be shod.

The women of the people in Syria ride astride a pad,
with long stirrups or none.   They frequently use the
men's saddle.   There is nothing odd about their seat as
about that of their Egyptian sisters.   They seem much at
home on horseback, though it is the ass which is especially
their mount.

The various Arabians I have ridden have been excellent
of their kind.   When not spoiled by or for the English
tourists by being taught to trot and jog, they have had
easy gaits, nice mouths, and good manners.   Many of
them have for their size a good deal in front of you, and
give you the impression of carrying you easily, though
they are usually much under fifteen hands, and weigh
little for their inches.   They have fine heads and necks,
little delicate ears which are lively but not nervous, and
a general air of good-nature and ability to go.   But they
do not give one the same sense of immense power which
a rangy thorough-bred will do, in magnificence of stride or
in the general action of head and shoulders as he gallops
away from under you.   Except for the habit of throwing
up the head, a trick bred of gag-bits, the Arabians are
most agreeable to mount.   If you will get one used to a bit
and bridoon, which is easy to be done, he will come " in
hand " quicker than most of our horses and carry his head
just right.   Still, it remains true that in gaits the Arabians
lag far behind our racer in stride, far behind our Southern

POOR BEDOUINS OF MOAB

saddle-beasts in training. As you look at them they appear tall; when you come to mount your foot goes readily into the stirrup, while at home you must usually
stretch well up to get the left foot in. Their small barrel
is proven by the fact that the immense amount of padding
under the saddle and flaps does not spread your legs too
much. At home we like a saddle-flap to be close to the
horse's side. It rarely is so in the Orient.

The climate of Syria is chilly in winter, and the horse
of the desert puts on almost as long a coat as the bronco
of our north-western plains. In the spring, until he has
scoured off this coat on the fresh grass, he is a lamentable
object to look upon. The old flea-bitten gray mare in the
illustration shows small signs of blood in her staring coat
and woful appearance; but in a few weeks she may be as
glossy as silk, despite her years; and perchance she can
now out-travel many a May-bird. The Bedouin spear is
quite a feature of this part of the world. Its great length
reconciles one to the historically stated size of the Macedonian sarissa—twenty-one feet. It seems as if one could
scarcely use so unwieldy a weapon, but in it the Bedouin
reposes almost as much confidence as in his fire-arm; and
in view of the common condition of the latter it is no
wonder. The background shows the stony upland common in the desert. The camel's-hair tent is a family inheritance; it is almost indestructible.

The clothes of the Bedouin are much like those of all
Arabs, but the *tout ensemble* lacks the grace which the
burnoose lends to his cousin of Algeria and Tunis. The
garments are mere bags, as elsewhere, either upsidedown
or right side up. The trousers have already been sartorially noticed, though there be many styles of these, from
the skirt-bags of the Syrian to the peg-tops of the Jew.
The upper garments are strictly on the same pattern, with

holes cut at the bottom of the to-be-inverted bag for arms
and head, and a slit in front, from the neck down, for
ease of putting on. Much may be added to the bag in
the way of embroidery and other ornament, but the pattern remains. The Bedouin does not generally wear nether
bags like the African, though the Syrian of the towns is
wont to do so; his upper bags are long and various, and
he wears as many as the season demands, or his purse
affords.

The Bedouin has the same fine physique that the nomad Arab everywhere boasts. It might be said, with
slight fear of exaggeration, that, on the whole—bar those
who are ground down by misery—the Arab is the hand-
somest man on earth. In mere beauty most critics would
be apt to put the Hindoo first; but he lacks the alert man-
liness of the Arab. Like his horse, the latter partakes of
the thorough-bred character. The standing, walking, running, lounging Arab is graceful, erect, alert, pleasing; and
his brown skin, when you know him, becomes singularly
attractive. Even when sitting cross-legged, he is as picturesque in figure as in costume. But when squatting on
his hams, in the way all semi-chairless nations sit—as the
poor whites sit in our Southern States — he loses his
flavor; and yet it must be a most convenient position.
One can take it anywhere, at any time, be apparently
quite at ease, and have but the feet touching the ground.
It is a distinct loss to our comfort that we are not taught
this habit, as well as to sit cross-legged, in our youth. It
does not prevent one's using benches and chairs; it merely
adds an additional and ubiquitous means of taking rest.
The dignity of the cross-legged seat is generally acknowledged; one might dispute that of the squat.

We ought not to take leave of the Orient proper without
a word about the palanquin rider. In a land where there

PALANQUIN CAMEL

are no roads, where all travel and traffic is by saddle and sumpter-beasts, the palanquin is the equivalent of our coupé. It is by no means as uncomfortable as it appears. Comfort is relative. An Oriental lady cannot take her ease and go so far as she might in a Pullman-car, or eke a travelling carriage over smooth roads; but on a camel one can journey ten hours a day, at an average of three miles an hour, with great comfort, over the merest mountain paths. When you try to double up in speed you must be habituated to the motion from childhood to stand the fatigue. A single camel palanquin is not as luxurious as one borne by two camels; but there is much room for change of position in even this. The palanquin looks unwieldy, but being made of reed and wicker-work it is light, and with its two travellers will not weigh more than four hundred pounds. The porter-camel can carry five hundred; a runner not much over half the weight, if he is to go far and fast.

LXI

Much of what has been said about the Arab in Syria applies to the Arab of western Asia Minor. He has perhaps not as marked characteristics, neither has his steed, but both bear quite a distinct resemblance to the Syrian. Wherever the horse is at his best, so, barring the lack of civilization, is the Arab; but, whatever may be said in favor of the Arab, we can never forget that he has ruined, agriculturally, financially, socially, morally, every country he has conquered. Even the breeding of the Arabian horse cannot make up for this wholesale havoc. The Moors, who at one time accomplished so much, and left their impress on so many lands, seem to have been the exception which proves the rule. Morocco of to-day, Algiers, Tunis, Tripoli, Egypt, Arabia, Syria, are all a desert in comparison to what we know from history that they were in olden days. Nor, with the character of the Arab as he has shown it in the past, does it seem probable that any improvement will be made in the future. Whether all this be not due to religious causes rather than racial, it may be hard to say. The Turk has accomplished the same devastation.

The Mohammedan must, however, be given credit for exemplary fidelity in some matters, as for his annual fast during the month of Ramazan. From an hour before sunrise until the sun has set he may neither eat, nor drink, nor smoke; and, strange to say, for a solid month he honestly does this thing, though he makes merry all through

TWO-CAMEL PALANQUIN

the nights as a compensation.   In Constantinople, should
a man openly break his fast, he would be arrested, and
fined or imprisoned.   The fast is not obligatory in the
case of weak men or of women or youth.   But when a
lad grows to be twelve or thirteen his soul rests not until
he has won permission to keep Ramazan.   On working-
men it is hard, especially when Ramazan comes in the hot
months, as, being by the Moslem lunar calendar made a
shifting feast, it does about a third of the time.   On soldiers it is still more hard; and though in war-time Ramazan is more honored in the breach than in the observ-
ance—much as Sunday was in our Civil War in the way
of battles—in times of peace the sentry does his rounds
unfed and thirsty.

I have a hearty respect for the best Mohammedan
element.   I have found them as liberal, sensible, and
gentle-minded as the lower classes can be fanatical—a
fact I ascertained to my sorrow when they stoned me and
my son out of Hebron last year.   One day in Jerusalem
I had a long and interesting discussion with an Arab
gentleman, which drifted from travelling to social matters,
from social to political, and from political to religious.   I
found no grain of prejudice in the man.   To him, as to all
Moslems, Abram was one of the great and holy men of
the past, Christ was one of the wisest teachers.   "But,"
said he, most reasonably, "we Mohammedans do not think
that you Christians of the present day teach the just and
beautiful doctrines of Jesus.   We look around us and we
see many sects, each expounding a separate dogma; we
look at the Mohammedans, and we find them believing
absolutely the same doctrines in every section of the
world.   The Koran means but one thing to all of us;
there have practically never been quarrels as to what it
contains.   So ought it to be with the Bible, which, to me,

so far as relates to the teachings of Christ, appears to be plain and simple, and I have studied it much. But is it so? I go into one of your most sacred temples, the Church of the Holy Sepulchre, to search for the simple truths I find in the Gospels, and what do I see? One altar erected in one section of the edifice by the Armenians, another in another section by the Greeks, a third in a third section by the Copts; again one by the Roman Catholics. No priest or communicant of any one of these sects will religiously mix with one of any other; and at Easter, the most holy day for all for them, I see the theological rivalry of these several sects at so white a heat that the Government is compelled to put a company or two of Turkish troops — Mohammedans — within the portals of this Christian church to prevent bloodshed on the very steps of the altar. This leads me to think, not that the Christ was wanting in the true spirit of prophecy, but that His followers have lost touch with His true teachings; it leads me to think that true Christianity had disappeared in the maze of doctrinal rivalry. And when again I contemplate the fact that half of the Christian world has seceded from the mother-church — I refer to the Protestants—that this seceding half is divided into yet more sects, all differing in many points of belief— well," he continued. with a smile, "I am reconciled to our one undisputed belief, which seems to suit both the lowly and those who think—at least, as well as what the Christians of to-day can teach us." What was there for me to say? He had covered the ground completely. I had no answer.

There is not much in Syria proper which distinguishes it from Palestine, but the farther north you go the farther you get away from the perfect type of horse; the farther east you go the more you lose the stanchness

which characterizes the Arabian. You might call the
Arabian desert the centre-point from which the horse has
got distributed; at too great a distance, without special
efforts to keep it pure, the stock gets diluted or lost. If
you wander, for instance, towards Kurdistan, you will find
a tough little horse, but he is no longer the Arabian of
the desert. He is more of a steppes runt. There is the
same peculiar family resemblance in the common horse
of almost all countries which there is everywhere to the
vin du pays. The bronco and Medoc express the types,
which vary as the inhabitants vary. Better care produces
a better article. We see the little mean Texan grow fat
and handsome when put into the stable of the polo-play-
ing swell; we should again see him, not less tough but
the very picture of wretchedness, if put for a month into
the brutal hands of an Indian or a Mexican. We see the
excellent Chianti of Italy degenerate into the vile pitch-
flavored κρασὶ ρετσινᾶτο of Greece. So with the horse or
the wine of the country everywhere.

Some of the oddest equestrian habits which a horseman
has ever imagined are to be found in lands abutting on
the home of the Arabian, though, indeed, the Arab has
himself enough of oddities. The Kurds ride a tree covered with plaited straw, quite flat, and padded with blankets. This they never remove from their horses, except occasionally to dry it out. The horse is kept saddled day
and night, summer and winter. This seems incredible,
but it is literally true. In Turkestan the horse's entire
body, from the ears back, is kept covered up with the bib-
lical number of blankets—seven—which he likewise wears
at all times, and which are supposed to sweat him out and
keep him in condition. The saddle is placed on the top
of these. The habits of horsemen in such countries vary
after a curious fashion. The Kurds sit in their straw, pad-

like saddle, with very short stirrups, and employ a severe bit. The Circassians also ride in a straw-covered saddle, but with an exceptionally high cantle and pommel, and with extra long stirrup-leathers, forked-radish or cowboy style. The Cossack again rides with short stirrup, as well as the Persian, and neither the latter nor the Circassian uses, as a rule, a bit, but a simple rope halter; while the Cossack uses an easy bit. Wherever the Arabian is in his glory you find substantially the same seat, already described; as soon as you wander away from the Arabian type you find as great a variety of equine habits as of dress.

The Persian horse, although a neighbor, appears to be a creature of quite different blood. He is taller and leggier than the Arabian, and has comparatively little stamina. The Kurds and Turcomans use a horse which is said to be the produce of Arabian sires on Persian dams, and this horse seems to gain the endurance of the desert blood, which it sadly needs. One does not expect much from Persians, and the horse corresponds to one's notions.

To wander for a moment while on the subject of Persia, it is said that when available funds run short in that despot-ridden land, the governors of the several provinces are paid by a firman granting them control of a given number of lashes. A viceroy is appointed with a salary and emoluments of, say, four thousand lashes per annum. He reaches his capital, and after making himself agreeable to his new subjects and getting settled in his duties, which are generally confined to ascertaining out of whom he can squeeze moneys, he sends word to the rich men of his district that he shall begin to apportion his salary. "To you, M. or N., of the wisdom and generosity of His Most Gracious Majesty the Shah, whom Allah preserve! and of my own loving-kindness, I award but two hundred of my four thousand annual lashes. These will be duly administered for your soul's health to-morrow at sunset. Allah Hu! Great is the Shah!" The clause to be read between the lines is: "If you desire to commute, my dear fellow, I shall be most happy to welcome you. I shall be in at almost any time to-day or to-morrow morning." M. or N., who may be a wealthy trader or a noble brigand, naturally enough prefers to pay with his purse rather than his person; he loses no time in accepting the polite invitation, and no doubt after interminable discussion as to amount and terms, endless gesticulation, and unlimited coffee, finishes by buying himself off with a good round sum, payable in whatsoever coin is current—flocks and herds, jewels, women, slaves, or grain. The viceroy repeats the stratagem on others, and finds himself rich in short measure, and is glad enough to go halves with his royal master. In a country where the Government steals from every rich citizen, where these do the same by the first comer, where brigandage pure and simple is the daily rule, this to us novel salary-scheme works to a charm. The annual budget is an easy one to cipher out. At all events, the method suits the people—and the Shah.

LXII

ONE is always led to imagine that the Arabian you find in Constantinople—in the imperial stables, or among the rich or high in place and power—is the *crême de la crême.* But, in truth, while you do find some very splendid specimens of horse-flesh under the shadow of the Sublime Porte, most of the best of them are not Arabians. I have rarely seen a finer lot of mounts than at Selamlik, one beautiful Friday last April, when His Imperial Majesty, accompanied by his ministers and generals, and escorted by a *corps d'élite* of the Turkish army, went from the palace, in state, to the mosque, where he might humble himself in prayer.

And let me here interpolate a word about the Sultan. His Majesty is currently imagined to allow his ministers to do all his work, while he himself lives a life of luxurious indolence, moving from one palace to another with his large and well-filled harem. The very reverse is the rule. The one man in all the Turkish dominions who works morning, noon, and night, whose mind never rests from effort to carry his people through the difficulties which beset bad system and lack of means, is the monarch. The ministers work little, the Sultan incessantly. Not only is this well understood, but my old schoolmate, heretofore referred to, is in daily attendance on his Majesty, and my ideas, gleaned from him, have given me a hearty respect for the personality of the present Bearer of the Crescent. Since his accession he has scarcely left his

A HUNGARIAN THOROUGH-BRED

palace in Pera; here he labors with honest fidelity to effect the impossible; for the bad Turkish customs are like the laws of the Medes and Persians. The system is as rotten as the people are hard to teach. Moreover, the Sultan is the simplest and most unrequiring man in his dominions. The unpretentious courtesy of his personal bearing, his apparent lack of egotism, his rather pale, nervous, overworked face are dignity itself. I have never witnessed a more patriarchal ceremony, or one of higher tone than this quiet procession of Selamlik.

To come back to the horses, I could not recognize in many of those I there saw the characteristics of desert blood; I suspected the truth, and was, on inquiry, told that they were largely imported or of imported stock.

The Arabian is not considered heavy enough for the Turkish cavalry in Europe; a Hungarian horse is bought or bred for the army, and, to a considerable extent, crossed with Arabian blood. It seems most natural to use the Arabian as the sire; but the experiment, I was told, is being tried of putting Arabian mares (where they manage to get any but scrubs I do not know) to the stallion from Hungary, the latter being largely impregnated by the English thorough-bred. This horse is for the man. Many of the officers—in Turkey all swells have military rank—import well-bred ones from various countries; and though you see a number of typical and very beautiful Arabians, especially in the Sultan's stud, you are out of the domain of the unalloyed article. And as to general grading, one may any day see a lot of saddle-beasts ridden in and out of our Southern towns, which in every saddle quality are superior to what I saw at Selamlik. The horses would not be splendidly caparisoned, nor the riders gorgeously clad, but the style and gait and blood would tell the story. The New York Horse Show is not

25*

approached in its exhibit of high grade saddle-horses by anything to be found in the Orient.

His Imperial Majesty, however, rides chiefly Arabians; and in the Selamlik procession there were led after his carriage a number of these, all white, richly mounted, and with a gold-bedecked blanket thrown over each, so that should he choose to return to the palace on horseback he might have his selection. The beauty of these horses seemed to elicit universal but injudicious admiration; they were more to be admired for their sleek, well-groomed appearance, and for their general air of extreme docility, than for any qualities they showed in the procession. A fine team of white Hanoverians in a low hung phaeton was also on hand, in case his Majesty should elect to drive himself back to the palace, as on this occasion he did.

The Turkish seat (in Europe at least) is no longer Oriental. It has become exclusively military. This is natural enough in a military autocracy. The English saddle, or some modification of it, and the extra long stirrup-leather—which is a simple perversion of the useful or appropriate in a flat saddle—is the regular thing. The short seat has become so universal that it has invaded the imperial stables, and the stud-grooms all ride, in their fancy liveries, strictly *à la militaire*. This is as heartily to be condemned as the Frenchman in gala uniform riding a to-cover gait.

On the whole, I do not like the flat saddle for the soldier. It does not, it is not intended to, give an upright seat. The knee is often back of instead of gripping the stirrup-leather, and the knee-pad on the saddle-flap might as well be on the horse's ears for any good it does with such short leathers. The flat saddle is cut for an entirely different seat. Hunting produced the English saddle; its

ONE OF THE SULTAN'S RIDING HORSES

use by a military man is a mere fad. I have seen many
more " unmilitary " seats—if there still be such a thing—
since the introduction among soldiers of the English saddle than before. It seems to breed a loosish seat—I by no
means say a bad one, but a free-and-easy method—the
very best in its place, but quite too slipshod for the soldier. A man naturally leans forward in a flat saddle
rather than sits erect, and so long as we insist on a soldier
being well set-up, why not make him ride erect as well?
The perfect seat and method for a soldier is, I maintain,
the one which enables him to preserve an upright, well-
set-up position in the saddle, to ride with one hand, at
need without any, to have his sword-arm at all times free,
and on occasions both. I have nowhere seen so near an
approach to this seat and method as in the officers of
our own regular cavalry, and they ride McClellan or
Whitman saddles. It is quite possible for the soldier to
have it, and yet not hang down his arm like a pump-
handle and stick out his thumb, as the merry caricaturist
will have it that he does. And as to effectiveness, the
proof of the pudding is in the eating, and it would puzzle
the best cavalry of any nation to follow some of our
veteran squadrons across the Bad Lands in pursuit of a
band of bucks on the war-path, or, for the matter of that,
to hold head to them when caught.

A soldier in Europe used to be a soldier, afoot or ahorse-
back. Now he is not unwont to be a dawdling kind of a
rider, and he threatens in many places to become as bad
a footman. Ramrod setting-up and pipe-clay may both
be overdone; but the new tactics may also go too far in
relying on individual intelligence and initiative. A good
setting-up, mounted or not, does a man no harm, and it
should be conserved for what it is really worth. Officers
and men both threaten to slouch too much. Because the

modern idea is skirmish drill, there is no need to lose the military bearing of the old elbow-touch days. I have of late abroad seen altogether too many soldiers of all ranks with very poor carriage. On the whole, we need never be ashamed of the West Point bearing, nor of the manners of our old regular soldiers. And, by-the-way, my friend, did it ever occur to you that, next to the manners of a cultured man of the world, the manners of a self-respecting old soldier were the best to be found? Keep your eye out and see if I am not right. And then seek for the reason.

LXIII

CONSTANTINOPLE is now a European city, as well in style as in geography. It is fast losing all its Orientalism. The fez is the only thing left which is universal. A crowd still remains, as of old, "a sea of fezzes." But the original Constantinople leg-gear has begun to cede to the convenience of "pants"—always the first and costly step in the downfall of national costumes and customs. Trousers are bad enough; pants are intolerable. Alas, that the landing-place of our brave old knee-breeched Puritan ancestors should have been desecrated by a three-dollar pair!

In a certain fashion, the trouser is the type of all human growth or backsliding. With the loss of the knee-breeches we lost the stateliness of the olden times; with the advent of "pants," gentlemen have become "gents." Wherever, nowadays, men are careful of their trouser creases, and of the proper length and flow of the garment over the instep, we find the telephone and the electric light and art and letters. Where, as in the Orient, the matter of six inches in the length of either leg of the prevailing trouser is of no material consequence; where the cut of the leg-clothing is quite disregarded, and a respectable or a rich man may appear in public with a ridiculous pair of cotton drawers in lieu of the well-brushed and well-fitted broadcloth, we find fanaticism, caste, and retrogression. May not the trouser be considered a measure of human endeavor and success, moral, material, and æsthetic? I submit this as a debatable point.

The Turkish cavalryman rides a gelding. The line of demarcation in the common use of the stallion and the gelding appears to be the Mediterranean and the Ægean Sea; in other words, in Europe you find the gelding, in Asia and Africa the stallion. The Hungarian gelding is a larger, bonier horse than the Arabian, averaging, per. haps, a scant fifteen two, generally dark in color, with fairly good points, but far from the whip-cord legs of the Arabian, and a poor tail and head. He is considered serviceable. The Arabian cannot be said to be highly regarded in Turkey, except as a pleasure horse. Carriage-horses are frequently bought among the Russian trotting-stock; they are black, and high steppers. The Turkish cavalry looks well as a body, but many of the men ride poorly. There are a great many Germans among the officers, who are doing well for it, but the arm is of recent erection.

At another great ceremony, the visit of the Sultan to the Treasury in the Old Seraglio on the fifteenth of Ramazan, to pray on the mantle of Mohammed, which is therein carefully preserved, and only taken out once a year, I had a chance to gauge the general run of the horses of Constantinople. The world and his wife (or rather his wives) were present. Everything on four legs turned out. The average struck me as very low. Among some exceedingly good ones there were altogether too many weedy, wretched little ponies under thirteen hands high. The harems of the whole city were on hand, and the attendants and eunuchs rode trashy stock of the meanest description. The livery-stables were emptied to carry the in-door female population out for an airing, and I doubt if you could have found so many poor specimens of the equine race in even a South American city, which is saying a great deal. The every-day hack of Constanti-

AN OLD ARABIAN FROM THE SULTAN'S STABLE

nople, as can be plainly seen, is an offshoot of Arabia; but I was not favorably impressed by the influence of desert blood on the horse under civilized conditions of hard work. The average size, weight, and serviceability would have been far greater in America. During the day I saw but one or two clean, fine-bred Arabians among the many thousands out. The army and bureaucrats appeared to monopolize the good horses, and there was but a small force of cavalry on duty to line the streets through which his Majesty passed, so that the common stock was the more unduly prominent.

Many men in Constantinople ride an English saddle, but still cling to the enormous Oriental blanket which comes back over the horse's loins and is made of a long, hairy, woollen fabric, generally red and white. It is extremely ugly. The saddle and blanket do not match. They represent a transition stage. The plate-shoe throughout Turkey in Europe has been almost driven out by the French shoe. The plate they used to employ in Turkey, unlike the plate of the desert, had as many as six nails inside and six outside, sometimes only five, or five outside and four inside, well distributed.

The Sultan's stables contain many fine Arabians. Some are extremely old. I saw one which had carried no less than four sultans—Abdul-Medjid, way back in 1860; and Abdul-Aziz, Murad, and Abdul-Hamid since. I was presented with an interesting series of pictures of them. Not a few have the curious marks on barrel and haunch and arm, which, by a queer superstition, are often inflicted on Arabians "to make them gallop faster," as they say; though what this means I am unable to tell, unless they give each two or three year old one special test (as is done in racing stables), and select those who show up the best; and to make them go the faster use a knife-blade

rowel.   Others explain the cuts in a different way, but it
is a blind matter at best, less explicable even than the
white foot business in Syria.   The cut on the barrel is a
long and semicircular one from below upward, as if made
by the heel armed with a vicious spur.   Into the cut is
rubbed (again they say) powdered glass to make an ugly

OLD ARAB OF THE SULTAN'S STABLE ON ARABIAN

scar, much as the German student indulges in unlimited
Kneipen to make the cuts received at *Pauken* heal up
slowly and into rough, and therefore much esteemed scars.
On a white horse the scar I have described is peculiarly
distressing.   The other cuts are straight horizontal ones
half-way up the buttock and arm.   There seems to be

neither rhyme nor reason in the trick. We brand a
bronco to mark ownership; these cuts are a mere outcome
of silly superstition.

Here is the counterfeit presentment of an old Arab
who belongs to the imperial stables, and who is sent
from time to time to the desert to bring back horses. He
retains his normal dress and bestrides a fine specimen of
a high-type Arabian. Most of the stud-grooms wear a
costume as little like an Arab as can be imagined, much
ornamented, and handsome enough in its way. The jacket and leg-gear are the Syrian, and highly wrought in
gold. The feet are incased in boots. The fez is worn,
as with every one in Turkey, from the Sultan to the
sweep.

LXIV

THE Greek in some respects approaches more to the European than to the Oriental civilization, but in his equestrianism he may well be added to the latter, though he properly belongs to neither. There is perhaps no odder-looking rider than a Greek peasant on a pack-saddle. The saddle is made so as to be equally adapted to pack or to riding, and while fairly good for the one is wretched for the other. Unlike those of all other peoples, this saddle, instead of being placed in the middle of the back or towards the rump, is made to fit so that the centre of gravity lies directly over the place where the English pommel sits—*i.e.*, exactly back of the top of the withers. When the Greek rides this horror of a saddle he is perched directly over the horse's withers, with his legs hanging way in front of the animal's. The saddle comes no farther rearward than the middle of the back. The seat, owing to its width, is so uncomfortable that the man is apt to ride sideways more often than astride.

Just where this trick originated it is hard to say. The common Oriental habit is to get the load too far to the rear. In fact, with donkeys it is usual for natives to ride on the weakest part of the back, just over the kidneys, because the place where the beast is most limber is the easiest to the man. With the Greek we have the horse's fore-legs loaded down to a dangerous extent, while the haunches have less than their fair share of work. A stumble would be far from a luxury, with the freight all in the bows, to speak nautically.

The Greek dress, until you get used to it, is too lady-like to be pleasing. The close-falling kilt of Scotland is natural enough. But as in Greece the kilt is made in such ample folds, and starched to so stiff an extent that it stands out absolutely like a ballet-girl's skirt, one never quite gets rid of a certain flavor of hermaphroditism, so to speak, until one has long been among the people. It is bad enough when the Greek wears the picturesque Thessalian leggings; but when, as in Albania, he wears what the old Rollo books used to call "pantelettes," one's ideas are turned topsy-turvy, even more than in Tunis, where one sees a pretty Jewess calmly parading up and down the bazaars in tight trousers and short sack-coat, all wonderfully wrought in gold embroidery. In either case, unless your judgment is very firmly fixed, you have to sit down and reflect for a moment, or pull yourself together in some other fashion.

The Greek is a high-tuned fellow. Though the blood of the modern Greek is rather Albanian—as also is his dress—than traceable to the heroic Hellene of twenty centuries ago, no prince of the blood can be more proud of his lineage, which he deludes himself into believing to be purity itself. The Greek peasant will strut by you with the most kingly air ; he looks down with a kindly but ill-disguised contempt upon the American tourist who could buy up a whole village of his ilk and scarcely know he owned it. He has many really fine qualities, this Greek, coupled to some we are not wont to admire, such as inordinate vanity. And in his wonderful garb on a hard-trotting horse, so near the withers that he gets threefold the motion he would get if he sat in the middle of the back, he is truly a spectacle for gods and men.

The Greek rides the veriest runt of a horse, though it has endurance. The fine little Thessalian chunk, of the era of Phidias, which was certainly alive and kicking in the days of Alexander—for was it not he that won the battles of the great Macedonian?—has long since disappeared. No wonder. The forests were all chopped down æons ago; as a consequence the brooks and rivers dried up and the land gradually became a desert. This is the condition everywhere in the Orient. It is a treeless, waterless waste. Thousands of places which, like Jericho when Antony made a present of it to Cleopatra, we know to have been among the most beautiful spots outside of Paradise, are now a howling wilderness of sand and rock. Any American who has travelled through the Orient must assuredly return home an advocate for forestry laws, a pronounced enemy to the ruthless lumberman who is fast sapping the sources of our noble rivers, and well equipped to vote for making public reservations of such essential forest-stretches as the Adirondacks or the wilderness around Moosehead Lake. It is only a question of time, if the destruction of our forests continues, when the Hudson River will cease to be navigable, when the beautiful granite streams of the White Mountains will be torrents in winter and dry beds in summer. The trouble lies in the fact that we Americans either will not believe this fact or that we work on the principle of after us the deluge—of which "the devil take the hindmost" is the more common equivalent. If we go on, it will be "after us hades." Oh, for another Peter the Hermit to preach a crusade on the preservation of our forests!

So soon as the land dried up, so did all that it produced and nourished. To-day Greece is fit, on all its hill-sides, to feed nothing but sheep and goats. The latter eat every shoot of vegetation; trees cannot grow. The Greek com-

MODERN GREEK COSTUME

plains that he has no water for irrigation, but he will not work for the future; he will not only not plant trees, but will not conserve those which themselves strive to grow. So soon as a pine-tree struggles up, as many do, to a size big enough to produce resin, he scores it to death to secure enough of its life-blood to keep his nasty wine, heedless of the fact that if he would let a few grow bigger, they would produce resin in abundance and water besides.

So died out the noble little Thessalian, whom Homer has immortalized in the horses of Diomed with flowing manes, and to whom Phidias has lent eternity on the splendid frieze of the Parthenon; who has written his own name in history on the pages which narrate the heroism at the Granicus, the struggle for life at Arbela, the charges seven times repeated at the Hydaspes. By-the-way, it is rather curious that, accurate as the horses of Phidias are in the sequence of step which the photograph alone has revealed to modern artists, they are faulty in projecting the fore-feet so far beyond the head. No horse can hold his head so high as to throw his fore-feet far beyond it. In no photographs, even of high-headed horses, are the fore-feet in any gait even out to a line dropped perpendicularly from the horse's nose. But for all that, Phidias came nearer to giving us the anatomically correct action of the horse than any one prior to mechanical Muybridge ever succeeded in doing.

LXV

On the Adriatic coast of Turkey, in Albania and Dalmatia, the horse of the country is the same small mean runt you meet with in every poverty-stricken land. He is not without his advantages. He eats little, needs and gets no grooming, stabling, or care; has a vast deal of endurance—of blows, neglect, and ill-treatment—and carries as big a load for his size as a bronco. But the bronco can run and keep it up; the little country brute of the Eastern Adriatic can barely work out of a walk; nor has he any gaits. He is a poor lot, much like the population which breeds him.

The origin of the best strain of Arabian blood has been related by some romancer. While Mohammed was fighting his way from his humble origin to greatness, he once was compelled for three days to lead his corps of twenty thousand cavalry without a drop of water. At last from a hill-top they descried the silver streak of a distant river, and after a short farther march, Mohammed ordered his trumpeter to blow the call to dismount and loose the horses. The poor brutes, starving for water, at once sprang into a mad gallop towards the longed - for goal. No sooner loosened than there came the alarm—false as it happened — of a sudden ambush. To horse! was instantly blown and repeated by a hundred bugles. But the demand was too great; the parched throats were not to be refused; the stampede grew wilder and wilder, as twenty thousand steeds pushed desperately for the river-

banks before them. Of all the frantic crowd but five
mares responded to the call. To these noble steeds duty
was higher than suffering. They turned in their tracks,
came bravely back, pleading in their eyes and anguish in
their shrunken flanks, and stood before the prophet. Love
for their masters and a sense of obedience had conquered
their distress, but their bloodshot eyes told of a fearful
torment, the more pathetic for their dumbness. The danger was over, the faithful mares were at once released,
but Mohammed selected these five for his own use, and
they were the dams of one of the great races of the
desert. From them, goes on the legend, have sprung the
best of the Arabian steeds. It can, however, scarcely be
claimed that the average horse of the land of the rising
sun comes up to this ideal. He must have been bred from
the nineteen thousand nine hundred and ninety-five.

On the whole, I must sum up the horse of the Orient
as of far from the high grade which is generally understood. The splendid specimens are less splendid than our
prize-winners or our well-known sires; the common herd
is common enough. The general run is exceedingly attractive, but scarcely as good performers as our own equal
class. Beyond the borders of civilization they are not
higher than the bronco; in the busy haunts of men they
are distinctly lower than our own common horse, certainly so for the purposes of our varied commercial and social
demands. The exceptional specimens, which partake of
the peculiar grace of carriage of the Arabian of art, are
more pleasing than a similar creature would be with us;
but to the horseman's eye their points will score for less.
Size being taken into consideration throws the balance
clearly to our side.

The rider of the Orient is what man is everywhere when
he lives in daily communion with his horse, but he is not

an intelligent horseman.   If you want to select a score of
men who, after short practice at every style, could show
the best performance in racing, hunting, polo - playing,
road - riding, herding, cavalry drill or work, escort duty,
fantasïya riding, or in any of the usual pleasures or duties
of the Occident or the Orient, these men are far and away
easier to find in the States than in any country where the
influence of the Arabian is still predominant.

LXVI

Before we leave this interesting part of the world to seek for oddities in riding among the Brahmans and the Buddhists, let us cast a glance at a rider who, from our childhood, has been known to us as a synonym of all that is wild and terrible—the Cossack.

Both Turkey and Russia have a large force of irregular mounted troops. These are not for the most part in constant service, but hold themselves in readiness to mobilize at any moment. Such are the army corps of Kurdish cavalry in Asia Minor; and many of the Cossack troops are agriculturists and soldiers at the same time. While organized on substantially the same basis, so much heed is paid to tribal habits that no two bodies of these troops are quite identical.

The boys of the Cossack villages from early youth look eagerly forward to their four years of active service, and seek to prepare for distinguishing themselves while in the ranks. All Cossacks consider horses as their proudest possession. They have plenty of them, and when he joins his squadron the recruit is held to furnish everything but his rifle. As against this he is allowed certain marked privileges beyond the common peasantry who enlist in the infantry, and what he loses in service is wont to be replaced by the Government.

The training of the Cossack lad is a constant preparation for what is considered most valuable in their peculiar tactics—that is, to throw his horse instantly, and use him

as a rampart from behind which he can fire; to mount
rapidly and attack with the sabre; to use the sabre in any
position or at any gait; to fire rapidly and with good aim
at any speed and in any position; to turn from the attack
at a gallop and seek shelter. In order to accomplish this
end, the Cossacks are as lads exercised in horse-vaulting,
which they call *jigitofka*, and this exercise is carried to
a high degree of excellence.

The ambitious Cossack lad, like the Indian, soon gets
to know every horse in his village, and the adaptability
of each one to the quick turns and twists of the *jigitofka*.
Surefootedness is a prime quality in his little steed, for on
it the Cossack must rely in many of his vaulting exercises; speed comes next, coupled with endurance; and in
other qualities he agrees with what all horse-lovers deem
essential.

There is a preparatory camp of instruction for these
Cossack lads when they have attained a certain age and
skill; and when a boy returns from it he is called a *jigit*
or vaulter. At this camp emulation is rampant, and the
exercises call out all the lads can do. They pick up objects from the ground; they jump obstacles standing in
the saddle, or with their shoulder in the saddle and feet in
air; they throw their horses at a gallop, or, strictly speaking, they stop them suddenly and make them lie down, a
thing which is done so rapidly that the first phrase almost
describes the feat; they pick up wounded men when going
at speed; they mount and dismount at full gallop; they leap
from one horse to another; they ride two or more men on
one horse and change horses at speed; they perform *in
petto* all they must do in active service on a large scale.
All these things are what our Indians do, varied in manner to suit a people equally wild, but of a different class.
The throwing of horses—but not at speed—was at one

COSSACK OF THE GUARD—FIELD TRIM

time introduced into some of our cavalry regiments; Indians always do it.

In addition to the vaulting exercises, the Cossack excels, especially in the Caucasus, in the *djereet*, or dart-throwing at a gallop. This is an old Oriental practice, recently revived. The rider gallops up to the target, which is a ball or a ring, casts his dart at some twenty paces, and immediately turns to seek shelter. Except among the Tartars, no people plays *djereet* so well as the Cossacks.

The Cossack bit is usually an easy one, though there be Cossacks and Cossacks, and they cover all Russia in Europe and in Asia, and all Turkey in Asia. The saddle, in lieu of being placed as close to the horse's back as it can be, is so constructed as to make the man sit very high above the horse—what seems to us absurdly high—and this height is increased as much as possible by blankets. The stirrups are so hung as to bring the rider's toes on a line directly under his ear, and his knees are much bent. He holds on by his heels and calves, not his knees. The Cossacks defend this seat by saying that when so placed the rider is compelled to learn to balance himself, and that the seat is consequently firmer. This latter opinion cannot be maintained. Nothing can give you as much firmness as closeness to the horse; the point is not really worth discussion. The Cossack habit creates a difficulty in order to train the man by making him overcome it. That the best training consists in overcoming obstacles is true, but this does not make the balance seat any better because the saddle is high. You might as well assert that a rope-dancer is more secure on his rope than on the ground.

The Cossacks also claim that their seat is easier on long marches, but our cavalry experience belies this. The Cossacks have not made well-recorded marches equal to ours,

so far as I can learn.   On the whole, the seat does not
appeal to me as a good one.   I firmly believe that the
same amount of work devoted to a seat more like our own
would produce better results.   But there is no denying
the Cossacks the ability to ride, and as a semi-civilized
light cavalry they are unequalled.

LXVII

It is related of a naturally reticent but observant old tar, who had definitely returned to his native village from many trips to foreign shores, that on being asked to give his assembled friends some account of the manners and customs of a certain savage tribe in one of the rarely visited islands of the south Pacific, he shifted his quid to the starboard side of his mouth, and, after considerable preliminary humming and hawing, gave vent to four words: "Manners, none; customs, nasty." In like fashion I propose to tell you—but at somewhat more length—about the riders of a land which, in comparison with those we have recently visited together, has no riders.

India is not a land of horsemen. How can you expect a man who for sole garb wraps a dirty piece of cotton cloth about his loins, wears ear, finger, and toe rings, and ties up his long black hair in a Psyche knot, to be a horseman? Our American Indian, whose full dress is sometimes a paper collar and a pair of cavalry spurs, shows at least a natural tendency to equestrianism; not so the pathetic-eyed Hindoo. Practically, over the entire extent of the Indian peninsula, the animal which the cow-boy picturesquely classifies as a beef-critter is (to speak Celtically) the horse of the country. The bullock does everything for the Hindoo as the ass does everything for the denizen of Egypt or Syria. He is as universal in his capacity to help man in his struggle for existence as the little burro of Mexico; and when he is not sacred he

27

is one of the most useful, as he is always one of the most picturesque, creatures in the service of man.

Our idea of any member of the bovine race is associated with clumsiness. We can scarcely imagine even a Jersey heifer hitched to a trotting-sulky. But the working bullock of India is not only quick and handy, but he is a rapid walker; and the light-hitch bullock can go a very lively gait. He moves as easily as a deer, and is safely guided by his nose-ring bridle by throwing the single rope-rein over to either side of his hump and giving it a pull. I have seen a pair walking four and a half miles an hour; they can trot a seven or an eight mile gait, and keep on doing it. They are really attractive animals, with their placid, pleasant faces, sleek mouse-colored hides, round bodies, and fine limbs; and the hump, which is on all cattle in India—which was there when Alexander conquered the Punjaub—becomes a rather pleasing incident in their outline when you get used to it. They bear their yoke well, physically and morally, and are equally good at traction and under a pack. The buffalo —our buffalo is a bison, you remember—does the heavier work, and is somewhat of a slouch, though strong and patient. There are donkeys in many parts of India; but the ass is not all things to all men as the bullock is. Droves of asses and bullocks mixed (you can hardly tell them apart) work very amicably carrying stone, or grain, or merchandise of any kind; and the bhistie, or water-carrier, is always a bullock or a buffalo. The small bullock measures scarcely higher than the ass, and many are no bigger than big dogs. A large number have the fine-bred look you see in our choice cattle; but in the south they score fancy patterns all over them, much to the detriment of their looks; and the driver is apt to be a "tail-twister," and often permanently injures that appendage.

The bullock has driven out both the horse and the ass as a general utility beast, and India is not a land of riders mainly because the bullock works better in a cart than under saddle, and because three - quarters of the land is one vast plain on which roads can readily be kept in good condition. There is, of course, a large cavalry force belonging to the Indian army; but to descant on the mounted troops of the British forces, wherever they may be recruited or serve, is to rehash much of what I have heretofore said about other cavalry. The fact that it is in India by no means makes it Hindoo cavalry; it is patterned on the army system at home. The Sepoys, and especially some of the Sikhs, are often extremely interesting; but not being to the manner born, they are, in riding, gradually growing to the European pattern. In fact, everything is. The introduction of cheap tapestry Brussels to replace the lovely hand-made rugs of yore, and of yet cheaper imported furniture to stand in the stead of the soft divan of the last generation, is working havoc. Telegraph and railway and steamer are doing their inevitable duty; and when a Parsee merchant offers you "a rare old bit of native work," you can almost smell Birmingham or Manchester on it. No one denies the value of steam transportation or the telegraph; but they do destroy many beauties which the strictly useful cannot replace.

The Hindoo is not much of a rider in the sense of the Indian or the Arab, and yet one sees an occasional interesting specimen in some country districts. In Bombay, save a rare mounted policeman, you find none but European riders, generally on Arabian horses, or some product of Arabian blood. In Calcutta you see more walers —as are called the Australian range horses; and in the inland cities, where there are garrisons, the waler is

common. Wherever the English go, thither follow polo,
racing, athletics. Even at Singapore, within forty miles
of the equator, the irrepressible Briton—may his shadow
never grow less!—carries out his regular programme of
sport, and in India all the games of the mother-country
are played, and tent-pegging and pig-sticking are in great
esteem. But this is not Hindoo horsemanship.

There are many Arabians imported into India across
to Kurrachee or Bombay. A few reach Madras. A small
part of the British cavalry is mounted on them, though
the regulation horse is either the waler—contracted for in
large numbers and delivered in Calcutta—or the country-
bred. In Bombay there is an immense sale-stable of
Arabians, where several hundred are at times collected.
This horse commands a much better price than I should
expect. I was asked from three to six hundred rupees—
one to two hundred dollars at current exchange—for
only fairish specimens. This is double the price of the
same horse in Syria. How much it could have been beaten
down I do not know. It is curious how, from the Arabian Desert, this nimble little creature radiates in every
direction, carrying the impress of his blood wherever he
goes, and improving every native breed with which he
comes in contact.

The native Indian horse is not a remarkable creature.
They run of all sizes and shapes; but though a few big
ones come from the Katiwar and Cutchi country, they
average small and of rather slim structure. They look as
if little had been done for them for many generations and
that little only of recent years. I have seen a few in
the interior which were said to be native horses that appeared strong and able, but rather ungainly in points.
If the native horse was available, or could be raised in sufficient numbers, it is clear that the cavalry would not be

mounted to such an extent on walers, not only because native industries are naturally encouraged, but because the
waler, though he is of decent size and has some endurance, reaches India always partially, often wholly, unbroken, generally goes through a long course of acclimation, and is not universally liked. By unbroken I do not
mean that he is as bad as our unbusted bronco, but he
is bad enough to give a deal of trouble. I have met
English officers who thought very well of the country-
bred horses of India, and purchased them for their own
use. The Arabian, they say, does not have to go
through an acclimation influenza; he is always gentle
and well trained.

Still, Australia has and furnishes good stock. It is the
English horse taken thither and bred on the ranges.
Some excellent racers have come from Australia to India
at half the price their equals would cost in the mother-
country, and have won much money.

There is no type of rider in India as there is apt to be
in other lands. You see in the same province, in the
same town, a dozen different styles. In Rajputana, for
instance, the men ride with a somewhat natural seat, but
many depress their heels in a way to outdo a military
martinet, while others will thrust their legs way out like
a Mexican on his muscle. The heels are not so uniformly
dug into the horse's flanks as among the Arabs, though
one sees many men whose sole reliance is on a heel grip,
and who seem to have no idea of what their thighs and
knees are for. You see as many old condemned army
saddles as you see native trees, but they are in some places
hidden by a cotton slip-cover like a country grandmother's spare-room chair, in others by a piece of bedquilt tied
on or strapped into place, so that you cannot see what
the man is riding as he passes by you. As a rule the bit

is a simple one—a snaffle or a double ring, sometimes a
chain bit, but always of European manufacture. One
rarely sees a gag, and yet more rarely a native-made bit.

Northern India might well be dubbed the land of bedquilts. What old house-keepers still call "comforters"
are, in cold weather, never out of your sight. Every native, unless he is poor, has one to sleep in—a red, yellow,
green, or Cashmere pattern, cotton-padded, quilted spread
—and this serves as his burnoose, bar grace, whenever he
sallies forth. If he be well-to-do, he has him a long coat
made of the same stuff, and when he parades up and down
on a chilly day, he makes you think of a perambulating
feather-bed, all made up. In Bengal there are not so
many bedquilts. You see a population apparently better
off, and many men wear Cashmere shawls in every stage
of decadence. In lower Bengal the people look well fed.
You no longer see the canary-bird leg and spare frame;
the coolies are fairly rounded up and muscular; and the
same remark applies to the Madras Presidency.

LXVIII

LET me draw you a picture of a Hindoo rider. Imagine this bedquilt individual on horseback. He has a turban of Turkey red, marvellously wound in a hundred folds around his head, and literally as big as a half-bushel basket; a pea-green comforter is thrown about him, and he wears a pair of tight violet cotton trousers on legs without the semblance of a calf; while over his saddle a blue quilted padding raises him far above his horse's back. His stirrup-leathers are wound with yellow cotton cloth, and a pair of huge crimson shoes finish off his nether members. Imagine his dark-brown skin, black piercing eyes, and a long mustache and beard stained brick color, and combed and *fixatived* in a sidewise and upward curve, the like of which one never sees except in a picture of Blue-beard; imagine him sitting a horse with so many and awkward ways of going that he cannot be said to have any gait except a walk—a horse naturally of a dirty white, but touched up with about a hundred spots of dull red paint all over his body and legs, with a tail dyed green, and wearing a broad blue bead necklace and a jangling silver chain; add to the man's equipment a small round inlaid shield of about the size and defensive value of a tin dish-pan, and a twelve-foot reed spear of equal offensive value; imagine all this internecine color carried off with an ingenuous equipoise and air of general and genuine self-satisfaction which leads you to suppose that the man owns half the earth, and you have a Rajput of distinction. He is really an impressive spectacle, this rider ; no picture which does not give color can yield any distinct impression of him. But he is not properly a horseman ; he is a man on horseback merely. He can, I dare say, ride in his fashion ; but he has no kind of a horse, nor any knowledge which will help him teach himself or it. Neither have his ancestors had any, and the consequence is plain. Farther north, nearer the Himalayas, there are tribes of quasi-horsemen, but not in the provinces usually known to tourists as British India. This rawness in color is, by-the-way, natural to the Hindoo. You see it in all the decorations of his palaces and his temples.

I saw a lot of horses in the stable of his Highness the Maharajah, at Jeypore. They came, the grooms informed me as they unblanketed and named each one, from every section of India, from Arabia, Morocco, and Burmah, and some from Europe. The majority were native. The stable was a long, shed-like structure, on one side of a huge quadrangle, massively built of stone, and highly ornate. It had no partitions throughout its entire length, but back of each horse was an arch some seven feet wide and fifteen high, while the mangers were built into the stone-wall opposite. The horses stood on the ground, which was not solid and cool, but warm and stamped into dust like very fine dry sand, fully three inches deep. The season being chilly, each arch was closed in by a straw-woven mat hung over it like a curtain. The horses were all blanketed with an extremely thick wadded cotton blanket, over which a second thinner one was thrown and girthed ; and each horse, under its fancy halter, had its face and eyes entirely covered up by a piece of loose-woven cotton cloth, " to prevent his seeing the flies," as the grooms said, and I presume to prevent his getting worried and unnecessarily stamping at them. This practice of blindfolding them

in the stall and then taking them out into the glaring
sun of India seemed to me singularly bad for their eyes.
I fancy the covering may serve to keep the flies from settling on the horse's eyes and producing inflammation; but
this was not the reason given.

The thing that would strike you as the oddest was the
style of hobbling—universal here, and used in whole or in
part in many Oriental stables. A twenty-foot road ran
outside the stable, back of the arches. On the farther
side of this road, opposite each arch, was a stone post,
around which was fastened two ropes, just long enough to
run across the road and into the stable to the point where
the horse's hind-feet would comfortably stand. Each rope
ended in a flat woven loop, which was passed around the
horse's fetlock-joint, so that he could neither stamp nor
kick flies, nor move his hind-legs to change his position,
nor lie down. His halter ropes were fastened to rings
in the ground below each end of the manger, say five feet
apart. He might as well have stood in the stocks. The
horses were some ten feet from each other.

They were fed on hay, rather too short and fine to suit
our notions (the kind which in New England we call good
cow-hay), dried peas, and a queer-looking, small species of
oats, all of which were given largely in mashes; and as a
consequence the horses were all overfat—as fat as the usual circus horse that is fed up to ride bareback. Except
one Arabian and a couple of Burmah ponies, I did not
see a decent set of legs under a single one of the horses.
They were all supposed to be saddle-beasts.

I asked which was the Maharajah's favorite. To my
surprise I was pointed out an English horse, over seventeen hands high, all but as fat as a London brewer's dray-
horse, and with very coarse legs, unclipped. Unless for
size, why he should be a favorite it was hard to imagine;

one could perceive no evidence of any saddle quality. In the mountains his Highness rides his Burmese ponies. I did not see any of the horses led out, and a horse in the stall is rather a deceptive thing to look at. They may have been better than they appeared.

The little country horse which you see drawing the native springless cart, or used for a pack, or ridden, is usually the meanest kind of a runt imaginable, whose ancestry, hard-worked, badly fed, and never cared for, has transmitted to him crooked legs and an ill-shapen body—I am not sure that I have ever seen a worse. But he is scarcely in our line, for he could by no means be twisted into the semblance of a saddle-beast.

LXIX

AND yet, when you get up into Nepaul, or on the borders of Thibet, in the foot-hills of the Himalayas, you find a sturdy, round, able pony of eleven or twelve hands, stocky, and weighing a good deal for his inches, which will carry you at a good walk, a rapid amble, or a strong, steady trot. He much resembles the Burmese pony, but is supposed to be the same animal as the Hindoo plains pony. Whatever his origin, the mountain air seems to have given him strength and roundness, as it has to the Mongolian men and women who inhabit these hills. As a general rule, you may notice that the long-bodied, short-legged mammal is produced by the hills, the long-legged and smaller-bodied mammal by the plains. It requires, so to speak, a good deal of boiler capacity to drive even a small engine up the sharp slopes of the hilly country. The plains dweller does not need to get up so much steam to propel him. The pony ridden by the young King of Nepaul shows the type. One might call the little fellow, as a generic name, the Himalaya pony.

The woman, by-the-way, is the cooly of the Himalaya region. She shoulders, or rather backs, a heavy trunk, which she holds by a rope passed under it and over the top of her head, and will carry from a hundred to a hundred and twenty pounds, her own weight almost, for a considerable distance. I have heretofore said that the Lord never made an animal except the ass which could stagger along for a day's work under its own weight; but

I must come close to excepting the Thibetan or Nepaulese woman. The children of six or seven begin carrying packs, small at first but gradually increased ; by the time a girl is twelve or thirteen, she is a full-fledged cooly. She works all day for the merest pittance ; carries stone for building or wood for burning, bamboo for huts or straw for thatch, traveller's packs or railway luggage ; and if after years of toil she can save enough to buy a silver prayer-box to hang on a string of cornelian and turkis beads around her neck, and to fee the priest to write and bless a prayer to put in it, she is happy. Nor is this a great ambition. Cornelian and turkis are found in every hill-side, and silver is all too cheap. I have been told that these little giants—they are rarely more than five feet high—can carry a hundred and fifty pounds and upwards. I have seen a string of them carrying from eighty to one hundred and twenty pounds each. The band over the head ends by making a distinct depression in the skull. But no matter, the Mongols in this Himalaya region are a sturdy and an intelligent race.

Among them are many different tribes—Lepchas, Nepaulese, Bhooteas, and others; and farther north the Goorkhas, who make the best soldiers the British have found in their Indian possessions, not excepting even the Sikhs. All these Himalaya races appear to partake of the freedom-loving hardihood and manly courage of mountaineers in every part of the world. They are centuries ahead of their Mongolian cousins, the Chinese — or is it behind them ? The Goorkhas are said to be capital fighters, to possess, indeed, the genuine *gaudium certaminis*, a thing the Chinaman most notably lacks.

Many of the customs of these Himalaya Mongols are peculiar, but they are readily understood. I have often heard of the Thibetan prayer-wheel, and had imagined it

KING OF NEPAUL

the most mechanical of religious devices. But I find that it amounts to no more than a species of rosary. It consists of a small cylindrical box, perhaps three inches in diameter by four long, through the centre of which runs a spindle with a wooden handle. A three-inch chain with weighted end is fastened to one side of the box, and its centrifugal force will keep the box revolving easily on the spindle. The owner pays the priest to write him a suitable prayer, which may be for the recovery of one sick, for the repose of a deceased relative, or for forgiveness of sins. This prayer he puts into the box, and then twirls it about, while he recites (pardon misspelling): "Oo manee pay mee hoon!" (O God, hear my prayer!) Wherein this is more idolatrous than the fingering of beads, or genuflections, or bowings, or the sign of the cross, or kissing relics, or than any mere form of any religion, I fail to see. It is a simple means of keeping the simple devotee faithful in the performance of a holy duty. The box, by-the-way, has usually the words of the ejaculation engraved on its margin.

The Thibetans have perhaps the queerest of all customs in disposing of their dead—or, at least, many of the tribes have. No doubt the Hindoos, especially in view of their hot climate, use the wisest method of burial—to wit, burning. The Hindoo body is placed on an ordinary pile of wood, and the fire is lighted by a relative with certain ceremonies; the ashes are cast into the nearest river, and thrice happy he who is burned on the banks of the holy Ganges. The Parsees, on the other hand, consider the elements—fire, earth, water—as too sacred to be polluted by dead bodies. They expose their dead in Towers of Silence, where the vultures devour them — an operation which lasts a bare hour. The Thibetans cut up their dead into small pieces, and cast these forth to the birds and beasts, and the richer the deceased the smaller he is cut up. This sounds very horrible, but, unless cremation is practised, are not all dead given over to some creature to feed on?

And so with nearly all religious customs. They seem odd, often what we characterize as heathenish, but they are really no worse than many of ours—who should know better. The howling dervishes, if properly considered, are truly devout worshippers, and make no more noisy demonstrations than some of our revivalists at home, even when they work themselves up to real religious fury in their cry of "Allah Hu! Hu! Hu!" (Allah, He is God! He! He!) The twirling dervishes are assuredly more dignified in their services than many troops of the Salvation Army; and, after all, did not David dance before the Ark? Do not all nations sing their praises?

In this connection I must tell you of one of the most curious cases of misapprehended religious fervor that ever came to my notice. Years ago, I was once taxing an old negro, deacon of a colored church in Washington near which I lived, with the fact that his congregation made an undue racket in their Sunday evening services. "Meejor," said the old man, seriously and respectfully, "doan' you know de Lawd's Prayer?" "Why, of course, Uncle Dan; but what has that got to do with it?" I queried. "Meejor," he replied, with evident sorrow for my apparent ignorance expressed on his good old black face, "doan de Lawd's Prayer say 'Hollered be Dy Name?'" This colored brother honestly believed that the second clause of our daily invocation was a direct command to praise the Lord with loud hosannas, and no doubt so did the entire church. I was silenced. There was no time to instruct Uncle Dan in the A B C of religion.

Reverence is much the same the world over, but it is

manifested in different ways. It was, they say, a good old
Puritan lady of the bluest sect who once remarked that
she was "going to Boston Wednesday *D. V.*, or Thursday
whether or no." She meant not to fly in the face of Provi-
dence, but she was of the trust-in-God and keep-your-
powder-dry order. With most of us, by-the-way, D. V. is
wont to stand for something more in the financial way—
something akin to *Dato Vento*—"If I can raise the wind."
But here I am, trespassing again, and most inexcusably.

LXX

WHILE the Hindoo cannot be classed among the riders of the world, it would seem that at least once in the course of his life he is bound to make his appearance on horseback. It is commonly said at home that no man fails to get at least one carriage ride while above-ground, though it may be on the day of his funeral; and similarly the Hindoo, in many localities, on his marriage day always appears on horseback. The bride leads the procession in a palanquin. Unlike our brides, she is by far less an object of curiosity than the groom; nor is she dressed so beautifully or borne in such magnificence. It is a rare circus that can turn out so gorgeously caparisoned a beast as the horse that bears the groom. His head is crowned with a tossing plume; his face and neck are covered with gold brocade from which hang innumerable bright-hued tassels; he wears a wide pad-like saddle, over which is thrown a gold-brocade blanket which hides his entire rump, and hangs down to his hocks; and from the sides of it depend huge clusters of gay tassels as big as cauliflowers. On this gaudy creature sits the happy groom, usually a lad under twelve, clad in equally stunning garb, and with his face hidden by a veil of gold fringe; for, though the bride on this day may show her face, so may not he. His horse is led by two men; while others fan him, still others hold long-handled sunshades over his precious head, and many attendants surround him. When the contracting parties are rich, all this magnificence is real. The kincob,

or gold-thread woven cloth, is as expensive as it is beautiful, and the horse's rig may have cost many thousand
rupees. When they are poor, it is no less showy, but runs
fast into the tawdriness which besets all shams and imita-
tions.

In the Benares region I saw a number of goodish horses
very neatly equipped. I took them to be native, with an
impress of Arabian blood—the latter is always unmistakable—and to belong to Hindoos from the north-west provinces, who had come down to bathe in the sacred Ganges
on the ghats of the Holy City. These horses had a fancy
red or yellow bridle, with a double-ring chain bit, and a
standing martingale of wide red cotton cloth inserted into
a loose sort of rope with flowing ends. The saddle was
stitched in white and red and yellow patterns, with a wide
padded saddle-cloth of soft woollen goods; and while the
tree proper may have been of wood, the pommel and
cantle and seat were made of heavily-padded and quilted
woollen goods, cleverly fashioned into the guise of a saddle.
It looked quite soft and easy. Leathers and stirrups were
of common pattern, but five or six thick party-colored
ropes passed loosely back over the horse's rump, and were
gathered at the tail as a sort of ornamental breeching,
while his mane hung in many braids, which were length-
ened to three or four feet by jute-cord worked in with
the hair, and were then looped up to the saddle-bow.
Altogether, the steed was admirably caparisoned in his
own barbaric fashion, but the general effect was spoiled
by the hideous bedquilt in which his master ensconced
himself. The rider was scarcely the peer of the horse.
When the hotter weather compels him to shed his outer
integument he must be more picturesque. But nothing
can equal the grace of the Algerian burnoose.

Among the military one sees an occasional upstanding

and good-looking horse; but among the natives of India
a good horse is so rare that one must set the two hundred
and fifty millions of this great peninsula down in equine
matters as far below the rank of other Orientals. The
little mountain pony is almost the only thing one sees
which has any attractive points; the plains horse averages low. All those worth having go into the army.

Polo is much more of a national sport in India than it
is in Europe. The English adopted it barely thirty years
ago; but they have assimilated it, as they do everything
that savors of athletics. The little Manipuri pony illustrated is a fair specimen of what is used in the native
sport. The Europeans sometimes import a small Arabian
for polo; but the native has to be content with the best
of the clever ponies of the country. This little specimen
is not fast; you cannot play a racing game with him;
but he is nimble and intelligent, and makes good sport.
The native is an expert. Polo rules vary considerably
from ours, but the game is pursued with great enthusiasm
and skill. There may not be so many cracked heads or
mallet-shy ponies, for the Hindoo character quite lacks the
brutal side which degrades while it improves all sport;
but the native game is quite as well worth watching as
many a game at Hurlingham.

This little Manipuri is unquestionably allied to the
Burmah pony. He has the same chunky, short-legged
skeleton and the weight-carrying power which characterizes the Burmese, apart from the fact that his habitat is
close by. Polo is played in many sections, and this same
pony is often a favorite with the English.

Pig-sticking is said by those addicted to the sport to be
the most splendid one which can be pursued in the saddle.
I have heard even old fox-hunters give voice to this opinion. When you are running down a fine old boar, and,

MANIPURI POLO-PONY

some two or three hundred yards ahead of you, he turns
and viciously awaits your arrival; when, by a sudden shy
or a fluke of your spear, your pony may get ripped up
and killed, or you may get thrown and end with an ugly
wound yourself, they say there is enough excitement
lent to the sport to place it easily at the head of equestrian pleasures. An old boar will often turn and face a
dozen pursuers, and will charge as furiously as any animal on four legs. I regret to say that I have never had
an opportunity to do any pig-sticking; though, as I have
done boar-hunting with dogs in Silesia, I well know the
value of this distinctly noble beast. I have seen him
eviscerate half the dogs in a big pack and send the others
to the right-about in a tussle of less than sixty seconds,
and then stand his ground until the huntsmen gave him
the *coup-de-grace.*

The sole inducement to raise a good horse in India is
that he may be sold into the army. There is practically
no sale for a draught-horse where bullocks do all the
work. The horses which draw the cabs in the large cities
are mostly from cast-off army stock, or army "culls."
The little runts are used in odd bamboo carts for passenger conveyance all over India; but by no chance do you
ever see a good and sizable horse in a native's hands,
unless he be a rich one or a powerful. Nor can it be said
that the Indian horse has any special gaits. If he drifts
into the army he acquires the trot and canter; all other
gaits would be taboo. So long as he remains native
property, he ambles or racks, but in a rather inexpert
manner. The Indian is not enough of a horseman to cultivate the gait. Even the donkeys are rarely ridden, and
as if to imitate their English rulers, under loads they as
often trot as amble.

LXXI

THE French have managed to make Algeria a French province; it will take the British longer to Anglicize India; but their hand lies heavy on the land. Though equal before the law, the native "has no rights which a white man is bound to respect," and the way in which he is repressed is, with due deference to the Briton, more worthy of criticism than our much-rebuked Southern method of bulldozing the negroes. The Hindoo may do nothing of his own free will; Government takes so fatherly an interest in him that he is fenced in at every turn, and prevented from doing this, that, or the other. He is hustled aside as our negro cannot be, and there is a sort of moral Post no Bills on every street corner. It reminds one of the celebrated witticism of the Louis XIV. era, when there was a "Défense" to do something on every hoarding, and a multitude had assembled at a new miracle-working shrine in numbers which threatened to become a nuisance. Some one posted up during the night near the spot a placard reading:

"De Par Le Roy, Défense à Dieu
De Faire Miracles Eu ce Lieu."

Our good cousins have a sad trick of berating us because the few millions of negroes in America are not admitted by the whites to social equality; and they allege that we have done nothing to raise the negro since his emancipation. But, with their usual obtuseness, they for-

get that here is nearly a fifth part of the population of the
world under their care, who are held down and despised
far worse than our black man and brother. And yet the
Hindoo is an Aryan cousin. What a mote and what a
beam!

The Hindoo is free enough in theory, but he is kept
down in a markedly high-handed way. The Southerner
really takes an interest in the negro. It pays to do it.
Not so the Briton in the Hindoo. And while in a certain
sense the latter has intelligence and some artistic qualities
beyond the American negro, his religion will prevent his
rising as the negro is eventually bound to do. It cannot
be said, indeed, that the Briton does much of anything to
raise the race. Of course he improves the land. He
builds water-works and railways and telegraphs. He is
just and liberal. All this reacts in a general way on the
people. India is distinctly mending her ways. But in
the matter of personal intercourse with the native, he
is far more of a sinner than the worst of the Southern
brigadiers.

In order to provide work for the immense population
at a mere living wage, labor of all kinds is subdivided in
a manner we cannot understand. You hire your "bearer"
or travelling servant, a very intelligent sort of man, for a
rupee and a half (forty-five cents) a day, and he boards
himself. A friend of mine in Madras keeps thirty-six
servants to do the work which my six at home do quite
as well. One man will sweep out the rooms, but will not
dust them; another will bring you fresh water, but his
caste forbids him to throw out the slops; a third will perform the most menial work, but will not touch a plate
which a Christian has eaten off. Each horse my friend
keeps must have a syce and a grass-cutter, usually the syce's
wife; and he needs a coachman for every two carriages

besides.   And yet all these servants cost but about the
wages of my six, and they all of them lodge and board
and clothe themselves, which mine do not.

Labor in India is extraordinarily cheap.   You hire a
servant to wait on you in a hotel for four annas (eight
cents) a day, and have no care as to his keep or shelter.
But the cumulative labor in the country is sometimes
absurdly dear.   On leaving the Great Eastern Hotel to go
to the P. & O. steamer last spring, I had two small trunks
and two smaller hold-alls.   At home one porter would
have shouldered a trunk and carried a hold-all; in two
trips he would have loaded them on a cab, and would
have been well paid with ten or fifteen cents; in England
or France with less.   But a "bearer"—*lucus a non*—
never bears anything except abuse.   There followed him
into my room no less than seven coolies.   Two hoisted a
trunk on their heads and marched off quadruped fashion;
two others did the like with the other trunk; the fifth
and sixth took each a hold-all on his head; the seventh
carried my umbrella, and the bearer looked on.   Down we
tramped, nine in all of us; the four things were loaded on
a two-bullock cart with two drivers, and I was put in a
cab with a driver and a syce.   Thirteen full-grown men
thus escorted the four bundles, or, to express it in more
correct terms, it took a dozen men, two bullocks, one
horse, and two vehicles to see me and my four small bits
of luggage to the boat.   Total disbursement, exclusive of
the cab, one rupee and ten annas, or just about fifty cents.
I was ruined by Hindoo cheap labor, but I could not go
for the heathen Hindoo on account of his plurality, let
alone custom.

The two coolies carrying a trunk on their heads reminds me of a wonderful answer once given in court by
old Harvey Waters, the mechanical expert.   It was the

case of Ross Winans, who had got a patent on a truck-car—*i.e.*, a passenger-car mounted on two trucks, instead of having the axles running in boxes fixed to the car, as is still the habit in all Europe. The truck-car will run on a shorter curve and on a rougher road-bed, and Ross Winans thought that he held the entire railway system of the States in the hollow of his hand. The patent was attacked, and Harvey Waters was expert for Winans. Mr. William Whiting was counsel for the party opposing the patent, and had shown that it had been usual to transport long pieces of merchandise or tree-trunks or lumber on two small four-wheeled cars, to which each end of the long thing would be lashed. He sought to make Mr. Waters acknowledge that a passenger-car on two trucks was the same thing as a big log lashed on two small cars; but could not do so. After a very long cross-examination, in which Waters's clear method of statement quite baffled the lawyer's acumen, Mr. Whiting said: " Will you please tell the court, Mr. Waters, wherein resides the difference between a log lashed to two four-wheeled cars and a passenger-car riding on two trucks?" Old Waters thought an instant, and then looking up with his glistening black eyes, and running his fingers through his snow-white hair, answered, " Mr. Whiting, a log lashed to two trucks is no more a passenger-car riding on two trucks than two men carrying a log between them on their shoulders are a quadruped !" This astonishingly keen reply told the story better—made the case clearer—than a whole day of legal refinements had been able to do. Harvey Waters was as wonderful as his scythe-rolling machine.

Among the very best of the Eastern populations which now owe fealty to Great Britain are the Burmese. They are very much like their native ponies, small, but muscu-

lar and stocky, with excellent endurance and the very
best of manners. The Burmese are Mongols, but even
in Lower Burmah the healthful influence of their original uplands in the Himalayas is clearly to be traced.
The men are strong, and many of the women are pretty;
they are quite another race from their Hindoo neighbors.
Why they did not ages ago conquer the entire Indian
peninsula it is hard to say, unless they prefer their own
rugged hills. The Burmah pony has all the characteristics of the Burmah man; and he is said often to possess road-speed, probably not, however, in our sense. He
finds his way all over India under the pseudonym of
Pegu pony.

The aspect of Southern differs materially from that of
Northern India. The soft, moist, tropical heat keeps the
native's pores open and seems to make him a cleaner mortal. He strikes one as better fed—it is an ambition here
to grow fat; his huts are neater, and altogether he fills
your ideas of decency to a greater degree. By decency I
do not refer to clothes. If the bathing-suit of a modern
belle can go in a bonbon box, so will the full dress of a
Hindoo go in a thimble. A string around his waist, with
a breech-cloth scarcely as big as a handkerchief tied to it
front and rear, is all he needs. He wears no turban except in the extreme summer heat, and goes about looking
for all the world like an old black-bronze statue. The
children remain as the Lord made them. The women are
always scrupulously clad, if diaphanously. But though
the Hindoo sometimes rides a bullock, he is rarely enough
astride a horse. His little native jutka pony is barely
worth notice; he is not half as good a goer as the trotting
bullock.

In Madras the waler is omnipresent. He is fair for
carriage work, not more. A pair of good-going sixteen-

hand walers command twelve hundred rupees; a good-looking, well-trained saddle-beast, a thousand.

As we leave the land of the Brahman, we feel that it is the least of a land of riders of any we have seen. The Hindoo cannot be called a horseman.

LXXII

WHEN, in coming from India, you reach the land of the Mongol, you are first of all struck by the sturdiness of the people. The Malay Peninsula shows you a population of athletes. Nowhere outside of Japan have I seen such a collection of muscular legs; the 'ricksha men have an abnormal underpinning, and the naked-torsoed coolies are a pleasure to behold, though perhaps they lack the thorough-bred type which you find in our own men in training, with its exceptional depth of lung-space. It is fortunate for Europe that the Turanian race is conservative instead of enterprising. If, with its numbers and physique and habits of obedience, it had the colonizing spirit and good leadership, it would sweep over Europe like an avalanche. But it is scarcely possible that a people which for so many thousand years has been content to starve at home will seek an outlet across the tremendous mountain barriers of Central Asia.

The bullock as the horse of the country disappears after you round the Malay Peninsula, and we are greeted by the same little pony which has excited our admiration in the Himalayas, and in Burmah and Pegu. When you reach Cochin China, or Annam, or Tonquin (I am not enough of a geographer or a politician to tell where one ends and the other begins, for in territorial divisions nations seem nowadays to be playing at hide-and-seek all over the world), you run across a race of men which needs no beast of burden. Indeed, they have not the where-

withal to feed it. These Mongols are essentially foot-
men; the coolies are the sumpter-animals; they have neither bullock nor horse nor ass for labor; man does all the
work; the horse is a mere luxury. The population of the
plains is so dense that there is food only for man. But in
the high lands the little Himalaya pony may be found;
he has wandered along the water-shed and spurs of the
"backbone of the earth" to Siam and beyond, and has
lost none of his sterling qualities.

He is indeed a wonderful little creature, this Himalaya
pony. I do not know how otherwise to name him; but
whether he be called the Burmah, or the Pegu, or the
Annam pony, he is in race as markedly the same as the
Barb of the Libyan is the cousin of the Arabian of the
Syrian desert. He varies in size. In Burmah he is often
nearly fourteen hands; in Cochin China he is barely twelve.
He is amiable and intelligent, has the same solid qualities
which all pony races seem to inherit, and, for his inches,
will carry or drag a wonderful weight. A man of over
two hundred pounds will ride a little eleven-hands pony
all day; a rat of less size will draw a cab with four passen-
gers inside and two men on the shafts. There is no S. P.
C. A. in the Far East.

As it decreases in size all horse-flesh gains immensely in
proportionate ability to labor. The same rule applies, in
fact, to all creatures. The flea can jump a hundred times
his own height or length; imagine an elephant lightly
hopping from the Champ de Mars to the top of the Tour
Eiffel and back again! The same ratio does not hold in
mammals; but the pony can certainly do twice the work
of the cart-horse in proportion to his avoirdupois, and this
is the case with every race of ponies. Some hybrid animals (such as the Spanish jennet) lack this peculiar quality; but the rule is sound.

I attended some races in Saigon, the French town of
Cochin China. They struck me as rather funny, for all
the entries were these same little rats, and the time made
was slow enough; but the plucky ponies proved clearly
that they had endurance, and speed according to their
kind. There were, among other events, trotting races in
harness and under saddle; and, providing the horse went
anything but a gallop, it was looked on as within the law.
In one saddle-race, with only two entries, one pony paced
and the other single-footed. The latter was a phenomenal little beast, and won the trotting-race in as fine a
three-minute rack as you ever saw, with the side-wheeler
at his tail. The whole thing was as interesting as it was
ludicrous.

Practically, no one rides in these Mongolian countries.
Only a stray mandarin who wants to put on an extra bit
of dignity uses a saddle-beast, and then he does not ride;
he occupies, as it were, a box-seat on the four-footed conveyance—a phrase, by-the-way, which recalls the lady who
is said to have gone out riding on her pet trained tiger,
and on the return-trip to have occupied an inside seat.
The mandarin has rarely a well-caparisoned mount. He
himself is as gaudy as the birds of his native land, but his
knees wobble to and fro and his toes point in every direction in and out of season. He does not ride, he gets transported by the horse.

The French officers serving with the army of Tonquin
and its dependencies ride the Himalaya pony; and all the
beasts they use in the artillery and trains are of this race;
but the native uses him little. No other horse can take
his place. The Government buys ponies at about thirty
Mexican dollars ($20 of our money) a head; an officer
pays forty to sixty for a good one; and the universal testimony is that he is unexcelled.

Curiously, the Arabian, who thrives in every other part of the world, has failed here. The French have essayed to acclimate him, but he has proven useless. The specimens brought over from Algeria, at a cost of over a hundred and fifty dollars each, went to pieces before they had rendered any service; and some officers who bought them for ten or twenty dollars at the Government sale, and tried to get this value out of them, practically had their trouble for their pains.

This pony needs little care in any weather or under any exposure. He is as surefooted as a Bad Lands bronco, a rather exceptionally good roadster, and hard to kill. He has lots of grit, and you can put him right along without fear of injury. He is not a small horse like the bronco: he is a pony with the real pony head, body, and legs; but he has a well-rounded crest, and carries a rather better than average tail. When this is squared, and his mane hogged, he is as neat-turned a little fellow as you may want to see. Few except whole horses are used.

LXXIII

THE Celestial is less of a horseman than even the Hindoo. There are scarce a dozen public horses in Hong-Kong; in Canton there is not one kept for public use, for there are no streets wide enough for him to travel on. In Shanghai there are a few cabs to supplement the 'rickshas and the queer passenger-wheelbarrow on which the Chinese take their outings or pay their social duties; but the only riders one sees in any part of China are military men, or residents, who ride à l'Anglaise.

Riders may be said to be habitual or accidental. So soon as you leave Arabia to the west of you, the latter condition obtains. In the far East no one who must not ever thinks of riding, unless he be a European stranded away from home by official duty or by commerce. One cannot wonder that, with this lack of appreciation of his good qualities, the Chinese pony has become a wretched specimen. On the whole, I do not know anywhere, but in Japan, a horse which shows so poorly. He is coarse in every sense. Even when clipped he still looks coarse. A large percentage are white or of light color, and they all resemble each other like eggs in a basket. This pony averages little over fourteen hands, if that. His head is large and meaty, though exhibiting in the face no signs of vice. His neck is put on so that he cannot by any possibility carry a good head; and as at all gaits and in all positions it sticks out in linear prolongation of his backbone, so he has no throttle, and his head is affixed to his neck as the head of a hammer is fixed on its handle. His body is clumsy, and his hair rough. The mane is thick, and the long, bushy tail is curly and carried close. His legs show neither bone nor sinew, and his feet look flat, though I have seen few lame ones. He is ungainly to a degree, and far removed from the Burmah pattern, which, while partaking of all the points that ponies exhibit all over the world, is neat turned, and boasts a good crest and well-carried tail. The fact is that the Himalaya pony will not wander far from his hills and retain his identity. The same thing has happened in China that has happened in India, but in a greater degree; and in neither case has man tried to breed for a good stock.

The Chinese pony may have endurance; but no animal so meanly constructed by Nature can possess the grit of the finer-made creature. Blood will tell. Not but what he will respond to good treatment. Some foreign residents manage to improve his looks, and, no doubt, to a certain degree, his qualities. But whenever you see a good one he is apt to be an imported pony.

I have met Europeans who speak well of the Chinese pony. The best specimens come from Mongolia, where, they say, a few Arabians which were brought to China by the English army in the fifties eventually turned up and gave a good impress to the native stock. This statement does not accord with the French experience in Tonquin, nor does the Arabian blood show here in the remotest degree—though it invariably does elsewhere, at once and permanently.

The Chinese pony is brought in herds to Hong-Kong and Shanghai from Mongolia, and is sold for from ten to fifty Mexican dollars. A good one can be got for sixty, and from that upwards. Why, *en passant*, can Mexico manage to palm off her dollars on the entire distant East,

while our handsome trade-dollar cannot be forced on the
people? The pony arrives half broken, but he may be
trained to fair utility, and many people make a decent
hack of him. Some say he can jump, but this cannot be
what we mean by jumping. At his best he is far below
his Himalaya cousin. His appearance proves it. Some
individuals, without points, may turn out to be good; but
I never knew a race of horses without points—or of men
either—who were worth their salt.

Nothing but necessity, or the desire to cut a figure—an
incentive, by the way, of the most potent among all human beings—can possibly get a Chinaman astride a pony.
I am not referring to the Tartars; they are another folk.
But John Chinaman, as we know him, the inhabitant of
the region to which Hong-Kong and Shanghai serve as
outlets, the pidgeon-English, "chin-chin" Mongol, is no
horseman. There are race-tracks in both these great
ports, but the sport is sustained by the foreign population, not by the Chinese. You may see a Chinaman ex-
ercising his master's horse, and clad in the garb of the
British groom; but he is the exception, and acquires
horsemanship in an imitative fashion.

The Mandarin on horseback is a sight for gods and
men. He is pompous enough in his element; but astride
a horse his dignity may be expressed by a minus quantity. To us this is very evident; but to the never-riding
Chinaman no doubt the mounted Mandarin gains in importance as he gains in height. He objects to being shot
at by a kodak, does the Mandarin, and still more to being
deliberately posed by the man with the tripod apparatus;
but he makes an interesting picture. His inverted wash-
bowl hat of scarlet silk has a rich black fringe loosely
flowing upon it, while a peacock feather sticks out from
it like a rudder to the rear. His inner gown of bright

yellow brocade, as he sits in the saddle, hangs like the very best pattern of the divided skirt so vainly longed for by our fair equestriennes. Over this goes a loose but stiff silk shirt-like garment of more modest hue, which hangs down only to the pony's back, and his cork-soled shoes are thrust into gilt stirrups, with his knees much bent but his lower leg nearly perpendicular. If he goes

CHINESE MANDARIN

out of a walk, however, he will cling with all the legs and heels he can command. His omnipresent fan he has momentarily exchanged for a lash-whip, and his general air of uneasiness is in keeping with the ill-kempt condition of his pony, who seems utterly indifferent as to whether he bears a Mandarin or a cooly. Barring a necklace of big beads, or sometimes sleigh-bells, and a thick saddle-cloth of gaudy color, the pony is meanly equipped; and he is

uniformly led by an attendant, though why, it is hard to
see.   An umbrella - bearer and other servants surround
the Mandarin, lest the many-headed should press too closely upon his Immaculate Transparency.   Thus mounted
and equipped he goes to and from the Joss-house—the
cynosure of neighboring eyes, and in his own the mirror
of purity.

   The Chinaman is a very able mortal, in his way.   It is
astonishing what excellent and reliable work he can do
at the rate of twenty-five cents a day for skilled labor.
He will copy you a coat, a clock, a steamer; he will
stall-feed and cook you a rat that you shall roll for as
sweet a morsel under your tongue as a gray squirrel; or
he will prepare you a puppy that shall serve you for a
sucking-pig.   He touches nothing that he does not adorn,
from philosophic thinking to cheating at cards.   Confu-
cius was a Chinaman; so was Ah Sin.   He has his limi-
tations, to be sure.   His coat may rip; his clock may not
keep time; his steamer may not go.   He rarely perfects
anything; "will pass" is his motto.   It costs him an
effort to get to the true inwardness of things.   Take the
case of the abacus.   You buy three articles at ten cents
each; the Chinese shopkeeper cannot tell you that the
sum is thirty cents (in America it would be "three for a
quarter," I suppose), but he goes at his abacus, and after
rattling away a few seconds, exclaims "Dirty cent!" with
a smile of triumph.   I went one day into the splendid
building of the Hong-Kong and Shanghai Banking Cor-
poration, capital ever so many millions, to get some notes
changed—$440 at 1% discount.   One must assume that
the employés of this concern are men of the highest ability in their line; but my particular clerk, though a man
of fifty and evidently in authority, could not tell me that
he must deduct $4.40 for the 1%, and give me back

$435.60; he had to fiddle away for ten or twelve seconds
at the abacus. In the brocade-shop of Laon-Kai-Fook &
Co. I bought 3¼ yards of goods at $1.60 a yard. It was
easy for me to say $5.20 at once, and I laid that amount
on the counter; but the clerk doubtfully shook his head,
and going at the abacus, in a short while evolved the same
sum total. Yet he will do intricate sums in interest and
discount as readily as he does the 3 + 10. The abacus
spoils his mental arithmetic as many books destroy the
memory; but it averages well.

Now, the moral of all this is that the Chinaman rides
his horse much as he does his figuring—not by under-
standing the animal and the work to be done, but by the
use of a sort of equine abacus. If the pony shies, he has
to rattle out the best thing to do by a mechanical process,
or get "rattled" himself. His intuitions, his horse-sense
are *nil*. What wonder he is no rider!

Which last phrase reminds me of the old story that
John Brougham is said to have once told on Lester Wallack, in payment for some practical joke by the latter.
It was at an actors' dinner, and in his after-dinner speech
Brougham said that he had lately had a dream. "I had
died," said he, "and was laboriously plodding up towards
the gates of Paradise, foot-sore and weary, along the dusty
highway, with a lot of other pilgrims, all manifestly from
among the lowly in station, when I heard the sound of
wheels behind me and the blare of a horn; and, turning,
I saw coming towards me a fine crimson coach and four
spanking bays, the leaders cantering and the wheelers on
a strong, square trot, as stylish as you please. Stepping
aside, to my surprise I perceived Lester Wallack on the
box, tooling the team in a masterly manner; and as he
passed, heedless of my shout of recognition, flicking a fly
from his off-leader's nigh ear with the nonchalance of an

artist of the first water. I watched them as they bowled along at a fifteen-mile gait, fancying it too bad that I should thus be left behind by one of my old friends and one of my own ilk; and, *mirabile dictu*, as they neared the outer portals, these were swung wide open as a welcome, and the coach-and-four rumbled in. Some hour or so later I reached the gates and humbly knocked at the small side-wicket. After a while a sort of little ticket-window was cautiously opened and St. Peter put out his head. 'Who's there?' 'It is I, St. Peter, John Brougham,' I replied, with fear and trembling. 'Where from?' 'New York.' 'H'm—profession?' 'Actor.' 'Oh, don't come bothering here!' said the saint, testily, rattling his keys; 'first turn to the left, broad road, downhill; we've no room in this place for theatre-folks,' and was about to slam the window in my face, when I hastily exclaimed, 'But, good St. Peter, I just saw Lester Wallack drive through the beautiful big gates in gorgeous style.' 'Lester Wallack, did you say?' mused St. Peter—'Lester Wallack? Why, *he's* no actor!' "

This story may be like a jewel of gold in a—well, misplaced; but 'tis a good story.

It is due to the Chinese merchant to say that, even if he has no horse-sense, he is business-like and reliable. No Chinaman's note ever goes to protest at the banks; and the man who handles the cash all over the far East, even in Japan, invariably wears a pigtail.

LXXIV

The every-day Japanese pony is a buffoon, the clown of the equine circus. His character seems to come from a lack of appreciation of what a horse is fit for on the part of this amiable people. When you see a rider dismount at a hill, walk up himself and push his horse, stopping to rub the sweat off his nag's face at intervals; or when you see him perform half his journey afoot on a hot day, walking along beside and fanning his horse meanwhile, you may indeed conceive a high opinion of the man's sweet reasonableness, but you do not gain in respect for the brute as a saddle-beast. Wouldn't a cowboy grin at such an exhibition? No wonder the pony is a perfect Jack-pudding.

His appearance corresponds with his character. Perhaps there is no animal which more distinctly belies the noble qualities of the race. If the Chinese pony lacks good points, the common run of the Japanese may be said to have none at all. Generally of a dirty brown color, this horse has a shock of coarse mane about his neck and ears and face which would do honor to a Dandie Dinmont terrier. Since the Japanese themselves have begun to adopt European customs, they have given up the picturesque paint-brush queue, which used to be brought from behind up over the head and pointed at you like the barrel of a Smith & Wesson, and now get their polls cropped about twice a year. After some six months' growth, the thick raven hair with which the Jap is blessed stands up like nothing in the world so much as a coarse black clothes-brush; and the Japanese pony's head is an exaggeration of his master's. Old pictures show that this has always been so. The shaggy mane and forelock is not like that of a good pony; it is not only unkempt, but scarcely possible to comb; it exhibits the lowest form of breeding, and the rest of his appearance corresponds. He is, however, much larger and apparently stronger than the Chinese pony.

There is no typical Japanese rider at the present day. The daimio of old has gone into the army, and rides according to the modern dispensation; the samurai have degenerated into policemen. They are out of our category. Polo may be said no longer to exist. The fact that there is a Polo Club—an aristocratic survival of Old Japan—and that a formal game is now and then played—much as we hold a Forefathers' Ball—merely serves to prove the rule. I have said above that the Japanese exceed all other players in skill at polo. This is true; but I must limit the statement to that part of the game which consists of handling the ball. In the part which covers horsemanship they are far behind.

You may not remember the fact that Japanese polo, which has been played since the seventh century, is a fine game of skill rather than a hammering athletic sport. The polo mallet is really a sort of small racket with a long bamboo handle, and with the net loose enough to enable the player to catch up and by a circular motion of the wrist retain the ball. It weighs under two ounces, and the ball under one. Fourteen players range themselves in two files down each side of the long enclosure. Goal is a fence at the farther end of the ground, in which is a round hole eighteen inches in diameter, holding a net pocket; and the object of each player is to put the balls of his side, with which he starts and is kept provided, into goal, and to prevent his opponents from so doing with their own. A barrier keeps the players from coming within eighteen feet of goal. Seven balls goaled on either side finishes the first stage of the game, when one ball alone, for the side having so scored, is kept on the field. If this side can also goal this last ball, it wins. Games lasting over half an hour are drawn. The game is very full of nicety, but lacks the vigor of ours.

In olden times — and olden times in Japan date only back of 1855, when Commodore Perry so lustily knocked at her doors—there was a rider in this land of the rising sun. Tradition and art combine to prove his existence. He may have been a daimio or baron; he may have belonged to the samurai or gentry, which was also the warrior class. As every one who has ever seen a Japanese picture-book will remember, this rider is generally represented by the old artists in a peculiarly fierce attitude, and with an expression which the vulgar imagine to be evoked by the determination to conquer some mighty enemy, to slay some grewsome dragon, or to face some gibbering, squeaking ghost, the most fiendish of all Japanese fiends; but to my horseman's eye the expression clearly denotes a determination to stick to the saddle for the next half-hour or perish in the attempt. The act of riding appears to have been more terrible to the ancient Japanese warrior than the enemy. If the daimio rode as he is depicted as riding, he was not even a man on horseback; he was a man who might stay on horseback or might not. Like John Leech's Frenchman describing his experiences in the hunting-field, he might explain: "Ven she joamp easy, I am; *mais* ven she joamp so 'ar-r-rd, I do not r-r-remain."

But he had a noteworthy saddle, this daimio—a saddle of gold lacquer. This may not sound very wonderful, but do you know what gold lacquer is? You pick up a little shiny yellow box as light as a feather at a curio-dealer's, a box which to your inexperienced eye looks worth fifty cents, and ask its price. "One hundred dollars," comes the answer. You think the man is joking, and offer him five, and keep on increasing up to fifty, sixty, perhaps eighty, and still you will not get that box. There is many a gold-lacquer box too small to hold even a few quires of note-paper, and without any fictitious archæological value, which a thousand-dollar bill will not purchase; and I recently saw, in that wonderful curio-store of Ikeda's in Kyoto, eight thousand dollars offered and refused for a not very large cabinet. The offer came from a well-known English nobleman. Until you know the labor which goes into it, and its durability, and acquire the taste for its refined beauty, you have no idea of what gold lacquer can be. It is the most indestructible product of human skill. Though made solely by repeated coatings of an ill-smelling sort of varnish on a wood frame, a needle will not scratch it nor a live coal burn it. Some lacquer sent by the Mikado to the Vienna Exposition went down off the coast on its return home, and lay eighteen months in the sea-water before it was fished up. When opened, though its coverings had been at once soaked through, and though the metal hinges were deeply corroded, the gold lacquer was found to be as perfect as the day it had been finished—two hundred years ago. His lacquer is somewhat of an index to the character of a Japanese. Both contain much honest gold.

Now, though the daimio may have been less of a rider than the Indian in his home-made elkhorn tree, he often sat in a gold-lacquer saddle, which represented the work of a score of men for a decade, and very beautiful it was. Its construction was odd. The pommel was like an enor-

mous two-pronged fork with short tines much spread; the
cantle was the same, but somewhat wider, and with tines
more spread. These were held together by two side-
pieces placed against them end on, and lashed to them by
gay silk cords passed through holes perforated in each.
and with dangling tassels. The saddle was never a firm.
solid whole; the parts were illy held to each other, and
nothing but a mass of blankets saved the horse from a constant sore back. The daimio sat as loosely in the saddle
as it sat loosely on the horse, and rode with a more than
Oriental seat, leaning forward over the withers and perched
away above the horse, much as I can remember the effigy
of Akbar, the Great Mogul, at Madame Tussaud's Wax
Works. His feet were thrust into the biggest metal stirrups which, I think, have ever existed, and which weigh
six to ten pounds apiece. They are made like a huge pair
of slippers without heels or counters, and with the sides
cut out, while the heavy silk cord which served in lieu of
leathers passed through an eye at the instep. These stirrups can often be bought at the curio-stores. They are
generally of iron, ornamented with fine damascene work
of gold and silver. To us less artistic people it seems
queer to decorate with precious metals so common a material as iron; but the Japanese thinks only of the effect,
using all metals indifferently to work out his scheme; and
iron lends itself wonderfully well to decoration. The daimio's bit was a queer affair, a cross between a curb and a
double-ring snaffle, and was hung in a simple bridle of silk
cord. His bridle-reins were often tied to his sash on either
side of him—a fact which perhaps argues more for his
ability to guide his pony than I have above admitted.
The pony was shod with straw sandals or not at all. The
daimio wore a dress of marvellous goods, with his crest
between the shoulder-blades, and embroidered all over

with flowers and storks and dragons, and ample enough
to cover half his horse as well as to hide his own person.
He was a gay bird, indeed, but nothing in the old pictures,
or in the modern horse, shows him to have been much of
a rider.

The modern Japanese horse is properly a beast of burden; so is the bullock; so are the men and women. But
there are few horses and fewer bullocks, while men and
women are plenty. It seems to me that the Japanese
works harder than any other peasant in the world. The
loads he drags on his long two-wheeled cart are enormous; the speed and endurance of the jinricksha cooly
surpass those of any other. He is built for hard work.
With an extra big body in proportion to his small stature,
he has legs which are wonderful for their muscular development; and he seems to be able to keep at his work
without distress. The 'ricksha man neither sweats nor
puffs, even after a long pull. A set of tandems took my
party sixteen long miles one morning in two hours and
twenty minutes, over a rise of four hundred feet; they
went the last three miles downhill at a full run, apparently for the fun of it; and when they pulled up not one of
the eight men was even breathing hard. The home trip
was at an equally lively pace. The demand has called out
a supply of runners. There is no need of a light draught-
horse in Japan.

The Japanese is essentially a strong man of his inches,
and has endurance unspoiled by bad national habits. The
athletes are very able; but until I saw them, I never
could explain to myself how men who eat and drink
themselves into mountains of fat could retain their powers of wrestling. On seeing the imperial champion, a
man of perhaps five feet seven — this is tall for a Jap,
whose average height is little over five feet — and weigh-

ing, I should judge, at least two hundred and fifty pounds,
with fat, indeed, hanging down in big loops over his belt,
I exclaimed that it was not possible for such a man to
wrestle. And I was right; according to our rules he
could not wrestle at all. But Japanese matches require
far less endurance than our own long collar-and-elbow
matches, or than any style admissible among us. A Japanese bout lasts often but five or ten seconds; rarely a
hundred; and bouts are never more than best two in
three. The idea of rules which will keep a man at work
for two hours or more has not occurred to them. So
many things end a bout that the fat man runs no chance
of getting winded; he scarcely has to use his lungs. The
ring is not much over a dozen feet in diameter, and if he
can force his lighter opponent out of it, or throw him in
any manner whatever, or force him on one knee, he wins.
A fall in Japan means any fall; a man need not be put
flat on his back. The fat man himself is hard to move;
you cannot get a hold on his slippery, bulky corporosity;
so long as he has to make no running fight which will ex-
haust him, he is master of the situation. But in a match
that called on him for lung power he would be nowhere,
despite his mere strength and weight. A lively antago-
nist who would jump all round him and keep him moving
would soon tire him out.

Though the average Japanese nag is a poor specimen,
an occasional army officer has a fairly decent pony, well
kept and neatly saddled. A few European residents in
the treaty-ports and Tokyo keep saddle-beasts, but they
are far from good. There are some at livery in the big
cities; but not one of those I have seen would you or I
condescend to throw a leg across at home. A fairish cob
may now and then be observed in a victoria or a dog-cart;
and when he is groomed and harnessed properly he is better

than the mere *cheval du pays*.   But this is due to European
influences.   The horse carries a low head, and though his
croup is high, he is apt to hug his tail.   From the little
experience I have had with him, I should judge him to
tire easily.   Despite his appearance, however, the country
horse plods along willingly, and rarely suffers at the hands
of his master from anything but lack of food — a want
equally partaken by the man.

LXXV

But I fear I may be losing my *chiar-oscuro:* to say that there is no modern Japanese rider except the cavalryman, that there is no evidence of there ever having been a horseman in the best sense, and to stop there, savors of injustice to this wonderful people. There is no more interesting population in the world. We may indulge in a good-natured laugh at the odd way in which the modern Jap combines his graceful kimono and his odd national clogs with a hideous bean-pot of antiquated pattern, and worn any way but the right way; or we may scream our protest at his chopping down venerable cryptomerias along the highways in his eagerness to make room for the rigid horror of telegraph-poles; but the fact remains that the Japanese are a marvellous race, which has done marvellous work.

It is a singular reflection how this nation, starting from the same point as our own woad-painted ancestors, has wrought out a civilization quite as perfect in its way—judging from the Greek standard probably more perfect than the European, for it was an æsthetic rather than a material one—and yet as different from ours as black from white. Of course, at the present day, Japan, with a territory and a population as large as Great Britain and Ireland, cannot take the place she aspires to in the society of nations without conforming to the tenets of our semi-mechanical, semi-intellectual civilization. This she is now busied with doing, and has made remarkable strides in

30

acclimating our steam and electricity. But her own civilization was quite another, as were also her morals, religion, habits.

Like every other purely human structure, the term civilization is relative. So, for the matter of that, is morals.
So is religion. So is cleanliness. If the end of civilization
be to make men happy and contented, then Japan has had
the greater. If morals be to do nothing of which you
need be ashamed in the eyes of your own particular world,
then the Japanese moral code is quite as good as ours.
If the end of religion be to make men and women good
members of society, and to prepare them for rest in whatever future state they may be called to, then the Shinto-
Buddhism of Japan has accomplished it. If to bathe several times a day be cleanliness, then the Japanese is the
cleanest of mortals.

But though a highly civilized being, the Japanese has
always done things in, to us, a topsy-turvy way. As
Chamberlain points out, the beginning of a book is on our
last page. A big full-stop heads every newspaper paragraph. Men make merry with wine before, not after dinner, and sweets precede meat. Boats are hauled up on
the beach stern-foremost. People wear white for mourn-
ing. They carry babies on their backs, not in their arms.
Keys turn left-handed. A carpenter planes and saws towards him, and builds the roof of a house first. It is an
act of politeness to remove your shoes, not your hat.
The Japanese dries himself with a damp towel, and dries
his lacquer in a damp room. He mounts his horse from
the off side; all buckles are placed on the off side, and
when the horse is stabled, he is backed into the stall and
fed in a tub where our drain is wont to be. His very
language is what we should style perverse. If you want
to ask how many guests there are in the hotel, you say:

"Under roof honorable guests how many as to?" the last two words suggesting the *quant à* of the French. For all this, to us, utterly wrong-headed method, the Japanese, when Perry's black ships first approached their shores, were a wonderfully civilized people.

It has been truly remarked that the Japanese are great in small things, and small in great things. Their art is true and exquisite, but it is not a broad art like that of Athens or the Renaissance. They cannot erect a Parthenon or a St. Peter's, for theirs is a land of earthquakes; still their architecture and the setting of their temples are noble, and they can decorate as no one else ever has. They have done wonders in small work: their lacquer, ivories, porcelains, embroideries, are marvellous; but they have never created a Hermes or a David; they have never conceived a Panathenaic Procession or a Parnassus. In landscape-gardening they are masters; in landscape-architecture, if the distinction may be allowed me, we have better work. The Mito and the Hama Gardens in Tokyo are, each in its way, perfect; but neither has size nor breadth of treatment such as one may see in Central Park.

There can scarcely be said to be a positive code of morals. The Decalogue did not prevent Solomon from having three hundred wives and seven hundred concubines—I believe that was the number. You cannot maintain that the Hindoo mother, who, in the frenzy of worship, tears from her breast the sucking child and casts it to the sacred crocodile in the Ganges—the greatest act of self-immolation of which a human being is capable—is guilty of infanticide. So with the Japanese. The present crown-prince is the son of a concubine, but he is none the less crown-prince. How far back do we have to go in English history to find an equal origin of many noble families who now consider their blood pure ichor? How long ago did the delightful old system of "bundling" obtain in our own midst? What we choose to call female modesty is a subservience to a certain code of conventionalism. The Japanese woman has one of her own. So long as she walks pigeon-toed as an outward symbol of correct morals, she may tear all our ordinary rules of modesty to shreds. But the Japanese woman is none the less truly modest. The country girl will enter a common public bath with men, clad solely in her own ideas of decency, because she has no private bath at home, and to bathe is a perfectly natural thing to do; but she will not uncover a square inch of her neck or arms to secure the admiration of men. If her kimono flops aside in the wind she may show her naked leg half way up the thigh; but she will not protrude a toe from beneath her garments from mere coquettishness. The geisha-girl is full clad, and dances mainly with her arms; she would scorn to show her person or to do high-kicking, as our ballet-girls do; and yet she belongs to the class which we frown from our midst as play-actors. The Japanese rule is simple. Nakedness is not immodesty at proper times, such as the hour of bathing; nakedness, in whole or in part, to incite desire, is the grossest form of immodesty. The Japanese maiden would blush to see our sea-side girl go into the breakers with a suit made of half a yard of serge; but she would go in as the Lord made her without a notion of impropriety. In other words, the Japanese woman treats the entire subject of clothes *au naturel*. Her ideas are very similar to those of the ancient Greeks, whom we do not go out of our way to abuse for their lack of what we call modesty.

So with cleanliness. So long as he bathes from one to half a dozen times a day (as he literally does), the Jap cares little whether he changes his linen or not. We do the reverse — bathe less often but change every day or two. Which is the better habit? Now, while the Japanese homes are all as clean as a lady's boudoir, is their idea of sanitation ours, and the smells in Japan often recall Coleridge's impromptu rhyme anent Cologne of old:

> "In Köln, a town of monks and bones,
> And pavements fanged with murderous stones,
> And rags and hags and hideous wenches,
> I counted two and seventy stenches—
> All well defined and several stinks!
> Ye Nymphs, who rule o'er sewers and sinks,
> The River Rhine, it is well known,
> Doth wash the City of Cologne.
> But tell me, Nymphs, what power divine
> Shall henceforth wash the River Rhine?"

Truly, their ways (as they were) are not as our ways. But they are fast getting "civilized." Even that horror of modern entertainments, the swallow-tailed waiter (why will he not migrate with the other swallows?), threatens to make Japan an abiding-place. Not so very long ago, a Japanese gentleman would invite his friends to a tea-house (male friends, of course; no lady was ever invited to dinner) and give them a charming repast, enlivened by the songs and dances of the most attractive geishas—who, as a class, are the most accomplished women in Japan. Nowadays he asks them to a European table, after-dinner speeches and all. Is this a gain?

By-the-way, this after-dinner speaking reminds me of one of the very best things I ever heard said on such an occasion—but not in Japan. It was at a Papyrus dinner in Boston, when the guest of the evening was a gentleman who is now one of our leading young college presidents. I cannot quote his felicitous words, but the

30*

idea was this: "I have always thought," he remarked, when he was rather unwillingly got on his legs after the Loving Cup had passed around, "as Daniel was sitting in the lions' den, looking dubiously at his glaring, heavy-maned hosts, and wondering when the performance was going to begin, that one of his chief causes for self-gratulation must have been the agreeable fact that in all human probability he would not be called upon for an *after-dinner* speech."

The Jap is a sentimentalist of the first water—in a way we Anglo-Saxons do not understand. He fairly worships his cherry blossoms; the first two weeks in April are a constant fête for the entire population; and prince and peasant, side by side, will write scraps of poetry on scraps of paper and tie them, each to a twig of his favorite tree. Adjoining my country-place at home is the Weld Farm, renowned for its champagne cider. There is no more superb sight in Japan than the two hundred acres of apple-trees on Weld Farm in full bloom; but what Yankee ever tied a piece of poetry to an apple-tree? His character, his education, his tendencies, all lead him to prefer the cider. The Japs are quite crazy over flowers. If a man were proven before a Japanese jury to have committed murder in the first degree, and was also shown to be peculiarly devoted to cherry blossoms or chrysanthemums, I doubt if any twelve men could find it in their hearts to bring in a verdict of guilty. But halt! so far as our subject goes,

> "The flowers that bloom in the spring, Tra-la,
> Have nothing to do with the case."

LXXVI

WELL, after this unwarranted interpolation, what more
about Japanese horses? Not much; but there are some
queer tricks which they have with animals in that country which are interesting as contrasting theirs with our
methods of management. The bulls they use for draught
wear the usual nose-ring, and have their tails tied around
to one side, under the impression, no doubt, that if he
cannot lash himself into fury with his tail, a bull cannot
misbehave. It is something of an Irish bull, this starting
in on horses and ending where I have; but as we have
got so far, it may not be amiss to point out the fact that
our idea that bulls and stallions are necessarily hard to
manage is a mistaken one. When kept for breeding, they
may indeed become so; but all over the Orient they are
in common use; and when they are not put to service
they are as tractable as our steers and geldings. But you
must keep them at work, and with their own sex.

Another queer Japanese trick with sumpter-horses is to
tie their heads back to the girth by so tight a martingale
that they can neither get their heads up nor down, nor
stretch out their noses. The head is held in a complete
vice. The animal, thus hampered, cannot possibly labor
to good effect. The horse's tail is sometimes tied around
to his girth in the same way as the bull's.

A certain dread of the horse is very noticeable in the
Japanese way of using him. I have seen a well-behaved
young driving-horse, which would work kindly and re-

liably in a snaffle-bridle, bitted with so severe a curb that
he was worried out of any sense he had; and to offset
the awkward way in which he would act, the driver
would have a footman run beside him all the way, help
him turn corners, and hold back the carriage down the
least incline.   You and I would have driven him anywhere single-handed; but his Japanese owners made the
poor colt twitchy and nervous by their own nervousness.
The same quality appears in their putting nose-rings on
cows.   And yet the Jap is a courageous fellow; it is only
enterprise he lacks.

The straw shoes, with which the horse and bull and man
are alike shod, are peculiar to the Japanese.   They last
barely a day or two, but they cost nothing, and any one
can make them.   They give a curiously clumsy look to
the feet of the animals, but they prevent the horse from
interfering.   If a horse is shod our way, and happens to
lose a shoe, on goes a straw substitute, and the odd shoe
gives him a peculiarly one-sided look.

It is not over-polite, perhaps, to say of the Japanese
that he lacks good looks as much as his horse; but the
fact remains that he is not a handsome mortal.   For all
that, the old adage, "Handsome is as handsome does,"
distinctly applies to him, for no man is more patient, more
amiable, more helpful, more loyal than the Japanese.   The
men are strongly Mongolian in face, and have almost uniformly ugly mouths.   I have generally observed that artistic races acquire sensitive mouths; but to the Japanese
this rule does not apply.   The women are far less pronounced in type, and average better looking; really pretty
women are no rarity; but in figure they are too short-
legged to come within the Attic standard.   Moreover,
the constant use of clogs gives them an extremely un-
graceful gait; and when they walk in their stocking-feet,

MONGOLIAN HORSEMAN

as they all do at home, they are still awkward. Like all undersized mammals, they have heads which are too big; they are, so to speak, of a regular pony build.

Still, they are very charming, the Japanese women, and graceful in their way. The dancing of the geisha-girls is full of meaning and singularly attractive; and while, like Chaucer's nun, who "intuned in hir nose ful swetely," their singing is monotonous, it, too, has its good side. A geisha never shrieks, as all too many of our singers do; and, after all, may not the style of singing be a mere matter of taste? A superb soprano aria sent the members of an early Japanese embassy to Europe into peals of laughter, and yet we are forced to acknowledge their keen artistic instinct. In grace and dignity and exquisite pantomime, the dancers are far and away beyond our own, whose posturing and kicking are nowadays mostly directed at the occupants of the orchestra stalls, much as a well-known preacher was once said to have delivered the most eloquent prayer ever addressed to a Boston audience. The Japanese woman's dress is pretty, if not graceful. The skirts, cut scant so as discreetly to clothe the person in whatever position she may assume—and she squats half the time—lack the pleasant lines of the best European fashions.

But if manners make the man (and woman) in beauty as well as charm, then the Japanese stand distinctly at the head of the list. So delightful a people can nowhere else be found; and if they lack grace of person, they possess grace of manner in superabundant measure, and the truest form of politeness. That this has always been so is testified to by no less a witness than St. Francis Xavier, who was in Japan in the sixteenth century. "This nation is the delight of my soul," he writes. On the other hand, the æsthetic Japanese has neither the accuracy, re-

liability, nor general νους of his disagreeable cousin in
China. This seems to be the universal testimony.

I much fear that the foregoing pages would have be-
trayed the globe-trotter, had I not, in my Preface, already
confessed to being one. Unlike the Frenchman, who asserted that he had lived in each of the capitals of the
world all his life, I have not spent my days studying
au fond every country I have been fortunate enough to
get a glimpse of. After all, globe-trotting is no more
than the reading of many books instead of the study of
one science. And is not to be full of many books or
countries an enviable satiety—if, indeed, one ever becomes
satiated? Globe-trotting is not only an interesting occupation *per se*, but if your powers of observation and as-
similation are good, your mental book-shelves become
gradually filled with

"A twenty bokes cloathe in blake or rede"

which never cease to give you pleasure so long as heart
(or head) failure can be staved off.

As I am supposed to be writing on the horse and horsemanship of Japan, I will say, in conclusion, that the gaits
of the Japanese horse—*i.e.*, the only one you ever see
much of, the army horse—have of late been reduced down
to the severity of the British trot. Left to himself, he
will naturally amble or rack. The soldiers ride much of
the time with two hands, in the ranks and out. One sees
a squadron of lancers passing by, and half the men will be
using both their hands to guide their horses. How shall
they manage sword and lance? Is not this two-handed
military riding a contradiction in terms? And yet the
habit seems to be growing. Why it is that the nation
with the least military experience of any of the Great
Powers should be able to force her habits on all the others,

I cannot see. That the English are in fact the best sportsmen in the saddle seems to be held to be a proof that
they are the best horsemen, which they decidedly are not.
Nor, indeed, has English cavalry had the chance to exhibit
any excellence it may possess since the days of Balaclava.

LXXVII

MIDWAY across the stormy Pacific (a contradictory but accurate description, by-the-way,) one encounters, in the Sandwich Islands, two types of riders quite interesting enough to claim a moment's notice. The first, or bullock-riders, are solely from the people. There is no native horse in Hawaii. The Polynesian first-comers brought cattle with them, but no horses. Those you now find have since been fetched from Australia and California, and bear the European stamp. The bullock is used to a certain extent for saddle-work, for the country paths are, as a rule, too narrow or too ill-kept for vehicles of any kind. He is saddled much as a horse would be, and with a common horn-pommel tree; he is bridled solely with a nose-ring, the rope from which is passed upward and between his horns to the rider's hands. He is not a fine-bred fellow, this bullock, neither rapid nor easy of gait; but he serves his turn. The bullock of India might be made a really passable saddle-beast; not so this one. Still he is employed by the natives both for pack and riding. He walks well, and jogs in a rather clumsy fashion; and as all bullocks are more intelligent than you suppose, he is readily guided by moving bridle rope to right or left.

The other rider may perhaps furnish us with the missing link between the side-saddle of to-day and the seat to which our *fin de siècle* Amazons aspire. She sits simply and atrociously astraddle. Such a guy as she usually is in her riding-dress it is hard to imagine—be she afoot or

HAWAIIAN BULLOCK-RIDERS

a-horseback. This is partly due to the fact that in these volcanic isles woman has not been wont to be much more clad than her native hills; and she has not yet learned how to dress. Her toilet, to be sure, when she has been semi-Americanized. is not quite so simple as that of the indigenous Hula girl, who is robed in her own hair, a short ballet-skirt of straw, and perhaps a wreath of flowers; but it takes her a short time only to get ready for a ride. Any kind of a hat, any kind of a jacket, guiltless of corsets—in fact, what she commonly wears—remains; and then, bound about the waist over the latter, she adds a divided skirt, or rather a pair of huge overalls, twice as long as the rider's legs and four times as big around. Bar starch, they are the same as those in which the Japanese actor struts his short hour upon the stage—struts, because in such garments he can do naught else. When our equestrienne moves about in this leg-gear, she looks like a pudgy, but extremely long-legged man walking on his knees. When she has mounted, which she does with no great effort, or grace either, she is merely a man in the usual saddle, with the most uncouth of "togs," which hang down on either side to within a few inches of the ground. The rider sticks her toes in the stirrups, stuff and all, and otherwise. except for some flowers with which she adorns herself and her horse, is more original to look at than soul-filling. The whole rig is ungainly enough and not to be rashly imitated—though, indeed, it may be improved by being what we should call "tailor-made."

But from this questionable beauty there is an evolution into a decidedly neat riding-suit, in which I saw several young American ladies cantering about Honolulu, and very prettily they looked. A neat, horseman-like hat, and a jacket neither too close nor so loose as to appear baggy, was finished off by a divided skirt of cloth heavy enough

31

to fall and stay in place by its own weight, and cut so snugly in the seat as not to drag upward when in the saddle. This skirt—though I had no chance to make a sartorial investigation —must have been a mere pair of excessively loose trousers, gradually widening to the feet, which latter, when mounted, could just be seen. The lassies used the common man's rig, and rode upright and well.

Still, nothing that I have ever seen since has impressed me so strongly as a beautiful portrait of herself which a lovely old lady once showed me, some forty years ago, in Silesia. She was painted riding astride, as all women in her youth had done in that part of the world, with long flowing Turkish-style trousers, and mounted on a spirited Arabian. It may have been the impressionableness of youth—the inflammability, I might say—which has made the portrait keep its place so freshly in my mind, but I remember it well, and as the sole pattern worthy of copying which I have ever seen. This was a picture, however. I have never seen a woman astride a horse whom I thought a good model for universal imitation.

HAWAIIAN AMAZON RIDER

LXXVIII

But after passing in review the Riders of Many Lands, when I again set foot on shore in the United States I could not but feel that this country of ours is the home *par excellence* of horsemen. The idea is not, I think, bred solely of national pride; my readers will surely absolve me from narrowness or provincialism in the matter of equitation, or from any set scheme to rob other nations of their due. I am happy to admit, for it is manifestly true, that the best sportsman in the saddle is the Briton. As a cross-country rider, as a polo-player, as a breeder and rider of race-horses at home, in tent-pegging or pig-sticking abroad, he is, on the whole, unequalled. On the other hand, the German is as far and away ahead of him in military riding—that is, in the drilling of bodies of horse—as the Frenchman is ahead of him in the niceties of breaking, training, and manége-riding. Where to place the Arab it is hard to say. With all due respect to the man or the race that produced the original strain of blood on which we all rely for our speed and endurance, I do not think that the best Arab is as good a rider as the best European or American; while the average Arab is, in efficiency, far below our riders under parallel conditions. The Cossack makes, no doubt, the best half-barbaric light cavalry in the world, and in his element is hard to equal; and the Australian—from all reports, though I regret to say that I cannot speak from personal observation—is a close second to our plains-rider. But, after all said, it must be allowed that in some matters equine we Americans are pre-eminent. The word "allowed" is, perchance, too strong. I know that some Britons—bless their cramped Saxon obstinate blindness!—will not *allow* that we Americans have ever done anything — be it in electricity, machinery, or trotting-horses. Not even our republican institutions or our public schools have any merit or originality; that we can build or sail yachts is to them a mere fiction. But apart from this distinct type of all-owning, all-controlling, all-inventing, all-comprehending Briton, I have generally found that the Briton who truly "knows and knows that he knows" is glad to admit virtue and ability wherever he may find it. And, eliminating the Briton who "knows not and knows not that he knows not," I will venture to claim that in distance-riding, which is perhaps the very highest form of horsemanship, we Americans are quite unapproached—our army-marches and express-rides have clearly demonstrated this fact; that in rough-riding no man alive comes near the cowboy, and that in road-riding and breeding of saddle-beasts the Southerner "beats all creation." It might be more scholarly to make the superlatives a trifle less obtrusive; but, on the whole, they may stand. Added to all this the fact that we have enriched the world by a brand-new type in the trotter, and that in racing and in polo and hunting we are fast catching up with our English cousins; and while I do not wish to "claim everything," I think—to recur to my original word—that it must be allowed that in all-round ability to breed, train, and ride the horse to the very best advantage, the American is *primus inter pares.*

THE END

www.ingramcontent.com/pod-product-compliance
Lightning Source LLC
Chambersburg PA
CBHW032011110726
47901CB00004B/1041